W9-AZP-415

A ROMAN CONQUEST

"Take the gift, Rhianna. They require no debt on your part, no expectations, save that you think of me when you wear them."

She sighed her defeat. "As you wish. I thank you for them."

"And does the acceptance of my gift also mean you accept its companion?"

Rhianna tensed, sensing his sudden change of tactics. "Ah, here it comes. I should have known—"

"No, it's not what you think. I only hope for the granting of what was also requested that Lughnasa day—your friendship."

Friendship, Rhianna thought. So simple a word, so fraught with complexities. Yet had he not earned it time and again, with his kindness, his courage, his willingness to sacrifice himself for her?

Her gaze locked with his. "Aye, Marcus. For what worth there is in it, I'll be your friend."

He smiled, his large hand capturing her chin. His head lowered, covering her mouth, the strong hardness of his lips melding with the yielding softness of hers.

Sweet spirals of delight shot through Rhianna. She gave herself up to the need to feel, yet again, the powerful strength of his arms about her.

With a small cry she came to him, wrenching her mouth away to bury her face against the corded muscles of his chest. More than anything, more than life itself, Rhianna needed to touch him, to hold him. 'Twas more than just a simple desire for friendship—she knew this well—though friendship was all she could ever dare allow. Yet still she clung to him, savoring the deeply needed if forbidden solace of his body . . .

Praise for Kathleen Morgan's
ENCHANT THE HEAVENS

"Kathleen Morgan brings history to life, peopling it with vivid characters and weaving it through with classic romance!"
—Linda Lang Bartell, author of *Tender Rogue*

". . . a superbly crafted love story, rich with Celtic lore and poetic imagery—a feast for true romantics. Rhianna is everything a heroine should be—beautiful, courageous, intelligent with the extra bonus of being a charismatic leader devoted to her people. Marcus is her perfect match. . . . a magnificent epic . . ."
—Katharine Kincaid, author of *Windsong*

"Kathleen Morgan successfully scribes a fast-paced historical romance as fascinating and romantically exciting as readers have come to expect from such an expert craftsperson."
—*Affaire de Coeur*

Kathleen Morgan

Enchant The Heavens

ZEBRA BOOKS
KENSINGTON PUBLISHING CORP.

ZEBRA BOOKS are published by

Kensington Publishing Corp.
850 Third Avenue
New York, NY 10022

Copyright © 1995 by Kathleen Morgan

All rights reserved. No part of this book may be reproduced in any form or by any means without the prior written consent of the Publisher, excepting brief quotes used in reviews.

If you purchased this book without a cover, you should be aware that this book is stolen property. It was reported as "unsold and destroyed" to the Publisher and neither the Author nor the Publisher has received any payment for this "stripped book."

Zebra and the Z logo Reg. U.S. Pat. & TM Off.

First Printing: January, 1995

Printed in the United States of America

To a Jennifer of years ago, who loved this book and wanted to buy it. And to Jennifer of today, who loved this book and could *buy it. Times change, markets evolve, but I never doubted ENCHANT THE HEAVEN's day would come.* Never.

And to Mary Ellen Johnson, a gifted writer in her own right. Your generosity in offering guidance to a new and very ignorant author was deeply appreciated. I always meant to dedicate this book to you, too. It just took nine years longer than I first imagined.

Prologue

Britannia, early May, A.D. 55

Bonfires blazed on the hills, spreading through the gorse and field hedges, criss-crossing the land with walls of flame and billowing clouds of smoke. In the distance, skin drums throbbed and horns wailed. All heralded the Celtic feast of Beltane, celebration of the birth of spring, fertility, and the return of great magic.

An old man dressed in flowing white robes turned from the scene of blazing countryside. 'Twas time, Cunagus the Druid thought. Time to teach his granddaughter her powers. Time for her to embark on the next journey in the circle of her life, just as the year had turned once more in its own continuum of dying and rebirth. Time . . . for her sake and that of their people.

"You were named for Rhiannon," he said, walking back to the sacred circle to sit beside his granddaughter. A huge copper cauldron, suspended atop a wood fire, steamed before them. "Rhiannon, the Great Queen, the goddess of birds and horses. Yet you are doubly blessed, in name as in powers, for you also have the Gift."

Twelve-year-old Rhianna glanced up from the picture she was sketching in the dirt. "The Gift, Grandfather?" Her brilliant blue eyes mirrored her trust and love. "Is it mayhap the gift of flight? Ah, how I'd love to soar with the hawks and eagles!"

Cunagus smiled, his face warming with affection. "Nay, child, 'tisn't such a gift. 'Tis the power to see into the future, to bear the message of the gods to your people." He extracted a packet of herbs from a small pouch hanging at his waist. " 'Tis time, in the fullness of your budding womanhood, to open yourself to it. Are you ready? Are you willing to learn?"

Rhianna frowned, her youthful brow wrinkling in thought. "And this learning, Grandfather? Will it be difficult?"

"No one can predict what the gods will ask of you, Rhianna. 'Twill all depend on you, and how fully you open your heart. But whatever 'tis, 'tis meant to teach, to inform. 'Tis meant for the good of all. Will you trust me in this?"

Her head of pale gold hair bobbed in eager assent. "Aye, Grandfather. For you, anything."

The Druid poured out a palmful of herbs from his packet and tossed them into the boiling cauldron. With a hiss the leaves sank into the roiling liquid, blended, then dissolved. A scent of sweet bay, juniper, and thyme filled the air.

Cunagus took up a small, earthenware bowl and dipped it into the steaming brew. He handed it to his granddaughter. "Close your eyes and breathe, Rhianna. Breathe and see," he urged, his voice slowing to a soothing, hypnotic cadence. "Fill yourself with the power of the herbs of vision. Accept, listen . . . and understand."

The air turned quiet and heavy. Rhianna clasped the vessel to her, its heat, its smooth, gaily painted bulk reassuringly solid in her hands. The bowl's herbal essence wafted up, filling her nostrils. She breathed deeply, her eyes closing as the heady scents encompassed her, lulling her into a state of deep relaxation.

Her head began to whirl. She felt herself falling, tumbling

into an abyss of bright lights and beautiful sounds. Then they stilled, disappeared. The present faded to a world of white brilliance wherein stood a solitary man.

He was beautiful, his features radiant in the sunlit, snow-shrouded forest. He crouched upon the frozen ground at the edge of a clearing, the gold torc glinting about his neck. His eyes, when he smiled, held the promise of springtide, fruitfulness and love.

Rhianna glanced down at herself and saw she, too, had changed. Her body was now that of a woman. Bemused, she stepped closer, drawn to the beautiful man.

A gust of air stirred the light powder of snow beneath her feet, swirling a curtain of white flakes around her. Rhianna's view blurred . . . but through the crystalline haze she saw him change. His face lengthened into a grotesque snout. His flawless skin roughened to that of hide.

Then the wind died. The beautiful man was gone.

In his place stood a white boar. Tiny, cruel eyes returned Rhianna's horrified gaze. With an ominous grunt, the beast charged. The heavy pounding of its hooves reverberated in the silent woods.

Time slowed as the boar thundered onward, drawing ever near. Rhianna glanced about her. There was no hope of escape. No hope . . .

She took a step backward and stumbled. Her mouth moved, but no sound escaped. The boar's rank scent, so close now, mixed with the acrid taint of her fear. Then, unexpectedly, a man's laughter rose on the wind, swelling to crazed proportions, mingling and melding with the incessant thrumming of hoofbeats.

The laughter came from behind her. Rhianna tried to turn, to discover who the man was, but couldn't. Her body refused to respond. Her limbs went numb, cold. Her strength ebbed away.

Run! Rhianna thought, the cacophonies consuming, panicking her. She shoved awkwardly to her feet, but it was too late. Something sharp and burning tore into her back. The laughter rose, deafening her. Blood gushed out, warm, sticky, and wet. She fell forward, her agonized scream piercing the air.

"Rhianna? Rhianna, lass?"

Through the swirling mists a voice called. She moaned. Her arms flailed, warding off what remained of the hideous vision.

"Rhianna. Wake up, lass."

Her lashes fluttered open. She stared, wide-eyed and shocked. There, leaning over her in the dim firelight, was her grandfather.

"You're safe, lass. The vision is over."

Rhianna groaned and crept into the warm haven of Cunagus' arms, shaking uncontrollably. He smoothed the tousled hair from her damp forehead and kissed her. "No more of the vision," he soothed. " 'Twas but your first. Time enough to fathom it later."

"N-nay." Rhianna shook her head. " 'Twas my first *and* last. 'Twas too terrible! I can never go through that again!"

" 'Tis only terrible if you choose to interpret it that way. In time, when you learn more—"

She pushed away and sat up. A fierce resolve, far beyond that of her tender years, burned suddenly in her eyes. "I've no wish to learn more, Grandfather. And I tell you this now. I won't. Not now, or ever!"

One

Britannia, early August, A.D. 60

Soaring high on the air currents, a swift, powerful goshawk claimed dominion of the skies. "Kek, kek, kek," he cried. Brown wings dipped and the bird shot earthward to skim the trees. Then, as swiftly as he had fallen, the goshawk rose, his creamy belly feathers glinting in the late morning sun. Carried aloft by the wind, the bird transcended dizzying heights before diving, yet again, toward the distant land.

Something moved below, a shimmer of red and gold. The goshawk's gaze sharpened, focused on the object. With a piercing cry, the bird veered about and flew away.

From her vantage point atop a nearby hill, Rhianna watched the goshawk's departure. Freedom, she thought, a sudden, heart-deep longing swelling within her. Surely 'twas the most glorious of fates! To be as independent as that mighty bird. To fly away and owe no man pledge. To find one's honor, one's happiness, in the unfettered intoxication of the heavens.

She gazed into the sky for one last, lingering moment, then sighed. Turning, Rhianna glanced down the hill at her two friends.

"Come on, Rhianna," brown-haired Ura called from the mass of blackberry brambles growing at the forest's edge.

"We've three baskets of berries to fill and 'tis nearly midday. If we don't hurry, we'll miss the festival wrestling."

Reminded of the true purpose of this day's outing, Rhianna grimaced. To appease her mother's anger, after the discovery of her daughter's recent excursion to spy on a Roman encampment with some of the clan warriors, Rhianna had thought the most prudent course was to disappear for a time and join her friends in berry picking. Proper woman's work, and exactly the sort of feminine behavior her mother expected of her only daughter.

Gathering the long skirt of her red tunic-dress, Rhianna ran down the hill. The force of the breeze whipped her waist-length hair back in a shimmering trail of gold. Eyes, as brilliantly blue as the late summer sky, scanned the lush meadow, the land of her clan. Trinovante land.

Rhianna's pace slackened as, once again, the beauty of it all overwhelmed her. Ah, how she loved her home—and loved this day—the feast of Lughnasa, the celebration of First Fruits! A fitting time, indeed, to honor the Lady of the Harvest, to thank the earth for its generous bounty. From the morn's tender rays to the splendor of the waning eve, Lughnasa was the fulfillment of the year, a symbolic culmination of life offered to the land and people.

Her hand moved to the dagger sheathed at her side. Aye, her land, her life, Rhianna thought fiercely. A life she'd gladly offer in her people's defense, if ever the opportunity presented itself.

A wren called thrice from a nearby ash tree, its song hauntingly sweet. Rhianna drew to a halt. An omen? The Druids taught that the bird's call, given three times, if heard from the east, foretold the coming of someone of import. If heard from the south, it boded evil.

She glanced up at the position of the sun. Relief flooded her. The wren called from the east. Thank the Goddess!

In that instant of joyous gratitude, everything slowed . . . stilled. A warmth, wholly apart from the heat of the sun, surged through her. The ancient beliefs, the reverence for the land and all it contained, acquired a sudden, piercing clarity.

An oath welled up, sacred and binding. *Naught, neither human love nor life itself,* Rhianna vowed, *shall separate me from the dear Mother Earth, or her children, the Trinovante.*

Girlish laughter intruded on her poignant thoughts. With a painful wrench of mind and body, Rhianna forced her sluggish limbs to move, joining her friends at the blackberry bushes.

Cordaella fisted her hands on her hips and gave a shake of her red curls. "By the Goddess, Rhianna, but you're as wild as an untried colt, hiking up your skirt and racing down the hill like that. When *will* you remember we're young women now and not permitted such unseemly behavior?"

Rhianna threw back her head and laughed. "And when have I ever done what was expected? 'Tis why mother hounds me all the time. But truly, Cordaella, do I harm anyone by my actions, apart from a few raised brows and clucking tongues?"

"Nonetheless, you should put away your sword and spear, stop your incessant battle practice with your brothers," Cordaella muttered. " 'Tis . . . 'tis unseemly for a betrothed woman!"

A betrothed woman . . .

A sudden despair darkened Rhianna's heart, then was gone. Her mouth twisted wryly. "As if Cador cares one way or another about my behavior. Don't delude yourself that he weds me for anything other than my position as chieftain's daughter."

"Nonetheless . . ." her friend persisted.

Rhianna sighed. "Don't prick at me so, Cordaella. Life is beautiful. While I may, I intend to live it to the fullest!"

"Aye, stop being such a mother hen, Cordaella," Ura chided, turning admiring eyes to Rhianna. "Rhianna knows her duty to the clan. Let her enjoy herself. She'll have time enough to settle down once she is wed."

Cordaella gave a snort of disdain. "I begrudge Rhianna naught, but her position as chieftain's daughter doesn't absolve her from her responsibilities. Times are hard, these years since the Romans conquered our land, and I fear events will soon lead to another war. 'Tis past time Rhianna grew up, put aside her childish dreams and faced life as a woman."

"I'll bear whatever burden my people ask and do so gladly—if and when that day comes," Rhianna replied in stout rebuttal. "But why such a long face on Festival Day? What could possibly mar our beloved Lughnasa?"

Cordaella turned back to the brambles and began picking berries. "The appearance of the Red Crests, for one," she shot over her shoulder. " 'Tis certain the Romans will pay us a visit. Tribune Helvius Albinus would never miss the opportunity to rub salt into the wounds of our subjugation."

"The Morrigan take him!" Rhianna muttered, evoking the curse of the Goddess of Death. She began to pick berries, her actions jerky and irritated. "Ah, how I hate him! He knows our honor demands we extend hospitality to all, no matter how vile or despicable. Yet does he return even the smallest bit of respect we offer him as guest? Nay! He uses every opportunity to mock us, leering and groping after our women, denigrating our men."

Once more, her hand sought out her dagger. "If, the next time he visits our hill fort, he tries to touch me, I swear I'll slide this between his ribs!"

"Rhianna!" Cordaella and Ura breathed in unison. They glanced about as if expecting a cohort of Roman soldiers to appear from the trees.

"Blessed Sweet Goddess!" Rhianna glanced at her two friends and shook her head. "What a pair of timid does! On the one hand you speak of war, Cordaella, and on the other you want to run and hide. Well, when the time comes, *I* shall ride with the warriors against mighty Rome."

"If your father allows it," Cordaella sniffed. "Your brothers may have well seen to your warrior's training these past years, but you know the Trinovante don't permit their women in battle, save in the direst of circumstances. Easy words, *your* talk of war, when you'll probably never have to fight."

Storm-dark blue eyes riveted on Cordaella. "Are you implying I'd not raise arms to defend our clan?"

" 'Tis certain you would." Apprehensively, Ura looked from one to the other. "You would lead the warriors if you could, Rhianna. Cordaella knows that. Don't you, Cordaella?"

Cordaella eyed Rhianna, then, exhaling a deep breath, resumed her berry picking. "Aye, I know, I know. 'Tisn't Rhianna's lack of courage that's the issue here. 'Tis the easy talk of war. I fear we follow our hearts overmuch. Successful battles are best fought with one's head."

"And when has following one's head been of profit in dealing with Rome?" Rhianna demanded, tamping down her anger with an effort. "Look at King Prasutagus of the Iceni. He tried to ensure a portion of his kingdom for his family by willing half to the Emperor Nero and half to his own two daughters. Yet now that he's dead, I've heard rumors the Romans plan to have it all. I could cut out their hearts for what that will soon do to Boudicca!"

"Exactly the kind of act that would drag us into another war with Rome!" Cordaella countered triumphantly.

Rhianna's mouth twisted in irritation. "So, tell me, all wise and knowing Cordaella. How will using one's head help the plight of Queen Boudicca and her children?"

"There is still hope some good will come of the negotiations. And even half a kingdom is better than a bloody war resulting in the loss of it all."

"Nay, nay, my friend." Rhianna firmly shook her head. "Honor is everything. To beg Rome for what is rightfully ours is a fool's quest. I, for one, will never bow to those dogs."

Ura popped a ripe berry into her mouth, leaned over and surveyed the contents of her two friends' baskets. "Well, all this heated talk is doing little to pick the blackberries. Come, 'tis past time we were finished. If we don't hurry—"

A crackling of underbrush, followed by a discordant snorting, interrupted her. As one, the three girls wheeled about. Berry baskets fell, unnoticed, from their hands.

At the edge of the thick stand of ash trees was a huge, bristle-backed white boar, sharp tusks gleaming. For a horrible moment all stood motionless, humans and beast alike. Then, with a series of low grunts, the creature lowered his head and charged—toward the blackberry bushes and three terrified girls.

Dry, choking dust swirled around the band of Roman cavalry as they advanced down the dirt road. At the head rode two red-cloaked officers in horsehair-crested helmets, both wearing the insignia of the high rank of tribune. Behind them followed twenty auxiliaries. All bore bone-handled short-swords, with shields and long spears completing the weaponry of the enlisted men. In full battle garb, from the leather corselets covering their chests and upper torsos to the thin metal greaves protecting their shins, the bronze-helmeted men presented a formidable appearance.

"So, Tribune Albinus, enlighten my ignorance." As his strong legs expertly guided his horse along, Marcus Suetonius Paullinus wiped the sweat from his brow. "If I'm successfully to assume your command, it's imperative I learn as much as I can about the current situation here."

The one called Albinus, swarthy and as lean as a cat, cast a thin-lipped smile at the man riding beside him. "One would think, Tribune Paullinus, the nephew of the Roman provincial governor would need no assistance in dealing with these barbaric Britanni. Even the most ignorant of officers could surely manage the Trinovante for the short span of a year. Especially," he added, his mouth twisting cynically, "when the reward of a distinguished career in Rome awaits."

At the barb in the senior tribune's words, Marcus bit back a sharp retort, reminding himself for the hundredth time in the past two days that he could afford to be gracious. *He* wasn't the one recalled to Rome for mismanagement of provincial affairs. *He* wasn't the one repeatedly reported for his insensitive treatment of the local Britanni, for his blatant rapes of the women and frequently unwarranted executions of the men. No, quite the contrary. Albinus' dismissal as *Praefectus Alae* of Camulodunum's garrison had only served to further Marcus' military career.

A small smile flitted across his face. His uncle had indeed favored him when he'd been summoned from Gaul as Albinus' replacement as commander of the cavalry unit of auxiliaries. The prestigious assignment had all but sealed the success of his last year of required service in the army and guaranteed his political future in the Roman Senate.

The task before him, however, was far from simple. For too many years now, greed and heavy-handed administration had stirred the cauldron of Britanni discontent. Something had to be done soon or the flames of war would once more scorch the land.

Take control before it's too late. . . . The memory of his uncle's words five days earlier sent an odd prickle rippling down Marcus' spine. There was too much at stake to allow some half-wild, battle-crazed race of people to ruin his plans.

He glanced at Albinus. *I must succeed, and the work before me is awesome enough without alienating an important source of information. A source who seeks to sabotage even my earliest efforts.*

"More the reason to learn as much as I can," Marcus replied, forcing a smile. "Even a year is time enough to make serious blunders with such volatile people. Tell me, Tribune Albinus. What are the Trinovante like?"

Thin lips puckered with annoyance. "The Trinovante?" Albinus paused to lean to the side and spit on the road for emphasis. "They are Celts, as are all the tribes of Britannia. Need I say more? You know as well as I what proud, warlike people they are—living only for honor and a glorious death in battle."

A hard look flared in his eyes. "You've just arrived from a command in Gaul. If rumors be true, you handled yourself admirably there. Deal with these Trinovantes as you did the Gaullish Celts. Remind them at every turn where their place lies, break their spirit by whittling away at their land holdings, their wealth. *That* is the only way to control a barbaric people."

That is how you controlled them and have brought them to the brink of war instead, Marcus thought grimly. *But while they remain at peace, I'll deal with these Trinovante more reasonably. No one, not even a barbarian, reacts well to having his pride ground in the dust.* I *intend to succeed, both for Rome and myself. You, on the other hand, Albinus, are a fool and have earned the fool's reward.*

Marcus' hands tightened on his reins, but the expression he shot the other tribune was only mildly curious. "Is this expedition to their Harvest Festival one example of your means of control?"

"The Feast of Lughnasa? In a sense, yes." Albinus gave a harsh laugh. "The Trinovante dearly resent the Roman presence at their sacred festivals, yet dare not protest. I, myself, enjoy the day immensely. There are horse races, wrestling, and feasting, not to mention the opportunity for some pleasurable interludes with the native women."

Marcus bit back a grimace of disgust. "I find it hard to believe you find willing maidens among these people."

"Did I say they were willing? There are ways, my young tribune. Remember, I am the hand of Rome. Who would dare oppose me?" Albinus paused, his eyes glinting lustfully. "There is yet one maid whose charms I mean to savor before I leave this cold, unfriendly—"

Shrill screams pierced the air. Marcus halted the men, then wheeled his horse about in the direction of the cries. Two disheveled girls, one red-haired, the other brunette, broke through the trees.

At the sight of Albinus leading a troop of Roman cavalry, the two girls pulled up short. The brown-haired one's frantic gaze scanned the men, finally alighting on Marcus. She ran toward him.

"Help us, help us, my lord!" she cried. "Our friend! The boar! Help her!" She pointed back through the trees.

In respect for his position as senior officer, if not for the man himself, Marcus glanced at Albinus for direction. The other tribune merely shrugged. "I'll not risk even one of my men. It could well be a trap. The Britanni are famous for them."

"Are you then willing to ignore the possibility there truly is a girl back there? Have you determined to let her die?"

Albinus cocked a sardonic brow. "And didn't I make myself clear, Tribune? If you, on the other hand, wish to take such a chance . . ."

Marcus hesitated but an instant, then grabbed a spear from the nearest soldier. Spinning his mount around, he pressed the animal forward in the direction the girl had indicated.

He charged through the woods at a reckless pace. There was little time if the maid's words were true. The girl still facing the boar could already be dead, gored to a bloody mass of flesh and bone.

Marcus urged his horse onward. A flash of crimson, a shimmer of long, pale gold hair caught his eye. Harsh snorting, followed by an angry squeal of pain, echoed through the forest. In the next instant man and horse broke into a clearing.

There, but fifty feet away with her back to him, stood the girl. In her upraised hands she clutched a stout tree limb. She took a step forward. At the action, the back of a long, shapely leg was fleetingly exposed through the torn dress.

A sudden, discordant snort drew Marcus' attention to the boar. The beast stood at the opposite end of the clearing, the hilt of a dagger plunged deep in its back. The thrust had been sure, slowing the boar's movements with its position high between the shoulder blades, but wasn't fatal. Surprise, that the girl would have dared so close a pass and had the skill to plunge her dagger so deeply, flashed through him. She was a bold one, even for a Britanni . . .

Rhianna heard the new sounds behind her. Goddess, let it be help, she prayed, then refocused her attention on the maddened boar. Twice already, since she'd stabbed her dagger in the animal's back, she'd evaded its attack. Resounding blows on its thick skull with her club hadn't seemed to make much of an impact, however.

The boar was quick and crafty. 'Twas only a matter of time before it caught her in a false move. A shiver ran through her.

A false move . . . as in her visions.

To steady the hands clenched about the tree limb, to calm the sudden acceleration of her heart, Rhianna concentrated on the pig's tiny, coal-black eyes. 'Twas there she'd find the signal of its next attack. Yet as the seconds passed, nothing happened.

Curse the beast! Rhianna thought, struggling past the rising hysteria. Why didn't it move? Naught was worse than the waiting! She opened her mouth to taunt it, to urge it on, to put an end to the suspense, when the boar charged.

Behind her a pounding of hoofbeats rose, intensified, melding with the surging beat of her heart. A wild thrumming reverberated beneath her feet, encompassing her in a prison of sound—and her own rank fear. Rhianna wanted to turn, to flee, but that was not the warrior's way. The enemy was before her; the only honor permitted was to face it.

The boar drew closer. Rhianna's fingers gouged into the wooden club. There was no hope of escape. As she braced herself for the creature's attack, the grim realization pounded through her head. No escape . . . until one of them was—

A sudden sound from behind caught her off guard. An arm snaked about her waist and Rhianna was jerked from the ground. The club dropped from her suddenly nerveless fingers.

She twisted about, caught a glimpse of a bronze-helmeted

face and swirling red cloak. Roman! Her rescuer was a Roman!

The man shoved her before him. Then, with only the pressure of his legs, he urged his mount forward. He lifted a spear, firmly wedging it beneath his arm. In that instant before the weapon made contact, the Roman jerked his horse out of the direct line of attack.

Leaning into the spear, he drove it into the boar's thick hide. The barbed point tore through flesh and organs. With an agonized squeal, the beast dropped to the ground.

In a quick haunch-turn, the man guided his horse back to the boar. Leaning over, he wrenched his spear free. The fallen beast's stubby legs jerked spasmodically, its lifeblood staining the earth in crimson spurts.

For a long, breathless moment, Marcus and Rhianna stared down at the animal. Then, as if by mutual accord, they looked at each other. Wary blue eyes met those of calm, green-gold.

Suddenly, Rhianna remembered who was holding her. Despite the realization that she owed the Roman a debt of gratitude, she couldn't bear to be near him. She squirmed, pressing her hands against the hard leather covering his chest.

"Unhand me. Put me down this instant!" Rhianna cried in the competent Latin Cunagus had taught her. She pushed with all her might against the restraining force of his arm.

"Without even a thank-you?"

Rhianna glared back at him. "I'll thank you to put me down!"

The Roman's mouth curved into a smile. "And what if I don't? What will you do then, fair lady?"

In reply, she struggled futilely against the corded strength of his arm. When that failed, Rhianna grasped the dagger sheathed at his waist and pulled it free. As she raised the weapon to stab him, the Roman's grip loosened. Rhianna plummeted to the earth, landing beside the nervously prancing horse.

Sleek, white thighs peeked from beneath her bunched-up skirt. With an angry, embarrassed movement, Rhianna yanked the material back down.

"Well, I suppose that's one way to answer a question," the Roman observed mildly.

She glowered up at him.

"Next time, however, I'd suggest you not attempt to punctuate it with that." He motioned toward the dagger still vibrating, point down, in the grass.

Rhianna climbed to her feet. "What I do or don't choose to do is my affair."

"Such as taking on a boar with only a knife?"

"I needed no help with the boar. I was doing just fine without you!"

"Indeed?" His glance skimmed her trim, supple body. Marcus' interest sharpened.

The girl lifted defiant eyes, her long hair a flaxen tumble about her shoulders. Curved, rosy lips, slightly parted, graced an ivory-complected, nearly oval face. Her nose, wrinkling in haughty disdain, appeared well-formed and pert. And, though the neckline of her tunic-dress was high, the gown couldn't disguise the small but firmly jutting breasts, nor the folds of fabric over the trim hips and long, slender legs.

In spite of himself, desire flooded Marcus. A seductive young creature, this Celtic maid. His smile widened.

Warmth flushed Rhianna's cheeks. How dare he look at her like that, the Roman dog! Yet how could she stop him from that—and worse—alone here in the forest?

The possibility of such a fate filled Rhianna with grim determination. She'd die before losing her honor to a Roman—and take him with her in the bargain!

Tilting her chin in what she hoped was a bold manner, Rhianna stared up at him. Though she could see little of the hair beneath his helmet, she guessed it to be black. His skin was bronzed by wind and sun, his chest and shoulders broad and muscular. He sat his horse with an easy grace, his legs bare beneath his pleated tunic.

Rhianna studied him for any chink in his armor—and found none. The Roman was indeed formidable, she admitted, struggling to bolster her ebbing bravado, but she wasn't ignorant in the ways of battle. If she could take him by surprise—

"This is a most entertaining visit," her companion remarked dryly, interrupting Rhianna's violent train of thought, "but if you've no further need of my services, I'd like to rejoin my men." He edged his horse sideways until he was but a foot from Rhianna. Leaning over, he offered his hand.

She eyed him with suspicion. "And what has any of that to do with me?"

"Your two friends await you on the road where I left my troop. It would reassure them you're safe if we return together." He shot her a wolfish grin. "Otherwise, they may envision your fate as far worse than being ripped apart by a boar. And, despite your possible desires to the contrary, I don't wish to begin my new command with accusations of ravishment laid at my feet."

"M-my desires to the contrary? Why, you . . . you insufferable dog!" Rhianna stomped her foot. Her hands fisted at her sides. "To think I'd even let you touch me, much less want it! Why, you're . . . you're—"

"So pleased to be of service in rescuing such a lovely lady?" A trace of laughter hovered at the edge of his words.

"Aye! I mean, nay!"

Rhianna hesitated. Guilt pricked the edge of her conscience. Despicable Roman though he was, he *had* saved her life. She owed him more than the poor gratitude she was now showing.

She struggled to master her temper. "I'm grateful for the rescue, my lord," Rhianna began again, her tone more subdued, "but my body must never be construed as payment for my life."

"And did I ask it of you?"

Rhianna paused, momentarily taken aback. "Nay, I suppose you didn't."

"Then calm your fears. My tastes don't run to unwilling maidens. And I've no plans to indulge in any new predilections during my year in Britannia." He again offered his hand. "Now come. Let us be on our way."

"Thank you, but nay. I prefer to walk." Tossing her hair across her shoulders in a golden gesture of defiance, Rhianna turned and strode off in the direction from which he had come.

Marcus watched her, admiring the tantalizing sway of her hips and the flash of bare leg through the long rent in the back of her gown. She was a fetching morsel by any standard, Roman or otherwise. If he'd had the time, a long, carefully planned seduction of her would have been a most pleasurable challenge.

But such endeavors would only interfere with his plans. Plans he had no intention of threatening by anything more than a superficial involvement with the Britanni. Rome and his future were what mattered—not an affair with a pretty maid or some passing assignment in a barbaric land far from home.

Marcus guided his horse to the dead pig. Dismounting, he pulled his dagger from the ground and resheathed it. Next, he wrenched the girl's from the boar.

Wiping it clean on the grass, Marcus shoved it beneath

his belt. He paused to stare down at the animal. A white boar. His brow furrowed in a thoughtful frown. Didn't the Britanni consider it the most sacred of beasts, a god in animal form?

Well, no matter. He'd more pressing things to concern him than some Celtic superstition. Marcus lithely regained his horse's back and galloped after the girl, the bloodied spear clasped in his hand.

Two

"Rhianna! Rhianna!"

Ura was the first to see her flaxen-haired friend break through the trees. She ran to her.

"Oh, Rhianna," Ura sobbed, clasping her by the arms. "I was so afraid for you. My heart died when you ordered us to leave you to face the boar alone. By the Blessed Goddess, I will never desert you again, no matter what you say!"

"You didn't desert me, my friend." Tenderly Rhianna wiped the tears from the brown-haired girl's cheeks. "Someone had to go for help. I knew I could hold off the boar for a time."

"You were fortunate, and that's the truth of it," Cordaella interjected, stepping forward to join her friends. Her features mirrored her exasperation. "Truly, Rhianna, you put too much store in your warrior's prowess. If we had been forced to run all the way back to the fort . . ." At the set, stubborn look on Rhianna's face, she sighed her defeat. "Well, why should I hope to convince you? Nothing I have ever said has penetrated that obstinate head of yours."

A deep, masculine chuckle rose from behind them. "Obstinate is too mild a word for the likes of her." The Roman reined in his horse beside Cordaella. "I hope you other two ladies prove more amenable to reason."

Rhianna glared up at him, nonplused with his surprising

facility with the Britanni tongue. Then her composure returned. She stepped between the Roman and her friends.

He arched a questioning brow. "Yes, lady?"

"What might you desire of my friends, Roman? I am their leader and speak for all."

The Roman's green eyes narrowed. "And I say you overstep your bounds. The claim of a leader should be assumed with the greatest of care. How you present yourself can well affect the fates of your followers, for good or ill."

Perceiving the ruthless, implacable aspects of the man, Rhianna stiffened before the veiled warning. A true son of Rome, she thought, anger stirring her courage anew. Well, let him see he failed to frighten even her.

"As daughter of the Trinovante clan chieftain, I'm fully aware of the responsibilities of leadership," she stated, proudly lifting her chin to meet his icy gaze. " 'Tis a trust I was born to; a sacred tie to the land that is *my* rightful home. Not," she added, "a dubious distinction granted some dog worrying over someone else's bone."

An angry murmur rippled through the soldiers. At the blatant insult to the Roman presence in the land, Marcus' patience shredded. His jaw went hard as Rhianna's friends grabbed at her arms, pleading with her in low, anxious voices. In response she turned and whispered something to them he couldn't hear. Then she shook free of their clasp.

"My friends and I are expected home shortly." The challenge to him was implicit in her deceptively soft words. "If you are finished with us . . ."

In a quick motion, Marcus bent down and grasped her arm, drawing Rhianna to him. For a long, silent moment they stared at each other, so close their breaths met and melded.

"Never doubt, even for an instant, I've finished with you, lady." His voice, couched in a velvet tone, was edged, nonetheless, in steel. Though loath to frighten her, Marcus felt he had no choice but to dampen the girl's pride a bit. If the Celts desired respect, they must render it as well.

"I may be a dog worrying someone else's bone, but I still possess the ultimate authority over you and your people." As if to give emphasis to his next words, his grip tightened. "And, as long as it's within my power, peace between Rome and the Trinovante *shall* be maintained. I'll not have hotheads on either side threatening that." Marcus gave her a small shake. "Do you understand me, wench? Do you?"

Rhianna shot him a mutinous look. "Aye, Roman. I understand."

He released her and straightened in the saddle. "Fare you well then, chieftain's daughter—until we meet again. And you can be assured we will."

Smoldering blue eyes glared up at him for a long moment, and Marcus knew she was on the verge of yet another angry retort. Then, with a haughty flounce of her head, she turned to her friends.

"Come, let us be on our way," Rhianna snapped. "We've claimed far too much of these soldiers' precious time."

Albinus rode over. "Really, Tribune Paullinus," he smirked as he watched the trio hurry off, "you really should consider a change of tactics if you plan on controlling the men of their clan. Why, your words barely touched those girls, especially that imperious little witch, Rhianna."

Marcus shot him a cool glance. "She's no fool, despite her haughty mien. The maid will carry my message well, or I'll see further to her education."

"So, she stirs your blood, too, does she? Just remember, my claim was staked upon her first." Albinus paused to eye the bloody spear still clasped in Marcus' hand. "How far lies this boar? A more appropriate gift for the Trinovante I couldn't imagine. Let us bring the beast to the festival."

The festival of Lughnasa, Marcus thought. He had almost forgotten.

The image of a wild, slim beauty, her brilliant blue eyes sparkling in defiance, flashed through his mind. A beauty Albinus had made more than evident he meant to have. But Albinus had been mistaken before. There'd be no more challenges to his new position, Marcus vowed, not from a Britanni maid, nor from one of his lust-driven countrymen.

A grim smile touched his lips. "As you say, Tribune. The gift of meat bearing with it the gift of a life." He paused, suddenly thoughtful. "Perhaps this festival will prove more fruitful than I'd originally imagined. Far, far more fruitful . . ."

"A boar? A Roman rescued you from a boar?"

Riderch, chieftain of the Clan Trinovante, scanned the faces of the three maids clustered around him in the hill fort, his strong, weathered features mirroring his surprise. Garbed in a green-linen, thigh-length tunic and a green-and-blue-checkered cloak, a heavy, gold torc about his neck denoting his noble standing in the clan, he stood before them, a man of stature and bearing.

Ura cut in excitedly before Rhianna could reply. "Aye, my lord. When I approached him, pleading for help, he immediately responded. Later, when I'd a time to pause and consider, his behavior struck me as most strange—for a Roman, I mean."

Riderch arched a bushy, graying brow. "Indeed? And did this surprising Roman possess a name? I've a mind to thank him for my daughter's rescue."

Rhianna made an exasperated sound. "He gave no introduction, other than garbing himself in the arrogant manners of Rome. I doubt he'll expect any show of gratitude."

Her father frowned in displeasure, his long, silver-threaded mustache dipping low to graze his chin. "The man saved your life. I care not a wit who he is. Have you forgotten your honor, to deny him the thanks he's fairly earned?"

An uncommon warmth flooded Rhianna. She bowed her head. Her father was right. Once again she'd allowed her hasty judgments to blind her to what truly mattered. Courage, kindness, and a sense of fair play were worthy of respect in anyone, friend or foe.

"Your pardon, my lord," she murmured. "The man has indeed earned our gratitude." She lifted her eyes. "And especially *my* gratitude."

A knowing smile teased the corners of Riderch's mouth. "Don't fail to remember that, my fiery-tongued lass, the next time you see him. Your lack of memory can be quite convenient when the proper opportunity presents itself." He stroked his chin. "Now, tell me. Did this Roman ride with others of his kind?"

His daughter shrugged. "He was with that cur Albinus and a troop of soldiers. That is all I know, except . . ." She hesitated. "He did mention something about having authority over us and that he was starting a new command."

"So, the rumors are true. Albinus has been relieved of his duties. It seems you, sweet lass, have been rescued by the new tribune."

"I care not what his rank is. He's still a Roman and a loathsome blight on our land!"

"Rhianna," her father warned.

"Am I not allowed the freedom of my opinions? Fear not, Father. I don't deny my debt to the man. If ever he enters our fort, he will find me as gentle as a turtle dove, as sweet as a bee's comb dripping honey."

Riderch gave a disbelieving snort. "You may well regret those lofty words before this day wanes. Though you girls outdistanced the Romans with the shortcut through the forest, I'd wager the new tribune journeys here even now."

At Rhianna's look of distress, Riderch laughed. "Why the dismal face, daughter? You know Albinus has attended our Lughnasa festival each year since assuming his post at Camulodunum. Wouldn't it seem logical he'd bring along his replacement?"

A shout from the sentry at the fort's forward ramparts precluded further speculation. Riderch motioned toward the nearby cluster of round, timber-framed buildings. "Off with you girls. The Red Crests approach and will be here soon. 'Tis time for me to prepare a greeting for our Roman guests and for you to don your festival gauds."

"Father, a moment more." Rhianna moved closer. "Ura's tale omitted one thing. The boar. 'Twas white."

Riderch's jaw tightened. "White, you say? So, your vision has at last come to pass."

"There is one thing more." She hesitated for a moment, then forged on. "The vision and actual event weren't exactly the same. I heard no laughter, and there was no man present . . . until the Roman arrived."

Her father frowned. "Strange. Cunagus will have to be told of this, but not today." He gave Rhianna a small shove forward. "Go, lass. The wrestling will begin in a short time and Cador is sure to be the victor of the games. You'll not wish to miss that."

The three girls walked away. Cordaella, who had remained uncharacteristically silent during the entire interchange, glanced at Rhianna. A knowing smirk twisted her lips.

"You'll not want to miss *that* victory, will you, Rhianna?" Cordaella taunted. "Cador might choose another for his victor's due and you'd lose your only chance to lie with that lusty warrior before you wed."

Rhianna shot her a scathing look. The red-haired girl laughed, then ran across the large enclosure of thatched-roof huts to her family's own dwelling.

Ura laid a gentle hand on Rhianna's arm. " 'Tisn't your wish to lie with Cador this eve, is it?"

"Nay, Ura." Rhianna sighed. "Nor will it ever be."

'Twas never my intent to take Cador as husband, she thought with a sudden surge of misery. Cordaella was the one in love with him, who found him irresistibly attractive. But not she. Never Cador, the mighty, arrogant warrior, surrounded by his fawning band of young, hot-headed warriors . . .

At seventeen, Rhianna was in her prime marrying years. But she also realized her dreams were different from most girls. Freedom from the mundane duties of a wife was her dearest desire. Honor in battle, glorious service to her people, were what had filled her thoughts and fantasies from her earliest years.

Yet here she was, on the verge of marriage in two months' time, the only honor left her the acceptance of a man she'd never have willingly chosen. By custom, Celtic women selected their own mates, enjoying freedoms denied females of other nations. Indeed, if her father had been other than clan chieftain, Rhianna would never have been faced with such a decision.

There had been little choice, though, once Riderch had revealed Cador's political machinations within the clan and desire for the chieftainship. Only a marriage to the chieftain's daughter would appease him, would avert a challenge to her father that could well end in his death. And times were too unstable now to permit a man like Cador to gain the chieftainship, not to mention risk her father's life.

As much as Rhianna loathed the man and dreaded the thought of wedding him, how could she do less for her clan, her beloved Trinovante? A true warrior fought his battles where they arose, faced whatever befell him with honor and courage. In light of that reality, all her fine aspirations dwindled to nothing, as nebulous, as elusive as the faeries said to dwell in the forest depths.

"Sometimes 'tis hard to do one's duty for the clan," Ura observed, unconsciously echoing Rhianna's thoughts.

Rhianna watched Cordaella disappear into her house before turning back to Ura. She forced a laugh. "Don't look so sad. Worse things could happen than being bedded by one's betrothed. And mayhap Cador won't win the victory."

She patted Ura's hand before gently disengaging it from her arm. "Go, see to your festival garb. I'll join you presently."

Rhianna ran off before Ura could reply, unwilling to allow her personal problems to further mar the joy of Lughnasa. Passing several clusters of huts, she headed toward a rectangular, more ornately decorated house set apart from the others. As she passed her family's outdoor fire pit, the tantalizing aroma of baking bread reached her nostrils. Rhianna's mouth watered in anticipation of the feasting to come.

The interior of her house was dim, lit only by the sunshine streaming in from long, narrow windows and the open doorway. In the center of the huge room stood a large, stone hearth. Suspended high above it was the roof wheel holding the family's supply of meat, conveniently smoked whenever fires burned.

The main room was empty save for the languorous sway of brightly colored woven hangings, suspended from the lower support beams, and the skulking form of a dog as it climbed down from one of the boxbeds. Good, Rhianna thought as she headed toward her own bed. If she were lucky, she could dress and make her escape before her mother arrived.

Sweeping back the curtains enclosing her boxbed compartment, Rhianna slipped inside. The tiny room was fashioned from the area where the roof sloped steeply beneath the supporting pillars of the house's outer wall. Though barely enough space for a bed and clothes storage chest, Rhianna found it a cozy haven, a snug, warm spot where she could retire from the commotion and lack of privacy of the common room.

Stripping off her torn dress, she hung it on a nearby hook. 'Twas sorely in need of mending, but there was no time for that now. Opening her oaken chest with the carved form of a wild pony galloping across its lid, Rhianna rummaged through her pile of neatly folded gowns.

She pulled out a deep-blue linen dress trimmed at the hem with a wide crimson-and-cream braid. The embroidered birds on the braid almost sprang from the background, ready to soar into the skies. The gown was one of her favorites.

Stepping into the sleeveless tunic-dress, Rhianna fastened each of the open shoulders with a gold fibula, its clasps also fashioned in the form of birds. Her maiden's girdle was quickly tied around her waist. After placing the open-ended, gold torc denoting her rank as chieftain's daughter about her neck, she clasped a thin bracelet of twisted gold around her right forearm.

Next, she retrieved a small cloth bag from the chest. From it Rhianna withdrew her hairbrush, bronze hand mirror, and a generous length of ribbon dyed the same shade of blue as her dress. In a few nimble movements she wove her hair into a single tight braid, then quickly returned her things to the chest.

A flurry of commotion at the tall, wooden main gate caught Rhianna's attention as she headed across the timber-enclosed hill fort. She passed several more clusters of family dwellings as well as the animal pens and underground feed storage pits that honeycombed the fortress, paying scant heed to the people hurrying to and fro in preparation for the festival games to come. Already, the mounted forms of the two Red Crest officers were halted before her father. With a determined set of her slender shoulders, Rhianna forced herself to maintain her course in their direction.

As she approached, the Romans dismounted. The one who had rescued her was as tall as he was powerful, towering over Albinus by at least a head.

Father will like that, Rhianna thought. A Roman he can look straight in the eye. Introductions were being made and she quickened her pace, straining to catch the new Red Crest's name.

". . . Marcus Suetonius Paullinus, soon to be the next *Praefectus Alae* of the garrison at Camulodunum," Albinus was saying. "If the name sounds familiar, it is because his uncle, General Gaius Suetonius Paullinus, is our provincial governor." At Riderch's startled expression, smug triumph wreathed Albinus' swarthy features.

Marcus offered his arm in a gesture of greeting, quietly noting the Trinovante chieftain's surprise. Obviously his uncle wasn't looked upon favorably by the Trinovante, either. After a long moment, Riderch grasped his proffered arm.

Rhianna well understood her father's hesitation. Not only was he unsettled by the Roman's relationship to the despised provincial governor, but Albinus and his predecessors had never extended even such a simple courtesy as a handclasp.

An ember of hope flared within her breast. Mayhap this Roman might be different . . .

The men's conversation faded as they acknowledged Rhianna's arrival. Her glance moved politely from one Roman to the next before returning to her father. The brief moment, however, had been long enough to note the open admiration on the face of the one called Paullinus and the feral, calculating gleam in the eyes of Albinus.

Riderch's arm encircled her shoulders in a proudly protective gesture. "My daughter, Rhianna." He smiled at Marcus. "I understand I have you to thank for rescuing my most precious of possessions."

Marcus pulled off his helmet and raked his fingers through his hair. "I'm honored to have been of service, my lord."

He turned to Rhianna, his right arm rising to his chest in close-fisted salute. Then he withdrew her dagger from beneath his cloak and handed it back to her. "Lady, I thought you might need this, in the event you came upon future boars."

She accepted her dagger. "I'd not thought to be so blessed by your presence twice in the same day, my lord," Rhianna said, smiling, returning his greeting as if it were the most natural thing in the world.

Marcus' eyes narrowed. Was the girl once more plying that sharp tongue of hers? The blue eyes staring back at him, however, were pleasantly bland. He decided it best to accept her salutations at face value.

His gaze skimmed her. The color of her dress intensified eyes already as blue as the summer sky, and the light fabric clung to every rounded curve of her body. With her long, pale gold hair gathered into a demure braid, she was no longer the fiery, wildly beautiful girl of the forest. She was now a regal, seductive woman.

Rhianna returned his glance. With the helmet off, the Roman appeared almost boyish with his tousled mass of slightly damp, black curls. Her gaze leisurely perused his face, observing the square jaw; generous mouth; firm, sensual lips; and the strong, straight nose.

With some surprise she noted a long, jagged scar. Heretofore hidden by the cheek-piece of his helmet, the old wound meandered from the edge of his left eyebrow until it faded into the smoothly shaved expanse of his lower jaw. The only flaw, Rhianna mused, in an otherwise flawless face . . .

The discordant clearing of a throat shattered the mutual inspection. With a small start, Rhianna glanced at her father. Riderch's long mustache was lifted in a questioning smile. At the realization of how her behavior toward the tall Roman must appear, a traitorous warmth stained her cheeks.

Noting her embarrassment, Marcus waved over the two men bearing the boar carcass. Its huge body suspended from a stout tree branch, the animal seemed even more imposing and horrible dead than alive.

He gestured to it. "A small gift for your festival, Lord Riderch. Is it permissible to consume a white boar? Your people revere them as sacred, don't they?"

" 'Twill be well appreciated, Roman." The Trinovante chuckled. "That 'tis a white boar only increases its value. 'Tis believed the partaking of its flesh conveys special powers, enhancing one's courage and prowess in battle. I, most particularly, will savor the beast, knowing the loss of its life bought my daughter's."

The harsh wail of a long, animal-headed carnyx pierced the air. At the unexpected sound of the trumpet, Marcus' brows lifted in unspoken query.

" 'Tis the call to the festival wrestling," Riderch explained.

"The finest of our young men vie for the victor's due. Only the most powerful and cunning of warriors can ever hope to win." The chieftain paused, his glance sweeping the hard-muscled form of the younger Roman. " 'Twould be a great honor, Tribune Paullinus," he continued carefully, "if you'd consent to participate in the games. A token of the good intentions of your new command, shall we say?"

What is the old man's game? Marcus wondered. Did the Trinovante sincerely intend the offer as a gesture of gratitude for saving his daughter? Or did his true motives lie deeper, embedded in the depths of his hatred for Rome? To see the new tribune summarily defeated could also suit the chieftain's plans, both as a humiliation of Rome and its newest representative. Refusing the Trinovante's offer would be a delicate task, but the wisest one in the long run.

"You honor me by your invitation," Marcus began, when Albinus smoothly cut in.

"Surely you cannot be serious?" The senior tribune laughed disparagingly, meeting Riderch's narrowed gaze with a glittering one of his own. "Roman soldiers needn't prove their good intentions to anyone! *We* are the conquerors. You need only concern yourself with unquestioning obedience." Albinus turned to Marcus. "What say you, Tribune? Do I not speak for Rome in this?"

Marcus tensed. There was no mistaking the mocking challenge in Albinus' eyes. Though, to the two Trinovante, the senior tribune's interference might be construed as a rescue of his compatriot, Marcus knew better. The man's true intent was to bring the rapidly worsening confrontation to a head—and force Marcus into a no-win situation. He, too, it seemed, still pursued his agenda in the waning days of his command.

"You erred in your offer of hospitality, Father," Rhianna jeered, apparently eager to offer her own thoughts on Marcus' participation. "Obviously, the new tribune intends to continue the current policies of his predecessor."

He swung around to face her. "I'm my own man, lady," Marcus growled, a frigid wrath in his eyes. "Rome's policies can be adapted to many situations—and in many ways."

"Can they now?" Rhianna stepped forward to meet him face-to-face. "And how will you adapt to this particular situation, Red Crest? There seem but two choices. Will or won't you wrestle against our men?"

"Lady, I warned you before—"

"Rhianna, enough!" Her father grasped her arm and pulled her back to his side. "The tribune doesn't need your sharp tongue pricking at him. He must make his own decision—and live with the consequences."

"As must we all, Lord Riderch," Marcus agreed tautly, continuing to eye Rhianna. Then, with a sudden resolve, his mind was made. "I accept your offer. My wrestling skills suffer from want of practice, but I'll strive to do my best."

Riderch grinned, visibly relieved. "Good, then 'tis settled. The contestants are gathering. I'll find someone to assist in your preparations—"

"One moment more." Marcus' teeth flashed white in a lazy grin, though his gaze never left Rhianna's face. "You spoke of vying for the victor's due. What is the prize?"

"Why, the choice of one of our clan's maidens, to serve all the victor's needs for the day—and night."

"And the choice is of any maiden," Marcus prodded carefully, "no matter her standing in the clan?"

Irritation tightened the corners of Riderch's mouth. "Of course. 'Tis a matter of honor, for the clan as well as the maid chosen."

"Then I tell you now, Lord Riderch," Marcus said, his gaze meeting and holding the Trinovante's, "that if I win the wrestling, I intend to choose Rhianna as my victor's due. Does your fabled Celtic honor extend to the granting of your own daughter to a Roman?"

Rhianna choked back an outraged cry and leaped at Marcus. Her father barely managed to restrain her. "You would dare throw my honest offer of friendship back in my face by insulting my daughter?" he demanded. "She is already promised to another!"

"Indeed?" Marcus shrugged. "And aren't Celts permitted to take lovers before they wed? I don't want to marry her. I just want her for a night's pleasure. That *is* the purpose of the victor's due, isn't it?"

With Albinus snickering in the background, Marcus subjected Riderch to a savage scrutiny. "But then the real point of the matter is whether your offer was truly made in friendship or as a ploy to humiliate me. Which was it, Lord Riderch?"

Rhianna glanced from her father to the Roman and saw the tension building. That realization, more than the restraint of her father's arms, reined in her anger. There was no way to guess how long the Red Crest's temper would hold, but she knew Riderch was near the end of his patience.

As difficult as it was to admit, her father may have met his match in the younger man. She refused, however, to allow the Roman to use her as a pawn a moment longer.

"Accept his bargain, Father." Rhianna gave a disparaging laugh. " 'Tis well known the Red Crests aren't famed for their wrestling ability. There's no danger to me or my maidenhood from a Roman who dares go against our men."

Riderch turned to his daughter, pulling her over to the gate and out of earshot of the two tribunes. He shot a quick glance at the younger Roman, who waited in watchful silence. "Cador won't be happy with this."

"He needn't know; and once he wins, 'twill be a moot point at any rate."

"If you wish it so, lass," Riderch agreed glumly, his shoulders slumping. "But I don't like it. I misjudged Paullinus when I invited him into the wrestling. I thought to take him down a notch in his Roman arrogance—one way or another—and now find the tables turned." He expelled a deep breath. "By the Goddess, all my fine maneuverings have done naught but place you in jeopardy!"

Rhianna gave his hand a quick squeeze. "Don't worry, Father. The Roman will not win."

He managed a crooked smile. "Most likely not, but nonetheless . . ." Riderch indicated that she accompany him back to the Romans. Once there, he immediately confronted Marcus. "The bargain is made, Tribune. *If* you win the wrestling, Rhianna will be your victor's due."

"A most potent incentive, to be sure, Lord Riderch." Marcus paused to eye Rhianna closely, gaining nothing for his efforts but an impassive stare, before turning back to the chieftain. "I'll need help in the preparations. It's only fitting Rhianna aid me. Don't you agree?"

Riderch clamped down on an angry retort, noting, as he had when Rhianna and the tribune had first been introduced, that hungry light burning in the other man's eyes. Though a part of him felt shamed at so cold-blooded a consideration, another part was suddenly hopeful, heartened. The Roman wanted Rhianna, yet the need 'twas more than just the stirrings of a young man's lust. And mayhap, just mayhap, that weakness could be used to the Trinovantes' advantage. He was desperate enough to risk it.

" 'Tis indeed fitting," he forced himself to reply, boldly meeting the tribune's gaze. "I won't have it said you lost for want of proper instruction."

He gave his startled daughter a small nudge forward. "Go, lass. Take the tribune to the ring."

Rhianna's stomach sank with a sickening thud. Once again, she had allowed her sharp tongue to draw her into an unpleasant situation. Well, there was naught to be done but face up to the consequences, consequences she knew would, at worst, now entail tolerating the man's presence for the afternoon.

She graced the Roman with a scathing glance. "By your leave, my lord." She indicated to Marcus that he should accompany her.

He grinned and joined her, following through the milling crowds of gaily dressed people headed toward a large, roughly fenced-in area of close-cropped grass. The little spitfire would learn her lesson before this day was over, he mused in silent satisfaction. As would Albinus and the Trinovante chieftain.

Yet, though he fully intended to win Rhianna to make his point, Marcus had no intention of taking her maidenhood. He only wanted to earn her obedience—and the obedience of her father and people—in as expeditious a manner as possible. Turning the table on the proud Riderch and his headstrong daughter, Marcus supposed, as well as putting Albinus in his place, was as good as any way to begin his command as *Praefectus Alae.* Good, if not painless, he thought with a wry grimace, recalling the brutal wrestling matches to come.

Rhianna halted near the entrance to the wrestling arena, where piles of male garments as well as several large wooden bowls filled with silvery fluid had been laid out, and turned to the Roman. "Disrobe here. One of our lads will assure your equipment's safety until your return."

Marcus' gaze skimmed the near-naked bodies of the Celts warming up in the ring, then shot her an amused glance.

"Our men aren't in the habit of exercising before women in such scant attire."

"Well, *our* men are and we women find no affront in it. You agreed to participate, Roman. Don't offend us further by refusing to abide by our customs."

A deep, rich laugh answered her. The Roman unfastened the leather buckles of his corselet. "As you wish, Rhianna. I'd be hard-pressed to refuse such a delicately couched request, especially since I know it's due to your eagerness to assess my body for the night to come."

"M-my eagerness!" Outrage flared within her as she accepted the two halves of his corselet, but Rhianna bit back further reply. Though he was naught more than an arrogant boor, he was still a guest. She wondered how many times she'd have to remind herself of that before the afternoon was over.

Marcus' sword belt and scabbard, shin greaves, and heavy military sandals came next. By the time Rhianna straightened to face him again, the thin belt girding his short-sleeved, gray woolen tunic was in his hand. She accepted it from him. He pulled the garment over his head.

As he busied himself folding his tunic, Rhianna's gaze widened in reluctant admiration. Except for the brief linen loincloth, the Roman's body was now fully exposed. His smoothly muscled frame appeared as fit as that of any of the Trinovante's finest warriors. Wide of shoulder, with a broad chest covered by a generous thatch of black hair, his body tapered into a narrow waist and hip.

Her glance quickly passed over the taut, rippling abdomen and cloth-covered groin down to long, steel-tempered legs. Several scars on his chest and thighs marred the magnificence of his body not a wit. On the contrary, they only enhanced his prowess, raised as she was to glory courage in battle.

"Would you care to check my teeth?"

"What?" Rhianna jerked her gaze back to the Roman's. "What do you mean?"

"I only thought you might like to complete the examination by looking at my teeth. No horse at auction could have received a more thorough inspection than you just gave me."

"Why, you crude—"

"Careful, Rhianna." Marcus held up a warning hand, a roguish grin on his face. "Others are watching, including your father. It wouldn't be seemly to start the wrestling on a premature note."

She opened her mouth to reply, then clamped it shut. Stalking over to one of the large bowls, Rhianna quickly retrieved it and returned to Marcus' side.

He eyed the fluid suspiciously. "What's that?"

"Oil. Men, vain creatures that they are, use it to display their muscles to the greatest possible advantage." Rhianna dipped her hand into the unctuous liquid. "Turn around and let me smear your back. The judges are already pairing opponents."

Marcus turned and offered his back. Rhianna spread the oil over the muscular expanse presented her, marveling at the texture of his skin, so warm and alive beneath her hand. The scent of musk—fabled for its magical powers of energy and strength—gradually filled the air. The oil, warmed by the heat of his body, Rhianna realized, had released its special, sense-stimulating fragrance. Quickly, she moved to the backs of his arms and finally squatted to do his legs.

"Turn around," she ordered at last, standing once more.

Immediately confronted with a massive, hairy chest, Rhianna swallowed hard. His masculine scent mingled with the musk-laden oil, wafting to her nostrils, flooding her with a strange excitement. She tamped that down, both furious and confused by her reaction.

This is ridiculous, Rhianna thought. 'Twasn't as if she'd never seen a half-naked man before or spread oil on a male body. Curse the man! He was even more unsettling now than he'd been in the forest, when she'd been alone and at his mercy. She took a step backward, hoping the distance would still the strange pounding of her heart.

His gaze caught Rhianna's, the look he sent her plummeting straight to the depths of her soul. She felt him tremble as her hand touched his chest. The brush of his crisp hair against Rhianna's fingertips sent a jolt of molten fire coursing through her. On and on the fire flowed, until the searing heat reached the very core of her being.

Against her will, a warm lassitude swept over her. Struggling past the strange lethargy, it was all Rhianna could do to complete the work of smoothing the erotically scented oil over the rest of the Roman's tautly strung body. Finally, she forced herself to move away.

She glanced toward the middle of the arena where her father stood talking to the two judges and gesturing in the Roman's direction. Multicolored banners suspended about the enclosure snapped in the erratic gusts of wind, lending a vibrantly agitated emphasis to the gay tumult of surging bodies. All, Trinovante and Roman alike, appeared eager for the wrestling to begin.

'Twas strange, Rhianna thought. Before, she, too, would have found the festive atmosphere exciting, even blood-stirring. But not now. Everything had suddenly paled in comparison to the past moments with the Roman.

"Y-you are ready." She choked out the words, her eyes

drawn back to his by some oddly compelling force. "My father awaits you."

The Roman's gaze locked with hers, his eyes darkening to glittering bits of jade. A muscle worked in his jaw. With sudden insight, Rhianna realized he was as excited, as unexpectedly stimulated, as she. A premonitory warning prickled down her spine.

With a mouth gone dry, she watched him walk to the ring. His corded, well-oiled body gleamed in the strong midday sun, his movements athletic, full of power and vitality. Rhianna followed, ignoring the looks and whispered comments of the people who had gathered to watch what, to them, must have been the sideshow of a Trinovante maid tending a Roman. She gritted her teeth against the surge of embarrassment and, instead, forced her strangely nerveless body to turn toward the rough-hewn fence delineating the wrestling arena.

Rhianna grasped the wooden rail and clenched it until her fingers turned knuckle-white. Her stomach churned; her challenge, so lightly given, now rushed back to haunt her. *Accept his bargain, Father. There's no danger to me.*

She deeply regretted now the looseness of her tongue. The Roman would be a formidable opponent for any of their men. That much had been evident as she had run her hands over his battle-hardened body.

Then the memory blurred, sharpening once more into a scene of the Roman's body, this time gloriously, magnificently naked, clasping her equally naked body to his. Rhianna's breath came in ragged gasps as the familiar, unwanted comprehension flooded her. 'Twas the Gift, visiting her once again.

"Don't fight it, lass," a gentle, age-thickened voice urged. "Accept, listen, and understand."

"N-nay!" With a superhuman effort, Rhianna threw off the vision's hold and turned to face her grandfather. "Nay, I cannot! 'Tis *your* gift, not mine."

Wise old eyes, framed by an ancient face and long, white hair, gazed down at her in loving compassion. " 'Tis yours as well, Granddaughter. You must accept it. 'Tis your destiny. A destiny preordained by the gods."

"Nay." She shook her head, her eyes filling with tears. " 'Tis no destiny; 'tis a tragedy. The greatest tragedy of my life!"

Cunagus smiled sadly. " 'Twon't change what is preordained, lass. 'Twill only hinder the acceptance and the Gift's benefit to both you and our people." With a swirl of long, white robes, he walked away.

Rhianna watched until the beloved form of her grandfather had passed into the crowd, then turned back to the arena. Frantically, she sought out the mighty form of Cador in the gathering of contestants. He swaggered, flexing his well-oiled muscles, laughing and joking with the other contestants as if his victory were a foregone conclusion.

A victory that had suddenly assumed staggering proportions.

Let him win. He *must* win, Rhianna beseeched the Mother Goddess, her antipathy for the man fading beneath a rising, far more terrifying realization. Her life on this hallowed feast of Lughnasa, she sensed with a sickening swell of despair, had reached a shattering crossroads. Indeed, if she and Cador did not join tonight, any hope of a normal life was doomed.

Doomed—as surely as her destiny would then forever entwine with that of the Roman.

Three

Scanning the sheer bulk of his opponent, Marcus inwardly groaned. The Trinovante, it seemed, were determined to put a swift and resounding end to his participation. While the sticklers responsible for the game's fair play circled the perimeters of the individual wrestling rings, the signal was given to begin.

With a roar echoed by the crowd of Romans and Trinovante watching from the fence line, the blond giant leaped forward. Huge, beefy arms attempted to capture him, but Marcus feinted to the left, drawing his foe off balance. He slung an arm about the Trinovante's neck, neatly tripped the man, and quickly wrestled him to the ground.

A stickler squatted to view the pin. He grunted his assent. The match was over.

Marcus rose and waved to his wildly cheering men. Then, as his glance moved around the arena, his eyes met Rhianna's. She stood on the women's side surrounded by other brightly garbed and jostling women, the loose tendrils of her flaxen braid floating about her face on the breeze. Their gazes locked. Marcus grinned in triumph. She looked away.

Though oddly disappointed, Marcus squelched that emotion as ridiculous. What had he expected? She already despised him, and his threat to bed her if he won had only angered her further. But those moments, when Rhianna's hand was upon him smearing the oil, had been heady and exciting. He could have sworn they'd been equally so for her.

Marcus turned to await the assignment of his next opponent. This time the man was more equal in height and breadth of shoulder, with a crafty gleam to his eyes. Unlike the first Celt, he wore the gold torc of the nobility.

Rhianna watched as her cousin, Idris, strode into the ring. She cared little for him, although the thought of his defeating the Roman was still pleasant to contemplate. Idris had been a thorn in her flesh since childhood. The son of Riderch's younger sister, Idris was nothing more than a strutting peacock. And that he was Cador's closest friend did little to alleviate Rhianna's uneasy dislike.

Like his friend, Idris coveted the chieftainship. Everything he did was clothed in the trappings of that ambition, an ambition for a position he had as legitimate a claim to as Rhianna's family. Trinovante custom had always allowed for selection of clan leader from within three generations of a common ancestor, men and women alike.

Not that women were often chosen. There were a few ruling queens, like Cartimandua of the Brigantes and now, Boudicca, but those opportunities rarely arose.

The stickler signaled and the two men lunged at each other. Excitement thrummed through Rhianna. Ah, if only she could join in the wrestling! Even now, the women contestants were warming up for their own matches. 'Twas a poor imitation of battle, but a release of bridled energy and aggression of a sorts, nonetheless. But nay, instead she was relegated to serving as some Roman's handmaid.

Squelching her sudden swell of frustration, Rhianna focused her attention back on the occupants of the ring. It became rapidly apparent the Roman would have more difficulty besting Idris. As they grappled, Rhianna fervently prayed the Roman would be beaten. Still, the tide turned slowly against her cousin. Then a shout rose from one of the other rings and her attention strayed.

Tall, blond Cador, his powerful body glistening with a mixture of oil and sweat, had just won his match. Arms flung up in triumph, he turned to the fierce adulation of the crowd. His searching gaze found Rhianna's. He shot her a possessive, knowing smile.

She returned his greeting with a small wave. Then her glance moved quickly from his, careening straight into the intently frowning one of the Roman. He stared back at her, the recent victor of his second match, his stance taut and guarded. He'd noticed the interchange between her and Cador. A strange nervousness fluttered in the pit of Rhianna's stomach.

Then he smiled, the look just as possessive, just as knowing as Cador's had been. Men, Rhianna thought in disgust. No matter their allegiance, they were all the same.

With an angry toss of her head, she directed her attention to the third-round pairings. From the original group only five remained. The Roman, unfortunately, was one of them. As last year's champion and the odd man, Cador wasn't required to participate in the next two competitions.

Her oldest brother, Cerdic, was one of the two pairings and would wrestle against another clansman. He had recently recovered from a brutal fall from his chariot and was barely healed, but had still stubbornly insisted on participating in the games. Rhianna loved him with a younger sister's worship of an older brother but knew, nonetheless, this time Cerdic had overreached himself. He'd be lucky if he made it past this next round.

The tall Roman was pitted against the fort smithy. Rhianna

eyed the blacksmith's bulging arms and strong, sturdy legs and decided the Red Crest had finally met his match. With that thought she dismissed him and concentrated on her brother's bout.

The comments of Ura, however, kept her apprised of the contest in the other ring.

"Oooh, look at that poor man!" the brown-haired girl squealed. "That vicious Roman will break his arm. Ah, wait. Maglor has slipped from his grasp. H-he's got the Roman in a headlock. He's trying to wrestle him to the ground." Ura screamed. "Ah, nay! The Roman's squirmed loose . . ."

Rhianna found it increasingly difficult to keep her attention fixed on her brother. Blessed Goddess, she thought in rising irritation, what did it matter what happened to the Roman anyway? If he, by some stroke of fortune, managed to keep winning, she'd be forced to watch his eventual match with Cador. Ah, if only Ura wouldn't shriek so!

A tap on the shoulder drew Rhianna from her unsettling musings. She glanced over at Cordaella.

A strange light danced in the red-haired girl's eyes. "The Roman is winning. You had an opportunity to examine his body. What do you think of his chances against mighty Cador?"

Rhianna graced her with a withering look. "You act as if I willingly assisted him. 'Twas hardly the way of it."

"Was it now? I was nearby, Rhianna. I saw the looks you sent the Roman and the fire burning in his eyes for you. You are fortunate Cador was not about. He would not take kindly to his betrothed lusting after a Roman."

"I don't care what Cador thinks. He may be my betrothed, but he has yet to become my husband."

"Nor will he, if he finds occasion to doubt your vows to him." Cordaella arched a slender brow. "What if the Roman should win and claim you as his due? You'd be honor-bound to lie with him." She twirled a strand of auburn hair around her finger. "I wonder, would Cador still want you after a Roman soiled your maiden's flesh?"

"Cordaella!" Ura's shocked voice intruded on the discussion. "How could you even think such a thing?" She patted Rhianna on the arm. "Don't fret, my friend. You haven't a worry. Cador will surely win . . ."

At Rhianna's piercing look, Ura's voice faded.

A loud cry sprang from the crowd. Cerdic's opponent had defeated him at last.

Rhianna dared a glance to where the Roman still struggled. Though both men were rapidly tiring, it was evident the Red Crest would ultimately emerge the victor. Rhianna groaned inwardly. Things were becoming more complicated with each passing moment.

A firm grip settled on her arm. "Come, child. I need a few moments of your time," Savren, her mother, said. "Cerdic's defeated, and Cador won't wrestle in this next round. Help me with the bread and other victuals for the feast. I'll have you back before the victor's match."

Relieved to be free of Cordaella's biting words, for once Rhianna followed her mother across the fort without protest. As they wove through the brightly garbed crowd, many dressed in the beloved Celtic stripes and checks, Rhianna's thoughts flew. Were Cordaella's accusations true? Had her response to the Roman, a reaction that both confused and frightened her, really been so obvious? And, worst of all, had the Roman noticed?

A hot blush warmed her cheeks. What *was* it about him that compelled her to act so? He was a physically admirable man, but there were many who rivaled him in that respect—Cador included.

Cador.

Rhianna turned the name over in her mind, mentally worrying it for some hint of why it should suddenly unsettle her so. Did the answer lie buried in her repugnance for him? Did she loathe Cador so deeply she'd prefer a Roman?

Shame filled her. What manner of woman was she to flee her clan responsibilities because the choice of her betrothed didn't suit her?

The Gift's fearful intuition swept through her once more, confirming those and even deeper fears. She felt hot, then cold, and the world threatened to fade.

Blessed Mother, Rhianna prayed silently. *I beg of you, take the choice from me! Let Cador win this day and seal my fate. Now, before 'tis too late—*

"Daughter, what ails you?"

Rhianna dragged a puzzled gaze to her mother. Savren stared back, concern narrowing her eyes. Her heart commenced a triphammer beat. Was it possible? Did her mother know of the bargain made with the Roman?

"A-ails me? Why, naught." Rhianna halted before their cone-shaped, outdoor fire pit, taut with apprehension of what her mother might say next. "Isn't the bread ready?"

"Aye, 'tis ready. Come, hold the platter near while I remove the loaves from the oven."

Rhianna exhaled a small breath of relief and moved to help her mother. They worked together, laying six long, round-edged loaves of brown bread on the wooden plank. Faint tendrils of steam wafted fragrant aromas to their noses. Behind them, a tumult of voices erupted from the wrestling arena. Rhianna glanced up, then resumed wrapping cloths around the bread.

"The shouts sounded joyful," Savren murmured. "Mayhap the Roman is at last defeated. Though he fights as bravely as any Celt, it galls me to have him win. Well, no matter. Our men will soon see to his defeat." She glanced at Rhianna. "Has it been difficult for you? Tolerating the Roman's presence in the name of hospitality?"

Rhianna shook her head. "Nay. I'd rather his presence than that worm Albinus. And, as Father said, I owe him some measure of gratitude for rescuing me."

As she wrapped the loaves, she lowered her head, grateful for even the smallest excuse to avoid her mother's scrutiny. *Please, please let her move to another subject before I betray myself,* she thought.

"I only hope Cador understands," her mother continued blithely. "It must sit poorly with him to see his betrothed as some Roman's handmaid. I wonder what your father was thinking, to make such a request of you. Cador is proud. If he should put you aside . . ."

She doesn't know of Father's bargain with the Roman, Rhianna thought, or she'd be far from this calm. And there'd be no need for her ever to know. Cador would soon see to the solution to all of their problems.

"Calm your fears, Mother." Rhianna tucked the cloth about the last loaf. "Cador's no fool. He values his chance for the chieftainship too highly not to wed me. He won't put aside our betrothal."

"Nay, Cador is no fool, and neither am I!"

At the sharp reproach in her mother's voice, Rhianna's head snapped up.

"Do you think, daughter, I've not heeded your reluctance to wed Cador, your aversion to the man? 'Tis of no import, though." A sudden despair hovered on the edge of Savren's words. "Higher things than the whims of a spoiled girl are at stake here. Remember that, Rhianna, and thank the Goddess 'twas Cador who asked for you. For the sake of your father and our clan, you could do worse."

Suddenly, some memory seemed to assail her. Savren grabbed Rhianna's arm, pulling her close. "Do naught that would endanger us. Do you hear me? Naught!"

"A-aye, Mother," Rhianna stammered, unnerved by the desperate vehemence in her voice. "I have already sworn to wed Cador. What else can I—"

"Mama! Rhianna!"

The excited voice of Emrys, Rhianna's youngest brother, intruded. Before the two women could rise to their feet, he and his older brother Kenow slid to a halt before the fire pit.

"The fourth round! 'Tis over!" the twelve year-old lad blurted in one breath. "The . . . the Roman. He . . . he will meet Cador in the victor's match. Hurry and come. They may have already begun."

Rhianna's heart sank. Goddess, what else could go wrong today? 'Twas impossible that the Roman should have succeeded this far! Now, her only hope lay in Cador.

Kenow, at nineteen already as tall and solid as a young oak, grabbed Rhianna's arm. "Aye, hurry. Cador told me to fetch you. He wants his betrothed present when he grinds the Roman's face in the dust." A grin creased his sunburned face. "As we'll soon be doing to all Romans who dare set foot in our land."

"Kenow!" his mother cautioned angrily. "Hold your tongue. Have you forgotten those very Romans are in our midst? Lughnasa is a sacred time. Let there be no talk of war."

Her son hung his head, his shaggy brown locks falling to hide the crimson flush tinging his cheeks. "The excitement . . . I forgot myself."

Rhianna moved to his side and tucked his arm under hers. Far better that both of them escape Savren's razor-sharp tongue. "And have you also forgotten the match is about to begin? Come along with you. I, too, dearly wish to see the Roman defeated. Let's carry the loaves to the feasting tables for mother, then be on our way."

With blond, freckle-faced Emrys tagging behind, a large wooden bowl of curded cheese in his arms, Rhianna and Kenow hurried to the long rows of tables. After depositing the food, they ran to the arena. The two men were already in the ring, listening to the judge's final instructions.

As Rhianna worked her way to the front of the fence line on the women's side, she caught the Roman's attention. His head turned. Dark hair matted damply to his forehead; rivulets of sweat trickled down a grime-encrusted face and body. He looked bruised, weary, yet the fierce light burning in his green-gold eyes was proud and resolute.

He'll never give up, Rhianna realized, not until the last breath leaves his body. As he'll pursue anything he ever desires . . .

The knowledge sent a tiny shiver through her. Why, at the most inopportune moments, did that cursed Gift choose to reveal itself—and about the Roman, no less? She wanted naught to do with him, now or ever. He was naught to her. Naught!

She tore her gaze from his. Cador, a confident smile on his handsome, long-mustached face, nodded to the judge. He was rested, his lean-muscled body cleansed of the earlier rounds of dirt and sweat.

Rhianna compared the two men. An equal match, to be sure, if the Roman had been provided the same chance to rest as Cador. But in the condition he was now in? Had he even been given a cool drink before having to face this last and most formidable of adversaries?

Guilt tugged at Rhianna's heart. He'd had no one to see

to his needs, and that charge had been hers. No matter what her feelings for him or how much she wished for his defeat, she'd failed in clan hospitality. The Goddess would surely frown on her fortunes this day.

At the judge's signal, the two men hurled themselves at each other. The dull thud of flesh meeting flesh resounded throughout the crowd. They grappled, muscled arms and legs straining in an effort to gain a solid foothold. Fresh sweat soon gleamed atop the oiled surface of their bodies. Neither appeared to move as one's effort was met, and equaled, by the other's.

When it became evident neither man could gain the advantage, a stickler stepped forward to break the hold. Once more the two opponents leaped at each other. The Roman's breath rasped hard now, its harshness carrying to Rhianna's ears.

'Tis all a game, she realized. Cador's wrestling strategy was to spare himself while nibbling away at the Roman's rapidly waning strength. Not the most honorable way to win a contest, but winning was all that ever mattered to Cador.

A flicker of movement, then the slap of flesh cracked through the crowd as Marcus blocked the Celt's grab. Before Cador could recover, Marcus sprang at him. His weary muscles flexing to their limits, he heaved the Celt into the air. Cador's feet flew out from under him. Locked together, the two men tumbled to the ground. Marcus managed to land on top.

With an angry cry, his opponent lurched upward, throwing his head full force into Marcus' face. Stunned by the pain and blinded by the blood that welled rapidly from the freshly torn flesh over his left brow, Marcus loosened his grip.

It was all the Trinovante needed. With a triumphant snarl

he twisted to deliver a sharp, surreptitious jab to Marcus' groin.

Only raw instinct maintained Marcus' clasp. His legs jerked up in a spasm of agony. As he fought for breath, the other man bodily rolled them over.

The end was near. If the Trinovante succeeded in pinning one of his shoulders, Marcus knew he'd never break free. With his last ounce of strength, he, too, twisted and fought, managing to land on top again, facing upward. The effort only seemed to worsen his situation as Cador's arm moved to lock around him.

A stickler stepped forward to break the hold, but the judge motioned him back. The Celt's arm crooked about Marcus' neck. Suddenly, he found himself throttled.

Each time Marcus raised his hands to break the stranglehold, Cador would try to flip him over onto his stomach. Forced to lower his hands to maintain his precarious balance, he could do little to extricate himself from the strangling grip.

The sky blurred. A gray mist encroached at the edges of his vision. Yet even in that moment of defeat, Marcus refused to yield. Never . . . not while there was breath left in his body . . .

Rhianna's own breath came in painful gulps as she watched the scene in the arena. Blessed Goddess, would the Roman let Cador kill him rather than yield?

She looked to the judge. He made no move to halt the contest. Cold despair rose within. Would *no one* help the Roman? Were they all blind to his impending death?

Despite the loathsome pact she'd made with him, he didn't deserve to die like this. He had saved her life. Yet Cador would kill him if he didn't yield. The blood lust was upon him, that heady, mind-drugging ecstasy of battle. Cador couldn't stop himself now if he wanted to.

She opened her mouth to cry out, to beg the judge to halt the match, when the Roman, with one last, superhuman lunge, jerked from Cador's grasp. Rolling over, he flung himself upon his opponent. Cador bellowed in rage but the Roman managed to hold him down. The stickler bent low to examine the pin.

Rhianna's breath caught in her throat. Her heart pounded within her chest. Let it be finished, she prayed. She could bear no more. Let him win—no matter the consequences!

The stickler finally signaled. The match was over. From the auxiliaries' side of the fence joyous bedlam reigned. Albinus, conspicuously silent and sullen, stood a short distance from the others.

He's not pleased, Rhianna realized. The two tribunes weren't friends though they served the same emperor. The thought filled her with a curious elation, but she dared not delve too deeply into the basis for her feelings. Not after the past, emotion-laden minutes.

Her father walked onto the field, an oak-leaf wreath in his hand. The crown of victory, woven from the greenery of the tree most sacred to the Celts, was presented at Lughnasa to the champions of the various athletic contests. The Roman climbed awkwardly to his feet. Cador, though unhurt, remained flat on his back, his face contorted with rage.

Marcus offered his hand to the blond Trinovante. "You fought mightily. I pray we never face each other in battle."

Pale blue eyes opened to glare up at him. "Another time, Roman, and you won't be so lucky!" Ignoring the outstretched hand, Cador rose and stalked away.

Riderch halted before Marcus, his frowning gaze following Cador's retreating form. "I beg you not attribute Cador's conduct as that of all Trinovante," he growled, turning back to Marcus. "You have won this victor's crown fairly and are esteemed the most powerful man of this Lughnasa." He raised the wreath above the Roman's head. "Accept this token of our respect and the victor's due that accompanies it."

Marcus stepped forward and bowed his head. The twisted circlet of oak leaves was placed upon his brow. As if by some covert signal, the crowd, Romans and Trinovante alike, broke into a cheer. At the noisy acclaim, Marcus' strained, weary expression transformed into a wide smile.

Only at Lughnasa, Rhianna thought, the prickle of tears burning at the back of her throat. Only on sacred festival grounds, at rare moments in the year, did one see the barriers of tribal animosities and long-standing enmities, that now included the presence of a foreign power like Rome, tumble down and men come together as brothers. Yet reality being what it was, the consequences of the Roman's victory could not long be buried beneath the outpouring of universal fellowship. The victor's due had yet to be granted.

A hush settled over the gathering. Riderch waited for the crowd to calm, his glance skimming the assemblage. Then, he once more faced the Roman.

"Is it still your wish to have my daughter?"

Marcus returned the chieftain's icy gaze, steeling himself to the other man's plight. Why should he feel pity for the Trinovante? It was he who had goaded him into the wrestling. Now, let him pay the price for this day's entertainment.

"Yes, it is."

The muscles of Riderch's jaw tightened. No matter the gravity of his own personal sacrifice, he would grant the tribune his victor's due. Ancient tradition demanded it; Trinovante honor would uphold it. "Then have her you will."

He turned and raised his arms. The crowd fell silent. "The

Tribune Paullinus has won the wrestling," he cried. "For his victor's due he has chosen, from all the maidens of our clan, to honor my daughter, Rhianna." A single gasp rose from the silent crowd. Riderch knew it was Savren. He hardened his heart to her pain, as he already had to his own.

"Come, daughter." He motioned Rhianna forward from her place at the fence. "The Roman has chosen."

Rhianna paled but, curiously, felt no fear, no emotion at all. Her fate had been sealed from the moment she and the Roman had met. No amount of lamenting would change what was preordained.

Preordained. As was her Gift. Bitter as it was to contemplate, Cunagus had spoken true.

Far better to accept and see it through. It was only one day in her life, after all, and many women had lain with men other than their betrothed. She stepped from the fence and entered the arena. As she did, an angry voice shouted "Nay!" before being quickly stifled.

Cador. Rhianna recalled Cordaella's earlier words. Would he indeed still want her after tonight?

It didn't matter. No one would think less of her. On the contrary, if the victor had been other than a Roman, she'd have been the envy of all the women.

Rhianna halted before the two men, her gaze storm-dark and proud. Her father took her hand, placing it within the larger one of the Roman. He watched as the strong brown fingers closed over those of his daughter.

"Take this maid as your victor's due," Riderch proclaimed, his voice heavy with emotion as he uttered the ceremonial words. "For this day and night she is yours. But only on this, our beloved feast of Lughnasa. On the morrow, she is ours once more."

Rhianna's glance caught and held the Roman's. His eyes

burned brightly, as if stoked by some savage, inner fire. She knew it for what it was. She met his heated gaze with a cool one of her own.

I am not afraid, Rhianna silently answered him. *I'll not quail before you no matter what you do to me. Honor is everything and I am Trinovante. Nay, Roman, you've won naught. Naught at all.*

Rhianna halted before a large bower fashioned from tree boughs and interwoven vines. Situated in a distant corner of the hill fort far from the other houses, the dwelling's four sides were enclosed by woven hangings, brightly striped in shades of saffron and green. Though intended as a cozy, comfortable little hideaway, the care lavished in its construction was wasted on Rhianna.

She turned to the Roman. "As champion, this place is yours until the morrow."

He glanced at it briefly and nodded. "Let us make use of it then. I've a wish to cleanse myself of this dust and sweat before I walk again among your people."

She smiled thinly and stepped through the bower's opening. Marcus followed.

The tent's interior was comfortably furnished. A large, intricately swirled blue-and-cream carpet covered the hard-packed earth. Upon the rug sat three wooden chairs and a table laden with two earthenware pitchers, mugs, and a bowl of fruit. Several braziers were already stocked with kindling to light the night and a spacious pallet lay over to one side, heaped high with furs and cushions.

The Roman's eyes riveted on the bed. Rhianna's hands tightened around his armor and clothing. Blessed Goddess, what was he thinking? Would he take her even now, in the shaming light of day?

She inhaled a fortifying breath. No matter what he demanded, she must never show fear, never beg for mercy. She turned to face him.

His gaze met hers, his eyes dark and unfathomable. A small, questioning smile touched his mouth. Hot color rose in her cheeks.

Rhianna gestured to the pallet. “For your repose whenever you desire and where you . . . I mean, *we* will sleep tonight.”

He bowed his acknowledgment. “I thank you for the consideration.”

Anger flamed, spilling over into her voice. “ ’Tis no consideration, Roman. ’Tis your victor’s due, and we honor our customs above all.”

“Even above your hatred for me? Isn’t that what you really meant to say, Rhianna?”

She hesitated, unwilling to utter further words that might be construed as inhospitable. “You won and, without protest, the bargain was paid. Let the rest be. I’ve no wish to be rude, but I’ll not lie.”

“I’ve never asked you to lie, Rhianna,” came the soft reply.

“Then accept what you’ve achieved, as I have, Roman. Accept and probe no deeper. ’Tis the best course for the both of us.” She laid his clothing and equipment on a nearby chair. “I’ll fetch water and cloths for washing. There’s beer and spring water for your refreshment until I return.”

Rhianna quickly exited the bower and headed back across the fort for her supplies. Her tumultuous emotions, however, were no calmer by the time she returned.

Marcus glanced up, mug in hand, as she paused in the bower’s doorway, the hanging pulled up and out of her way. His gaze raked her slender form. By the gods, but she was lovely! Backlit by the sunlight streaming in, her hair was a golden nimbus about her head and the clinging fabric of her dress a tauntingly sheer accent to the long, nubile shadow of her legs.

His loins tightened. Choking back a frustrated curse, Marcus forced his gaze back up to her face. "Have I mentioned how beautifully that dress sets off your eyes?" he inquired, his voice husky with barely repressed desire.

Pointedly ignoring his remark, Rhianna's glance strayed to the two pitchers on the table beside him. Marcus' gaze joined hers. Both containers lay on their sides, quite empty.

She shook her head; her mouth twisted. " 'Twould be wise to imbibe less of our beer. 'Tis more potent then it first seems and your thirst could betray you. The water might have been a better choice to begin with."

He arched a dark brow in feigned dismay. "But, sweet lady, I *did* start with the water. It was gone soon after you left. There was no other choice but to turn to the beer." He raised his earthenware mug to her, his grin slightly lopsided. "And a fine, potently brewed beer it is, too."

The Roman was no different than any of their men, once he'd had too much to drink. Rhianna strode over and placed the bowl of wash water, cloths, and a small box on the table beside him. "Well, as soon as I tend that cut over your eye and help you clean up, I'll bring you more drinking water."

She moistened one of the cloths and began the cleansing of his face. Though she concentrated hard on her task, especially the careful washing of the jagged wound that slashed across his left brow, Rhianna was intensely aware of his scrutiny. His gaze, as soft as a caress, slowly traversed her body. As it passed from one spot to the next, she grew warm and tingling.

A thought sprung, unbidden, to her mind. If he could do

so much with a look, what would it be like to lie with him, to feel his hands and mouth upon her body . . . to feel his flesh join with hers?

A strange dryness rose in her throat. Rhianna swallowed hard. She threw the soiled cloth into the bowl, the force of the act mirroring the emphasis with which she flung aside the shameful ideas.

She glared down at her tormentor. "Why do you persist in looking at me like that?"

Grudging respect for her direct assault gleamed in his eyes. "Have I offended you? I meant no harm. Though Roman, I'm still a man, a man who can't help admiring a lovely woman."

"Well, I find no pleasure in it. Please stop."

He shot her an incredulous look. "Indeed? I wonder if you'd say that if I were that warrior I battled for the championship. I saw how he looked at you. He's your betrothed, isn't he?"

"And why is that of interest? Surely there are greater matters to concern you than the affairs of an insignificant Trinovante maid."

"Do you love him?"

She stiffened. "You presume too much, Roman. Even Trinovante hospitality has its limits."

Marcus shrugged, seemingly unperturbed. "Then I withdraw the question—for now." He lifted his cup to his lips then paused, a wicked look sparkling in his eyes. "Strange, though, that you make so much of such a simple question. The true reason intrigues me."

Rhianna's fists clenched at her sides and she choked back an insulting curse. By the Goddess, the sooner she could remove herself from this infuriating Roman's presence, the better! She resumed her cleansing of his blood-clotted wound, this time with less gentleness.

All she could obtain from her rougher efforts, however, was an occasional grimace. Rhianna's anger slowly subsided. Gradually, a more practical, feminine wisdom replaced the stronger feelings.

This was simply another battle of sorts and, though the Roman might ultimately take her body, he must never pierce the shield of her heart. High emotions on her part only encouraged him, and that was never the way of a warrior. Far better to thwart him by calm indifference.

The realization comforted her. A soft smile replaced the tight-lipped frown. At last Rhianna threw down the cloth and examined her work. The wound was clean, the grime and sweat gone from his face. She picked up the small box, rummaging through its contents until she found the healing ointment wrapped in a large oak leaf. She dabbed the wound with some of the unguent.

"There, all finished." Replacing the oak leaf and other supplies in the box, Rhianna tucked the container under her arm and picked up an empty pitcher. A strong brown hand stayed her.

She frowned down at him. "Is there something else, Roman?"

"Don't be angry with me, Rhianna. Your ill will is the last thing I'd wish."

Eyes, warm and compelling, locked with hers. His scent, a bracing mix of man, sweat, and musk-laden oil, wafted up to her. Caught in the mesmerizing aura that was so uniquely his, Rhianna's first impulse, to inform him that ill will was all there could ever be between them, died on her lips. Strangely, the words just wouldn't come. Suddenly, 'twas hard even to think coherently.

Rhianna sighed, calling herself back to the reality of the situation. The Roman was physically attractive. She was a hot-blooded maid. And the events of the impending night were impossible to ignore. 'Twas as simple as that.

"I bear you no ill will," she forced herself to reply. "To deny my respect for your strength and courage would be less than honest."

"And does this respect allow for friendship?"

Her eyes widened. She felt like a trapped bird, caught in the ensnaring depths of his bewitching smile. Rhianna wrenched her gaze away.

He asked for naught more than a token of friendship, she told herself. Surely 'twould do no harm. Yet, even as she parted her lips to reply, a small voice raised itself from the depths of her soul.

'Tisn't possible, it cried in rising indignation. *'Tisn't a warrior's way. Render him respect for the formidable foe he is, but never, ever, trust nor friendship.*

Her resolve hardened. "There's no hope of friendship for us. Only equals dare that. And, as long as Rome subjugates my land, you can never view me as such."

A shadow, some remembrance, passed across his face. He released her hand and leaned back, once more the stoic, disciplined Roman soldier. "You're right, Rhianna. Rome *does* subjugate your land. And neither of us must ever forget that."

She stared down at him, the cruel truth of his words piercing her heart. Then anger, that she should even care, swept through her. Rhianna stepped away.

"Finish your bath. I'll go for more water." She brandished the pitcher as she turned and headed for the exit.

"But Rhianna," the Roman's voice followed her, a wicked, teasing note hovering about his words, "if we can't be friends, won't you at least assist with my bath? You promised . . ."

Her bitter, haughty laugh, drifting back on the summer breeze, was his only reply.

Four

He had donned the last of his armor by the time Rhianna returned. The sudden brightening as she swept back the door hanging caught Marcus' attention. He turned in one fluid motion, his smile widening as his glance snared on the pitcher clasped in the soft valley between her breasts.

"I'm flattered you guarded my water so carefully." He reached for the earthenware container. "It'll taste all the sweeter because of your vigilance."

Rhianna's mouth tightened in annoyance. "Must you persist in this insincere flattery? There's no need to court my cooperation. You've already assured my presence in your bed."

Marcus' smile died in the clenching of his jaw. He took the pitcher from her. "Your presence, yes, but not your willing participation. And, if you weren't so insensitive, you'd realize I've yet to be insincere with you."

"I-insensitive! Why, you're nothing more than an . . . an arrogant—"

"Enough, Rhianna!" Marcus strode to the table and grabbed a cup. With little care to the mess he was making, he poured himself a drink and swallowed it in one gulp.

Curse the woman! He felt like a babbling, gangly schoolboy in her presence—he, who'd been raised in the highest of Roman society, who'd never found a woman intimidating.

It was all quite simple, Marcus decided in disgust. For no logical reason, he'd allowed her to turn him into a brainless, slobbering fool!

Well, fool or not, it was time to set aside his growing lust and turn to the task he'd set himself—keeping the peace. His earlier intentions, never to demand the full settlement of his victor's due, had been wise. He must distance himself from her emotionally, his apparent acceptance of Rhianna and her body used *only* to teach the Trinovante a lesson.

Marcus set the cup and pitcher aside. He grabbed up his helmet and tucked it under his arm. "It seems we're doomed to constant bickering as long as we remain here. If you think you can bear my presence, I'd like to see the rest of your fort and learn more about your people."

"So you can better rule us?" With a mocking sweep of her arm, Rhianna bowed. "I am at your disposal in all things, my lord." She straightened and stalked out of the bower.

The happy tumult outside did little to soothe Rhianna's churning emotions, especially when the Roman joined her to walk at her side. Yet, after a time, her smoldering anger cooled and remorse flared in its place. Remorse and an uncharacteristic self-doubt and confusion.

Once again she had failed in her duty and treated the Roman rudely. Yet his words had been no worse than those of other young men. Why had she reacted so strongly?

True, he had presumed to an unwarranted familiarity in questioning her about her betrothal to Cador, in asking for her friendship. He had also looked at her with lust in his eyes. And he had called her insensitive . . .

Insensitive. Rhianna winced. Those words, even more than his heated glances and presumption, had shot their mark.

She had never intentionally been cruel to another. Never, that was, until she met him.

Shame flooded Rhianna. What was wrong with her that she should treat him, the man who had saved her life, like this? She turned and grasped his hand.

He halted, his dark brows rising in cool inquiry.

"Your pardon, lord," Rhianna began, willing to try once more, for the sake of honor and Trinovante hospitality, to make amends. "I beg—"

"Rhianna! Ah, there you are." Emrys bounded out from behind a hut, his eyes, the same shade as his sister's, flashing in youthful exuberance. "I've so much to tell you. Cador's livid and—"

As his glance caught the Roman's, Emrys' voice faded. "Ah, I beg pardon." He flushed in embarrassment and backed away. "I . . . I'd forgotten about your . . . guest."

"There's no reason to leave on my account, lad." Marcus smiled and motioned him forward. "Hopefully, Rhianna's not to be avoided because she's with me. She certainly has my permission to speak with her friends."

"Aye, Emrys. Come and walk with us." Rhianna pulled him to her side, grateful for her brother's distracting presence. She turned to the Roman. "Tribune Paullinus, this is my youngest brother."

"I'm honored." Marcus rendered the boy a salute.

Emrys' eyes widened. "And . . . and I, too, my lord." He hesitated. "A question. Would you permit a question?"

Marcus chuckled. "Ask as many as you wish."

"I watched you during the wrestling. I've heard the Greeks are masters of the sport, but I'd not thought a Roman capable of such expertise. Yet, you won today, besting our finest—"

"Emrys!" Rhianna cried, shocked at her brother's brazen insult to Roman manhood. When *would* the lad learn to guard his tongue? She paused, catching herself. But then, when would she, for that matter?

The Roman raised a hand, his laugh deep and warm. The rich sound resonated pleasantly through Rhianna. She glanced up at him, unable to repress a small smile of relief.

He grinned back with no trace of his former reserve. Her smile faded as an immediate and intense physical awareness of him assailed her. Of his pulse, quickening in the corded shaft of his throat. Of the sweetly intoxicating musk of his body wafting over. A frisson of that now familiar excitement shuddered through her.

The uncomfortable shuffling of Emrys' feet jerked Rhianna back. She turned to the red-faced boy.

"Er, your pardon, lord," her brother mumbled, his attention fixed on the Roman. "If I offended . . ."

"I found no offense in your question, lad," Marcus replied, dragging his own gaze from Rhianna. "You'd asked me about my wrestling abilities. It's true we Romans, as a whole, aren't as addicted to athletics as are the Greeks. But my tutor, for the majority of my youth, was a Greek. Fortunately for me, he was also a former wrestling champion."

"A wrestling champion?" Emrys' open-mouthed amazement echoed the admiration in his voice. "Small wonder you so easily bested our men."

Gingerly, Marcus touched the wound over his left brow and grimaced. "I'd hardly call the warrior Cador an easily bested opponent. For not knowing the finer points of Greek wrestling, you Celts are formidable adversaries."

Emrys' chest expanded visibly. "We are renowned for our fierceness in battle. All quail before us, even mighty—"

Rhianna plucked quickly at his arm. "Come along, little brother. Tribune Paullinus wishes to see our fort. The feast will begin at first darkness and time is short."

They walked through the massive and imposing fort, touring the ramparts which overlooked a fertile expanse of land dotted with small farmsteads that depended on the hill-mounted enclosure for their defense. Rhianna pointed out various buildings and storage granaries, the corrals where the horses were kept, as well as the winter pens for the sheep, goats, and pigs. Everything about the fort seemed to interest the Roman, no matter how commonplace and lacking in apparent military significance, and Rhianna found herself attempting to reply as clearly as possible. She marveled at the Roman's unflagging interest in such mundane aspects of their lives, wondering how any of this could possibly aid him in his role as *Praefectus Alae.*

With her usual impulsiveness she almost asked him that very question, save for her fear it would ignite yet another argument. Nay, Rhianna thought, covertly glancing at the Roman as they moved across the fort's spacious enclosure, far better to keep to more neutral topics and maintain the precarious truce.

The bright, gaily-colored trader's wagon, a simple box-like contrivance pulled by two oxen, came into view near the wrestling arena. Rhianna eyed it so avidly Marcus couldn't help but notice. Though he'd no interest in wares the shops of Camulodunum supplied, he gestured toward the wagon with feigned interest. "Could we pay a short visit to the trader?"

The startled look on Rhianna's face was well worth the effort. Marcus soon stepped back to allow her the freedom to sort through the enticingly arrayed supply of jewelry, housewares, cloth, and various trinkets that had been painstakingly acquired from all over the Roman Empire. As he waited, the sun, beginning to set, streaked the sky in dull shades of red and gold, its rays snaring in the shimmering strands of Rhianna's hair.

How exquisite she looks in this light, Marcus mused. A hauntingly lovely woman-child . . . and my victor's due. An image—of Rhianna naked and eager for him—flashed through his mind. The realization that his former resolve not to take her maidenhood was once more weakening followed swiftly in its wake.

Marcus stiffened, his hands fisting at his sides. Uneasiness coiled about his heart. Never before had he allowed anyone, neither man nor woman, to come between him and his goals. But the thought of holding Rhianna, of making love to her, was suddenly the sweetest and most potent of temptations.

And when had one night of simple lust ever interfered with his life before? he asked himself. He knew better than to risk his future for a woman or endanger his certain fame and fortune for a romantic interlude that could enmesh him in the lives of a people halfway across the world. After all, no matter what happened, she was only his for this single day . . .

Rhianna, unaware of the tormented conflicts warring within her dark-haired companion, rummaged happily through old Petrus, the Greek trader's, wares. Her glance passed over the highly prized red, Samian-ware cups and dishes, the delicate armlets and bracelets, the silver and gold hair-combs, the brooches of filigree work and necklaces of jet, amber, jasper, and amethyst, before moving onto an expertly crafted pair of bejeweled daggers. She admired them briefly, running a finger over the serpent and vine-engraved silver handles, then turned back to the Roman. As she did, a cunningly carved pair of bone earrings fashioned into tiny hawks caught her eye.

She picked them up to examine them more closely. Proud and free they are, Rhianna thought in delight, enchanting the heavens with the unfettered joy of flight. She held the earrings up to view in the hand mirror that suddenly appeared in the trader's hand.

"They are meant for you, they are, lass," the silver-haired Greek said. "See how they match your fibula, the braid on your gown? Have you no lover to buy them for you?"

Rhianna paled, her glance straying to the Roman. 'Twas too much to hope he hadn't heard the trader's good-hearted babblings.

A powerful intensity darkened his green-gold eyes. Her throat went dry.

He stepped up and gestured to the earrings. "How much?"

Petrus smiled. "For you, Tribune, but one denarius."

Marcus dug the coin from his pouch and tossed it to him. "Done." He took the earrings, offering them to Rhianna. "But a small token of my esteem, lady. To remind you that, no matter how vital a good dagger may be, you should never forget you're also a woman and need pretty things."

Rhianna eyed the earrings, so small and delicate in the broad expanse of his callused palm, and shook her head. "My thanks for your consideration, but I don't need a Roman telling me what I should and shouldn't be. And I've no wish to own what I cannot purchase." She closed his hand over the jewelry. "Save them for your wife."

His teeth flashed white in a lazy grin. "But I have no wife, Rhianna."

Surprise widened her eyes. "Oh, well . . . then some sweetheart, mayhap." Unaccountably, embarrassment filled her. She motioned for him to follow. "Come, the feasting will soon begin. As victor, you've earned a place at my father's right."

Marcus shrugged. It was evident the matter of the earrings was closed. He dropped them into his coin pouch. "And have I also earned the pleasure of having you sit with me at the feast?"

"Ah, Roman, will you never learn?" Exasperation threaded her voice. "You've only to ask and—"

"Rhianna!"

Cordaella and Ura stood near a cluster of huts, motioning her over. Rhianna glanced up at the Roman. "By your leave, if I might have just a few minutes . . ."

"Go to your friends, lady. I'll await you here."

She ran to join the two girls. Rhianna's last view of him, from over her shoulder as she reached her friends, was that of a tall, broad-shouldered Roman smiling back at her from his place at the trader's wagon.

The pungent scent of wood smoke from the huge stone hearth mingled with the savory aroma of roast boar. As the pig's carcass turned on the iron spit, the juices drawn from the cooking meat dripped and sputtered onto the crackling fire. Through the hazy light of wall torches and braziers set around the large, rectangular hall, women moved about, their arms laden with serving platters and pitchers of dark, foaming beer. Fair-haired men, sitting or reclining on skins strewn about in a roughly shaped circle, sang boastful songs as they downed cup after cup of the rich, heady brew.

In one corner, perched on a stool, sat the bard, his harp clasped in the crook of one arm, the fingers of his free hand plucking gently at taut strings. The sweet notes of his music barely carried to the noisy revelers, but Kamber wasn't concerned. Soon, the chieftain would call for him. Then all would fall silent to hear, once more, the ancient, sacred songs.

His dark eyes scanned the room, finally alighting on the flaxen-haired chieftain's daughter. Fair, headstrong Rhianna, Kamber thought with affection. What mysteries of the flesh awaited her this night? He watched as her dark companion turned to her, a soft smile etching the classic planes of his face.

The Roman. Powerful and brave he was, a fitting mate for the fiery maid. Yet Fate, so brutal, so impartial, seemed destined to intervene.

Kamber sighed. How frequently sad the human existence, he mused, bittersweet source of song and ritual, frustrating man at every turn . . .

His chieftain raised a hand. As Kamber's attention turned to him, the sounds of boisterous revelry faded.

Riderch smiled at his bard. "If it pleases you, poet-priest, a song of valor to honor this day's victor, the Tribune Paullinus." He lifted his cup in toast to the man sitting beside him, then downed its contents in one swallow.

Kamber rose and walked to the center of the large circle. Once more, the murmur of voices rose. Marcus offered his own cup in a private salute to the Trinovante chieftain. "You esteem me overmuch, my lord. The ability to wrestle another to the ground is hardly justification for such courtesy, especially," he added wryly, "when the victory could have easily gone the other way."

"Nay, Tribune." A look of respect gleamed in Riderch's eyes. "To a Trinovante, 'tis ample reason. More than brute strength is honored here. Courage and cunning are as vital, if not more so. We honor such attributes in warriors, abilities that have served us well for many centuries.

"Besides," his voice dropped several notches so his words

reached only Marcus' ears, "I desire your tribuneship begin on a cordial, mutually beneficial basis. 'Twould serve both our needs, would it not?"

Marcus smiled. After the freshened hostility over Rhianna and the victor's due, the implications lurking beneath the chieftain's words were more than he dared hope for. "Then the games are over between us? The attempts to manipulate and embarrass me?"

Riderch flushed. "Aye. I erred in my judgment of you. You are not at all what I first imagined you to be."

"Indeed?" Marcus cocked a dark brow. "And what am I, my lord?"

"A man of ambition who knows his own mind and has a sharp intelligence not easily manipulated by others. But a man, as well, who realizes 'tis far wiser to treat others with consideration and respect if he ever aspires to success."

"Success can be achieved in many ways." Marcus swirled the contents of his cup, then swallowed down the rest of his beer. "Albinus may deem his tour here successful. He kept your people under control, did he not?"

"Aye, that he did," Riderch muttered grimly, his fingers clenching about his own cup. "But Rome is also recalling him. And relations between my people and yours are all the worse for Albinus' presence." He leaned over, picked up the pitcher of beer sitting before them, and refilled Marcus' cup. "I can only assume, from Albinus' dismissal, that even Rome prefers a lighter hand on the backs of the Britanni if 'twill only keep the peace."

"Your assumption is well-founded, Lord Riderch." Marcus raised his cup to him, then took another deep draught of his beer. "And I'll tell you true. I've no personal ambition in my year here in Britannia, save to maintain peace at minimal cost to both sides."

"An ambition that would serve us both well." Riderch gazed thoughtfully into his now-empty cup, then set it aside. "Unfortunately, my young warriors are ever eager for a fight."

His voice lowered even more. "Mayhap I err in speaking of this, but I perceive qualities in you sadly lacking in the others and wager you'll take what I say this night in the spirit 'tis intended." His glance lifted. "My young men have always been a thorn in my side—but no more than that—until one rose to challenge my authority and question the judgment of striving to keep the peace. Combined with the ill-advised policies of your predecessors, not to mention the continuing difficulties with the Roman veterans at Camulodunum, the thin skins of my people have been rubbed raw. It may be too late even now, Tribune, but if you can help . . ."

"I'll do what I can. You have my oath on that. A war would only serve the self-seekers and callous scavengers on both sides." Marcus paused. "The leader of the faction within your tribe . . . It would help if I knew his name."

Riderch shook his head. "Nay, Tribune. Even for the sake of peace I'll not betray my own. Trust me in this. It has been taken care of."

"As you wish, my lord. I'll not interfere in your tribal matters unless I've no other choice." Marcus' glance strayed to where the bard now sat, poised expectantly on his wooden stool. "It seems your singer's ready."

"Ah, yes. But a moment more, Tribune."

Marcus cocked a dark brow. "Yes, Lord Riderch?"

"My daughter." He shot Rhianna a quick look. She was engrossed in conversation with her brother Cerdic. Riderch turned back to Marcus. "You will treat her gently this night, won't you? For all her proud, headstrong ways, she is still a maiden. What is given in the name of hospitality—"

"Shall be treated with the utmost respect," Marcus finished softly. He quashed the impulse to assure the Trinovante chieftain he'd no intention—and never had—of bedding Rhianna. It was still his secret, his final lesson to a man who'd dared try to use and humiliate him. And Marcus meant to maintain the illusion of that intent for a time longer. "I'm not a cruel nor crude man when it comes to women, my lord."

Riderch eyed him closely. "Aye, I can see that, Tribune. But my daughter's emotions are as fragile, as newly awakened as her body. And, Roman that you be, already she holds you in high esteem."

Marcus' mouth quirked wryly. "Indeed? She has a strange way of showing it."

The Trinovante smiled. "High emotions can sometimes be manifested in the most surprising of ways." At the flicker of surprise in the tribune's eyes, a grim satisfaction swelled in Riderch's breast. The bait had been dangled; 'twas time to see how deeply the Roman's lust would snare him.

Riderch turned and signaled. The hall once more fell silent. "A song, venerable Kamber," he called to his bard, barely able to contain the triumph that crept into his voice. "One of heroes and battle. One to fire the heart and warm the blood. Aye, give us a song of the glory of Celtic manhood."

Kamber bowed his head of bright red hair, his nimble fingers strumming the opening chords. "As you wish, Lord Riderch. Mayhap you'll find *The March of the Faerie Host* to your liking."

The notes, sharp and clear, streamed from the curved, oakwood harp, drifting to the farthest corners of the hall. The lilting melody that emanated was strong and bold, a perfect accompaniment to the words.

In well-devised battle array,
Ahead of their fair chieftain
They march amidst blue spears,
White curly-headed bands.

They scatter the battalions of the foe,
They ravage every land I have attacked.
Splendidly they march to combat
An impetuous, distinguished, avenging host!

No wonder though their strength be great:
Sons of kings and queens are one and all.
On all their heads are
Beautiful golden-yellow manes:

With smooth, comely bodies,
With bright blue-starred eyes.
With pure crystal teeth,
With thin red lips:

Good they are at man-slaying.

When the last strains had died from the vibrating strings, Kamber laid down his instrument. His glance slowly, lovingly scanned the gathering. Awestruck they were, yet proud of their heritage; a tradition passed from bard to bard solely by word of mouth. He'd seen it time and again, these many years of service to his clan, and had never failed to be struck by the power, the responsibility of his special skills. A sacred trust indeed, his wondrous ability to entertain, to instruct—yea, to inspire.

Once more the chieftain raised his hand, recalling the minds and hearts of his people. He gestured to the two men at the spit. "Carve off a hind quarter and bring our honored guest the hero's portion."

As he spoke he indicated the Roman sitting at his right. "And let no man contend with him for this." His eyes locked with Cador's across the circle. "Today, the Tribune's prowess has been amply demonstrated."

Marcus watched as his former adversary nodded his reluctant assent. Then, he turned to Rhianna who sat on his other side, uncharacteristically silent for a time now. "That was a warning to Cador, wasn't it? Your father was afraid his warrior would challenge me for the first choice of meat."

"Aye," she muttered uneasily. "A bloody dispute with Rome over a piece of boar is hardly appropriate on Lughnasa, no matter how dearly the hero's portion may be desired." A haunted look flared in her eyes. "My father knows Cador would never willingly accept the bestowal of such an honor upon you, though you've fairly earned it this day. 'Twas but his attempt to prevent further unpleasantness."

"My presence, it seems, is the source of a great deal of, ah . . . unpleasantness." He ran a weary hand through his curls. "I can understand the reluctance to accept a representative of Rome. Yet at the same time, I'd ask not to be prejudged. Allow my actions to speak for me."

"And do you think we care what your intentions are?" Rhianna demanded softly. " 'Tis of no import whether you're judged fairly. Our only concern is to be free of Rome, its good as well as bad."

Marcus shrugged. He refused to be drawn into another argument, and most assuredly not before her entire clan.

"Nonetheless, I am here and must be dealt with. Surely peaceful, mutually respectful relations would only serve to Trinovante advantage."

She sighed. "Aye, Roman, that much I concede."

The servers carrying the platter of meat halted before them. Marcus withdrew his dagger and carved a large slab of succulent roast boar, the clear juices running from its flesh with each slice of the knife. Carefully transferring the meat to his wooden platter, he cut himself a smaller portion. All eyes were upon him as he slowly raised the morsel to his mouth and took the first bite.

As if by signal the hall's occupants came to life, laughing and calling loudly for meat of their own. Marcus relaxed. He grinned at Rhianna.

Her own lips curved unconsciously upward. Blessed Goddess, she thought with a pang, but 'twas difficult to remain cold to him when he looked at her like that—so boyish, so open. And 'twas doubly hard to remember he was Roman.

As he continued to hold her gaze, his eyes darkened to a smoldering, sensual intensity. Rhianna's heart began a thudding beneath her breast. Her mouth went dry. For just the merest moment in time, she allowed herself to imbibe the heady thrill of his nearness. Ah, how good it felt! How—

Albinus squatted behind his compatriot. Startled, Rhianna shot him a brief look, then quickly averted her gaze. The old, barely contained loathing rose within her.

She glanced at the Roman sitting beside her. Strange, Rhianna marveled, that I can have such different feelings for two men I should hate equally.

"My congratulations, Tribune Paullinus." Albinus moved closer until his stale-beer odor nearly overpowered Rhianna. "This is the first opportunity I've had to offer my regard for today's victory. You've done well for having just arrived in Britannia a fortnight ago."

At the unexpected encounter with the senior tribune, Marcus glanced around the gathering. Had any noticed or overheard Albinus' words? It seemed not. All, including the chieftain, were hungrily engrossed in their meal.

Marcus turned to confront the man at his shoulder. "I thank you for the compliment, but perhaps another time—"

Albinus stared down at Rhianna, his bloodshot eyes raking her. "Yes, you've done *quite* well," he went on, oblivious to Marcus' interruption. "This maid will give you a fine ride before the night's done. Enjoy the sweetness of her fair flesh, my friend. Show her how a Roman—"

"Enough, Albinus!" Marcus snapped, his voice low and hard. "I don't need your crude advice. Keep to the subject of Rome and Roman affairs or don't speak to me at all."

Albinus blanched. His hands lifted in drunken placation. "Ah, so that's how it's to be. A minor success with these Trinovante and I'm no longer of use. Well, no matter. But a week more and I'll be free of this cursed island." Albinus' mouth pulled into a sour grin. "But you, *Tribune Paullinus,* though you may run in powerful circles, have yet a year to serve. Ample time for a fall from favor, ample time for arrogance to ruin a promising career."

Marcus resumed the cutting of his meat. "Perhaps, but I'll never live to see the day I rue my treatment of these people."

He plunged his dagger into a slice of boar and offered it to Rhianna. She accepted it, a soft smile lighting her face.

At the implied dismissal, Albinus tensed. His hand crept to his own dagger and, for a moment, he contemplated thrusting it into the other tribune's back. But only for a moment.

Albinus released his grasp of his weapon and leaned away. Revenge he'd have, he thought grimly, glancing from his dark-haired associate to Rhianna, but now it would serve a dual purpose.

Rising, he stalked out of the noisy, smoke-filled hall and into the warm summer night, his mind churning with plans. Yes, Albinus assured himself, a triumphant sneer twisting his swarthy features, he'd yet have it all—Paullinus' humiliation *and* the beautiful Rhianna.

Five

A thin slice of moon pierced the ebony sky, illuminating the path through the trees with dappling patches of light. As Rhianna made her way back to the bower, her pace slowed. She gazed up at the heavens. How beautiful the summer night. How peaceful the silent forest encompassing the fort. Would that her own soul could draw sustenance from that tranquillity, fortify her for what lay ahead.

After several hours more of music and feasting, all spent under the appreciative eye of the Roman, Rhianna had found she couldn't bear the tension a moment more. Neither the tension nor the excitement rippling through her every time he had looked at her. She knew her duty, could face it bravely as any warrior must. But the rising sense of anticipation, of desire!

She had harked back to those moments before the wrestling. The brief loincloth covering the Roman had done little to hide the ample swell of his manhood. Aye, he was superb, Rhianna had thought with a woman's instinct strong and sure. He would pleasure her like few others. Yet, she shouldn't think of him so. Shouldn't want him.

She sighed. Blessed Goddess, if only—

"Rhianna!"

A low-pitched voice rasped in the darkness. A large hand

snaked about her arm. Rhianna wheeled around, slamming into a hard male body. Cold eyes gleamed down at her.

"Cador! What are you doing here?"

"Waiting for you, sweet lass." He pulled her to him and kissed her, his tongue probing at her mouth. Rhianna tensed.

With a deep laugh, Cador stepped back. "Ever the unsullied virgin, eh, Rhianna? An admirable trait in one's betrothed, if not for the fact you'll soon surrender that same virginity to another."

His grasp tightened. His fingers gouged into the soft flesh of her arm. " 'Twould seem you've been too eager to lie with the Roman. Is that true, lass? Have you so quickly forgotten your betrothal vows?"

"Nay!" She struggled to free herself from his painful hold. " 'Tis the customs I obey, as would any maid of our clan. I haven't forgotten my promises to you."

"Then prove your loyalty." Cador shoved a small flagon into her hand. "Mix this in the Roman's drink."

Rhianna glanced down at the container. "What's in it?"

Cador grinned wolfishly. "A potion to cut short that proud tribune's career and spare your maiden's flesh. You are mine, lass. I'll not permit you to be sullied by another, much less a Roman." He bent her fingers around the flagon. "Go, do as I say. 'Tis past time you settled into a proper wife's role."

"Nay, Cador." Rhianna wrenched away in horror. "Not for you, nor anyone, will I do such a thing. 'Tis cowardly and dishonorable. 'Tis his right to claim me. To kill in such a way would shame us all."

With a feral sound, Cador struck her. The blow was hard, unexpected. Rhianna rocked back on her heels, nearly losing her balance.

Tears of pain filled her eyes, but her anger fueled her to

action. She grasped her dagger. This wasn't to be tolerated, Rhianna thought in a white-hot rage. She would kill him!

The weapon rose in the air and, from behind, was jerked from her clasp.

"Rhianna. No!"

From the depths of her fury she heard the deep, insistent voice of the Roman. She twisted in his clasp. She slapped him once, twice, before he captured her hand.

"Let me go!" Rhianna cried. "He must pay for striking me. My honor demands it!"

Marcus stared down into flashing eyes and knew her determination. If he didn't find a way to divert her rage, she'd surely harm herself attacking Cador. He shook his head. "No, Rhianna. You're wrong. You are mine for this night, and it's *my* duty to defend you."

He withdrew his sword. The metallic grating of iron filled the night with an ominous sound. It wrenched Rhianna back to reality. She grabbed Marcus' arm and stepped between the two men.

"Nay, Roman! He has no sword. 'Twould be murder." She gazed up at him imploringly. "Don't kill him. Please!"

"Don't beg for me, woman!" Cador spat, his mouth a cruel sneer in the moonlight. He shifted restlessly behind her. "I'm not afraid of a Roman dog, armed or not."

He glared past her to Marcus, his shoulders squared belligerently. "You tread where you've no right to go, Red Crest. If you think to ingratiate yourself with our chieftain and turn the tide of animosity against you and your kind, 'tis too late. A single wrestling match does not a victory make. And you and I are at war as surely as our people will soon be!"

Marcus resheathed his sword, his aim accomplished. "Get out of here before I forget myself and kill you anyway."

Cador's lips twitched in barely controlled fury. The tension grew, burgeoning as the minutes passed until it was nearly palpable. Rhianna glanced from one taut, angry man to the other. They were like two wolves, each eyeing the other for the opportune moment to attack.

'Tis more than mere enmity, she realized with a flash of insight. They battle as much over me as from personal hatred.

The thought infuriated her. Curse them both. She wasn't some prize slab of meat to be won by anyone!

"Cador, stop it," Rhianna ordered, determined to put an end to the ugly confrontation. "Leave us this instant."

He rounded on her, his big body trembling with rage. "You are mine, woman. For the sake of our clan, remember that. Remember—and do what must be done."

She stared at him a moment longer, then tugged at the Roman's arm. "Come, my lord. The eve grows late. Come with me to the bower."

He glanced down at her, his smile taut. "Yes, lady. Enough of the eve has been wasted in this insignificant dispute. It's past time I enjoy the sweetest fruits of this day's labor."

They left Cador impotently fuming and made their way to the bower. The braziers had been lit and the melding of shadows and flickering red-gold light sculpted the tent into a cozy, intimate retreat. Rhianna strode to the middle of the room, then turned to face Marcus, the forgotten flagon of poison still clasped in her hand. His glance swept her slim form, coming to rest on her clenched fist.

"What do you have there, lady?"

Rhianna jumped. "N-naught. I've naught."

Something about her reaction, about the fact she couldn't quite seem to meet his gaze, warned Marcus she lied. He covered the distance between them in a few, quick strides and pried open her hand. The little flagon lying there glinted amber in the firelight.

Marcus picked it up. "And what is this?"

"No more than a . . . a sleeping potion. To help you rest, if you've the need for it."

Blessed Goddess, let him delve no deeper, she prayed.

"A sleeping potion, is it?"

He rolled the vial between his thumb and forefinger, his brow furrowing in thought. Were Rhianna's words true? Was it indeed but a sleeping potion, or something far worse? A poison, perhaps? The implications of such an action sickened him. Was her hatred for him *that* strong?

Marcus smiled grimly. "How kind to think of my comfort, even to providing for a sound sleep." He walked over to the table, which held fresh pitchers of beer and water.

"What are you doing?" Rhianna tried to see his actions but his broad back hid his movements.

"Taking advantage of this fine sleeping potion, of course." He turned, the unstoppered flagon in one hand, a cup of beer in the other.

Apprehension swept through her. She watched him pour the vial's contents into the cup, then swirl it to mix it. Horror rose. The Roman meant to drink the poison!

Time slowed as he lifted the cup to his lips. Rhianna opened her mouth to speak, but couldn't. The words had solidified in her throat. An uncontrollable trembling shook her. With a superhuman effort, she forced her limbs to move.

"Nay!"

Her cry sliced through the air. The fatal cup lowered from the Roman's mouth, its contents untouched. A dark brow arched in unspoken challenge.

"What troubles you, lady? Surely you realize the potion won't affect me before I've taken my pleasure with you?" His eyes narrowed. "But then, that's hardly your true concern, is it?"

Marcus set aside the cup and flagon and advanced on her. "Did you really mean to kill me, Rhianna? Do you loathe me so deeply, you'd see me dead rather than touch you?"

"Nay, Roman. Never!" Desperately, she fought back the tears that sprung to her eyes. " 'Twould be poor gratitude for saving my life. The poison wasn't of my doing."

He stared down at her warily, his eyes shards of deepest jade. "Then whose was it?" Marcus grabbed her and gave her a small shake. "Tell me, Rhianna. Was it Cador?"

She lowered her head, hiding eyes that might betray. "Don't ask, for I cannot tell you. Clan honor would never permit my revealing that to you. 'Tis enough, I would not carry out the deed."

A callused hand cupped her chin gently to lift her head. Their eyes met. Something passed across the Roman's face, anger, then acceptance, then a smoldering scrutiny that heated rapidly to desire. A desire that spoke eloquently of hunger, passion—and something deeper.

Marcus knew it was time to stop, before one or both of them lost control. It was far too dangerous to push ahead, no matter how much he suddenly wanted to claim his victor's due. The look in Rhianna's eyes beckoned him to a heady oblivion, free of the constraints of family, nation, and personal dreams. Yet he had given his word to her father to relinquish her on the morrow and meant to keep it.

A kiss, he vowed. That was all he'd take. That, and a brief moment with her body pressed to his. The most meager of payments for his efforts this day, but all he dared risk. Then he would part from her, leave her a maiden still, and return to Camulodunum.

"After what you almost did to me," he forced himself to reply, "you make it hard for me to trust you. But trust you

I will. What matters this night isn't what others have done or wish to do, but what we do."

A guarded look crept into her eyes. "And what will we do?"

"Not what you seem so to dread. I'll not require that you fulfill your vow to me."

She gazed up at him, now startled and confused. "I don't understand."

"I won't make you lie with me. I won't take your maidenhood." Marcus released her, his hands falling to his sides. "I never meant to do so, at any rate. My demand was intended only to teach you and your father a lesson." He managed a sheepish grin. "To teach you of the might of Rome, so to speak."

Anger flared anew in Rhianna. "I grow weary of being the pawn in everyone's games."

"No doubt." Marcus sighed. "I regret my actions, lady. No matter how you angered me at times with your defiance, I was wrong to use you so. Can you forgive me?"

"Forgive you?" Reason warred with indignation as she considered his request, knowing she was as much to blame as he. Reason won. "The fault, I fear, must be shared," Rhianna finally admitted with a small smile. "I, too, acted foolishly at times."

He stepped close, a tender look gleaming in his striking eyes. "No more so than I, sweet lady."

Gazing up at him, standing so near that the heat of his big body encompassed her in a warm, soothing aura, Rhianna felt a strange tension rise, then spread through her body. His power and vitality—a raw, potent force—flowed around her, consuming her. It should have frightened her, but it didn't. She moved closer, driven by her own response.

The long scar, livid from the clenching of his jaw, formed

a narrow trail of crimson down the side of his face. Rhianna touched it, tracing the path with a hesitant, wondering finger.

He turned to meet her hand. Transfixed, she watched his mouth open, his firm, full lips gently grasp her thumb, then index finger. Watched him suckle the slender digits one by one, first carefully, then more boldly, more sensuously, with each passing moment.

She shuddered and gasped softly. The sound seemed to kindle something in the Roman. He hesitated, glanced up at her, indecision momentarily darkening his eyes. Then, with a low groan, he gathered Rhianna into his arms. His lips found hers, hard, slanting, greedy.

Curiously, his sudden aggression didn't disturb Rhianna. She responded with equal abandon, entwining her hands behind his neck, fiercely drinking in the sweetness of his kiss. It seemed but a natural culmination of the day's tension, a blessed easing of the ever-mounting emotions.

The coaxing enchantment of his mouth beguiled her. The increasingly intimate pressure of his body beckoned to her. The barriers of clan and country dissolved, melted by the burgeoning heat of a passion the like of which she'd never known before.

"Ah, Rhianna," Marcus whispered hoarsely, pulling back from the searing intensity of their kiss. His breath wafted over her face, a warm, stimulating caress across passion-sensitized flesh. "This is wrong. . . . I gave my word but, the gods forgive me, I want you!"

"Then take me," she whispered back, her words little more than a husky entreaty. "Though you may have never meant to bed me, I fully intend to honor my vow. Your promise has been fulfilled; there is no shame or sin now in taking what is offered."

Her words inflamed his barely contained desire. He should

draw back from her, Marcus thought. Now, before the last remnants of his control shattered. She was a maiden, betrothed to another man. She was the innocent, a pawn in the games men played for power and country. There was no honor in easing his lust upon her. No honor . . .

"And what of you?" Marcus asked instead, his heart pounding wildly within his chest. "Do you offer yourself because you want me, Rhianna? Or is it because it's expected of you? Because clan honor permits you nothing less?"

She hesitated, knowing the answer would change her life forever. The realization was terrifying, this presentiment, this *Gift* that once again shot through her. Yet to turn from her destiny, to deny it, would be to live a lie. 'Twas a coward's way—and she was no coward.

Her head lowered. A blush warmed her cheeks. In that moment, Rhianna felt helpless, vulnerable, yielding. She wanted and needed the Roman with a fierceness that was frightening, yet knew naught of him or what was truly in his heart. And suddenly, who and what he was, how he truly felt about her, mattered very much.

"Rhianna?"

The Roman's voice, rich-toned and deep, caressed her. A wave of affection, of longing, washed over her. Strangely, she felt safe with him, cherished as she'd never been cherished before.

Rhianna glanced up, meeting eyes that gleamed with a tender inquiry. " 'Tis more than clan honor, more than the fulfillment of others' expectations." She exhaled a soft, tremulous breath. "I offer myself because I want you. Aye, want you so very, very much."

A slight flush colored his tanned skin. His mouth curved upward into a beautiful smile. "Then have me you will."

Marcus gazed down at her, at the delicately carved features

muted to a soft, shadowy loveliness in the flickering firelight. Even in her maiden's innocence she faced him proudly, unashamed of her desire. He sensed that her lovemaking, once she'd tasted the secret pleasures of womanhood, would be just as free and giving. And he, before all others, would savor her passion, share her ecstasy.

His hands moved up her arms until he reached the fibulae joining the shoulders of her gown. After a brief fumbling as he divined the clasp's workings, Marcus unfastened the ornamental pins. The top half of Rhianna's tunic fell to drape at her waist.

The sight of her creamy flesh and firm, plump breasts with their pale, pink nipples was nearly his undoing. Before she could utter protest, Marcus' mouth closed over a softly pouting nipple. As his hands moved to free her maiden's girdle, he suckled the bud to throbbing hardness.

She moaned, the sound one of pure pleasure, mingling with the rustle of fabric as her gown cascaded to the floor. Marcus' lips moved to settle on the impudent twin of her now highly sensitized breast while his hands slid down along the gentle indentation of a naked, narrow waist. Slowly, tenderly, his fingers met and conquered the last barrier of cloth.

He stepped back then, unbuckling his heavy sword belt. Shedding it, Marcus loosened the smaller side buckles of his corselet. Only when he stood in tunic and sandals did he pull Rhianna back to him. His powerful thighs pressed against her, the fabric covering him doing little to hide the hard evidence of his desire. With a questing eagerness, his hand wound its way up gleamingly flawless skin until, at last, it joined with a firm, jutting breast.

As he fondled her with careful strokes, teasing the nipple until it once more hardened in excitement, Rhianna's hands clutched at the corded strength of his upper arms. Tremors wracked her body. Fire shot through her veins, engulfing her in a conflagration of unbearable delight. She wanted, needed him with every fiber of her being.

That he was Roman—and her enemy—no longer mattered. They were fire and tinder, hunger and sustenance. Together they would burn out the night, nourishing each other with young, eager, rapturous bodies.

"Ah, Goddess," she breathed, her hands clenching upon his chest. "Let me touch you. . . . I need to . . . feel you!"

A deep, rich chuckle rumbled through him. "Never have I met such unabashed enthusiasm in a maid. Is it, perhaps, but a happy harbinger of things to come?"

"You've only yourself to blame," Rhianna replied boldly. "You weave your manly spell around me, wielding your greater experience with such expertise I grow mad with desire. I am as clay in your hands. If I displease you, 'tis your duty to enlighten me."

He grinned down at her. "Have no fear, sweet lady. You please me in every way."

Marcus removed his sandals and belt. As Rhianna edged nearer, his hands paused at his undertunic. She lifted her face to him, her smiling eyes passion-dark and sensuous. "Pray, allow me to assist you, my lord."

Together, they pulled the garment from him. At the sight of the expanse of exposed masculine flesh, Rhianna felt a curious tightening low in her belly. His tall, powerful form, clad only in the briefest of loincloths, sent her blood coursing hotly through her veins. Gods, but she never wearied of looking at him!

Yet it was the bulge of his manhood, straining against the meager fabric covering his loins, that transfixed Rhianna this time. She watched as he slid the cloth down, freeing his huge, thick shaft. Her throat went dry.

Marcus stepped toward her, the epitome of the confident male. His strong, warm fingers clasped her shoulders, pulling her back to him.

An inexplicable impulse to run swept through Rhianna. Blessed Goddess, but he was too much man for her! She'd never be able to sheathe him within her body. She'd never be able to please him! She twisted in his grasp, but 'twas already too late.

The Roman's lips found hers. He probed at the soft barrier of her mouth, teasing her lips to part. When they finally did and his tongue met hers, fire exploded within Rhianna, vibrating through her in splintering bursts until it reached the core of her womanhood. The pure, carnal intimacy of his mouth, of his naked body pressed so hotly, so possessively against hers, banished the lingering mists of Rhianna's fears.

Excitement surged through her. Her hands roved boldly now, delighting in the rough-textured feel of him, the sleek, sinewy muscles that flexed and bulged under her questing fingers. "P-please," she quavered, her voice a breathless whisper. "Come to me. Join with me."

With a low growl, the Roman gathered her up in his arms and carried her over to the pallet. Kneeling, he gently laid Rhianna down, then covered her slim body with the heated, hard-muscled strength of his own. The throbbing weight of his arousal pressed against the sensitive apex of her thighs. Instinctively, Rhianna tensed.

"Trust me," Marcus rasped, knowing he was at the limits of his control. The effort to hold back, to deny himself the exquisite pleasure of penetration, made his skin glisten with moisture. "I'll be gentle with you, sweet lady. I swear it."

Rhianna exhaled a long, shuddering sigh. Once more their mouths joined. Casting aside all thought but that of the strong, magnificent man in her arms, she surrendered to the heady intoxication of possession.

At the slightest pressure of his knees, she opened herself to him. His kiss turned fierce, stoking the hot, aching fires building within her. He grasped himself then, guiding his sex to her. When his throbbing organ thrust into her virginal sheath, Rhianna gasped, tensed, then forced herself to arch to meet him. In one sharp, searing lunge, he buried his shaft within her.

Then Marcus stilled, tenderly stroking the silky head lying beneath him. "Lie still, sweet one," he whispered. "Give your body a few moments to adjust to mine."

"I-I'm all right," she said, though her trembling belied her words. " 'Tis such a small, sweet pain."

Marcus smiled. "Yes, and that sweetness will soon dispel the pain. That much I promise."

Her fingers dug into his back and she blinked back an unexpected rush of tears. "I believe you."

He began to move within her again, gently, slowly at first, gauging his actions to the response of her body. And, gradually, Rhianna relaxed, then began to move tentatively with him. Marcus guided her, teaching her all the ways to gain the greatest pleasure, prolonging their mutual torment as his hand snaked down between her legs to stroke her sensitive bud.

The sensations grew more intense, more overwhelming. Rhianna's movements became wild, abandoned. No longer did she know or care where he was leading her. She only wished to follow wherever he took her, knowing 'twould be wondrously, rapturously beautiful. She wrapped her legs about him, urging him deeper. Goddess, but she couldn't get enough of him!

The tempo of straining bodies increased. They thrust at

each other, ardently, passionately. The tension built to an exquisite crescendo. Breaths came ragged and rasping; skin turned sweat slick and hot; hands stroked and clasped and squeezed.

And then, with a guttural cry mingling with her own gasp of ecstasy, Marcus spilled his seed into Rhianna. In a blinding moment of glory, they spiraled out in a wild, joyous abandon, their shuddering, hungry bodies discovering an undreamed-of surcease—and a curious freedom in a possession soaring far beyond the heavens.

They lay there for a time afterward, immersed in their own thoughts. Rhianna snuggled beneath the furs, watching the braziers slowly burn out. Beside her, the sound of the Roman's deep, even breathing filled the bower. She knew, even before she glanced at him, that he, too, was awake.

Shadows flickered and danced on the bower walls, casting a reddish-yellow glow onto his broad, powerful back, highlighting the play of muscle and sinew along his arms and shoulders. He was so beautiful, such a good, gentle lover, she thought with a sudden, hot swell of tears. And she could never be with him again.

Rhianna choked back her despair, wondering at the strange emotion. He was a Roman, a deadly foe. What had transpired between them could never change that. She should still hate him.

He stirred beside her, then rolled over onto his back. In the rapidly darkening bower, he pillowed his arms beneath his head. "I've a question."

His deep voice, unexpectedly rising out of the darkness, startled her. Rhianna waited for the leaping rhythm of her pulse to slow before venturing a reply. "Aye? And what might that be?"

Marcus knew he shouldn't ask, much less care, but he did. Their joining had been a startlingly exquisite experience, bringing all his carefully built walls tumbling down. Walls he knew he must rebuild higher and stronger on the morrow.

But not tonight. Tonight, he'd allow them to lie where they were. Tonight, he'd permit himself to care.

"Cador," he said. "I asked you once before if you loved him. Will you answer me now?"

She hesitated but an instant. "Nay, Roman. I don't love him—and never will."

Though she couldn't see him, Rhianna felt his smile. The realization filled her with joy. In some small way, for some reason, he cared. Rhianna relaxed, clasping the secret knowledge to her.

"One thing more."

"Aye?"

"My name. It's Marcus. If it's not too repugnant for you, would you call me by it instead of 'Roman'? It would please me greatly."

She smiled. 'Twas so small a thing he requested after all the happiness he'd given her.

"Aye . . . Marcus." Rhianna turned away, pulling the furs around her shoulders. She felt safe, strangely content. A drowsy haze engulfed her.

"Sleep well," she murmured in gentle dismissal.

He scooted over and settled her into the curve of his body. "Sleep well, sweet lady," came his husky reply.

Six

The small garrison at Camulodunum scurried with activity. Dogs barked in excitement. Guards shouted their welcome. Groomsmen rushed out from the stables as the troop headed by the two tribunes drew to a halt.

His expression darkly preoccupied, Marcus swung off his horse. While his compatriot dealt with the reports of the centurion left in charge of the garrison, Marcus strode across the sun-drenched parade field enclosed by low-slung wattle and daub buildings to a larger, stucco-covered, and far more imposing edifice. He entered the quarters he currently shared with Albinus, strode into the *triclinium,* pulled off his helmet and tossed it onto a nearby wicker chair.

The tall, blond figure of his freeman, Cei, appeared in the doorway of the formal dining room. The man paused, frowned in concern when he met Marcus' scowling gaze, then crossed to a finely crafted marble table and took up a swan-necked flagon of wine. He poured a healthy libation into a goblet, then carried it over to his friend.

"Here, drink this." Cei shoved the ruby-colored liquid into Marcus' hand. " 'Twill put it in a better perspective, whatever 'tis."

The terse command had its desired effect. With a wry grin, Marcus accepted the cup and walked over to a set of three red, silk-covered dining couches arranged around a low table.

Taking a seat on the nearest one, Marcus sipped absently from his wine, putting the goblet aside only after he'd taken enough to satisfy the persistent Cei. Then, with an exasperated gesture, he ran his fingers through his sweat-damp curls.

"My thanks, Cei. You always know what I need before I've even guessed it myself." Marcus' hands moved to his sword belt. "Come, my friend. Help liberate me from this sweltering cocoon of armor."

In two quick strides Cei was at his side, accepting the sword belt as Marcus proceeded to remove his corselet and shin greaves. Unencumbered at last, Marcus threw himself down onto the couch. He heaved an immense sigh and pillowed his arms beneath his head. Deep in thought, he stared up at the timber-beamed ceiling.

He hadn't moved by the time Cei returned from cleaning, oiling, and replacing his master's equipment in the campaign chest. A frown of concern slanting his dark blond brows, the Gaul pulled a small stool over to the couch and sat down. "You tarried overlong at the Trinovante fort," he began without preamble. "What happened there?"

There was a slight hesitation from the figure on the couch. "I met a maid."

"A maid? Is that all this is about?" Cei chuckled softly. "I pray you bedded her well. 'Twas always enough to clear your head of a female before."

Marcus glanced at his freeman. "Yes, I bedded her; and no, it didn't help. Now, I can't get her out of my mind, though I know I must."

"And pray, who is the fetching maiden who has won the esteem of the mighty Paullinus?" Cei prodded mercilessly, a wicked gleam in his eyes. "Ailm swore you'd lose your heart someday but, until now, I never believed it possible."

At the mention of Cei's lovely wife, Marcus' somber expression warmed. "Don't taunt me, you who suffered the torments of the damned until Ailm agreed to wed. If anyone should understand . . ."

Cei grasped his friend's arm. "Forgive me. 'Twas cold-hearted to prick at you so. But to see you, ever so calm, so in control of every situation, reduced to such a . . . a common state as infatuation, well, it confounds me!"

"It's nothing more than lust, damn you," Marcus gritted the words through clenched teeth. "She's just . . . unusual, that's all."

"Indeed?" Cei leaned closer, cocking his head in bemusement. "Come, tell me of the maid. Mayhap I can find some way through your dilemma."

"There's not much to tell." Marcus sighed. "Her name's Rhianna and she's a fiery-tongued, headstrong beauty."

Cei quirked a disbelieving brow. "And what of it? You've tamed your fair share of willful females. Why is this one any different?"

Marcus' gaze riveted back on the ceiling. "Because she's a Celt, a chieftain's daughter, and she hates Rome. Not to mention she's already betrothed to another."

His manservant expelled an appreciative whistle. " 'Tis a fine muddle you've entangled yourself in, my friend. But no matter. If she's the maid you want, by the Good God you shall have her."

The faintest glimmer of a smile brushed Marcus' face. "Who would have thought the few denarii spent to buy you from a slave market would've also purchased such loyalty and concern for my needs? I'm grateful, Cei, but this is one problem best avoided."

" 'Twasn't my purchase that bought our friendship. 'Twas rather the gift of freedom and your unswerving respect for me as a man. You have always seen to my happiness, even to the procurement of permission for Ailm to accompany us to Britannia. I'd be a poor friend if I failed you now."

"And once again, my thanks for your concern." Marcus swung to a sitting position, his heavy military sandals rapping smartly on the brightly tiled, mosaic floor. "If the time ever comes, I'll not fail to call upon you. But this isn't such a case. I'll get over Rhianna. There's no other choice. I've far more important issues to deal with than the bedding of a comely maid."

His glance moved to the window. Through the glazed panes he saw Albinus stop to talk with a mounted messenger, then gesture toward their quarters. Right now the thought of spending another moment in the other tribune's presence was more than Marcus could bear.

He turned to Cei. "Gather my bath articles and a clean tunic and meet me at the *thermae.* The morn is nearly spent, and I've a wish to cleanse myself before attending to this day's duties. Thanks to that greedy, deceitful Albinus, there's pressing business in Camulodunum that'll require more than a few days to settle."

Cei grimaced. "I admire your control in dealing with that tribune. I'd have bashed in his head long ago."

Marcus' mouth twisted in wry humor. "My thanks for your offer, but there's more at stake here than the fulfillment of my own desires. Raw emotions effect nothing but chaos. I must bring control to this region. The task is great enough without wasting further time and energy on a man who'll soon be gone."

"Aye, 'tis a difficult task your uncle has set you," Cei agreed. "But, as provincial governor, has he not promised his support in whatever you undertake?"

"In a half-hearted way," Marcus admitted glumly. "The bulk of his troops, as well as his own attention, though, is currently directed to the final conquest and subjugation of the tribes of North Wales. I can hardly ask my uncle for assistance when he'll soon be over two hundred and fifty miles away. And, though I'll have full authority over the troops and the citizenry of Camulodunum once Albinus departs Britannia, the provincial procurator, Decianus Catus, is essentially an independent entity unto himself."

"Decianus Catus." Cei murmured the name half under his breath. "Isn't he the one involved in the attempt to unseat the Iceni queen from her kingdom and land holdings? 'Tis rumored all that restrains him from his greedy takeover is the official word from Rome." The blond Celt frowned. "Truly, my lord, what can you, what can any man do, with a provincial governor who lacks the skill to govern well and a procurator whose only interest is in fattening his own purse?"

Marcus leaned forward. His head lowered, his arms resting on his legs as if he were suddenly weighted with a burden too great to bear. "My only recourse, it seems, is to win the trust of the Trinovante and Iceni. Yet, as difficult as that may be, it'll prove a far easier task than convincing Roman officials of the self-destructive course they have set us all upon."

His head snapped up and he rose lithely. "A self-destructive course, indeed," Marcus muttered, shrugging off the vestiges of his despair, "for Camulodunum is but one of several indefensible towns in this region, with the bulk of the Roman army far away, engaged in battles of its own. If I can just buy a little time until my uncle returns—"

A staccato rapping at the massive oak door interrupted further discussion. Cei left to receive the visitor. To pass the interval until his return, Marcus drained the contents of his goblet. The outer door finally closed. The Celt hurried into the room.

"A missive, posted from Germania." He handed the scroll to Marcus.

Marcus broke the wax seal and unrolled the parchment. As he read, his tense expression slowly faded. A look of joy ignited in the warm depths of his eyes, spreading across the chiseled planes of his face until it reached his mouth. The firm, generous lips curved into a smile.

"Quintus! He's being posted to Britannia within the fortnight as a legionary tribune with the Ninth Hispana." Marcus rerolled the scroll and tossed it to Cei. "I haven't seen him since we served together in Germania over two years ago. Ah, what scrapes we used to get into as lads! Quintus was always the impulsive one. Still is for that matter." He laughed. "Well, they say it's impetuosity that wins the battle decorations, and Quintus has certainly earned his share and more. I'm sure I'll never hear the end of it when he arrives. By the gods, though I love that man—as he does me—our affection has never kept us from the fiercest of rivalries."

Cei smiled. "Yet, as *Praefectus Alae,* you're one step ahead of him in the *tres militae.* How will that affect your competition?"

Marcus shrugged at his manservant's mention of his final appointment in the required triad of a tribune's military service. "It'll only make Quintus strive the harder. Come," he motioned, "let's find Ailm. I intend on honoring Quintus with a fine banquet. And, with your wife's attention to detail, two week's notice for a feast will be barely enough time."

Rhianna shivered. Though the rays of the east-born sun had long since topped the leafy canopy of birch trees, the night's chill still clung to the pond's dark waters. She sank lower. The liquid lapped about her bare shoulders, offering scant protection from the gentle breeze cooling her water-kissed skin.

A glorious morn, fresh and golden, heavy with the promise of yet another warm, late summer's day. The land lay gilded in splendor, like the wheat in the fields, plump and ripe, eager to yield its fruitful bounty. Ripe . . . fruitful . . . like Gunnella, fresh from the birth of her son, Dagolit.

The memory of the babe cradled in his mother's arms, warm and sweet-smelling from her milk, flooded Rhianna with a poignant tenderness. Dear, tiny Dagolit. Cerdic's first-born—and her nephew.

The thought of bearing her own child—Marcus' child—filled her with a woman's yearning. A son, dark of hair, green of eye, just like his father. A son who'd grow to be as strong, as proud—

Girlish laughter intruded on her romantic reverie. With an angry toss of her head, Rhianna flung the considerations aside. 'Twas over between her and the Roman. She must forget him. She must.

She raised slightly in the water, her hair, water-darkened to deep honey, clinging in thick, damp tendrils to her naked breasts. Her glance moved to her friends, Gunnella, Ura, Cordaella, and diminutive Onn.

All stood in the darkly ruffled waters, their gazes riveted expectantly on her. Rhianna flushed. They awaited but her full attention before the childbirth purification could begin.

She looked up at Savren, long-gowned and frowning, standing on the bank. With a resolute squaring of her shoulders, Rhianna made her way to join the other girls in the semi-circle around Gunnella. All eyes lifted to the impressive form of the chieftain's wife.

In her hands Savren held a cup carved from the sacred oak, smooth and lustrous with use, lovingly caressed by generations of clan women who had carried out this selfsame ritual. Bending down, Savren dipped the container into the gently rocking water, then raised it over her head.

"From loin of man to woman's womb," she intoned, "in loving union the seed is sown. We come here today to celebrate a babe's birth and cleanse the mother from all childbearing taint. Yet even as we purify, we also honor, for she has borne the pains bravely so the clan might flourish and the tribe grow strong."

Savren stepped down into the pond and made her way to where Gunnella stood, her milk-swollen breasts barely covered by the lapping water. The older woman raised the cup above the young mother's head and poured the libation over her. Then she handed it to Cordaella. Around the half-circle the vessel passed, each one repeating the ceremonial cleansing.

Rhianna's turn came at last. Grasping its oaken glossiness, she dipped the cup into the shimmering pond. As she pulled it forth, a reflection danced in its depths, one she recognized as her own. Yet though she stood immersed in a pond, Ura and Cordaella at her side, the scene surrounding them was different, foreign. Her own breasts were blue-veined and swollen, her belly flaccid from . . . childbirth.

The world whirled crazily. As before, the Gift descended upon her, fleetingly claiming control of her mind, her thoughts, her will. Rhianna groaned and shook her head to clear the disquieting vision.

Blessed Goddess, once again she had looked into the future—and seen her woman's fate! 'Twas expected she someday bear children. That much she could accept. But who was her babe's father, and why had she given birth in a strange land, far from her beloved home?

The water's depths held the answer to those questions and

many others, but she dared not look further. Rhianna lifted the cup and emptied its contents, contents suddenly pervaded with hidden, haunting secrets, onto Gunnella's head.

"Give it to me, child."

Her mother's voice, edged with concern, drew Rhianna from her preoccupation with the cup. Wordlessly, she handed it to her.

Savren scanned them all. " 'Tis time you departed the pond, sacred and healing though it be. To tarry longer would risk a chill. Come, dress, then we'll journey home."

Still caught up in the strength-sapping aftermath of the Gift, Rhianna forced her limbs to move, to follow the others out of the pool. She rubbed herself dry, hoping the fierce toweling would rouse her blood and clear her mind. Yet even when the last sandal was tied and her gown in place, she still lacked the will to leave. Wrapping her cloak about her shoulders, Rhianna sank onto a large flat rock beside the pool. She sighed, the sound heavy with exhaustion.

The act caught Savren's attention. "Rise, daughter. 'Tis time we were on our way. Young Dagolit will soon be squalling for his mother."

Rhianna glanced up. "Nay, I must rest here awhile longer. Go on without me. I'll follow soon.

Her mother frowned. "As you wish, daughter. But do not tarry overlong. Your tasks await, no matter the time of your return."

Savren signaled for Ura to lead the group back to the fort, the sacred rowan branch held high before her. As the women wended their way through the birch grove, Rhianna shot them one last look, then lowered her head to rest upon her knees.

Ah, if only I could blot out the memory of that vision, she cried to herself. If only I'd misunderstood or not understood at all. Never have I sought the Gift of Foreknowledge—and today, less than ever.

In the past the presentiment had foretold things that, while sometimes unpleasant, were easy to accept. Things that seemed inevitable, even eagerly desired, like her duty to clan and country. But today that same ability had alluded to a future beyond endurance, when it foretold she would someday leave her beloved land.

With a small cry, Rhianna buried her head in her hands, grinding her fists into her eyes to block out the ugly specter of her fate. Still it rose to taunt her, mocking Rhianna with her inability to avoid what was preordained—and the futility of even trying.

"You seem perturbed, Tribune Paullinus."

Marcus glanced over at the man riding beside him. "Perturbed, Tribune Albinus?" He arched a dark brow. "Hardly. I'm just surprised that, on the day before your departure from Britannia, you'd express a desire to visit the Trinovante fort. I'd have expected you more inclined to a joyous celebration in some tavern in Camulodunum."

Albinus smirked. "Fear not. Once my farewells are said and a few unfinished tasks seen to, I anticipate a long evening of revelry." His eyes narrowed speculatively. "And what of you? Surely your business with the chieftain won't require the entire day, yet here you are on the road and it's barely mid-morn. Can your eagerness perhaps be attributed to a certain flaxen-haired chieftain's daughter?"

"My duties as *Praefectus Alae* leave me little opportunity for social visits," Marcus replied dryly, maintaining an iron control over his rising irritation at Albinus' needling. "Though it's hardly any of your concern, my interlude with the lovely Rhianna was over, once and for all, the day after Lughnasa."

Albinus sighed. "Well, even one tumble with that maid is more than I was able to achieve. You're a fortunate man, Paullinus."

Marcus gifted that comment with a cold stare. Though he'd managed to put Rhianna out of his mind as the days had passed, the anticipation of seeing her again now stirred his blood with fresh, unbidden memories.

That realization troubled him. He'd never allowed a woman to insinuate herself so easily, so thoroughly, into his thoughts. If this were simply a case of lust, it was the worst he'd ever had.

But lust notwithstanding, Marcus knew he needed all his wits about him if he were to be successful this day. He traveled to the Trinovante fort to confer with the chieftain on pressing matters, not to pay a social call on his daughter. And the news he brought with him was far from pleasant.

Though Riderch had asked for help with the return of Trinovante lands illegally acquired by the Roman veterans and a cessation to the heavy taxes levied against them for the construction of the Temple of Claudius in Camulodunum, there was little Marcus could do without his uncle's concurrence. And his uncle, obsessed with preparations for his upcoming military campaign against the Druid stronghold on the Isle of Mona, had little time and no interest in Trinovante concerns. Nothing could be done for the time being—or at least nothing that would garner swift, impressive results. All Marcus could offer was his word that no further Trinovante lands would be seized and, since the temple was nearing completion, the heavy taxes would soon be lightened. He only hoped it would be enough.

Up ahead, the timbered ramparts and protective outer ditch

of the tree-studded hill-fort came into view. At the approach of the Roman cavalry, a shout went up from the gate. A few minutes more and the chieftain appeared at the huge, open doors.

Albinus halted the men a few yards from Riderch. Swinging down from their horses, he and Marcus closed the distance in long, rapid strides. As Marcus approached the Trinovante chieftain, he extended his hand in greeting.

Riderch pointedly ignored Albinus and returned Marcus' gesture. "Welcome, Tribune Paullinus. You honor us with your visit."

"I've important matters to discuss, my lord." Marcus clasped the chieftain's hand. "I saw no purpose in delaying solutions to problems long overdue." He glanced around him. "Is there some place you and I might talk?"

"Aye." Riderch shot Albinus an inquiring look.

The other tribune smiled blandly. "If you'll forgive my absence at what, I'm sure, will be a most momentous meeting, I prefer to pay one last visit to your fort before my departure tomorrow." His mouth twisted in a sardonic smile. "By your leave, of course, Tribune Paullinus."

Marcus restrained an impulse to slap the mocking expression off the other tribune's face. Gods, tomorrow couldn't come soon enough! Yet Albinus' request suited his own needs. No good would be served permitting him to join the council. The issues were distressing enough without Albinus' grating presence.

He nodded. "As you wish, Tribune. The trumpeter will sound the call when we're ready to depart."

Albinus smiled thinly and strode away.

The two men watched his departure, then turned to face each other.

"Have you come with news of when our lands will be returned, Tribune?" Riderch demanded.

Marcus' mouth tightened. The might of Rome, he mused wryly, quailed few Celts—man or woman. The memory of Rhianna, defiant and proud, flashed through his mind. He shoved it aside.

"News I have, my lord," Marcus said, forcing a smile onto his lips, "but for your ears alone."

Riderch gave a short laugh. "So be it. Come." He motioned to a shady spot beneath a large ash tree. " 'Tis as good a place as any to talk, for none can overhear without our notice. Both my wife and daughter are engaged in a traditional ceremony and not presently in the fort to serve us. One of the other women will bring our refreshment."

Disappointment flooded Marcus. Rhianna wasn't in the fort. True, he'd no intention of seeking her out nor speaking with her, but he'd hoped for at least a glimpse . . .

Choking back his surprising surge of frustration, he followed after the chieftain, inwardly cursing himself for the disturbing muddle he was now in—a muddle he'd Riderch's flaxen-haired daughter to thank for.

Albinus sauntered about the fort, his movements slow and careless, belying the serious intent of his search. He meant to find the chieftain's daughter and, one way or another, trick her into coming with him. Away from the safety of the fort, he'd at last be able to take his pleasure with her. And, once he'd finished, it would be simple enough to kill her. With the few personal items he'd managed to have pilfered from the other tribune's quarters, he'd then set the blame on Paullinus.

At long last, he thought gleefully, he'd have that proud beauty *and* ruin Paullinus' career. By the time that tribune realized what had happened, *if* he even survived the Trinovante chieftain's rage, he, Albinus, would be well on his way to Rome.

The crime would, at the very least, result in a serious blot on Paullinus' heretofore exemplary military record. If fortune truly smiled, perhaps there would even be a punishment worthy of the nephew of the provincial governor—a discharge *missio ignominiosa.* A fitting reward, to be publicly flogged then drummed out of the army in disgrace, Albinus thought smugly. After all, hadn't he suffered nearly as much, losing his command to that wealthy young upstart?

Immersed in his darkly preoccupied thoughts, Albinus' steps carried him to the chieftain's house. No one was about but a boy of twelve intently engaged in whittling a chunk of wood.

"You, lad," Albinus commanded imperiously. "Fetch me the chieftain's daughter."

Emrys glanced up in surprise. He put down his knife and piece of wood. "You seek my sister Rhianna, lord?"

"And who else, boy? Bring her to me immediately."

Emrys shook his head. " 'Tisn't possible. She's not in the fort."

"Oh?" Albinus could barely restrain his interest. "And where is she, lad?"

"At the sacred pool in the forest with my mother and some other women." He indicated the direction. " 'Tis but a short ride from here."

"I know the place well." Albinus turned and strode away.

So, he thought in rising anticipation, the act would be easier than he'd planned. The wench was already far from the fort's protection. Even if she were with a few other women, it would be easy enough to frighten the rest away. In the excitement none would remember who it was who abducted

Rhianna, save that it was a Roman tribune. It would all look like Paullinus' work after he'd left a few judiciously placed pieces of the other tribune's clothing at the site.

Yes, Albinus assured himself as he headed back to his horse, this would indeed be a fitting end to his assignment in Britannia. His plan was foolproof. What couldn't be contrived, he thought, remembering the small troop of men accompanying them, could just as easily be bribed.

A half-hour later Marcus, accompanied by Riderch, headed back to where his troops waited in the shade of some trees. After a few brief instructions to his men, he gave the command to the trumpeter. "Sound the call for the Tribune Albinus."

The trumpeter hesitated, a puzzled expression wrinkling his youthful brow. "But my lord, the Tribune Albinus left a short time ago. He said he was on an errand for you, settling an old debt as it were, and that you had given your approval for him to leave." The young man swallowed convulsively. "W-was I amiss in not informing you?"

"No, you weren't amiss." Marcus frowned. "Tribune Albinus most probably finished his business and was eager to return to Camulodunum. Did he take any men with him?"

"No, my lord. He rode out alone."

Most unusual, even for Albinus, Marcus thought, to travel without protection in unfriendly lands. His glance caught that of the chieftain's. Riderch, too, seemed perturbed. Perhaps it would be prudent to head back to Camulodunum as soon as possible.

Marcus extended his hand in farewell. "My thanks for your time and understanding, my lord. You have my assurances that I'll do all—"

The sound of gay female voices drifted over from the main

gate. Both men turned toward the sounds. Ura, a tree branch in her hand, followed closely by an older woman—most likely the chieftain's wife by her fine dress, Marcus surmised—Cordaella, and some other young women, entered the enclosure. He searched for sign of Rhianna, knowing she'd accompanied her mother. The maid wasn't with them.

"Ah, they return at last from the purification ceremonies!" Riderch said.

"Purification ceremonies?"

The chieftain smiled. "Aye. My eldest son's wife recently gave birth. 'Tis the custom for the females of the family and a few close friends to accompany the new mother to a sacred pool for a ritualistic cleansing. Come, a moment more of your time to meet my wife and my daughter by marriage, Gunnella."

Marcus walked with Riderch over to the women, his gaze drawn to the chieftain's wife, who stared coldly back.

Riderch stepped forward and wrapped his arm about his wife's shoulders. "This is Savren, Tribune Paullinus. My mate and mother of my children."

"Domina," Marcus formally replied, rendering her a close-fisted salute and respectful bow.

Savren's thin-lipped expression never altered. "Tribune Paullinus."

The chieftain next turned to a pretty, chestnut-haired woman. "My son's wife, Gunnella."

"Lady, it is my pleasure." Marcus bowed, acknowledging the introduction.

Before the open-mouthed Gunnella could reply, Savren shrugged out of her husband's clasp. "Forgive us, Tribune, but I hear the babe crying for his mother. We've tarried overlong at the pool as 'twas. By your leave—"

"A moment, wife." Riderch halted her with an upraised

hand. "Where is Rhianna? She accompanied you to the pool, did she not?"

Savren expelled a small, exasperated breath. "Aye, husband. We left her there, no doubt to one of her endless dreamings. She'll be along soon."

At her words, a warning jangled inexplicably in Marcus' mind. *To settle an old debt.* Albinus' actions were too out of character for this to be mere coincidence, with Rhianna outside the fort, alone, and Albinus, who'd never hidden his desire for her, gone as well. Perhaps he was wrong, but—

Marcus turned to the Trinovante chieftain. "Your pardon, my lord, but I desire a moment of your daughter's time. Would you direct me to the pool?"

Riderch heard the urgency beneath the calmly stated words. "At the bottom of the hill is a trail through the trees. Take it. The pool lies at its end."

"Wait, husband." Savren made a hasty motion to halt him. " 'Tisn't fitting to permit this Roman to seek out our daughter."

"I give leave as chieftain, not as father," Riderch informed her sternly. He turned to Marcus. "Go, Tribune, with my bidding."

Marcus nodded curtly, then wheeled about and strode to where his men waited. In one lithe motion, he swung up onto his stallion. He glanced down at his auxiliaries. "Await me here."

He headed down the road, restraining the impulse to urge the animal into a run for fear of the concern it would cause in the gathering at the gate. Perhaps, in spite of the growing anxiety gnawing at his gut, there truly was no reason for worry. Perhaps Albinus had gone back to Camulodunum. Perhaps . . .

Finally, he reached the trail at the treeline. Once into the forest, Marcus threw all caution aside and kicked his mount into a dead run. Perhaps, indeed! Though he knew not from whence the certainty came, there was no longer any doubt as to its meaning. Rhianna was in mortal danger!

The sun rose to its zenith before full awareness returned. Ever so slowly, like a flower opening its bloom to the light of day, Rhianna's head rose from its position in her lap. Her arms unfolded to move once more at her sides.

She glanced about. In a rush, it all came back. The pool. Her vision.

Blessed Goddess—her vision! Reality washed over her, drowning Rhianna in a sea of misery. Ah, how could she bear it? How could she live with the knowledge of what fate held?

Yet how could she do less? 'Twould be dishonorable to flee her destiny. She lifted her chin in defiance. She'd not shrink from life no matter what it offered. She was Trinovante. Her lot was to serve her people, no matter the cost or sacrifice.

But never, despite her grandfather's urgings to the contrary, would she accept her Gift. Such abilities were not for her. She didn't understand them, nor want them. If the truth be told, the powers terrified her. There was enough in life to be dealt with as 'twas, without braving the Gift as well. Enough already she didn't want, to have to accept queer abilities that would set her even further apart from others.

Rhianna climbed to her feet, brushing off the small bits of leaves and dirt clinging to her gown. Her glance traveled to where her mother and friends had disappeared through the trees. 'Twas past time to make her way back to the fort. Mother would be angry if she tarried—

Someone moved through the trees. Rhianna tensed. Her hand slid to the dagger sheathed at her waist. Her heart began a staccato beating in her chest.

He wasn't at all adept, whoever he was. A soft footfall soon betrayed his position close by. With a fierce battle cry, Rhianna wheeled about, her dagger slashing through the air.

Faced with the assault of a blond she-cat, Albinus stumbled backward. His own soldier's training, however, quickly rose to the forefront. Though not a particularly bold fighter, he'd overcome many foes with his crafty, unsettling way of battle.

He threw up his hands in defeat. "Forgive me, lady. I'd no intention of alarming you."

Rhianna eyed him suspiciously. "I find that difficult to believe, Tribune. There's no reason for your presence here."

"Ah, but you're mistaken, fair maid." A smile spread across his swarthy face. "I'm here through no desire of my own, but of that of the Tribune Paullinus. He awaits back at the fort, eager to speak with you."

"Marcus? Marcus is here?"

Albinus nodded. "Yes. Now will you put away your weapon and accompany me?"

He lies, Rhianna thought, a frisson of renewed apprehension shooting through her. But what were his motives? Better to buy time and find out.

She arched a slender brow. "Then why didn't he come himself?"

Thin lips clamped shut and, for an instant, Rhianna feared she'd pushed him too far. Though her hand had lowered, the naked blade remained between them. Her stance altered, until she was poised on the balls of her feet.

"It wasn't my wish to act the errand boy," Albinus muttered sullenly, "but our tribune thinks his new position entitles him to certain privileges. Thank the gods I won't have to suffer his arrogant manners after today."

Rhianna schooled her features to hide the smile lurking beneath her studied nonchalance. She'd no sympathy for Albinus. If Marcus had succeeded in humbling the cruelly proud man, he had her undying gratitude. The hesitation at seeing him once again melted in a warm surge of anticipation, carrying with it her earlier restraint in Albinus' presence.

"Come then, let us seek the Tribune Paullinus." She gestured for him to lead, indicating the forest trail. "I'm expected at the fort and can't tarry overlong."

Grunting his assent, Albinus stepped out, his eyes glancing warily at the dagger Rhianna still clutched in her hand. Its presence altered his plans. With her behind him and armed, he'd now have to wait until she was distracted before attacking. But no matter. He could be patient when the prize was such a lovely, nubile wench. Indeed, hadn't he waited all these years for just this opportunity?

Yes, at last he'd take the chieftain's daughter. It was only fair, after all. Paullinus had amused himself with her without paying the price of three miserable years on this island as he had. It was but a just reward for all his years of faithful service.

Albinus' chance came as they approached the trees. A pheasant, its brightly hued, iridescent feathers flapping in the air, flew up from its hiding place in the bushes directly alongside Rhianna. In that instant of lowered guard Albinus struck. He wheeled around, one arm snaking about her neck. His other hand clamped over the wrist holding her dagger.

She managed a strangled cry before his grip cut off her air. As she struggled in his clasp, his fingers intensified the hold on her wrist until she thought he'd break her bones.

Rhianna fought back, kicking, flaying out with her free

arm. And, all the while, she refused to loosen her grip on the dagger. Her fingers grew numb. Finally, the dagger dropped to the ground.

With a triumphant snarl, Albinus imprisoned both her arms. Half-dragging, half-carrying her, he pulled Rhianna toward a grassy knoll lying just beyond the trees.

She managed to jab an elbow into his groin.

He let out a surprised grunt, then tightened his grasp on her even more. "You'll pay for that, witch!" He gripped her hair and yanked her head back.

Rhianna caught her breath. "U-unhand me, you d-dog!"

Albinus chuckled suggestively. "I'll handle you any way I choose—and you'll like it." Slowly, relentlessly, he forced her to the ground.

He ripped aside her cloak and groped for her breast. Rhianna bit him. Cursing, Albinus jerked away, leaving a long, jagged tear in his skin. He slapped her, his wounded hand smearing her face with blood. Once more his fingers splayed around her neck, bruising the ivory-hued flesh.

With his greater weight pinning her beneath him, one hand capturing both of her hands above her head, Rhianna could do little more then squirm in futile desperation. She fought the rising panic. What could she do? Would he kill her? Her powerlessness sickened her.

Yet even as she gathered the last vestiges of strength for a final effort, Albinus tore open the front of her gown. Goddess!

Crude, grasping fingers probed within the gaping fabric. His hand was everywhere, on her breasts, snaking down to rub across her belly and between her thighs. She groaned. Ah, better to die than have his filthy hands on her!

His mouth lowered to clamp over Rhianna's lips. His hard, jabbing tongue sought entry to her mouth. She clenched her teeth against him. Finally, he pulled back.

"Submit, you stubborn wench. It'll do you no good to play the little virgin." He leered down at her. "We both know the truth of that, don't we? Paullinus may have lacked the skill to please you, but I don't. Submit and discover the pleasure of lying with a real man."

"Nay!" Rhianna bit back a gasp as his hand moved to once more find her breast. "Never will I submit to you. You're a swine. I'll die first. My father will kill you for this!"

He slid his hand up to entwine in her hair, jerking her face back to his, and laughed. "Your father may indeed kill someone, but it won't be me. I've set the trap too well to implicate myself. Your people will have to turn their vengeance in another direction, onto a man most carefully picked by me."

"And who would that be?" she demanded in a choked whisper, even as a dreadful premonition twined about her heart.

Albinus' mouth lowered until it was a hot, rancid breath away. His stench wafted over Rhianna. Nausea flooded her.

"Why, your lover, of course," Albinus continued with grim satisfaction. "The Tribune Paullinus. I'll take the pleasure, and he'll bear the blame."

As if the thought added fuel to his passion, he ground his hardened shaft against her. "You feel me, don't you? You like it." He grinned down at her. "Paullinus may have been with you first, but it'll be my face, my touch, you'll carry to your grave!"

Then, his mouth set in a hard, savage smile, Albinus lowered himself down onto Rhianna, his plundering tongue but a loathsome harbinger of things to come.

Seven

A cry, quickly muffled, drifted to Marcus' ears. He halted his mount, straining to ascertain the direction of the sound. The forest remained perversely silent, save for the twittering birds and rustling leaves.

Seconds seemed hours as Marcus waited, his frustration mounting. Should he ride further or dismount and continue on foot? If he were near, it would be wiser to use more stealth. But what path to take, and how close was he to discovering her?

A faint sound teased his ears. It sounded like . . . like the nicker of a horse. Marcus swung off his stallion. With long, lithe strides, he sprinted through the trees.

He came upon a horse, tethered to a tree. It was Albinus'. A rage flared to life. The cur! This time Albinus had gone too far. He would pay for laying a hand on Rhianna!

Sounds of struggle drifted through the forest, then quickly faded. Marcus' pace quickened. There could be only one explanation for the prolonged silence.

He caught a glimpse of movement through the trees. Albinus, crouched low on a hillock. Straddling something. Something green and white. Then the object between Albinus' legs moved.

Rhianna!

At Marcus' hoarse war cry Albinus sprang to his feet. His

hand groped for his sword. The discordant sound of its unsheathing rang through the quiet woods.

Marcus halted, his own blade in hand. "Move away from her," he growled, "and lay down your sword."

Albinus glanced back at Rhianna. Already, she was scrambling away, clutching her torn gown closed. He chuckled and turned to the man before him. "But Tribune Paullinus, you promised me a tumble with the fair maid. Will you now go back on your word?"

"Liar!" His words echoed the fury contorting Marcus' features. "You toy with the wrong man if you hope to lay that at my feet." He swung his sword in a commanding motion. "Heed my words, Albinus. Lay down your weapon."

"And if I don't?" came the mocking reply. "What will you do? Murder me?"

"I'd hardly call a fight between two armed men murder."

Albinus laughed softly "What would a court of our peers call it if you killed me, you, the superior swordsman? Your uncle is renowned for his edict against fighting within the army. What would he say to a duel between two of his highest ranking officers, and over such an insignificant matter as this maid?"

Frustration flooded Marcus. Albinus spoke true. If he killed the man, it would be the worse for Rhianna and her people. His uncle would only use the incident as an excuse to impose even harsher measures against the Trinovante under the guise they were responsible for the tribune's death. But gods, how he wanted to carve the man's heart out!

He looked down at Rhianna. She stared back, wide-eyed but undaunted. Though her dress was torn, her face bloodied and neck bruised, it appeared she had managed to evade ravishment. What would she say if he allowed Albinus to escape without punishment? Even if he didn't satisfy his own need to beat that smirking grin off the man's face, didn't he owe her some retribution?

"Are you all right?" Marcus ground out the words through gritted teeth.

She nodded.

He stood there, torn between his need for revenge and the realities of the situation. As *Praefectus Alae,* he was responsible to higher things than the satisfaction of his own desires. He had no choice. Albinus must be allowed to leave unharmed.

Rhianna read his decision in the sudden slump to his broad shoulders. She opened her mouth to protest, then just as quickly clamped it shut again. There was naught she could do. Her dagger was out of reach and was useless against a sword at any rate. If Marcus failed to avenge her honor, she must bear the humiliation.

"Go, Albinus," Marcus finally snarled. "Get out of here and make certain I don't come upon you again before your departure tomorrow. I've had all I can stomach of you. For Rhianna and her people's sake, I'll spare your life. Our next meeting, however, will end in bloodshed."

Albinus smirked, then headed toward the forest path. Marcus watched until the other man passed Marcus' stallion, which had wandered from the forest to graze in the meadow. Then he resheathed his sword and turned back to Rhianna. He pulled her to her feet. "Someday you'll have your revenge. If he'd been of lesser rank, I could have had him flogged, but—"

"Roman, make your excuses to your uncle," she snapped, glaring up at him in outrage. "They are wasted on me. 'Tis a dishonor you've allowed, a disgrace no Celt would ever let pass. None, at least, save a coward."

Pain twisted his face, but so briefly Rhianna wasn't sure

she hadn't imagined it. 'Twas of no import anyway. Though he'd rescued her from Albinus, he'd permitted the other man to disgrace her. She'd expected more of him.

Rhianna jerked from his clasp. "Go, leave with your countryman. You are two of a kind—"

Out of the corner of her eye she saw Albinus move stealthily up, a short, circular-edged ax clutched in his hands. "Marcus! Beware!" Rhianna screamed.

Marcus shoved her out of harm's way and wheeled about, his hand moving to his sword. The ax, however, had already begun its downward descent. The blade sank through the hard leather of his corselet, gouging deep into his upper chest. Pain—searing, excruciating—lanced through him. Marcus stumbled backward. His sword dropped from his hand.

He gripped the ax handle and, with a grunt of pain, wrenched the blade free. Fighting past the white-hot flash of agony, Marcus sank to his knees. His head spun dizzily; his gut roiled. Then Albinus, drawn sword in hand, moved back into his line of vision.

Gods! Marcus cursed his own stupidity, even as the world around him began to dim. His ax. Albinus had used his own ax upon him! Was this to be his final battlefield then, with a coward as executioner? And Rhianna. What would become of Rhianna?

The instant the sword fell from Marcus' hand, Rhianna dropped to the ground and crept toward it. With Albinus' gaze fixed upon his opponent, he never noticed when she picked it up. Its bone handle felt cool and smooth in her grasp. An exultant strength pumped through her veins.

She climbed to her knees and shot Marcus a glance. Blood streamed down his chest, and his face was ashen. He could barely remain upright, save for the hand Albinus now entwined in his hair. And the man's other hand, gripping his sword, lifted high over his head in preparation for the killing blow.

With a cry, Rhianna lunged at Albinus, her weapon driving straight for his unprotected groin. The blade thrust upward, piercing, then plunging deep into the soft flesh.

Albinus froze. Pained horror contorted his features. Then his sword dropped.

He screamed—a long, anguished, spine-tingling sound. Blood spurted, spattering Rhianna. She released her grip on the sword. Albinus toppled over before her, impaling himself on the razor-sharp blade.

For what seemed an eternity he writhed on the ground, his cries gradually lessening to piteous sobs, and then, silence. A sound from behind wrenched Rhianna from her stunned fascination. She turned. Marcus, with a low moan, pitched, unconscious, to the earth.

The heady satisfaction of victory fled with the realization of Marcus' plight. She crawled to his side and turned him over, then quickly removed his corselet to fully expose the injury. Blood saturated a large portion of his tunic, but the tough leather chest armor had prevented a fatal wound.

She ripped the cloth to reveal the long gash in the furred expanse of his chest. Tearing a piece of his tunic away, Rhianna wadded the material against the wound, binding it with more cloth from her hem. Blood continued to stain the bandage until, at last, it slowed and finally stopped.

Relief filled her. At least he wouldn't bleed to death before she got him back to the fort. Rhianna ran down to the pool. After quickly laving her face and arms to remove Albinus' blood, she cupped her hands full of water and hurried back to Marcus. Dribbling only a little of the cooling fluid onto his face at a time, she managed gradually to rouse him.

He groaned as full consciousness returned. His hand clutched at the throbbing wound high on his chest.

Rhianna quickly restrained him. "Nay, Marcus. Don't touch it. You might quicken the bleeding."

His eyes flickered open. "Rhianna?"

"Aye?"

"Albinus?"

She hesitated for an instant. "He's dead."

He groaned again, but this time the sound seemed to spring from a deeper anguish. "It was his destiny . . . but it will make the . . . consequences no less dire. Curse the man! Why was he so . . . so set on the course of his own destruction?" Marcus grasped her by the shoulder. "Tell . . . no one . . . what happened here today. Do you hear me? I'll bear the . . . the blame for his death."

"Nay." Rhianna fiercely shook her head. " 'Twas my deed. I'll not allow you to suffer for it. Let them do with me what they will. Albinus deserved to die and I'm glad. Do you hear me? *Glad* I killed him!"

Awkwardly, Marcus levered himself to one elbow. "I'll not miss the man, either, but . . . but I'll not have you dragged into this sordid mess. It will only complicate things . . . stir hard feelings on both sides if the true tale comes out." He dragged in a pain-wracked breath. "Your people, as well as you, may suffer. Please, Rhianna. Let me deal with it. I know what to do and . . . and I swear, no harm will befall me because of it."

She stared back with dubious eyes. "I-I don't know. 'Tisn't honorable. I've been taught to accept the blame for my actions, good or bad."

"You've suffered enough this day, fair lady." Marcus grimaced against the agony in his shoulder. "Let me bear this for you. It's the least I can do . . . after so-so miserably failing to defend your honor."

Rhianna averted her gaze, unable to withstand the pained entreaty in his beautiful eyes. Blessed Goddess, how could she have ever doubted his courage? If he looked at her like that for just one more instant, she'd crumple onto his chest and weep like a babe!

Instead, Rhianna sighed her acquiescence. "As you wish. But only for the sake of my people," she added quickly.

"I understand. Now, come," he rasped, offering her his hand, "help me to stand. We must get back to the fort before . . . someone comes searching for us. I've a plan."

"And what might that be? I doubt you've much strength to accomplish anything too daring." Rhianna eyed him skeptically then, with a resigned shrug, helped pull him to his feet.

The sudden exertion proved too much for Marcus. They were forced to seek out a large boulder for him to lean against. He stood there for a long while, the sweat drenching his body and brow. "I'd hoped to . . . be able to make it to my horse," he gasped, "but I'm afraid you'll have to . . . bring him to me."

Rhianna studied Marcus. "Can you stand or should I help you back to the ground?"

He managed a weak smile. "Let me stand. You may never be able to get me back up . . . if I go down again." He made a feeble movement with his hand. "Now, go. I've little energy to spare . . ."

She headed for the white stallion and, as she passed her cloak lying on the ground where Albinus had torn it from her, grabbed it and flung it around her to cover her blood-spattered gown. Albinus' prone form received little more than a cursory glance. There were more important matters at hand than wasting further effort on one such as he.

Aye, Rhianna mused as she quickened her pace, the living had problems enough. And every time a certain tall Roman crossed her path, it seemed her life became a little more complicated—and the repercussions even more disconcerting.

Marcus reined in his horse at the base of the road leading to the hill fort. He glanced at Rhianna, who sat behind him, arms clasped tightly about his waist. Once again, his wounded shoulder began to throb. He shoved the pain aside and set his mind to the unpleasant task ahead.

"Get down, Rhianna. You must walk the rest of the way."

She stirred behind him. "Don't be a fool, Marcus. You need me to support you or you'll surely fall. The hill is steep."

"I'm not riding up to the fort. Once you're there, send my men down. I must get back to Camulodunum."

"But you're sorely wounded. How will you make it all the way back to Camulodunum? Please, Marcus. Come up to the fort and let us care for you."

"And risk the chance your people might discover what happened?" Marcus shook his head. "No, Rhianna. Besides, Albinus' body must be taken back and an official report made. The longer I tarry, the worse the consequences become. Now, please, get down. Your arguing taxes what little strength I have left."

Stung by the harshness of his words, even knowing it was his pain that sharpened them, Rhianna slid from the horse. She walked around the stallion until she could gaze up at Marcus.

Her heart ached at the sight of him. He looked as if, at

any second, he'd come tumbling off his mount. His features were drawn, his skin still pallid. Sweat glistened on his face, matting his dark curls damply to his forehead.

How could she let him go, ride away wounded and hurting, to a fate even more threatening? It seemed he was always protecting her from something, but this time it could prove his undoing. And if he left now, how would she ever know what became of him?

"Rhianna." Gently, he interrupted her poignant thoughts. "Do what I ask and trust me. It's for the best."

She squared her shoulders. Aye, 'twas for the best—for her and her people at least. And that was all that *should* matter. "Fare you well then, Roman." She turned to walk away.

"Rhianna."

She glanced back over her shoulder. "Aye?"

The merest shadow of a smile grazed his lips. "Marcus. You promised to call me Marcus."

Sadly, Rhianna returned his smile. "Aye, that I did. Fare you well . . . Marcus."

Before he could say more, she wheeled about and ran toward the fort. Tears blinded her, spilling over to be snatched away in her flight.

Marcus.

Ah, curse the man! He was everything she loathed—Roman and enemy. And yet to turn just now and leave him had nearly been her undoing.

'Twas too much to endure, too much to understand after such a day. With a wondering shake of her head, Rhianna quickened her pace, blotting out further thoughts of Marcus—and the strange, sweet stirrings of her heart.

* * *

It had taken but a moment to send the Roman troops after their leader. Afterward, Rhianna was able to slip into her house undetected. Relieved there'd be no awkward questions to answer, she went to draw the curtains of her boxbed.

" 'Tis past time you returned, daughter."

Rhianna's hand froze, gripping the cloak over her torn gown. Blessed Goddess, if Mother probed too deeply . . .

She turned, forcing her mouth into a sheepish smile. "I beg forgiveness. I . . . I sat on the rock and, with the sun's warmth heating it, I soon fell asleep. Permit me but a moment more and I'll be at my chores."

"Why do you wear a cloak on such a warm day?" Savren's eyes narrowed suspiciously. "Have you caught yourself a chill?"

"A-aye." Floundering for an acceptable excuse, Rhianna fell eagerly on the one her mother offered. " 'Tis naught to worry about, though. As soon as I change into a plainer gown, I'll set about my tasks with such vigor the exertion itself will drive my sickness away."

"Mayhap that would be wise. I know how you are, though. At the first sign of illness, promise me you'll come for one of my healing draughts."

At the mention of the vile-tasting concoction, Rhianna could barely restrain a grimace. "Aye, lady. I promise."

She watched Savren leave, relief at escaping detection making her knees weak. Rhianna fled to the safety of her boxbed. Removing her cloak, she glanced down at her tunic dress. Next to the blue one she'd worn at Lughnasa, it had been her best. But nevermore.

With a resigned sigh, Rhianna stripped it off and stuffed it in one corner of her wooden chest. She'd have to dispose of it soon, but not today.

Slipping on a simple gown dyed brown with the stain of

walnut shells, Rhianna turned to the task of subduing her tangled mane. One glance in the mirror elicited a horrified gasp. The imprint of fingers marked her throat. How had her mother failed to note the purpling bruises? The shadows of the sleeping area must have hidden them—'twas the only possible answer. But how to mask them until they faded?

Rummaging through her chest, Rhianna came upon some discarded lengths of fabric. Pulling a cloth knife from her sewing bag, she cut a swath of material left over from making the dress she now wore. She wrapped it around the lower portion of her neck, luckily the only area where Albinus had left his mark.

Rhianna studied her handiwork in the bronze hand mirror. Not the usual garb of a Trinovante woman, but 'twould have to suffice. If anyone commented on the new fashion, she'd tell them 'twas her way of fighting a sore throat. She'd seen some of the old women do just that, so her action, though a little eccentric, should pass without too much notice.

Had Marcus' attempts at hiding his wound been as easily accomplished? Once again she was struck by a need to go to him. 'Twas she who should stand before his judges and accept the blame for killing Albinus—a blame that, by all rights, was hers alone. But what could she hope to accomplish against the might of Rome?

Marcus had been right. Far better to leave it all to him. Rhianna replaced the grooming items and cloth knife in her chest. They seemed to be the only things in her life left that could be easily set to rest. Yet the necessity of maintaining some semblance of normalcy had to be acted upon.

Sweeping aside the bed hangings, Rhianna stepped out to face the world—as if nothing untoward had ever happened.

* * *

The hot summer sun beat down on the wheat field, its radiant beams dancing off the densely planted golden-brown stalks. Side by side the scythers worked, advancing down the rows with sickles glinting brightly. Behind them came the band-makers, women and older children, tying armfuls of the grain stalks into sheaves that they laid on the ground to await the stackers. Last in the parade of harvesters, the stackers gathered up the bundled swathes of wheat, propping them into upright shocks to dry in the sun.

Orderly and predictable, the ritual of harvest flowed from year to year. Lovingly, Rhianna scanned the scene. Like the land, 'twas one of the comforting, dependable aspects of life. Thank the Goddess for a few things to cling to in the midst of an existence as tumultuous, as ever-changing as the heavens.

Her back ached from long hours of bending. She paused from her sheaf-tying. After wiping the moisture from her brow, Rhianna drank from the leathern water skin hanging at her waist. The barley water slid down her parched throat in cool, undulating swallows. Refreshed at last, she replaced the skin bag and squinted up at the sun. Soon the call would come for the midday meal. Soon there'd be food to serve, others to talk to—and a blessed respite from the endless self-recrimination.

Ten days had passed since she'd watched Marcus ride away; and still the peace, the acceptance of his self-sacrifice, had failed to come. Sleepless nights had brought scant relief from the guilt and anguish. She wondered if anything, save the recourse of seeking him out, ever would. Yet he'd asked her to trust him, and she'd given her word.

Honor. Why had it suddenly become such a detestable thing? 'Twas all that stood between her and the growing need to ride to Camulodunum. Could honor possibly be of greater import than another's life? And was trust a higher good than accepting responsibility for one's actions?

A month ago the answers would have been so simple. But now? Over and over the questions roiled in Rhianna's mind, stirring the confusion until, like a muddied stand of water, nothing could penetrate its murky depths.

A sound—her mother's voice, sharp and annoyed—beckoned Rhianna back to the day's sweltering heat. She glanced about. Savren stood at the edge of the field, a small, green bundle in her hand.

Surprised that her mother would interrupt on harvest day, Rhianna waved to assure her she'd seen her signal, then finished tying together one last shock. The task complete, she gathered her long skirts and ran to where Savren waited. As she neared, the bundle of cloth in her mother's hand assumed a familiar appearance. Rhianna's heart sank.

Her gown, the one she'd worn that morn of Gunnella's purification. Goddess! She'd forgotten to dispose of it.

Savren held out the tunic dress, her blue eyes smoldering. "What happened that day at the pool?" she demanded in a low voice to avoid being overheard. "This gown is torn and blood-stained. Tell me. I command it."

Naught but the truth would satisfy her mother, and naught but the truth would be believed. Yet Marcus had asked her not to speak of it. Rhianna's chin lifted in stubborn defiance. " 'Tisn't mine to tell. All I can say is that, in the end, I escaped unharmed."

"And who has sworn you to such secrecy that you refuse me an explanation?" Savren shook the ruined dress in Rhianna's face. "No one, save the clan chieftain, can ask such a thing of a Trinovante. Was it your father who requested your silence?"

"Nay."

"Then who?"

"I cannot say."

Her mother grabbed Rhianna's arm. "Ah, but you will, daughter. Come, let us seek out your father."

Half-dragging Rhianna behind her, Savren set out toward the hill fort. Neither spoke as they hurried along, though the air between them fairly crackled with hostility. Possible explanations to extricate herself from her dilemma raced through Rhianna's mind, and just as many were tossed aside.

If her father as chieftain demanded it—and, at her mother's insistence, she knew he would—the truth would have to be told. Her only hope was to plead an oath-breaking. 'Twas the one thing that might save her.

They found Riderch sharpening his long, ceremonial sword on the weapon stone standing outside their house. At the sound of hurried footsteps, he turned from the tall column of carved rock and resheathed his blade. He caught sight of his wife and daughter. A broad smile spread across Riderch's long-mustached, weathered face.

"And to what do I owe the honor of such a visit on harvesting day?" he asked with a chuckle.

"A moment of privacy, my lord." Savren's voice lowered as her gaze scanned the various inhabitants scurrying about. " 'Tis a serious problem for your ears alone."

Riderch glanced from his wife to his daughter, his gray brows furrowing in concern. Ah, what was it this time? Would their bickering never end? When would they finally make peace?

He sighed, motioning toward their timbered dwelling. "Come. No one's about at this time of day. We can talk in the house."

Savren led the way, her grip on Rhianna's arm never lessening. Once inside, the older woman wheeled around, thrusting the ragged gown at her husband.

"Look at her tunic," she cried. " 'Twas the garment she wore the day of Gunnella's cleansing, the day the Romans visited. 'Tis ruined, torn beyond repair, and bloody. Yet our daughter refuses to tell me how it came to such a state. Ask her, Riderch. Ask her what happened that day at the pool."

Penetrating gray eyes turned to Rhianna. "Well, daughter. What have you to say for yourself? Did something happen at the pool after the other women left?"

The color drained from Rhianna's face. "I . . . I beg of you, Father. Don't ask. I'm forsworn not to speak of it."

"And who may forswear you but I?" came the gentle query.

Her head lowered in defeat.

" 'Twas the Tribune Paullinus, wasn't it?" Savren cut in. " 'Twasn't enough he had you as the victor's due. He had to seek you out at the pool and take you again. The cur! The swine!"

Rhianna's head jerked up. Blue fire flashed in her eyes. "Nay, 'twasn't Marcus. He has always treated me honorably."

"Then what did happen, child?" Her father gathered her face between his two large, callused palms. "If 'twasn't the Tribune Paullinus, who was it?"

Rhianna exhaled a long, shuddering breath. " 'Twas the Tribune Albinus."

"And did he ravish you?"

"Nay. Marcus rescued me." She hesitated. "But when Marcus' back was turned, Albinus attacked and sorely wounded him. I grabbed Marcus' sword when he dropped it and . . . and killed Albinus."

"Holy Mother!" Savren moaned from behind them. "She

has ruined us all. A Roman tribune. Our daughter has killed a Roman tribune!"

"Hush, woman." Riderch held up a silencing hand. "Rhianna hasn't finished her tale, have you, lass?" He peered at her intently. "Why wasn't this brought to my attention that very day? And if the Tribune Paullinus was wounded, why didn't you bring him to us for care?"

"Marcus feared the repercussions if our people discovered what Albinus had tried to do. He said 'twould be wiser for him to take the blame for Albinus' death. H-he made me swear not to tell anyone."

Her eyes filled with tears. "I tried, Father. I begged him to let us care for his wound. Ah, 'twas a grievous thing, that ax-blow to his chest! But he insisted on riding back to Camulodunum. Even now I don't know if he survived the journey or what became of him once he returned."

Riderch gathered his daughter into his arms. "And you're heartsick about it, aren't you?"

Rhianna nodded from the comforting haven of his chest, unable to staunch the tears a moment longer. "A-aye. 'T-tisn't fair he should s-suffer so dearly for my sake," she sobbed. "If-if only I knew wh-what befell him . . ."

"Then know you shall. The man deserves both our thanks." Her father leaned back to gaze into her tear-streaked face. "Let us pay your tribune a visit. I've a few tasks in the city anyway and, as the day is half-past, we can stay overnight."

He gave her a small shove. "Go, child. Prepare yourself. We depart for Camulodunum in an hour's time."

Eight

The little bay mare pranced erratically down the road, side-stepping and dancing about until Rhianna nearly lost patience. Time after time she reined in the spirited animal to forestall swerving into her father and brother Emrys' horses. Riderch smiled with paternal tolerance, but finally sandy-haired Emrys, after one especially unnerving near miss, snorted in aggravation.

"By the Goddess, Rhianna! Can't you keep your mount better controlled? You humor her far too much. She's but a horse, after all."

"Calm yourself, little brother," Rhianna laughed. "Demetia is a finely bred animal. Surely you don't expect her to plod along like a plow horse?" To placate him, however, she pulled away to ride alongside her father's gelding. Riderch chuckled, but said nothing.

Demetia senses my excitement, Rhianna thought. Even now, I can hardly believe I'm on my way to see Marcus. But only to assure myself he is well and no harm has come to him because of Albinus' death, she added quickly. 'Twas all a point of honor, and naught more. Once settled, she could put the unfortunate incident—and all thoughts of Marcus—behind her.

Yet still Rhianna feared the unpredictable reaction of her heart, fully realizing the effect his tall, powerful presence always had on her. Better that she'd never met the man. He lured her, like the haunting depths of some dark pool, toward things compelling and mysterious, yet fraught with danger.

Riderch noted the tiny frown that drew her delicate brows inward. " 'Twasn't ill meant, your mother's anger," he began, misinterpreting the source of his daughter's concern. " 'Twas her love for you that caused her to lash out. Try to understand."

Rhianna gave a bitter laugh, grateful to turn her thoughts elsewhere. "It seems I rarely please her these days. I see no love in Mother's actions. I see only fear I'll do something to endanger my marriage to Cador and ruin all her plans."

He shook his head. "Nay, lass. Savren but desires what any mother would for her daughter. A husband, a family . . . an acceptance of a woman's fate."

"And because I fight against my woman's fate, it angers her."

"Aye," her father admitted, his eyes warming with compassion. "Because of that, Savren thinks she has failed in her duties to you. It angers her, but even more so, it hurts her."

Rhianna sighed. "I'm sorry, Father. I wouldn't willingly hurt either one of you. But sometimes the call of one's heart . . ."

"I know, lass. I know. Yet there are times when, for the good of others, we must modify, if not completely alter, our dreams."

She turned her gaze to the scene around her, unwilling to dwell further on the harsh truth of her father's words. Reality though she knew them to be, Rhianna refused to allow his somber reminder to mar the excitement of a rare trip to town. As they neared Camulodunum and the coast, the land dipped gradually in elevation. From the higher, heavily forested hills and dales where the Trinovante lived, they came out upon two river valleys. There in the distance, nestled among miles of dikes, Rhianna could make out the city of Camulodunum, now little more than a Roman *colonia* for retired army veterans.

As they approached the town's west entry, the forms of half-timbered houses, interspersed with those of a more humble wattle and daub construction, came into view. Rhianna shook her head in wonder at the foolishness of a people living together without protection of walls. Why, even the hill fort was better fortified than this metropolis of Romanized Celts. 'Twas but another instance of Roman arrogance, she decided, to tear down ancient walls and live in an enemy land as if there were no danger.

Riderch reined in his horse beside the Roman soldier guarding Camulodunum's main entrance. "We seek the Tribune Paullinus."

At the mention of his leader's name, the man snapped to attention. "The tribune is in the garrison situated outside the city. Follow this road through Camulodunum, and it'll take you out the east gate. The garrison is there."

The chieftain nodded his thanks and urged his mount onward, Rhianna and Emrys following close behind. Scarcely had they entered the city when a surging mass of bodies engulfed them. Demetia shied violently, unnerved by the unaccustomed close quarters. It was all Rhianna could do to prevent her horse from trampling a few unwary townspeople. As they rode on, however, the crowd only increased in size.

Interspersed with soothing the high-strung mare and avoiding a myriad of unsuspecting bodies, Rhianna managed to take in the impressive chaos of Camulodunum. As they moved farther into the heart of the city, they passed what seemed like hundreds of shops, all overflowing with items to delight the feminine heart.

Booths of tanners and dyers, tailors, cobblers, pottery, and glassware as well as coppersmiths and workshops for other fine metals jammed the narrow thoroughfare. As they passed a baker's shop, the sweet aroma of baking bread wafted to Rhianna's nostrils. Her mouth watered at the haunches of meat hung for display in the butcher's booth.

Her hunger, suppressed by the excitement of the trip, once more sprung to the forefront. 'Twas late afternoon and she'd not eaten since early morn. Dare she ask her father to buy one of those enticing loaves of crusty brown bread?

Rhianna glanced at him, intending to suggest just that. He had already halted his gelding, his attention focused on a goldsmith's shop.

"Emrys, hold my horse." Riderch swung down from his mount. "I've a notion to buy your mother and Gunnella a trinket or two. Await me here."

He disappeared into the bowels of the little establishment. Rhianna returned Emrys' bemused grin, then directed her attention back to the baker's shop. If she hurried, there just might be time to procure a loaf before her father—

The harsh snap of a whip cracked through the air, followed closely by a man's angry voice, mouthing a vile string of curses. Rhianna craned her neck to scan the crowd. The man with the whip was easy to find, for a circle of interested onlookers had gathered around him. In the midst of the circle was an overloaded cart. A thin, scraggly horse was hooked to it, attempting, as best he could, to pull the wagon along. The animal's strength, however, was spent, and still its burly owner persisted in beating him.

No one made a move to intercede. Rhianna's indignation grew to a scalding fury. Too long had she lived with horses, been taught to cherish them as the valuable creatures they were, to so indifferently sit by and watch one be cruelly treated. If the people of Camulodunum were so callused to the suffering of a dumb beast, she most certainly wasn't.

She swung down from Demetia. "Here, hold these." Rhianna tossed her reins up to a startled Emrys. "Stay with the horses until Father returns." Spinning on her heel, she forced her way through the crowd to the cart and whip-wielding man.

Dressed in a shabby, grease-stained leather tunic and breeches, the brute posed a hulking, formidable barrier. Rhianna eyed him uncertainly for a moment before speaking. "Stop that this instant!"

Her voice rose sharply above the din. A hush settled over the bystanders. The man's arm, lifted yet again to whip the unfortunate horse, halted in mid-air. He turned slowly and came face to face with Rhianna.

His black little eyes, so much like those of a pig's, raked her slender form until she felt she stood unclothed before him. Her chin raised a fraction higher as, defiantly, she returned his stare.

"What did you say, wench?"

The question was uttered in a low, rasping voice, the implied dare to repeat her demand hovering on the edge of his words. Apprehension flickered through Rhianna. This might be more difficult than she'd imagined. As if she *ever* bothered to think before acting on her first impulses!

"Stop beating that horse." The sentence, though in itself bold, slipped out from a dry, constricted throat. Ah, well, she thought, what was done was done and her pride wouldn't permit her to back down now. "Can't you see he's too weak to pull such a heavy load? Either lighten the cart or find a stronger animal."

The filthy stranger eyed her, then threw back his head and laughed. The raucous, mocking sound grated on Rhianna.

Fool, he had done it now! Her hands clenched, rising to a position of stubborn belligerence on her hips.

Unnerved by the girl standing, uncowed, before his show of bravado, the man's laughter faded. He glared down at her. "Away with you, wench, before I lay the lash to your back as well. No one orders me about, and certainly no mere slip of a lass."

A beefy arm shoved her aside. In a blur of movement, Rhianna's dagger appeared in her hand, glittering menacingly. The man paused.

"Y-you dare threaten me with that small toy?" he sputtered in outrage. "I'll have your hide for that!"

Leaping back, he unfurled his long whip. A cold knot formed in Rhianna's stomach. She glanced about for help. No one stepped forward. A movement of red and the clink of horse trappings skirted the edge of her consciousness, but she had little time to ponder their significance. Even now, the man was throwing back his whip arm.

In the next instant Rhianna was jerked upward, landing against a corseleted chest. Stirred by the memory of a similar rescue, she pivoted around in relief. "Marcus! Thank the Goddess—"

Eyes in a bronze-helmeted face gazed back at her, but they were of quicksilver gray. The visage, though ruggedly handsome, wasn't that of Marcus. She stared in disbelief as an admiring smile lit the man's jaggedly hewn features. He hefted her more comfortably onto his lap, then turned to the owner of the scrawny horse.

"Does the Tribune Paullinus permit such conduct in his city that men feel free to horsewhip beautiful women?"

The unkempt horse-driver couldn't fail to divine the implied warning in the Roman's icy query. He took a step backward, his whip falling limply to the ground. As if eager for the confrontation to come, the crowd edged closer.

"S-she tried to keep me from a day's honest labor," he said with a weak attempt at bravado. The man glanced about him, seeking corroboration of his words. There was none. He turned back to the Roman, wet his lips nervously, then forged on. " 'Tis a simple, hard-working man I am. I meant no harm, truly I didn't. 'Twas but a ruse to frighten the lass."

The gray-eyed Roman twisted his head to contemplate Rhianna. "Is that the way of it, lady?"

"Nay!" Rhianna snapped, rapidly regaining her composure as well as indignation at yet another high-handed Roman. " 'Twasn't the way of it at all. His cart's overloaded and his beast not fit for the task. I but asked him to consider the animal."

"Asked me!" The grimy cartman pointed an indignant finger at Rhianna. "That sharp-tongued wench did little less than *demand* I immediately stop work and accede to her unreasonable request. Tell me this, Tribune," he said, noting, for the first time the Roman's high rank. "Man to man, would you let a haughty lass order you around?"

Laughter rumbled within the Roman's broad chest. "If she were as fair and delightfully rounded as this one, yes, I might consider it." He shot her a devilish glance. "But only in the bedchamber, of course."

As the tribune finished speaking, snickers and a few crude comments rose from the crowd surrounding them. Rhianna stiffened in outrage. How dare he insult her in such a manner, and before all these people no less! She squirmed in his grasp.

"Unhand me, you crude lout! Your armor will rot off your body before *that* ever happens." Her dagger appeared under his chin. "Let me go this instant or—"

"Or what, fair maid? Will you pierce me with that tiny knife of yours?"

She opened her mouth to confirm his suspicions, then thought better of it. Blessed Goddess, how had she managed to escape one peril only to fall into yet another? Well, there was no way out of it. She'd have to play the humble Roman subject if she were to evade this one's clutches.

"Nay, my lord." Rhianna lowered her head, the long sweep of dark lashes masking the rebellious flash of her eyes. She returned her dagger to its sheath. " 'Twasn't my intent to harm you, only to obtain your attention. Free me and I'll show you how ill-treated that unfortunate horse truly is."

"And have you slip back into the crowd and disappear? I think not, my fair-haired beauty." He glanced back at the horse-driver, motioning toward his animal. "Unload half of that cart's contents. Pay someone to guard the rest until your return. Though this little spitfire's diplomacy leaves much to be desired, she was right about the treatment of your horse. A more generous grain dole might prevent future problems."

The leather-garbed man opened his mouth to protest then, thinking better of it, clamped it shut. He instead shook his head and proceeded disgruntledly to carry out the tribune's command.

The gray-eyed Roman motioned for the crowd to disperse, then turned his attention to the more pleasant dilemma of the woman clasped in his arms. "Tell me your name, lady. You owe me something for my rescue."

Rhianna glared back at him. "I owe you naught, Roman. Do you hear me? Naught!"

His large, brown hand toyed with a wheat-colored lock of her hair. Ever so carefully, he wound it about his fingers, then began gently but insistently to pull her toward him. "A kiss then? Such a small token of your gratitude and then I promise to let you go."

"Nay!" Rhianna leaned back as far as his hold on her hair would allow. "No man of honor would force a kiss—"

"Quintus is more honorable than most," a rich-timbred voice interjected. "Resisting a beautiful woman is just beyond his power. Isn't it, Quintus?"

At the sound of the familiar voice, Rhianna twisted in her captor's clasp. "Marcus!"

The Roman called Quintus chuckled to himself as he released Rhianna's hair and guided his horse about to face Marcus. As their eyes met, a broad grin spread across his leanly carved features. "That may well be, but the inability to avoid chiding me for my small failings has always been beyond yours, my friend."

Rhianna glanced from Quintus to Marcus. "You *know* each other?"

Marcus nodded, a small smile hovering about his well-shaped lips. "We are lifelong friends and—"

"Rhianna! Thank the Goddess. There you are!"

Her father. Emrys. She'd forgotten all about them.

Rhianna's confusion transformed swiftly to cheek-warming discomfiture. What would her father think of her in yet another Roman's arms? She turned back to Quintus, a pleading look in her eyes.

" 'Tis my father. Please let me down."

A hint of laughter glinted in his silver eyes but, without protest, Quintus lowered her to the ground. As her father and brother wove their horses toward them through the milling throng of people who were once more going about their errands, Rhianna ran over to stand by the safety of Marcus' white stallion. How much had they seen of her escapade with the horse-driver and Marcus' friend? she wondered.

"I hadn't anticipated seeing you so soon, fair lady. A most unexpected pleasure, to be sure."

Marcus' voice, low and rich, intruded on Rhianna's troubled preoccupation. Her lashes flew up in surprise. All the emotions that had haunted her waking and sleeping moments for the past ten days came rushing back. Caught up in the spell of his splendid eyes, she could do little more than stare mutely up at him.

Fortunately, Riderch and Emrys arrived, leading Demetia behind them. Her father shook his head in long-suffering exasperation. "Daughter, can I not leave your side for a moment without your involving yourself in some disturbance?" He glanced over at Marcus. " 'Tis a blessing the Tribune Paullinus was once again near."

Marcus laughed. "This time, I fear, the credit must go to my dear friend, the Tribune Quintus Petronius Marcellus. He rescued Rhianna, or so I assumed was the purpose of her presence on his horse."

He shot his friend an appraising glance, knowing full well Quintus' fondness for a comely female. But this was one time his friend's more amorous tendencies wouldn't set well with him. Not well at all.

Riderch bowed in acknowledgment. " 'Tis an honor to meet a friend of the Tribune Paullinus."

Quintus silently returned the courtesy.

"And to what do *we* owe the honor of a visit from the chieftain of the Trinovante?" Marcus asked.

"Considering the events of your last visit to our fort, I felt compelled to seek you out and extend my thanks. Besides, my daughter was worried about you."

"Indeed?" A flicker of guarded interest flared in Marcus' eyes then, with the realization the older man knew all, he relaxed. "It has been taken care of, with surprisingly few repercussions. You needn't worry about any blame being laid at your door."

He turned then to Rhianna, a half-bemused, half-pleased smile creasing his face. "Are your father's words true, lady? Were you indeed worried about me?"

Her cheeks flushed warmly, but Rhianna refused to reveal the truth about her anxiety for him. "We had business in Camulodunum," she lied. " 'Twas but a simple courtesy to pay you a short visit."

Ignoring the startled looks her father and Emrys sent her way, she hurried on. " 'Tis apparent you've recovered nicely, though, and have resumed your command without difficulty. I am pleased. Now," she turned to Riderch, "I'm sure the tribune is quite busy with his many duties. Since we have errands of our own, let us be on our way."

"Wait." When she made a move to walk away, Marcus grasped Rhianna's arm. "Must you journey home this day?" His inquiring glance moved from one Trinovante to the other. "I'm having a banquet this eve in honor of the safe, if somewhat tardy, arrival of my friend, the Tribune Marcellus. My quarters are spacious and there's room for all. If you can, stay this night and let me repay your hospitality with a little of my own."

Riderch hesitated. "Your offer is most kind, Tribune Paullinus. We had planned on spending the night at an inn. To lodge with you would be an imposition."

"Nonsense. Come, allow me to lead all of you to the garrison."

Marcus released Rhianna's arm, the feel of her soft, smooth flesh stirring him yet again. Since the moment he'd seen her, clasped in Quintus' arms, the old, unsettling longing had flared to a now-familiar intensity. He *must* find time to speak privately with Rhianna, to discern the true extent of his attraction for her, to say the things even now swirling hotly, yet unformed, in his mind.

Riderch turned to his children. "Would that suit you—to accept the hospitality of the Tribune Paullinus?"

Though the query was addressed to both of them, Rhianna knew her father was really seeking her approval. She sensed his unease over her inordinate emotional response to the handsome, green-eyed tribune. 'Twas past time to ease his anxieties. And, in the easing, dispel her own as well.

She graced him with one of her brightest, most carefree smiles. "Aye, Father. 'Twould suit us well to accept the tribune's hospitality."

Though the entire populace of Camulodunum seemed out on market day, the rest of the ride to the garrison was, save for one exception, uneventful, if no less interesting. As they journeyed deeper into the city's center, the simple shops and houses were replaced increasingly by the more imposing Roman edifices. The important public buildings were constructed of marble of varying hues. The most impressive was the Temple of Claudius, residence of the Imperial Cult to the now-deceased, deified emperor.

Rhianna recognized the imposing white marble structure immediately. In the years of its construction, far too much discussion had raged among the Trinovante over the moneys unfairly extorted from all the tribes not to know it on sight. Long, broad, and rectangular, the temple was surrounded by a colonnade of tall, slender pillars topped with the popular capitals of carved acanthus leaves. The three points of the roof on both ends were fronted by winged figures of gold with elaborately hewn representations of the Emperor

Claudius and other personages depicted in bas relief on the facade.

Yet, as beautiful, as finely wrought as the temple was, the sight of it filled Rhianna with loathing. Too much of her people's hard-earned funds had been confiscated for any Trinovante to feel anything more than hatred for this symbol of Roman tyranny. As long as it stood, 'twas a bitter reminder of their subjugation.

Camulodunum—the fort of Camulos, the war god. Indeed, how *did* that Celtic deity feel about the humiliation of his sacred city? Rhianna's gaze swept the broad expanse of steps leading up to the temple proper. Her breath quickened. And, in a flash of premonition, she felt the Gift descend.

No longer were the steps snowy-1white and dotted with happy worshippers hurrying to and fro. Strewn upon that expanse of marble, like so many fallen leaves, were now the lifeless forms of men, women, and children. Clouds of black smoke billowed from the burning edifice but through the haze Rhianna glimpsed blood, staining the hapless people's clothes, trickling down the stairs.

Dread engulfed her. She clenched her eyes shut, fighting back the nausea surging to her throat, struggling to drive the terrifying vision from her mind.

Death. Destruction. Revenge! The horrible words reverberated through her skull as if Camulos himself had deigned to answer her despairing question.

Blessed Goddess! Rhianna thought in rising panic. Had she called down vengeance upon the city in her summoning of that merciless god? Or was this but a warning of what could be if events progressed unchecked?

'Twas too much, this unbidden, detestable power! The foreknowledge was useless in her hands, no matter what its purpose. She was but a maid, untutored, untested. No one would believe her.

Better her grandfather receive such enlightenment. He was Druid, his word, his wisdom accepted as truth. Mayhap he could influence the course of events. But not she. Never, ever she . . .

She forced her eyes to open and glanced nervously around. Had anyone noticed her odd preoccupation? Mayhap the Gift had passed in a fleeting instant or mayhap the others were too distracted with the tumult of the city, but none even looked her way. Relief flooded her. No one would ever have to know.

Yet even as that thought struck her, Rhianna knew this time the vision couldn't be kept to herself. Before, the Gift's visitation had revealed events involving only her. This time, the sights she'd seen might well have impact on her own people. Cunagus must be told, just as soon as they returned home. Whether she wished it or not, her powers were slowly forcing her to deal with them. For the sake of her people . . .

Immersed in her morose thoughts, Rhianna hardly noticed when they exited the town and entered the small, timber-enclosed garrison. As soon as the group reached the parade field and halted before a sprawling, stucco-fronted stone building, Marcus gave the signal to dismount.

He handed his horse to a groomsman and strode over to where Rhianna still sat atop her horse in frowning concentration. "Lady, is something amiss?"

At the light touch of his hand upon her leg, Rhianna's troubled thoughts cleared. She glanced down at Marcus. His flawless features were bathed in the rosy glow of the rapidly fading sun. She smiled tremulously and shook her head. "Nay, 'tis naught but the weariness of the day. I need but a short rest, and all will be well."

He raised his good arm to her, the other still stiff from his wound. "Come, then. What's needed is a reviving plunge in the women's *thermae.* A bath will do you good and, though I yearn for a time to talk with you, there's yet a few hours of pressing business to my day. Come down, Rhianna, and let Ailm tend to your needs."

Mayhap it was the utter fatigue of the long day, or just the draining aftermath of the Gift, but Rhianna slid off her horse to fall against Marcus' strong body. For the briefest instant he held her to him. Fortified by the rush of blood sent coursing through her veins by a suddenly overstimulated heart, Rhianna jerked back. A hot warmth flushed her cheeks.

She glanced at her father, afraid of his reaction. He was deep in conversation with Emrys and hadn't noticed.

Not so with the Tribune Marcellus. His gaze met hers in a quicksilver perusal. He quirked one black brow, his firm mouth curling on the edge of laughter. Almost as if—as if he were amused with her.

With a toss of her hair, Rhianna turned her back to him. The arrogance, the audacity of the man! Marcus' friend or no, she didn't like him.

She looked up at Marcus. His attention was riveted on his quarters, a smile of pleasure on his lips. Pricked by curiosity, Rhianna turned.

In the doorway, a russet cloud of hair cascading down about her shoulders, stood a slender young woman of Rhianna's age. Her warm brown eyes glowed with joy as she waved a small, delicately boned hand in greeting. She was exquisitely, flawlessly beautiful, Rhianna realized with a sudden pang. And, whoever she was, 'twas evident she shared a warm relationship with Marcus.

The knowledge wasn't comforting. Not comforting at all.

Marcus grasped her elbow. "Ah, Ailm awaits us even now."

Happy anticipation deepened the timbre of his voice. "Permit me to introduce you to her." As he spoke, he propelled Rhianna toward the doorway.

Ailm's eyes were unreadable in the door's shaded overhang. Marcus released his grip on Rhianna as they paused before her. "Ailm," he said, "this is the Lady Rhianna. Please prepare a room for her for the night. Afterward, if there's time, accompany her to our baths."

Rhianna made a sound of protest. Marcus silenced her with a well-placed finger. "Roman custom though it is, trust me when I assure you that you'll enjoy our baths. No one, no matter what his nationality, has ever failed to appreciate the invigorating effects of the *thermae*."

Rhianna sighed her acquiescence. "As you wish. And my father and brother, what of them?"

"My manservant, Cei, will see to their comfort." He paused to brush aside a windblown lock of hair from her eyes. "Fear not, Rhianna. Ailm will see to all your needs."

Marcus stepped back and saluted her. "Until this eve."

His long, athletic strides quickly carried him back to where Quintus awaited with their horses. With one last, lingering look, Rhianna turned to face the other woman.

Ailm inclined her head in a gesture of respect. "If you'll permit, I'll show you to your room."

"Aye, 'twould be appreciated," Rhianna replied stiffly. What was Ailm to Marcus? she wondered. Servant? Slave? The fact Marcus hadn't introduced her as his wife implied she must work for him instead, as did his request for Ailm to prepare a room and accompany Rhianna to the baths.

But what if the other woman also served him as mistress? Ah, why hadn't she ever considered such a possibility? The questions gnawed at Rhianna's vitals, until all that was left was an empty, aching void.

With a small movement of her head, the dark-haired woman indicated Rhianna should follow. Rhianna's tumultuous thoughts faded as she entered the building to be replaced by a wondering curiosity at its interior.

The walls, their surfaces smoothed with stucco, were painted with brilliant murals of peacocks and other exotic birds. And, as if not to be outdone, the floor gleamed in polished, many-hued splendor. Tessellated pavement, Rhianna had heard it called. Small, colored cubes of marble, sandstone, limestone, and brick pressed into plaster formed a cunning hunting scene on the hallway floor.

" 'Tis beautiful, is it not?"

Rhianna jerked her gaze from her study of the floor. "Aye, 'tis a fascinating art, this use of stone. I'd not thought Marcus a man of such extravagant taste, though."

Ailm laughed softly. Rhianna stiffened. She's laughing at me, laughing at her greater intimacy with Marcus and how much better she knows him. Her temper flared. "Pray, what is it you find so amusing?"

Instantly, the other woman's laughter ceased. " 'Tis naught but the memory of Marcus' dismay when first viewing his new quarters. Though of a very prominent and wealthy family, his concept of soldierly quarters, even for a tribune, was of a much plainer fashion." She gestured about her. "This was all the handiwork of the Tribune Albinus, not Marcus."

"Ah, I see." Rhianna's anger faded.

Ailm hesitated. "Would you care to visit your room?"

"What? Aye, let us continue." Nonplused, Rhianna noticed little of the rest of the journey. Yet once she stepped into her room, her surprise immediately returned.

Her bedchamber was even more elegant than that of the hallway. Besides the vibrant murals and tessellated floors, the room was furnished with the most opulent of furniture.

Against the farthest wall stood a delicately carved table of citrus wood with ivory legs, topped with a vase of Murrhine glass. In the middle of the room three divans nestled around a low-set table of deepest cherry wood, each plush couch covered in bright emerald-green brocade, their frames decorated with tortoise shell.

Yet 'twas the bed, of ornately formed bronze and draped with finely spun, pale-green fabric, that caught and held Rhianna's greatest regard. To be able to rest her weary body on its soft contours, if only for a short—

"Would you care to repose for a time?" Ailm's query was accompanied by an understanding smile. "I've a few more arrangements to make for this eve's banquet and I could return for you in an hour or so. Then, if you'd like, we could relax at the *thermae* before joining the men for the meal."

At Ailm's gentle thoughtfulness, gratitude flared in Rhianna. "Aye. 'Tis an excellent idea, Ailm. Come for me in an hour's time. I'll be ready."

The russet-haired woman turned and left the room.

Rhianna stared at the closed door. 'Twas difficult to hate Ailm, she realized, even if she had been the one to capture Marcus' heart. Ailm was gentle, even-tempered, kind. What man wouldn't find her more compelling than a fiery-tongued shrew as *she* frequently was?

That question caught her up short. Ah, Blessed Goddess, Rhianna thought as she walked over to the bed and sat down. When had she ever considered hating another woman or comparing herself in such an unfavorable light—and all because of a man? 'Twas too confusing, the tumult of feelings more than her exhausted mind could bear.

She unlaced her sandals and flung them aside. Then, with a sigh, Rhianna sank back onto the welcoming comfort of the bed—and promptly fell asleep.

Nine

An hour later, Rhianna halted before the doors to the bath.

"Is something amiss?" Ailm asked, noting her hesitation.

"Nay, naught's amiss. Let us enter."

With more resolve than she felt, Rhianna stepped through the doorway and into the antechamber of the large building. A warm blast of air greeted her, wafting over her like the caress of a soft summer's breeze. She stiffened, determined not to be undone by the famous Roman baths.

Rhianna glanced around her. Many rooms led off from the main entryway. Feminine laughter and the splashing of water emanated from several of the chambers.

She turned to Ailm. "Lead on. 'Tis my first time at a bath." *And* my last, she assured herself.

With a smile and motion of her hand, Ailm headed toward the door directly before them. A few minutes later, as Rhianna disrobed in the dressing area, she eyed her russet-haired companion, who stood there, still fully clothed. "Aren't you taking the baths, Ailm?"

"I am here for your pleasure, not my own."

Rhianna frowned. "Well, I want you to join me. I care not for Roman rules of conduct. If you aren't good enough for these baths, then neither am I." She picked up her gown. "What shall it be? Will you bathe with me or shall we leave?"

Ailm began to undress, hiding her happy smile with difficulty. "I'm honored you've invited me. Please, let us stay."

Rhianna glanced around. "Tell me of these baths. What am I expected to do?"

The other woman finished folding her gown, then placed it on the shelf next to Rhianna's. " 'Tis a simple series of steps, really," Ailm explained as they entered a large room, a generous rectangular pool in its center. Several women were immersed in the waters, while others reclined on benches lining the walls.

"This is the *tepidarium,* which is the warm bath." Ailm gestured about the chamber. "After a time we move on to the hot-air bath, then the steam bath and, finally, a cold bath to close one's pores. There are also rooms where you can be massaged with fragrant oils and scraped clean with curved instruments called *strigils.* By the time you leave, you feel marvelous. Your skin glows and you smell as if you've stepped from a flower garden."

"Sounds wonderful," Rhianna muttered dryly.

Despite her skepticism, however, a short time later, her experience proved the truth of Ailm's words. Sinking lower into the velvety warm waters, her long hair fanning out in a honey-colored halo about her, Rhianna reluctantly admitted a Roman bath was a far more pleasant way to bathe than immersing oneself in the chill depths of a natural pool. A small, blissful sigh escaped her.

" 'Tis glorious, is it not?"

Her glance met Ailm's. "Aye, 'tis." She hesitated, her curiosity beginning to prick her. "You're far from home, are you not, Ailm? As pleasant as all this might be, don't you still yearn for your own land and people?"

Her companion nodded. "Aye. I miss my home in Gaul sometimes more than I can bear."

"Then why—" Rhianna caught herself. How thoughtless to probe into another's private pain. "I-I'm sorry. 'Tisn't my right to ask such things. Mayhap you had no choice."

"No choice? I don't understand." Ailm's brows furrowed in puzzlement. "Ah, I see. You think I'm a slave." She smiled. "I am a freedwoman, Rhianna. Marcus keeps no slaves."

"I beg pardon." A warm flush stole into Rhianna's cheeks. " 'Twas foolish of me to have assumed that."

"No offense was taken," came the gentle reply. " 'Tis understandable."

Rhianna's heart warmed to the other girl's kindness. 'Twas impossible to resent Ailm. Her goodness overshadowed even her great beauty. If Marcus loved her, Rhianna couldn't help but wish them happiness.

"Have you any other questions about me, Rhianna?"

"Questions?" The directness of the query startled her. The only remaining enigma was too cruel, too insulting to ask. And, though she'd hundreds of questions about Marcus, those, too, were best left unsaid, lest her interest betray her.

She shook her head. "Nay, Ailm. I've none."

"Well, with your permission, I've a few." She eyed Rhianna, a mischievous twinkle in her dark eyes.

Rhianna shrugged, the water rippling into ever widening circles with the movement. "Ask. I've naught to hide."

For a long moment Ailm said nothing, seemingly intent on the swirling motions her outstretched arms were making in the water. "How did you meet Marcus?"

Rhianna tensed. Blessed Goddess, did Ailm know of Lughnasa Eve and the bed she and Marcus had shared? 'Twould be unkind to tell her, to cause this gentle being pain, even if Marcus *had* intended to betray his commitment to her. Better to avoid the topic completely, unless directly asked.

"How did I meet Marcus?" she repeated. "Why, in the middle of a forest. A wild boar attacked and Marcus rescued me . . ."

By the time the slightly revised tale was finished, both girls were waterlogged. Ailm requested no specific details about the victor's due and Rhianna didn't volunteer any. As they climbed out of the warm bath and headed toward the *calidarium,* Rhianna, thinking the difficult questions were over, relaxed and began actually to enjoy her companion's company.

Rather than immerse themselves in the steaming waters of the next room, they chose to recline on the benches surrounding the pool. Rhianna lay back and closed her eyes, delighting in the soothing waves of hot air that caressed every pore of her body.

Ailm, however, appeared determined to pick up the thread of their conversation. " 'Twas a strange thing indeed, Marcus' mood that day he first returned from your fort," she chatted along. "Cei would tell me little—he's so protective of his friendship with Marcus—but a few nights later after a superb bout of lovemaking, I finally wheedled the truth from him. 'Tis amazing what you can get out of a man after you've exhausted him in bed," she observed with a self-satisfied smile.

Rhianna sat up. Her mouth dropped open in stunned surprise. Was Ailm mistress to both Cei *and* Marcus? Blessed Goddess, and she'd thought Trinovante women were free-spirited! "Y-you bed Cei, too?" she gasped without thinking.

Dark, delicate brows arched in amusement. "Well, aye," Ailm remarked dryly. " 'Tis an old Celtic custom, sleeping with one's husband. I'd assumed our cousins across the sea engaged in similar ones."

"Well, of-of course we do," sputtered Rhianna. " 'Tis just that I thought—Ah, never mind."

"Nay, Rhianna. 'Tis apparent you've still unanswered questions. What did you mean when you asked if I bed Cei, too? Who else did you think—"

Amazement, then triumphant glee, wreathed Ailm's face. "You thought I was Marcus' mistress! By the Good God, won't he find that the funniest thing he's ever heard?" She began to laugh, her mirth growing until the tears streamed from her eyes.

Rhianna glanced about her. Already, several heads had turned to see what the commotion was about. She reached out to the other girl. "Ailm, please stop," she pleaded. "I know I deserve this, but . . . but people are watching."

Ailm managed to stifle herself into giggles. "I-I am sorry, but 'tis so amusing—Marcus and I, I mean. We love each other dearly, but only as sister and brother." She shot Rhianna a sly glance. "However, from what Cei has told me, his feelings for you are quite different."

Rhianna paled. A surprising surge of joy swept through her. "Surely Cei's mistaken. Why, Marcus and I hardly know each other and . . . and, well, I'm betrothed to another."

Ailm shrugged, but her eyes betrayed her skepticism. "Every time he returns from visiting your hill fort, he's moody, almost melancholy. And that, my lovely friend, isn't our calm, even-tempered Marcus." She graced Rhianna with an arch look. "Is it possible? Has our handsome tribune at last met his match?"

"Well, match or no, I'm not the woman for him. 'Tis hardly my plan to involve myself with a Roman, however kind and attractive he might be." Rhianna rose from her place on the bench. 'Twas definitely time to put an end to this conversation. "Shall we be going? Surely the time nears for the banquet, and I've a wish to try each bath."

Ailm laughed and climbed to her feet. "His plans, your plans," she said in mild exasperation as she led the way into the steam bath. "Aye, 'tis indeed time. Time to finally face the truths of the heart. Never doubt that love, my fair Rhianna, has its own pace and way of disrupting the best-laid plans. Both you and Marcus, I fear, still have that to learn."

As Marcus dismounted and tossed his reins to a groomsman, he noted Rhianna and Ailm pause in their journey across the courtyard. Both girls were damp-haired and prettily flushed from the baths but, in truth, Marcus saw only Rhianna. He smiled and, accompanied by Quintus, strode toward them.

"I see the *thermae* stood you in good stead." His voice, though he tried hard to hide it, was husky.

At his bold perusal, Rhianna averted her gaze. "Aye, my lord. I feel greatly refreshed."

He chuckled. "It's to be expected, after all. In time, Rome's ways sit well on most people's backs."

Her eyes snapped up. " 'Twill take more than some hot water to convince me Roman ways are better!"

An uncomfortable silence settled on the gathering. Quintus' mouth twisted into a wry grin. Ailm blanched.

Marcus, however, well-accustomed to Rhianna's flashes of temper, smothered his laugh behind his hand with a cough. "That may well be, lady, but surely there's no harm in utilizing what's best, no matter the source. No one nation can produce everything, yet all can and should profit. It's the only way we, as an empire, can advance."

"As a *Roman* empire, don't you mean?" She gave a harsh

laugh. "I see Rome's ploy for what 'tis. First conquer the land and people by force of arms, then finish us off by seducing us with all the Roman comforts and amenities."

He shrugged. "Rome may take the lands, but in return it offers culture and civilization—and a lasting peace where it rarely existed before. A fair trade, to my way of thinking."

"Aye," Rhianna agreed, loath to give ground yet realizing, at the same time, the futility of prolonging such an argument. " 'Tis all quite logical—to a Roman's way of thinking." She turned to Ailm. "You mentioned a visit to the kitchen before we dressed for the meal. Shouldn't we be going?"

Ailm glanced nervously from Rhianna to Marcus. He nodded his consent. She turned back to Rhianna. "A-aye."

With an insolent flounce of her damp tresses, Rhianna turned again to Marcus. He grinned back at her as if she were some petulant child.

Irritation filled her. Her attention strayed to Quintus. A similar opinion of her actions danced in the silver depths of his eyes. And Ailm, well, 'twas impossible even to catch her gaze.

Heat crept up Rhianna's neck and into her face. Blessed Goddess, when would she learn to guard her tongue? To rail at Marcus as if he were single-handedly responsible for the plight of her people was indeed childish. Yet to apologize to him before the others was more than she could bear.

"By your leave, my lord." The subdued tone of her words was all the atonement she'd offer. "Will you excuse Ailm and me?"

Marcus made a small bow. "Go, lady. I give you my leave, but on one condition."

"Aye?" Rhianna tensed. What would he say? Some word of reprimand to shame her?

"Promise you'll dine at my side this eve."

Relief swept through her with the refreshing force of a storm-washed wind, cleansing the last bit of rancor from her heart. 'Twas impossible to stay angry at him, Roman though he was. She smiled. At Marcus' answering response, it grew to a wide, heartfelt grin.

"Aye. My promise is most happily given."

Rhianna and Ailm left him then and made their way to the kitchen. The aroma of roasting meat immediately assailed Rhianna's nostrils. Her mouth watered.

Cooks bustled to and fro in the compact space, one stirring the large cauldrons over a charcoal-stoked raised hearth while two others minced and sliced at a worktable in the middle of the room. Several dishes were already set out, laden with delicacies Rhianna had never seen before.

Ailm caught the direction of her gaze. "Those will be the *gustus,*" she volunteered, indicating the two large platters arrayed with a variety of light dishes. "They are the appetizers. This," she motioned to one of the plates, "is an arrangement of stuffed and cooked dormice, boiled peacock eggs, and stuffed olives and prunes. All are imported from the Continent. On the other platter are various shellfish and artfully prepared vegetables. Do any tempt your palate?"

Rhianna nodded. "Aye, all of it. 'Tis a long time since I last ate."

The dark-haired girl extracted two shelled eggs from an extra bowl. "Here, mayhap these will take the bite from your hunger." She glanced at the hourglass perched on a high shelf. " 'Tis but a half-hour until mealtime. Come, we need to hurry if we're to be dressed in time."

Hungrily consuming the tasty peacock eggs, Rhianna followed Ailm out of the aromatic kitchen and down the hall to her room. Her companion paused at the portal of Rhianna's bedchamber. "Have you need of anything? A gown? Someone to dress your hair?"

Rhianna swallowed the last delicious morsel of egg before answering. "Nay. I brought a fresh tunic with me and, since my hair isn't yet dry, I'll brush it out and wear it unbound."

" 'Tis a wise choice, I think." Ailm's glance strayed to Rhianna's golden mane. "Most men prefer it that way, and Marcus is no exception. You've such beautiful hair; 'tis like fine gossamer threads."

Rhianna smiled self-consciously. "My thanks, Ailm. Cei must find your own hair lovely, as lustrous and flame-dark as 'tis."

The girl's lips curved into a soft, contented smile. "Aye, that he does. And 'tis enough, don't you think, that this eve we'll both please the men we love?"

Ailm disappeared down the hall before the full impact of her words dawned on Rhianna . . . *the men we love.*

Blessed Goddess, this was the second time Ailm had alluded to some deeper affection between her and Marcus! Well, 'twas ridiculous. Though 'twas evident Ailm loved her husband, the same couldn't be said of her and Marcus.

True, she respected him and admitted he easily stirred her desires, but that was hardly love. He was a powerful, virile young animal, and she a woman in her first flush of maturity. 'Twas only natural to find him attractive, to want him. But love . . .

Love had never been part of her plans—not with Cador, not with any man. All her heart, all her efforts, must be devoted to the land and the welfare of her people. There was no room for aught else, nor did she want it any other way.

'Twas only Ailm's dreaming, Rhianna reassured herself with a vehement toss of her head, some romantic wish for the man she considered brother. Clinging firmly to that determination, Rhianna entered her room.

Oil lamps threw flickering, burnished light about the spacious *triclinium,* permeating the farthest corners, dancing sensuously off the richly laden platters of food. In the background, two musicians plied their melodious trade, one intently blowing into a double-piped instrument, the other gently strumming a lyre-like cithera. The scent of lavender hung on the air, pervading the room with its delicate, haunting fragrance.

Rhianna paused in the doorway, her glance scanning the chamber. Marcus, Quintus, Riderch, and two strangers stood near a small table set with goblets and a large flagon of wine. Each clasped one of the long-stemmed cups. Across the room stood Cei, Ailm, and Emrys, engrossed in conversation.

She counted the chamber's occupants. Eight people. Knowing the Roman dining propensity for multiples of three, she surmised she was the last guest to arrive.

Inhaling a deep, steadying breath, Rhianna stepped into the room. Quintus was the first to notice her presence and greeted her with an admiring smile. His pause in the conversation immediately drew Marcus' attention.

Deciding it best to take command before his impulsive friend did, Marcus set down his goblet and strode to Rhianna. He appraised her lazily, from the hem of her simple, maroon-linen gown to the lustrous, curling cloud of pale gold hair. At last his gaze reached her face.

His eyes gleamed with admiration. "Ah, lady, how can one woman possess so much beauty? Remember your promise to dine beside me this eve. Otherwise, I fear I may be forced to fight my friends for even the smallest moment of your time."

She blushed, as much at his extravagant praise as from the fierce excitement his thorough inspection stirred. Unable to find words, much less a voice, Rhianna sought time to quell her fluttering heart by studying him in turn.

She'd never seen Marcus in a toga. Its stark white folds, draped over his shoulder, combined with the white undertunic striped at the hem with one broad purple band, complemented his dark good looks. Save for the loosely arranged linen, the toga was undecorated, clothing him in a simple dignity. He stood, powerful of body, broad of chest and shoulders, and Rhianna thought him beautiful.

"Well, old friend," Quintus interjected sardonically, coming up behind Marcus. "Is it to be slow starvation or are you going to begin the banquet? I'd thought this feast was in my honor, but perhaps 'twas intended instead just for the two of you?"

Marcus turned, drawing Rhianna with him. He grinned good-naturedly at his friend. "My deepest apologies, Quintus. I was momentarily besotted with this lady's breathtaking beauty. You, of all people, should understand how that could happen.

"But come," he said, raising his voice and motioning toward the banquet table, "let us partake of a fine meal and enjoy the pleasure of each other's company. It isn't often I've the honor of entertaining both old friends," he nodded at Quintus, "and new." His head inclined toward Riderch and then Rhianna. "Let the wine flow and the fellowship abound!"

Marcus led the way toward three low, broad couches, soft with cushions, clustered about a huge, round dining table. He paused at the center one, situated at right angles to the others, and looked at Rhianna.

"It holds three." He gestured at the couch. "Would you mind also sharing it with Quintus? Generally the guest of honor reclines with the host."

"Nay, I don't mind. I understand the customs, if not all the steps of the meal." Rhianna lowered herself upon the couch and leaned on her left side. "I pray you'll be kind enough to instruct me as we go along."

"Well, if Marcus doesn't," Quintus offered, reclining beside her, "I'd be happy to aid you in whatever manner I can."

Marcus' brows drew together like two dark birds of prey.

Noting the look, his friend grudgingly moved to open a space.

Marcus stretched his long frame between them. "Your services, my friend, however well-intentioned, won't be required this eve. If you recall, Rhianna promised to dine with me."

Gray eyes, for the merest instant, careened into Marcus'. A battle of wills ensued. Quintus broke contact first.

He eyed Rhianna for a brief moment more, then lifted his goblet to Marcus in grudging concession. "Lovely as she is, my friend, there are sure to be other maids of her quality in Britannia. But if you misstep with her even once . . ."

Marcus grinned, then clapped his hands twice. "Let the feast begin."

As the guests hungrily reached for the variety of *gustus* arranged before them, servants moved among the couches, refilling wine goblets, offering water bowls to cleanse greasy fingers, slicing bits of food to suit a particular taste. The main course consisted of several boiled and roasted meats, including fallow deer with onion sauce and rue; a ham dressed with figs and bay leaves, then rubbed with honey and baked in a pastry crust; and a huge platter of roast pigeons flavored with garlic and thyme. These were accompanied by warm loaves of soft bread and dishes of beans, peas, and a variety of salads, all fragrantly seasoned and appetizingly presented.

Rhianna had never tasted such fare. Not willing to miss anything, she thoroughly sampled each new dish. Marcus ate lightly, content to observe her hearty enjoyment of the food. He and Quintus discussed various topics while both men watched in fascination as Rhianna gobbled up one unusual delicacy after another. Only when the "second table" of desserts arrived, did she finally begin to slow.

"Ah, how lovely that looks," she murmured sadly, as her gaze swept the plate of cakes sweetened with honey and the huge glass bowl of fruit, "but I'm afraid I'm quite full."

"Marcus could provide you with an emetic, if you've a wish to empty your stomach and start over again," Quintus volunteered with a wry twist of his mouth.

At the thought of making herself vomit, Rhianna clasped her arms about her stomach. "Oooh, what a horrible thought! Do Romans truly do such things to themselves?"

Marcus chuckled. "Only a few, though it seems to be becoming the custom of late. Do I take your response to mean you'll decline the emetic?"

Rhianna nodded vigorously. "Aye. 'Tis better if I just suffer awhile with my overfull stomach. 'Twill teach me not to be so gluttonous in the future."

"That it will," agreed Quintus. The two men shared a conspiratorial grin.

The evening wore on and the wine flowed as abundantly as the conversation. Marcus rose and made a point of spending some time with each guest. But, as it became more and more evident Quintus had overindulged the grape brew and his more amorous tendencies toward Rhianna began to elicit some narrow-eyed looks from the Trinovante chieftain, Marcus, in an effort to forestall any difficulties, finally returned to Rhianna's side.

"Aye?" She turned the full force of her striking sky-blue eyes upon him.

Lost in the luminous depths, Marcus momentarily forgot what he was about to say. The altruistic impulse to protect her from the intoxicated overtures of his friend transformed into a much more self-serving need to spend time alone with her.

He took her by the arm. "Come with me out onto the porch. I've a need for some fresh air, and I'd like to share it with you."

Rhianna hesitated. The presence of his awesome form, stretched alongside hers this eve, had stirred heady feelings, memories of another time he'd lain close to her. Yet how could she refuse the sweet entreaty in those warmly smoldering eyes?

She couldn't. "As you wish."

They strolled out upon the covered porch that opened onto an enclosed courtyard. Though summer was fast fading, the night was still warm, blanketing the little interior garden in a comforting coverlet of darkness. Save for the silver light of the full moon, it would have been impossible to see each other as Marcus drew Rhianna from the noisy gaiety of the room and farther into the tile-paved courtyard.

The fountain in the enclosure's center splashed and splattered its contents into its seashell-shaped basin. From its perch atop one of a twin pair of birch trees, a wren unexpectedly trilled as Marcus and Rhianna's approach awakened it from its slumber. Realizing its mistake, the tiny bird quieted.

Marcus smiled down at Rhianna. "You seem to bring out the birds, no matter the time or place." He withdrew a wrapped parcel from his toga and offered it to her.

She glanced down at the package, so small in the expanse of his large, callused palm. "What is it?"

"A gift I once tried to give you. Please accept it. It was always meant for you."

Rhianna eyed him warily, then took the parcel from his hand. With careful movements, she unfolded the covering. 'Twas the bone earrings he'd bought her at Lughnasa.

"They are yours, Rhianna," Marcus explained huskily. "Though perhaps I haven't the right to give them to you, they could never belong to another. No matter how you might fight against it, you're a woman who deserves women's things."

He silenced her protest with a gentle finger upon her lips. "You proved it that Lughnasa night. Proved it in my arms and in your passion when our bodies joined. Admit it, sweet lady."

"Aye, 'tis true," she whispered, lifting her gaze to his. "I have never denied my womanhood. My battle has always been against the woman's expectations placed on me. Expectations you place on me as well. But they, too, ended that Lughnasa night."

Gazing down at her, standing so near, so vibrant and alive, Marcus was nearly undone with the urge to take her into his arms and kiss her. Gods, if he could ease just once more the needs that had haunted him ever since that first night together! "Must it be over? I'm a practical man. I'll not force expectations you've no inclination to follow. But what we had was so special . . ." He stroked the side of her face. "So very, very special. I used to think once with you would be enough, but I'm no longer so certain."

His hand encompassed hers and he folded her fingers around the earrings. "Take the gift, Rhianna. They require no debt on your part, no expectations, save that you think of me when you wear them."

She sighed her defeat. "As you wish. I thank you for them."

"And does the acceptance of my gift also mean you accept its companion?"

Rhianna tensed, sensing his sudden change of tactics. "Ah, here it comes. I should have known—"

"No, it's not what you think. I only hope for the granting of what was also requested that Lughnasa day—your friendship."

Friendship, Rhianna thought. So simple a word, so fraught with complexities. Yet had he not earned it time and again, with his kindness, his courage, his willingness to sacrifice himself for her?

Her gaze locked with his. "Aye, Marcus. For what worth there is in it, I'll be your friend."

He smiled, his large hand capturing her chin. His head lowered, covering her mouth, the strong hardness of his lips melding with the yielding softness of hers.

Sweet spirals of delight shot through Rhianna. She gave herself up to the need to feel, yet again, the powerful strength of his arms about her.

With a small cry she came to him, wrenching her mouth away to bury her face against the corded muscles of his chest. More than anything, more than life itself, Rhianna needed to touch him, to hold him. 'Twas more than just a simple desire for friendship—she knew this well—though friendship was all she could ever dare allow. Yet still she clung to him, savoring the deeply needed if forbidden solace of his body.

Marcus fingered a tendril of her hair. "This afternoon," his deep voice rumbled against her ear, "when your father said you'd journeyed here because you were worried about me and then you denied it—did you speak true?"

Rhianna's throat tightened. He'd so easily seen through

her lie, had he? Yet, to admit it could reveal feelings best kept hidden. "Why would you have cause to doubt it?"

"No cause, just a foolish hope you'd come to care a little for me."

She struggled to raise her guard against him. He'd barely won her admission of friendship and now wanted more. Mayhap she should laugh away his question, laden with its underlying implications, yet the dread of being cruel was more potent than her disturbing reactions to him.

"I care," she sighed. "Isn't it evident by my willingness to be your friend? Yet what does it really matter—my caring, I mean? Do you still wish to bed me? You can have me for the asking, whether I care for you or not. 'Tis a spoil of battle, a privilege of conquering another nation, is it not?"

Marcus expelled a frustrated breath and gripped her arms, shoving her back from him. "Yes, it *can* be a spoil of battle. And yes, I still wish to bed you." He stroked her arms in a sensual, stirring movement of fingers along soft flesh. "But don't bandy words with me, Rhianna. With you I feel stripped of my rank and position. You are the conqueror, not I. Can't you look past your hatred of Rome and consider me as just a man?"

She stared up at him. "I . . . I don't know. 'Tis too hard to think when you hold me so closely."

"Stay here," Marcus rasped, his expression suddenly anguished, intent. "Be my lover. Your people permit their women to take other men before they wed. Stay with me until this fire cools between us. When it's over, I swear I'll let you go back to Cador."

A sudden rage engulfed her. When 'twas over, he'd *let* her go back to Cador? The arrogance, the self-serving conceit of the man!

Yet, perversely, Rhianna found herself almost wanting to

accept his proposition, as simultaneously attractive and hurtfully repulsive as it was. 'Twas too much to fathom. She had to put some distance between them, regain the perspective she so easily lost in his presence.

"Let me go!" Rhianna struggled in his grasp. "I should have known 'twould come to this! Let me go!"

In spite of her words, Marcus sensed she was near the admission he longed to hear. If he released her now, she might fly away forever. He pulled her to him. "No, Rhianna," he breathed into the fragrant cloud of her hair. "I won't release you until you give me the answer we both know to be true. The gods forgive me, but I want you. If you've any compassion, any pity—"

"And what of *your* compassion?" In spite of her best efforts, tears clogged her voice. "Can't you see that too much separates us? You've naught to lose. I have everything. Why must you press me? Aren't your own women enough?"

"No other woman is enough anymore!" Marcus cried in a sudden outburst of agonized frustration. "Do you think I sought this torment, this confusion? Gods, Rhianna, meeting someone like you was the furthest thing from my mind." He made an exasperated motion with his hand. "This—you—were never in my plans!"

Plans.

What had Ailm said? Rhianna struggled to remember. *Love has its own pace and way of disrupting the best-laid plans.*

Was this what it all came down to then? But Marcus didn't love her or she, him. 'Twas as he had said. He only wished to bed her for a time longer, to ease his lust, and naught more.

Yet if this were only lust, why did it hurt so? There was no happiness, no peace in the revelation or its acceptance. And honor. Where was there any honor?

"Nay," Rhianna whispered, her determination growing with each anguished beat of her heart. " 'Tis wrong, no matter what you say, no matter what our customs might allow. I will not bed you again. Forget me, as I must you, for I won't betray my people or my vows to this land!"

She twisted violently until, to keep from hurting her, Marcus was forced to let her go. She fled him then, the bone earrings still clasped in her hand. Back to the brightly lit banquet room and the safety of the others Rhianna ran. Back to a life familiar and comforting, if no longer so safe, so sure.

Yet, in her heart, she knew her flight accomplished naught. Naught . . . save the purchase of just a little more time.

Ten

"You must have a talk with Cordaella," Cerdic muttered from atop his big gray gelding two days later. "Her behavior with Cador increasingly borders on the unseemly."

Rhianna paused in the act of mounting Demetia and shot a quick glance over her shoulder. There, not fifty feet away in the shaded overhang of the hill fort's horse sheds, Cordaella openly flirted with Cador. As Rhianna watched, the red-haired girl leaned close, touched the big blond warrior on the arm, then laughed seductively, her hand lingering overlong before she finally pulled away. In response, Cador lowered his head toward her, murmured something, then laughed as well.

With a disgusted snort, Rhianna turned to her mare and swung up onto her back. "And what would you have me tell her?" she tautly demanded of her older brother. "That Cador's mine and I want no other woman near him? 'Twould be a lie and well she knows it. Why, surely even Cador must bear no further illusions of my feelings for him." Rhianna gave a wry laugh. "The only advice I could truthfully give is that, for her own good, Cordaella stay away from him."

Cerdic shifted his bow and quiver of arrows to a more comfortable position on his back and motioned her forward. "Well, be that as it may, 'tisn't a topic best discussed within earshot of others. Let us be on our way. Gunnella expects several rabbits to fatten our meat stores, and I'm certain Mother would appreciate some fresh game as well."

At the reminder of her mother's parting words, Rhianna grimaced. "Aye, 'twas the only reason she gave me leave to go hunting this day." She sighed. "If she only knew how desperately I needed to get away, to clear my mind with some hearty exercise, even she might not have begrudged me this brief respite from all our women's tasks. But Mother has been in none too fine a mood with me since our return from Camulodunum yesterday."

"Indeed?" her brother asked, then guided his horse alongside Rhianna's as they left the fort and headed down the hill. For a time they rode in silence until they neared the forest. Then Cerdic slowed his horse's pace and glanced over at Rhianna, his aquamarine eyes dark with concern. "What troubles you, little sister? Mayhap I could help? I always have most times before."

Rhianna smiled back. "Aye, that you have, Cerdic, but there's little you can do for me now. I'm all but a woman and must face a woman's problems. 'Tisn't so easy as rescuing me from a runaway horse or teaching me swordplay without Mother's knowledge."

" 'Tis Cador and your betrothal, then?"

She looked away, her gaze, for a long, emotion-laden moment, following the flight of an eagle soaring high above the trees. She turned back to her brother. " 'Tis more than that."

"The Roman, then?"

Rhianna paled. "How did you know? Ah, by the Goddess, Cerdic, if Father and Mother were ever to suspect!"

"I doubt Mother knows, but Father has spoken to me of his concerns, asked me to talk with you. He saw things at Camulodunum that disturbed him . . . things between you and the Roman. He thought I could mayhap help you through this."

"You must think me a traitor and fool."

"Why, because you find some Roman attractive?" Cerdic shrugged. "Mayhap I should, but the new tribune seems an honorable man and his courage and physical prowess are equal to the best of our warriors. Enemy though he is, I can still respect him. Yet I also see grave trouble ahead if you continue on this path, little sister."

Rhianna's grip tightened about Demetia's reins. "Aye, well I know that." She hesitated. "He asked me to be his lover and said that after a time, when the passion cooled between us, he'd let me go back to Cador."

"And what did you tell him?"

"What *could* I tell him?" Rhianna halted her horse, a heart-deep anguish in her eyes. "As ignorant as I still am in loving, I knew 'twould break my heart to give myself to him and then eventually have to leave him and return to Cador. Besides, I couldn't do that to Father. For the sake of the clan, I know I must wed Cador. There has never been any other choice."

"Aye," Cerdic muttered grimly, "and 'tis an injustice I'd soon set to rights if ever I became chieftain. The man's a foul, self-serving—"

She leaned over and grasped him by the arm. "There you go again, trying to protect me. But this time, 'tisn't within your power." Rhianna smiled wanly. "Though 'tis deeply appreciated, as it has always been."

Cerdic smiled. "I love you, little sister. I only want your happiness."

Rhianna released his arm and nudged Demetia on. "I know that. I love you, too. But times are uncertain and we must both do what we can to protect our people. My feelings for the Roman *must* be set aside. I *must* wed Cador. And that I will do."

"You have always held the welfare of our clan uppermost in your heart," Cerdic softly said. "I've one word of advice more, though."

"Aye, and that is?"

"Stay away from the Roman henceforth. 'Tisn't wise to stir your emotions over him unnecessarily. He's a compelling man and far more experienced in the ways of women than you are of men. And he has little to lose, while you . . ."

Rhianna's chin lifted, her pride stung, yet knowing Cerdic spoke true. Her shoulders squared with a renewed resolve. "Your words have been heard and heeded, big brother. Now, haven't we some hunting to do? There's little point in prolonging this particular subject. 'Twill solve naught—"

From down the road they were traveling, a small band of people with an old man at its head leading a horse pulling a small cart appeared over the next rise. As Cerdic and Rhianna drew near, the form of another man, swathed in blood-stained bandages, could be seen lying among the meager belongings in the cart. Cerdic shot Rhianna a frowning glance and both urged their horses forward.

"From whence do you hail and where are you going?" Cerdic asked as he reined his stallion in to walk beside the old man leading the horse. "And what happened to the man in the cart?"

The man looked up at Cerdic. Frustration and an impotent anger burned in his dark brown eyes. "My name is Bov and the man in the cart is my son, Largen." With a weary wave of his hand, Bov indicated the two women and four children walking behind him. "Those are all that are left of my family—my wife, daughter-in-law, and grandchildren. We are Trinovante, like you, but from northern lands bordering those of the Iceni." His glance snared on the gold torc about Cerdic's throat. "You are of the house of the clan chieftain, are you not?"

Cerdic nodded. "Aye. Riderch is my father."

"Then we ask shelter with you and your clan. We have nowhere else to go." Bov's mouth twisted grimly. "In the process of searching for hidden arms, the procurator's men all but destroyed our small village. When Largen dared defy them, the Red Crests turned on him. Even now, he lies so sorely wounded we fear for his life."

"Then hurry and bring him to our hill fort," Rhianna said, drawing up beside Cerdic. "Our Druid, Cunagus, is an acclaimed healer. He will tend your son."

"Aye, come, we'll show you the quickest way back," Cerdic agreed. He paused. "Are the Romans you speak of mayhap following you?"

The old man shook his head, then turned to spit on the road. "Nay, I'd wager not, the heartless dogs. They appeared too intent on sweeping the countryside north of here for back taxes as well as weapons. The provincial procurator's none too happy with the slow payments of our rulers. Rumor has it he's particularly agrieved with Queen Boudicca." He laughed humorously. "Seems she hasn't been properly subservient or respectful of his high office. There's serious trouble brewing, I fear."

"Aye," Cerdic agreed tautly. "I fear as much, too." He turned his horse around and leaned close to Rhianna. "Lead them to the fort. I'll ride ahead and apprise Father of this. 'Tis best he know as soon as possible."

She nodded. 'Twas best, indeed, Rhianna thought, her own anger at Rome rising anew as Cerdic signaled his stallion back down the road to the hill fort. There was no way of predicting when Decianus Catus might turn his ire further south—and stir the seething cauldron of Britanni discontent at last to an explosive boil.

"Rhianna doesn't wish to see or speak with you."

At the blunt finality in Riderch's words, Marcus felt a primal rage swirl through him. He swung off his horse in one swift, resolute move and handed his reins to one of his men. Bearing down on the Trinovante chieftain, he met him eye to eye.

For a long moment Marcus struggled with his frustration. He'd been a fool to think he'd be free of Rhianna after that Lughnasa night. He'd been an even bigger fool to insult her by asking her to become his mistress, then magnanimously offering to send her back to Cador when their passion had cooled. Yet though his real feelings for Rhianna were hard to admit—and even harder for him to accept—Marcus would face it as he had everything else in his life.

Rhianna was his, this much he knew after her response in the garden. Though she'd flown back to her hill fort the next day, her escape had been more from her own emotions than from fear of him. They had come so far since that warm Lughnasa day, and now to be prevented from even speaking with her . . .

"A moment of her time. Surely it's not too great a boon to ask," Marcus persisted. "Three days have passed since our . . . misunderstanding. I wish only to make amends. I don't want bad feelings between us."

"Then respect her request and mine," came the stern reply. "My daughter will wed in a month's time. 'Tis important she prepare for the happy event in peace." At Marcus' attempt to protest, Riderch raised his hand for silence. "Your constant need to meet with her is unseemly. Though I owe you much in regards to Rhianna, I cannot allow this to continue."

Marcus jerked off his helmet and ran a hand through his black curls. "Why do you prevent her from free choice of a life mate? She cares for me—and I for her. Permit Rhianna time to accept that. Cador isn't the man for her."

"And you are?" Riderch stared at the man whose surprising affection for his daughter threatened all his carefully laid plans and still couldn't suppress a twinge of pity for his plight. He, himself, was at least partially to blame. His manipulations had forced them together time and again.

And now . . . Now, the Roman loved Rhianna. One would have to be blind and a fool not to see it, yet it didn't matter. It couldn't matter. Too much was at stake; his people's welfare was of greater consequence than the romantic needs of two young, headstrong people.

The gray-haired chieftain shook his head. "This is a Trinovante matter, Tribune, and I ask that you respect it. Thanks to the procurator's recent atrocities against my people, tempers are hot, patience is thin. If we are to work together, I must retain autonomy in all tribal affairs. You said you were willing to do all that was possible to preserve the peace. 'Tis time your fine words were put to the test."

A cold, shuttered expression settled over Marcus' features. "Some of my countrymen have gravely erred, but their actions are not and never shall be mine. You speak as if you doubt my sincerity, Lord Riderch. In a sense, that's understandable. I've yet to be fully proven to you. But to use my relationship with Rhianna as your test isn't the most prudent course, either."

He shoved his helmet back on his head and strode to his horse. As he remounted, his steel-edged glance once more sought out the chieftain's. "I grant you your request, but heed me well. A time more I'll give her—and you—but speak with Rhianna I will!"

Rendering a close-fisted salute across his chest, Marcus pivoted his white stallion to lead his men away. Riderch watched the troop head back down the hill and into the trees. Then, as he turned away, a swirl of white robes caught the edge of his vision.

"A determined young man, that Roman," Cunagus observed.

"Aye." Riderch sighed. "Not to mention brave, determined—"

"And in love."

Riderch's head turned in surprise. "Is it so obvious?"

Cunagus smiled. "Not to Rhianna, nor as yet to the tribune."

"Then we must keep it that way. I made a grave error when I first thought to use Rhianna to soften the tribune's heart. Now I must break the bonds between them before 'tis too late."

A distant look clouded the old Druid's eyes. " 'Twon't be an easy thing, if indeed 'tis possible at all. Their destinies are somehow entwined, though to what length . . ." He paused, as if trying to perceive some unclear image. The seconds dragged by. Finally, Cunagus shook his head. "I cannot be sure. Something prevents my Sight."

"She *must* marry Cador. You know that as well as I." Riderch's voice rose in frustrated entreaty. "*How* are their destinies entwined? Did Rhianna's dream of the white boar herald the Roman's arrival? And, if so, what did it mean? I must know if I'm to protect her from his influence. Ah, Cunagus, tell me what to do."

"Do what you must, and let the heavens judge." Cunagus expelled the words on a shuddering breath and gave up the

Gift's power. "A storm gathers on the horizon," he said, recalling Rhianna's revelation of her vision at the Temple of Claudius, "a bloody war with Rome. Whether Rhianna weds Cador or not, there is naught any of us can do to change that. Just as the Roman, or Rhianna, or you or I cannot turn from our own destinies. In the end, no matter who pays, the purchase price must still be satisfied."

"Then why am I all but forcing my daughter to wed a man she despises?"

"Because that, too, is part of Rhianna's destiny. Part of *her* purchase price."

The chieftain frowned. "Purchase price? For what?"

"For her happiness."

The old Druid walked away then, leaving Riderch battling with a growing sense of confusion and futility. Cunagus had offered no comfort. But then, the Gift of prophecy had never assured easy answers, or even pleasant ones. Those, Riderch thought bitterly, seemed in the hands of the players, and their fortunes but a whim of fate.

"These Britanni are proud, stubborn people. They respect only power. You must always approach them from a base of strength or they'll walk all over you, laughing behind their hands as they do. Remember that, Nephew."

Marcus set down his wine goblet. He knew this speech well. It was a common Roman outlook when it came to the Celts. An outlook that certainly motivated the provincial procurator *and* the governor.

"Have no fear, Uncle." He turned from the window overlooking the parade field and walked back to where the provincial governor sat at his desk, signing the last few documents prior to his departure. "I'll maintain the peace until your return. A few concessions, however, to salve long-festering wounds, would go far to ease the discontent. The issue of the renewed search for Britanni weapons, for one . . ."

"No!" Gaius Suetonius Paullinus vehemently shook his head. "You've already overstepped your bounds in the death of Albinus. To kill another tribune is a crime, no matter how despicable or ineffectual he was as a man or soldier. You risked much for the sake of some Britanni woman, as did I, in extricating you from your just if brutal punishment." The general looked up at his nephew. "I warn you, Marcus, don't press me further. I cannot risk the Britanni rearming themselves while I'm gone, and my sources warn they are doing just that. My tolerance for these people is already stretched to its limits. I'll not have you undermining me, as well.

"Besides, you've more than made apparent your good will and eagerness to work with these Britanni," his uncle continued in a more conciliatory tone. "I'll not beg their cooperation nor have you, as my representative, do so, either. *We* are the conquerors, not they. You asked for latitude in your role as *Praefectus Alae.* I've given all I can. Make the best of it."

The general threw down the thin reed pen and rose from his desk. "For the next several weeks I'll be with the Fourteenth Gemina. My hands will be full subduing that hornet's nest of Druid discontent on Mona. You *must* maintain a strong front in my absence."

At the continued lack of any effective authority, the old frustration returned. "And how am I to do that with my hands tied?" Marcus strode around the desk to confront his uncle. "The issue of their weapons aside, the Trinovante are seething at the loss of their lands and the heavy taxation to build a temple that's a monument to their humiliation. The Iceni await only the decree from Rome that'll strip their queen of her kingdom. And what do you leave me? Platitudes and a big stick!"

A dark flush suffused the governor's face. "Remember yourself, Tribune! Though you're my brother's son, your words strike perilously close to mutiny. *I* am the provincial governor and military commander of all troops in Britannia. *My* word is law in this land. You question where you have no right, and I'll not have it, even from one of my own blood! I say again. Do not press me further."

Marcus glared back at him, waging a fierce inner battle. His uncle was wrong, perhaps fatally so, and it was folly to blindly follow his course. Yet the strict military discipline and unquestioning adherence to the orders of a superior were the heart of the Roman Army, the secret of its amazing success. Had he not sworn an oath when he'd joined that same army, promising his unswerving loyalty to the emperor and his representatives? Wasn't that vow of greater import than the problems of a people halfway across the world—problems that would endure long after he was gone?

And his career? Had he so easily forgotten his promising Senate career? Gods, what was wrong with him to so lightly toss *that* aside?

Marcus bowed. "As you say, Uncle. I forgot myself in my zeal to serve Rome. It will be as you ask, even to the offering of my life if necessary."

The governor smiled and clasped his nephew's arm. "I pray that such an act won't ever be required. We Paullinus' share a proud heritage, one I've high hopes of your carrying on. Now come, see me and my legion off on our expedition to Mona. It's past time I was on my way."

"Have a care," Marcus offered as he followed his uncle across the room. "The Druid stronghold there is said to be powerful. I fear the people's reaction to an attack on the heart of their religion."

"I've no other choice." The governor's smile faded. "That cult's anti-Roman stance has been a thorn in our side since before the invasion. If the Britanni are ever to be completely subdued, we must subjugate their religion. Besides, you know our policy on human sacrifice."

"Yes," Marcus sighed. "It's certainly not one of the more savory features of Druidism."

They reached the door and paused. The governor offered his arm in farewell. "Take care of Camulodunum, Marcus."

Marcus returned the gesture, then watched his uncle stride away. In but a few minutes more the legion rode out, a billowing cloud of dust marking its wake. For a long while afterward Marcus lingered at the doorway, immersed in thought.

The Druids stood in mortal danger with such a resourceful and determined general as his uncle committed to their destruction. Yet what of the long-term consequences of such an act? Marcus knew the Celts' blind devotion to their religion well enough to predict an attack against their teaching center wouldn't be taken lightly. Surely there must have been other alternatives.

He quashed that futile thought. Right or wrong, his uncle had made the decision. It remained to be seen if the repercussions would reverberate back to Camulodunum before the legion's return.

Filled with a heavy foreboding, Marcus walked inside to retrieve his helmet. For the time being, there was little he could do about the matter of Mona. There was much he could accomplish regarding the issue of a certain Trinovante maid.

A week had passed since his brief contact with her father. Time enough had been wasted. This day he'd demand his meeting. His own needs, and that of Rhianna's, whether she knew it yet or not, would at last be met.

Rhianna scrubbed the soiled tunic, then rinsed it in the river's swirling current. Holding it up to view, she deemed it finally clean enough to wring out and throw into the clothes basket.

Men! she thought in exasperation. While they were busy dirtying themselves in hunting and weapons' practice, she was expected to join the other women in more appropriate women's work. Blessed Goddess, she was willing to work herself senseless for her clan, but why must it be in such tedious, commonplace tasks like washing laundry? Ah well, on the morrow she'd ride out with Cerdic and Kenow on a stag hunt. That was compensation of a sorts for today's labor.

And at least the labor, whether of women's work or that of a warrior, kept her mind and body busy. Too busy, thank the Goddess, to think of Marcus much of late. That, in itself, was a blessing. Her talk with Cerdic notwithstanding, Rhianna found it hard not to wonder how Marcus fared or ponder why he hadn't come to see her or at least sent some word. 'Twas for the best, of course, but still . . .

She wiped her brow with the back of a damp forearm. Ura, Gunnella, and several other women were lined along the bank beside her, all busily immersed in their work. Farther downstream, the children splashed in a shallow, rock-enclosed area of the river.

Rhianna frowned. Some of the older boys were tempting fate by clambering up on the larger rocks overhanging the treacherous rapids. If one of them should slip . . .

She leaned toward Ura to comment on the boys' foolhardy behavior when a childish scream rent the air. As all eyes turned in the direction of the spine-tingling sound, Rhianna leaped up and ran toward the rocks.

"Kitto," one of the terrified lads cried. "H-he lost his balance and . . ." His trembling hand indicated the river where a small, dark head could be seen bobbing in the dangerous current.

Seconds counted. Rhianna climbed up onto the farthest rock, slipped out of her sandals, and dove into the water. Strong strokes, aided by the river's flow, rapidly carried her to the unfortunate boy. As she grasped Kitto and turned her efforts to regaining the bank, however, the task became much more formidable.

The churning, violently turbulent waters farther out in the river buffeted them. White water broke over them time and again. Once, twice, Rhianna almost lost her grip on Kitto. The sodden weight of her gown dragged her down.

She glanced toward the shore. Ura and the other women stood watching helplessly. Why did they seem to be drifting yet farther away? Rhianna's breathing became ragged, painful. Even with Kitto's attempts to aid her, their progress toward the shore seemed minimal.

Muscles weakened as the minutes passed. Arms and legs ached with the increasingly futile efforts. Despair surged through her. Goddess, if they didn't reach land soon . . .

A sharp cry from shore wrenched Rhianna's gaze back to the river. There, bearing down upon them, was a huge, uprooted tree. Its outspread limbs stretched like so many gnarled, grasping fingers as the raging waters swept it along. Summoning all her strength, Rhianna lifted and virtually flung Kitto toward shore and out of the dead tree's path. An instant later, the tree struck her full force.

Her head whipped back. Pain lanced through her skull. A kaleidoscope of colors danced before her eyes. The tree twisted and turned with the roiling current, its branches entwining in the long length of Rhianna's hair.

She tore wildly at her hair, knowing full well her fate if she didn't escape. The trunk rolled in the water, slowly, inexorably dragging Rhianna beneath the surface.

Terror shot through her. She'd drown if the tree didn't turn back in time.

The seconds passed. Still, Rhianna couldn't free herself. Her lungs began to burn.

Dying.

She was dying and there wasn't anything she could do. But 'twasn't possible—her life was yet so fresh, so new. Surely it hadn't been meant to end like this!

In one last, desperate surge of strength Rhianna clawed at her entangled hair, ignoring the pain as she finally pulled free. With frantic strokes, she fought her way to the surface.

An outcropping of boulders appeared out of the swirling waters. Pivoting sharply around on contact, the tree wedged firmly between two rocks. A heavy limb broke loose.

With a jarring force, it struck Rhianna on the side of the head. Before she could react, blackness, ominous and unforgiving, swallowed her.

The parade of visitors going to and from the chieftain's house did little to ease Marcus' anxiety. He'd arrived at the hill fort only to discover Rhianna had nearly drowned and was even now lingering at the brink of life and death. If it hadn't been for the two boys who had managed to find a rope and pull her from the river . . .

With a tormented groan, Marcus cradled his head in his hands. By the gods, how many more times would he come close to losing her? It seemed the only place she would ever truly be safe was at his side. Yet Rhianna lay within and he remained out here—and no one would let him go to her.

As the hours passed and Marcus sat, unmoving, upon the wooden bench outside the front door, he counted no less than ten people entering and leaving. Only Cunagus, with a box of what Marcus guessed to be his healing tools, walked in and never again left the building.

For all practical purposes Marcus was ignored, reluctantly tolerated after his vehement insistence that he be allowed to stay until he knew Rhianna was out of danger. Savren shot him icy glares as she moved about her tasks but, aside from a brief interchange with Cador, the wait was otherwise long, dull, and wearying.

Filled with self-importance, Cador strode past him the first time he entered, casting Marcus a haughty glance. *Even he has more right to be with her than I,* Marcus thought glumly as he watched the blond man disappear into the house. *Save for my part in Rhianna's rescues, I am nothing to them. Nothing more than a loathsome blight on their fair land, to be borne but never accepted.*

He lowered his head to rest in his hands. *Fool. You've never been more a fool than when you thought to win Rhianna's love,* Marcus berated himself. *Her people will never accept you and without their approval, what chance do you have? Devoted as she is to her clan and family, which do you think she'll choose? Even Cador, as brutish as he is, is yet of her kind.*

Frustration, deep and despairing, washed over Marcus. *Gods,* he railed inwardly, *why have you dangled her, the most brave, beautiful and enticing of women, before me when you never meant to allow us to be together? And why do I sit here, risking everything for her, whom I'll never have?*

Through the turmoil of his anguish, Marcus gradually became aware of a presence standing before him. He rose to his feet, his hand moving instinctively to his sword. It was Cador, a mocking smirk on his face.

"Still here, Tribune?" he sneered. "One would think you'd have gone skulking back to your garrison a long while ago. 'Twill do you no good, you know. Riderch and I won't allow you to see her."

The line of Marcus' mouth tightened, the scar on the side of his face pulling the skin taut, but he buried the hatred burning within. Never would he give Cador the pleasure of guessing how deeply his words had cut or the secret despair his taunt had ripped open once more.

"I don't care what your thoughts on the matter are, Trinovante," he growled. "Now begone. I'd rather the silence of my own company than the braying of an ass like you."

"Dog!" Cador's hand snaked to his dagger. " 'Tis past time you learned—"

"Cador, cease!"

The command, uttered with an expectation of instant obedience, sliced through the air. Both Marcus and his opponent froze, their heads turning toward the source of the voice. Riderch glared back at them.

"My daughter is injured and deathly ill, and all you two can do is snap and growl at each other like wolves fighting over some fallen prey. For shame!"

Marcus exhaled a deep breath, willing himself to relax. "My apologies, Lord Riderch. You are right, of course. My behavior was indeed shameful."

The chieftain's gaze swung to Cador. "And you, warrior. What have you to say?"

"I'll not apologize for protecting my betrothed from this cur, who sniffs after her like she's some bitch in heat. 'Tis past time he was enlightened as to how Trinovante men feel about such conduct." He fingered the tip of his drawn dagger. "And I'm the man to do it."

"Have you forgotten the Tribune Paullinus is bound by our laws of hospitality whenever he sets foot in our fort?" Riderch demanded angrily. "Remember this well, Cador. As long as I'm chieftain, no harm will come to any man within these confines." He made a disgusted motion. "Now go. Rhianna has had enough excitement for one day and sleeps. The morrow is soon enough for another visit."

Cador's face flamed red. He wheeled about and stomped away.

Riderch turned to Marcus. "The crisis is past. Cunagus says Rhianna will live, though she'll carry a bruise for several weeks to remind her how close she came to dying." He paused, waiting for the tremor in his voice to subside. "It seems my daughter's and your paths are destined to cross again and again. Because of it and all I owe you, my request becomes all the harder. Yet I must ask you once again, as Rhianna's father and chieftain of my people, not to see my daughter until after she's wed." He extended his hand. "Take my arm on it and seal your word with the clasp."

Marcus gazed down at the hand offered him, knowing full well that if he accepted it, he must also give up Rhianna. But to allow that swine Cador to have her! The very consideration sent his gut to twisting. He glanced up at Riderch, his features contorted in pain. Marcus shook his head.

" 'Tis for the best," Rhianna's father persisted. "Love isn't always the answer—you are old enough to know that, even if Rhianna isn't. Do what's best for her, or I fear you'll destroy her."

"She's stronger than perhaps even you realize."

"Mayhap, but do you want to put it to a test? Make her choose between you and her people? Risk tearing her apart to find out?" Riderch sighed. "I think there's yet time for her. She doesn't fully realize the depth of her feelings for you. If you give her up now, at least she won't suffer. If you don't, in the end I fear both of you will. At least have pity on my daughter, Tribune."

Riderch was right, yet the admission gave Marcus no solace. He would never be accepted by her people, or she by his. That fact had been brought home in the hours he'd sat outside her house, awaiting word of Rhianna's fate.

Yet, even knowing this, why was it so hard to give her up?

On and on, like wave after wave crashing to oblivion on the shore, the thoughts of a life with Rhianna, a life never to be realized, pounded through Marcus' mind. And, like the ebbing tide, each hope died a quiet death on the sands of reality, easing back into the secret recesses of his heart.

He ran a rough hand through his dark curls, the action signaling his grudging acquiescence. "It will be as you ask."

In a resolute move that belied his inner turmoil, Marcus grasped the proffered hand. Eye to eye the two men stood, each one taking the other's measure.

Then, with a despairing jerk, Marcus released his hold. "One boon, Lord Riderch, before I go."

"Ask, and if 'tis within my power . . ."

"You told Cador that Rhianna slept. If that is true, I've a wish to look upon her one last time."

The words nearly choked him, as did the necessity of requesting permission to see the woman he loved. Yet aside from the muscle quivering in his jaw and the darker register that slipped into his voice, Marcus fought to appear calm, the consummate soldier, undaunted, unmoved.

Riderch nodded. "Aye, she sleeps. 'Tisn't so large a request that I could refuse." He motioned. "Come, but only for a moment."

Marcus followed the chieftain into the house, his heart thudding painfully in his chest. They passed Cunagus sitting near the hearth fire and headed to a curtain-enclosed corner, pausing only when Rhianna's mother stepped forward to bar the way.

"You bring *him* in here?" Savren demanded in outrage. "After all she's been through, you allow him to see her? Well, she's my child as well as yours. I won't allow it!"

Riderch moved her gently aside. "Woman, 'tis only for a moment. The Tribune wishes to ascertain our daughter will recover. Then he's promised to go. 'Tis a small return for what he has vowed me, so cease your endless yammering."

Marcus pushed aside the hanging where, only seconds ago, Rhianna's mother had stood guard like an overprotective lioness. In the shadowed little cubicle, lit only by the erratic flickering of a small oil lamp, was a carved wooden chest and a bed. On the bed, covered by a bear pelt, lay Rhianna.

After a long pause, during which Marcus waged the fiercest battle of his life, he stepped inside and walked over to her. The curtain fell to isolate them, for a brief moment in eternity, from the inhabitants of the house—and the rest of a cruelly insensitive world.

Eleven

"Well, daughter, what do you think?" Savren asked a week later as she shook out a length of fabric from two samples lying on the cloth merchant's table. "Do you prefer this blue cloth or the checkered one of crimson and cream for your marriage dress?" At Rhianna's look of indecision, she clucked her tongue impatiently. "Come, come, girl. We've been at this half the morn now and cannot tarry in Camulodunum much longer. We must be back at the fort by evening."

When no reply was forthcoming, Savren impatiently cleared her throat.

Rhianna's glance swung to her mother's. She sighed. Even the sights of busy Camulodunum were of more interest than choosing fabric for her marriage dress.

"What do I care how I look when wedding Cador?" Rhianna's mouth twisted wryly. "For all it matters to him, I could come wearing a rag and he'd take me."

"Do you wish for me to choose then, daughter?" Savren demanded tautly.

Rhianna smiled and shook her head. No good was served in dragging this unpleasant task out a moment longer or in stirring anew the long-standing conflicts with her mother. "The robin's-egg-blue wool will do nicely."

Savren opened her mouth to protest, then clamped it shut in surprise. "Good. As the marriage ceremony will occur at month's-end, and the leaves are fast fading, the heavier material would indeed be wisest."

The purchase made, the two women hurried to a cobbler's shop for a pair of new sandals. Everything, from head to toe, her mother declared, must be fine and new. As chieftain's daughter, to do less would bring shame upon their family.

Distractedly, Rhianna glanced back outside. A glimpse of a red-crested helmet and swirling crimson cape caught her eye. For a moment, her heart quickened in excitement. Was it Marcus? Would he see her and ride over to speak with her?

The Roman's head turned. It wasn't he.

Though disappointed, Rhianna still smiled. A uniform certainly didn't make the man. Though of impressive build and size, the officer didn't possess Marcus' breadth of chest and shoulder or his towering height. Indeed, was there any Roman in Britannia, besides mayhap Quintus, who equaled Marcus for sheer magnificence of body and bearing?

A fleeting remembrance of warm, green-gold eyes gazing down at her, of strong arms pressing her to a hard-muscled chest, flashed through Rhianna's mind. Had it been but a dream that night in the garden, when he'd held her to him and admitted no woman was enough for him anymore . . . not since he'd met her? Had it been but two weeks since she'd last seen him? It seemed a lifetime.

Nay, Rhianna mused sadly, as hard as she'd tried to put him out of her mind, to accept her destiny, there was no man alive who rivaled Marcus. Time hadn't made her resolve to set Marcus aside any easier. She was beginning to wonder if it ever would.

The cobbler's zealous attempts to sell them additional wares drew Rhianna back from her somber reverie. Though the little man tried mightily to force a pair of elegant, high-heeled Roman sandals on them, assuring Rhianna and her mother they were the height of fashion in Rome these days, both women remained adamant. A simple pair of leather shoes was all they'd come for and all they intended to buy.

Their parcels in hand, they soon rejoined the surging mass of shoppers. Barely had they made their way toward a silversmith's booth when Rhianna's name rang out. She glanced around. There, standing across the cobble-paved street, was Ailm.

At the sight of her friend, Rhianna smiled. She waved for Ailm to join them.

"Rhianna, how wonderful to see you again," the dark-haired girl said, arriving breathlessly at her side. "It has been far too long and I've so much to tell you." Her gaze strayed to the older woman standing beside Rhianna.

"Ah, let me introduce you to my mother," Rhianna hurried to offer, realizing her courtesy was lacking. Though Savren arched a brow when Rhianna made mention of Ailm's relationship to Marcus, her mother appeared to calm after her daughter hastened to add that Riderch already knew of and had accepted the two girls' friendship. After the greetings had been made, a pause fell upon the conversation.

Even Savren couldn't mistake the unspoken question. She shook her head in wry amusement. "I'd wager you girls would like a time to talk." She looked up at the sun. "Meet me back here in an hour, daughter. We must be on our way home by then." Already the two friends were inching away, their arms entwined. "Remember, Rhianna. No more than an hour," she called after them, but they were already gone.

"Are you hungry?" Ailm asked as they ran along. At Rhianna's affirmative nod, she pulled her over to a baker's booth. A few minutes later, a freshly baked loaf of brown bread tucked under her arm, Ailm was again leading her friend in yet another direction. They found a bench off the main street and sat down to share the bread.

"Marcus told me about your accident at the river," Ailm began without preliminary, glancing at the yellowing bruise on Rhianna's forehead. She tore off a large chunk of the crusty bread and handed it to her.

Rhianna busied herself breaking her share of the bread into pieces. "I've no memory of his visit. My brother Cerdic told me he had come, refusing to leave until he was certain I was out of danger. I've had no news of Marcus since."

A heavy silence ensued as Ailm quietly studied her.

"Say it," Rhianna finally exclaimed, unable to bear the scrutiny a moment longer. "Tell me what you're thinking before you burst. Then we can move on to more pleasant topics."

"What happened between you and Marcus?"

Rhianna shook her head. "Naught, Ailm. I-I told you. I haven't seen or heard from Marcus since our last visit here. Mayhap he's washed his hands of me, knowing I'm shortly to wed. 'Twas for the best, of course." Her voice lowered, her throat constricting with emotion. Goddess, if only she hadn't started talking about him! " 'Twould never have worked anyway."

Ailm shrugged. "Mayhap not. Marcus looked none too pleased upon his return that day. Later, I asked him when he'd next be seeing you. He told me never to speak your name again." Her brow wrinkled in puzzlement. "He seemed quite upset."

Rhianna paused to chew her bread, considering. "I can't fathom why he'd be angry with me. Though I couldn't give him what he asked, I thought we had parted as friends."

"Then let's discover the problem!" Ailm turned to Rhianna, her brown eyes sparkling with excitement. "A secret meeting—just you and Marcus! I'll arrange it all. Simply tell me where to have him and when."

"I don't know, Ailm." Rhianna frowned in misgiving. "Mayhap that's not such a good idea . . ."

Her friend shook her head, russet curls dancing gaily about her shoulders. "Nay, 'tis a *wonderful* idea. You care for Marcus and he, for you. 'Tis a shame to give up so easily on each other. Now, when shall we set the day?" She leaned forward in rising anticipation. "The morrow or the one after?"

"What a matchmaker you are!" Rhianna laughed. Suddenly, she didn't care what she'd formerly resolved. All she knew was she wanted to see Marcus again. "The day after will do nicely, by the pool near our fort. Marcus will know where to find it. Tell him I'll await him there at midday."

"Then so be it." Ailm rose from the bench. "Come, there's a jeweler's shop I *must* show you. I've found the most cunning jasper-stone ring there, and Cei's promised to buy it for my birthday." Impatiently, she tugged at Rhianna's arm. "Hurry, slow legs. Your hour will be over before you even finish eating."

With a groan, Rhianna climbed to her feet. Where Ailm found such boundless stores of enthusiasm, Rhianna didn't know. She shoved the last morsel of bread into her mouth and strode after her friend. One could only hope, Rhianna thought as she hurried along, that Ailm could generate that same fervor in Marcus for their meeting in two days' time.

Though the morning sun had burned away the heavy mists, its weak rays did little to warm the air. The multi-hued leaves hung limply on the trees like so many sodden little rags. The rapidly browning grass managed to retain much of the night's dampness, bedewing the hem of Rhianna's gown as she walked. An altogether depressing, gloomy autumn day, she mused glumly.

She looked up at the pale orb gleaming high in the heavens. Midday. Not the most propitious setting for a clandestine meeting. With a small shiver, Rhianna pulled her cloak more tightly about her. Neither propitious *nor* wise.

Though they hadn't as yet put words to their disfavor, save that day Cerdic had spoken to her for their father, of late her parents' warning against Marcus hovered at the edge of all their actions. Rhianna wondered now if they weren't at least part of the reason Marcus hadn't visited since her accident.

Well, no matter. In but a short time she'd have all the answers. The thought sent a frisson of disquiet through her. Indeed, did she really wish to know all the answers? What could she do anyway? Swear undying devotion and love?

A crazy mixture of fear and hope filled Rhianna. Blessed Goddess, what had she entangled herself in, agreeing to this meeting? Suddenly she wanted to run, to hide before Marcus arrived. Her traitorous legs wouldn't respond, however. She sighed her defeat. 'Twould be cowardly, at any rate.

The pounding of hoofbeats shattered the forest quiet. Rhianna turned in the direction of the sound, the words of greeting dying on her lips. Instead of Marcus and his white stallion, Cei and Ailm drew their mounts to a halt. Ailm quickly slid from her horse and ran to Rhianna's side.

"Marcus?" Rhianna hid her disappointment beneath an expression of studied calmness.

"He refused to come. He ordered me not to meddle in his affairs again." Ailm shot her husband a glance over her shoulder. "Cei's angry with me, too."

"Did Marcus say why he couldn't come? Does he wish to meet with me elsewhere, mayhap some other time?"

Ailm lowered her eyes. "Nay, my friend. From his reaction

to our little plan, I fear he has no intention of ever seeing you again."

For a moment, anger waged a bitter battle with reason. The anger swiftly prevailed. How dare he turn from her after as ardent a courtship as any besmitten suitor, Rhianna raged silently, after finally winning the reluctant admission of her friendship! Was that all she'd ever been to him—a challenge to be met, an obstacle to be overcome? By mountain and sea, he would not find it so!

She turned the full force of her resolve on Ailm. "So, the Tribune Paullinus wishes to put me aside without farewell or explanation? Well, he has seriously misjudged. I *shall* have my meeting!"

Rhianna stomped to where Demetia was tethered and soon returned with her horse. Ailm stared at her, the realization of what she planned slowly spreading across her face.

"I . . . I don't know if this is wise, Rhianna," she hesitantly began. "Cei might not allow—"

"I ask only for the protection of your company," Rhianna briskly interrupted her. "Am I not free to ride to Camulodunum of my own choosing, demand an audience with the *Praefectus Alae* if I so desire? Would Cei prefer I brave the roads alone?"

Ailm shook her head, her shoulders slumping in defeat. Rhianna was as fiercely proud and headstrong as Marcus. Why, by the Good God, she moaned silently, had she ever arranged to bring them together? She motioned for Rhianna to follow.

The soldier stood before the large, parchment-strewn desk and tentatively cleared his throat. Marcus, intently immersed in his work, chose to ignore the auxiliary's presence. The soldier cleared his throat a little louder. His commander lifted his head and sent him a sharp look. The young soldier went pale.

"What is it?" Marcus demanded irritably. "I'm buried alive in this detestable pile of reports," he said, gesturing about him, "and whatever it is, it had better be important enough to override my request for privacy."

"A-a lady, my lord."

"What?"

"A lady wishes to speak with you."

Marcus rose and leaned forward on his desk. "And you interrupted me because some woman wants to talk with me?"

The soldier swallowed convulsively. "S-she said, rather she *insisted,* you see her. She refuses to leave until you do. When I threatened to have her forcibly removed, she, er, drew a dagger. Forgive me, my lord, but after that I thought it prudent to seek your guidance."

The description fit only one woman. A small smile tugged at the corner of Marcus' mouth. He could hardly blame the man for being intimidated. Rhianna could be quite formidable . . .

He caught himself in the affectionate musings. No matter her reason for being here, he dared not see her. He had given his word. Though rendered reluctantly and endlessly regretted, he would stand by it. Marcus lowered himself back into his chair.

"My order stands. I'll see no one today. Send the lady away."

The auxiliary saluted and left the room. With a sigh, Marcus forced further thoughts of Rhianna from his mind and returned to his work.

* * *

"He will not see you, lady, and bids you leave."

"Not see me? Bids me leave?" Rhianna was momentarily speechless. She hadn't counted on Marcus' refusing to see her once she was physically here. A knot swelled to a painful size within her chest. Did he care so little he could so casually brush her aside? Had she been a fool in coming?

She climbed to her feet. "And you may tell the Tribune Paullinus," she said with quiet firmness, "that I won't leave until he *does* see me, if it takes all day—and night!"

The soldier stared down at her. Rhianna could see his mind wending its way through the mass of information until he reached one inescapable conclusion. Whatever the connection between the *Praefectus Alae* and her, he was having no more to do with it. Without further comment or protest, he turned and took his place of guard outside Marcus' office.

With a bemused shrug, Rhianna returned to the bench. Knowing Marcus, she sensed the wait would be long and tedious. He was, however, no more determined than she. His conscience would prick at him eventually and he'd be forced to come to her. In the meantime, all she could do was wait.

Marcus, ensconced at his desk the rest of the day, assumed, or perhaps just hoped, the matter had been resolved. No one dared the inner sanctum of his office to tell him otherwise until dusk wended its way across the garrison. Then his aide slipped in to light the oil lamps.

As the room was slowly illuminated, the *Praefectus Alae* lifted bleary eyes. He glanced around, realizing for the first time how late it was. He ran a hand wearily through his hair.

"That won't be necessary." Marcus gestured to the remaining unlit lamps. "I'm nearly finished with this last report. Your own day's been long enough without waiting on me. I'll see that everything's secured."

His aide hesitated. "There's one other still in the building, my lord."

Marcus cocked his head in surprise. "And who might that be?"

"The golden-haired lady. Try as we might, we couldn't budge her. She insisted on waiting."

"Gods!" Marcus groaned. The obstinate wench had won after all. He rose, the report forgotten. Well, if it was the truth she wanted, it was the truth she'd get.

Yet what of his promise to her father? Could he keep his word once he was in Rhianna's presence, close to her again? He must. Must remember it was best for her, no matter what she said or did.

He waved his aide out of the room and lingered a few minutes more while he extinguished the oil lamps. Then, with a resolute set of his shoulders, Marcus marched out to confront Rhianna.

Settled on the crudely wrought wooden bench, her cloak tucked around her, she stared back at him. In the rapidly waning light it was difficult to discern her expression, but Marcus could tell by the sudden tensing of her body that she was awake. He strode over.

"Why did you come after I sent Ailm to tell you not to?" he demanded harshly. "And why did you persist in remaining here after I gave orders for you to go?"

Rhianna rose. "And why weren't *you* man enough to tell me to my face, rather than hiding behind the backs of others? I thought more of you than that. I expected more of our friendship."

He exhaled an exasperated breath. "There was nothing I could have said that would have been any kinder. I thought but to spare you—"

"Spare me?" Rhianna gave a disparaging laugh. "Spare

me what? By the Goddess, to imagine that you cared and then, in but a few weeks' time, to find you had turned your back on me as if . . . as if I were beneath you! How much time would it have taken for the kindness of an explanation?" She snorted disdainfully. "Spare me your excuses, Tribune. All I ask is the truth."

"Then you shall have it. I cannot see you again."

"Cannot or will not?"

"Does it matter? The result's the same."

A small, clenched fist swung out to strike him on his corseleted chest. "You big buffoon! Of course it matters. If you think to misdirect me, think again."

He smiled.

Instantly, Rhianna's eyes narrowed. "What's so amusing, Roman?"

Marcus shrugged. "Nothing of import. I merely wondered why you refrained from using your dagger on me. If I recall correctly, it's your favorite weapon."

"If I thought my dagger could carve the truth from you . . ." She ground out the threat through tightly clenched teeth.

"Well, it won't and you know it." He grasped her by the arm. "Come. The night draws on and you can't stay here. The room you had in my quarters is yours again. On the morrow, I'll have you escorted back to your fort."

"Nay!" Rhianna jerked free. "I meant what I said. I'll not leave until I have your explanation."

Marcus took a step closer. "Woman, you push too hard. I owe you no more than I choose to give. Never forget that."

"I-I don't forget." In spite of her best efforts to control it, Rhianna's voice broke. "Mayhap that's why 'tis so hard to accept this change in you. The last time I saw you, there was a promise, an affection in you that stirred me to the depths of my being. Even now, I marvel over it and yearn to see it again—and again. Can you blame me for wondering what came between us?"

"No, I can't blame you, Rhianna." Marcus' gaze softened. "But at the same time, I can offer little comfort. I gave my word. Even now, speaking with you like this, I verge on its breaking. Let it suffice that I didn't willingly choose to part from you."

Her disbelief grew apace with her anger. Though he didn't name the one who had demanded the vow, 'twasn't hard to guess. All the years of endless inculcations of unselfish service to people and clan burned away before a white-hot rage. Goddess, she was so weary of always having to sublimate her own desires to that nebulous ideal of honor! She'd willingly die to protect the Trinovante, but must she also sacrifice her heart's desire—the man she loved?

Rhianna gasped. Love? Had she admitted it then at last? Did she love Marcus? Fear mixed with a wild excitement coursed through her. Did she *dare* love him? And yet, knowing what she now did, could she face life without him?

"Nay, Marcus," Rhianna whispered, " 'tisn't enough. Only the truth will ever be enough. I care not for your vow. My life and all its decisions are mine alone to make. From this moment forth, I gainsay my betrothal to Cador. From this moment forth, I choose only to follow the dictates of my heart."

She made it sound so easy, Marcus thought in an agony of conflicted emotions, gazing down at Rhianna. In her innocence, it probably was. But wouldn't he be cruel if, in his wider experience, he went along with her beautiful dreams? Didn't he owe her the benefit of his greater years, even if only to quash her ideals a little, to dampen her love? In the end, he'd be doing her a kindness in sending her back to where she truly belonged.

Yet where *did* she truly belong? he asked himself. Was there not a home to be found in the arms of a lover? And who could say it was of less import than the love of one's people? The truth lay in the heart of the one who loved. And wasn't the cruelest act of all to take that choice from her?

Yet he had given his word and risked the peace he so dearly desired between he and the Trinovante if he now went back on it. Wasn't there some path through this treacherous labyrinth of honor and justice? There must be and, on the morrow, he would strive to discover it. But tonight . . . tonight he found he could fight Rhianna no longer.

In the deepening twilight, Marcus drew her against him. "Noble ideals aren't always enough, are they, lady?" His warm breath caressed her face. "You were correct in saying my vow was invalid. It wasn't my place, nor even your father's, to plan the course of your life. You're a grown woman. The choice should be yours."

With a tender, wistful motion, Marcus stroked her cheek. "You said once you'd be my friend. Is there hope of someday being more?"

A blissful warmth flooded Rhianna. "Aye, and that day, I find, is already upon us." She turned her head to kiss his hand. "I love you, Roman."

"And I, you, sweet Britanni."

Through the darkness she saw his head move, felt his mouth settle gently over hers. With but the lightest brush of his lips, he sent a delicious shiver of excitement coursing through her. Rhianna came to him, hungrily, greedily pressing into his iron-thewed form. His tongue sought out her mouth, caressing the delicately molded contours. Rhianna's lips parted, welcoming his sweet invasion.

The kiss deepened, sending the pit of her stomach into a wild swirl. Rhianna's arms entwined about Marcus' neck and, as she moved yet closer, her body brushed against his groin. He sucked in a ragged breath.

Marcus pulled her hands from his neck. Firmly replacing them at her side, he stepped back.

"What's amiss, my love?" she asked over the loud hammering of her heart. "Did I do aught to offend you?"

"No, sweet lady. Far from it. I but feared the strength of my response if I held you a moment longer." Gently, Marcus grasped her arm. "Come. For your sake, it's best we don't tarry here. Let's go to my quarters."

Rhianna smiled, a sudden certitude filling her. It was right and good that they should be together—tonight and the rest of their lives. Somehow, someway, she would make her father see that. Somehow, someway, she and Marcus would find a solution to Cador. There was no need to live apart, to deny their love. There never had been.

"Aye, let us leave this place," she whispered. " 'Twould be far more pleasant—for the both of us—in your quarters."

They left the building and walked out into the crisp night air. At the sudden chill, Rhianna pulled her cloak tightly about her. Stars twinkled in the blackened sky, their cool, silver brilliance a sharp contrast to the warm yellow light from the barracks' windows.

So much like the disparity of my feelings, she thought. *My love for Marcus is a beautiful thing, as high, as holy as the sacred expanse of the heavens. Yet my need for him is like the comforting glow from the windows . . . simple, earthy, and, oh, so compelling. A strange, wonderful disparity,* she mused. And one that cried for union.

Her resolve deepened. Though Rhianna knew their love for each other wouldn't solve everything, she was willing to take a chance on it. Together, she felt certain they could solve the problems awaiting them.

But what if Marcus didn't wish to wed? She knew 'twasn't any military stricture that forbade his marrying. Though the enlisted Roman soldier wasn't permitted to wed during his term of service, those rules didn't apply to high-ranking officers such as tribunes. Mayhap instead 'twas below his station to wed a Britanni, no matter how nobly born.

With a small movement of her shoulders, Rhianna shrugged the doubts away. Marcus had said he loved her and, again and again, he had proven the depth of his honor. 'Twas long past time to trust him.

They entered his quarter's dimly lit entryway. On a small table an oil lamp glowed. Rhianna smiled. Ailm, ever thoughtful, must have placed it there. Marcus took up the lamp and led Rhianna down the hallway to the sleeping chambers, the lamp light throwing huge, undulating shadows against the walls. As they reached the room Rhianna knew to be his, she halted.

He glanced down at her.

"Must we sleep apart?" she softly asked. "We are already well-known to each other."

Marcus impaled her with his green-gold stare. "I'd no right to claim such liberty, that Lughnasa day."

"And now?"

"And now?" Marcus paused, a curious half-smile lifting the corners of his mouth. "Now, I've no right to ask a husband's due. We aren't wed—"

She leaned on tiptoe to brush his lips with her fingers. "Hush, my love. 'Tis of no import. In my heart, though I knew it not then, I was wed to you on Lughnasa. A priest will not strengthen our bond. 'Tis the vows *we* make, one to the other, that matter."

He gently removed her hand, kissing each slender digit as he did. "And would you not wed me?"

"Mayhap." Her heart gave a wild leap within her chest. "Are you asking, Roman?"

"Yes. Will you marry me, Rhianna?"

She smiled. "Aye, I'll wed you and gladly, my love."

Marcus placed the lamp in the little wall-alcove near the door. Then, with a small sound, he gathered her back to him. "Ah, lady, you do me great honor," he murmured, stroking the sleek mass of her hair. "It won't be easy for either of us, and we've much to plan, for never in my wildest dreams—"

"Nay," Rhianna interrupted him. "Let us not talk of plans and dreams just now. I've a need for your arms about me, your mouth on mine." She grasped his hand. "This eve, priest or no, let us consummate our love."

Silently, Marcus turned and guided her into his room. Moonlight flooded the chamber, streaming in through the large windows, bathing the room in a luminescent glow. In the shadows, Rhianna could make out the form of a huge wooden bed. She turned to Marcus.

Once more, he took her into his arms. He cupped her chin in tender possession, his gaze solemn, tender. "I love you, Rhianna of the Trinovantes, and pledge my troth for all eternity," Marcus said. "Though many the difficulties be in joining Roman to Britanni, I will never stop loving you. This I swear, on the honor of my family name and the golden eagle of Rome."

Her eyes lifted to his. "And I pledge my troth to you, Marcus Suetonius Paullinus, and swear to love you above all, even life itself. I'll bear your children gladly and grow old in your embrace. This I vow, on the honor of my people, the clan Trinovante."

Caught up in his impassioned gaze, Rhianna watched his

mouth descend. At the hungry hardness of Marcus' lips, a white hot flame shot through her. She melted into him, her knees suddenly weak.

He found the clasp joining her cloak and unfastened it. The heavy fabric slid from Rhianna's shoulders to pool at her feet. Then, on a shuddering sigh, Marcus moved back to take her with demanding mastery, his mouth, his touch, his very body exploring each soft, sweet aspect of her. His lips moved over Rhianna's as if he were greedily imbibing of a nectar like one long-starved. And, as his insistent tongue sought entry, her lips parted.

Ever so gently, Marcus' hand outlined the swell of Rhianna's breast. She gasped, a tremor of delight wracking her slender frame. His fingers crept inward until, at last, he captured a soft mound.

Her nipples tightened to hard, sensitized little peaks. She molded yet tighter to him and, through the thin fabric of his tunic, Rhianna felt the swollen evidence of his desire. At the touch of him, thick and long against her belly, a searing heat flared in the core of her womanhood.

Suddenly, the need to have Marcus naked, to feel him hard and hot within her, filled Rhianna with an intense, ardent yearning. She pushed back from him.

Surprise flickered in his eyes.

"I want you," she whispered. "Now."

He laughed then, the sound rich, throaty, and filled with a deep masculine pleasure. In a swift surge of powerful muscles, Marcus swung Rhianna up into his arms and carried her over to his bed. Together, they tumbled onto the plump mattress. With eager hands they undressed each other and soon lay naked in each other's arms.

Rhianna sighed blissfully, reveling in the hard, hair-roughened feel of Marcus' body. "Much, much better." She paused to slide her hand down the bulging expanse of his chest, past his tautly rippling abdomen to the dense nest of hair guarding his jutting manhood. Threading her fingers through the wiry curls, she grasped his thickened shaft. "Aye," Rhianna purred. "Much better indeed."

With a low chuckle, Marcus rolled her over onto her back and, before she could offer protest, much less react, he slid between her legs. "Better, indeed," he agreed huskily, "but the best, sweet Britanni, is yet to come."

And, with that, he proceeded to show her explicitly and ecstatically exactly what he meant.

The next morning, Marcus insisted on returning Rhianna to the hill fort. Riding at the head of a small troop of his auxiliaries, the men placed far enough behind to allow an interval of privacy, Marcus and Rhianna made their way through the forests of Trinovante land.

It was a glorious, fresh fall morn, the world ablaze with color. Drunk with the first flush of his newfound love, Marcus exchanged frequent, wondering glances with Rhianna. Somehow, he sensed she found the happy reality of their newly born commitment as hard to believe as he.

Each time Rhianna's mare would flatten her ears when his stallion drew near, Marcus smiled at Rhianna's delighted laughter. The little bay mare was a handful, he mused, as spirited and tempestuous as her lovely mistress.

Indeed, Rhianna was a never-ending challenge, a beautiful, vibrant woman who stirred the blood. Her fiery, passionate nature enhanced every waking moment and, he thought with a warm surge of contentment, every loving intimacy. He hadn't known what it truly felt like to be alive before he met Rhianna. Nothing, not his successful career in the Roman

Army nor his dreams of an even more successful one in the Roman Senate, could ever hope to compare.

It would be difficult to bring her back to Rome, to integrate her into Roman society, though. Heads would turn; tongues would wag at her exotic blond beauty and headstrong ways. But other men had done it, and so would he. Taking Rhianna as wife would only temporarily detour his plans, not destroy them.

He thought of their wedding vows made last night. Though sacred and binding, they weren't enough to seal their marriage in the eyes of Rome, much less the Trinovante. A small frown creased Marcus' brow. Though Rhianna had been optimistic regarding her father's eventual acceptance, he wasn't so certain.

After the vows made and given last night, the love shared, he would have to tread very carefully if he were to salvage whatever remained of his relationship with her father. Riderch was no fool. He would guess what had transpired between him and Rhianna. But Roman soldiers wed native women all the time. Surely the Trinovante chieftain could be brought to some sort of acceptance in time. All it required was a bit of tact and patience . . .

"Are you still of the same mind to tell your father of our decision?" Marcus shot her a considering look.

Rhianna glanced over in surprise. "I owe him that respect, my love."

Marcus sighed. "And if he says no, what then?"

" 'Twon't change my decision. We'll still wed."

"It would be better to approach this a bit more gradually, I think. He does have the power to physically restrain you from coming to me."

"And would you not fight your way to my side if that happened?" she teased.

"You know I would, but that would hardly improve Romano-Trinovante relations, would it?" Marcus glumly shook his head. "It isn't my way to skulk behind someone's back, but I'd still prefer to be formally wed before your father found out. He might accept it a little more easily then." He exhaled a frustrated breath. "Gods, if there were only some other course . . ."

"But there isn't," Rhianna reminded him crisply. "Have no fear, my love. I'll feel out my father before telling all. If 'tis necessary for our wedding to remain a secret, then so be it. But let us not begin our life together under a guilty shade. Mayhap we are wrong in how we do this, but 'tis the best we can do."

He nodded. "If you don't tell your father, we'll have to be wed by a Roman priest to keep your people from finding out. Does that distress you?"

Rhianna stared down the road. "I'd have wanted my grandfather to marry us, but if Father isn't to know, we dare not ask Cunagus. As much as he loves me, he'd be compelled to betray our plans. Mayhap someday, though, when my people have come to accept you . . ."

"I pray that day comes." Marcus caught a glimpse of the hill fort through the trees. "Then it's set, is it? Five days hence, after my return from Londinium and my meeting with the procurator, you'll join me by the forest pool at midday?"

Rhianna smiled at his worried fretting. "Aye. Would any maid forget her wedding day? Of course I'll await you there."

The trees rapidly thinned and the fertile pasturage surrounding the fort came into view. In spite of her brave words to the contrary, the closer they approached, the more Rhianna's anxiety grew. "Mayhap," she began, " 'twould be wiser if I rode the rest of the way alone. Father's sure to be angry and we don't—"

"No. If there's fault, it's as much mine as yours. I'll not slink away and let you bear the brunt of it all."

"I meant no insult to you, my love," Rhianna hastened to explain. "I only thought, knowing my father's temper once 'tis stirred, that 'twould prevent further animosity between you."

His tight expression relaxed. He smiled. "Fear not, sweet lady. I can bear the force of Riderch's anger, knowing it springs from a father's love." Marcus reined to a halt at the foot of the hill. He rode back to his men. "Remain here and await my return."

Rejoining Rhianna, he paused a moment, a reckless grin splitting his finely chiseled face. "Shall we be on our way, lady? Our chastisement awaits and will only worsen the longer we make your father wait up there." He indicated the irate figure of the Trinovante chieftain standing, arms akimbo, at the great wooden gate.

"Aye," she sighed. " 'Twon't improve with time. That much is certain." She nudged Demetia. The mare eagerly sprang forward.

The foreboding look on Riderch's face only deepened with increasing proximity. As they neared the gate he strode forward, purposely putting them out of easy earshot of the sentries. Riderch virtually ignored Rhianna, his glowering rage riveting, full force, on Marcus. "I see now how well a Roman honors his word. You have earned my contempt, Tribune."

"Father, 'tisn't what it—"

"Enough, daughter," Riderch growled, silencing her with an upraised hand. "You, I'll dispense with later. But first I've a liar to deal with, a man whom I thought was noble and trustworthy and whom I now find is a greater hypocrite than all the rest. You sicken me, Tribune," he snarled, his lips curling in disdain. "I want no further dealings with you."

Marcus sat his horse in impassive silence. Only when Riderch finally faded into speechless fury, did he reply. "As Rhianna said, it's not what it seems. In a sense I broke my word, but I'd little choice. I come not, however, to make excuses for my conduct, but to assure the safe return of your daughter. What I've done I stand by. My only regret is the loss of your respect and friendship."

"Fine words, as always," Riderch muttered, "but words I now hold little store in. Begone, Roman. I've naught further to say to you. You're not welcome here. The mantle of Trinovante hospitality, as long as I am chieftain, will never fall on you again."

"Father, nay!" Rhianna cried, knowing full well the implications of such a decree. Marcus could never enter the fort again. If he tried, he'd be in danger of his life. And if he were ever found alone, he'd be fair game for any of their warriors.

Riderch wheeled around to confront her. "And you, woman. Dare you now question the judgment of your clan chieftain? Haven't you brought enough shame on us that you must now argue with me? Get to our house before you heap further dishonor on yourself!"

The pain that lanced through Rhianna at the harshness of her father's words was beyond tears. Never had her father spoken to her like this; never had his rage seared her as now, shriveling her very soul with its scalding fury. She glanced questioningly at Marcus.

"Do as he says, Rhianna," came the gentle reply. At her hesitation, he smiled. "Fear not. No harm will befall me."

At the visual interchange between the tribune and his daughter, a numbing fear brushed Riderch's spine. Had he lost her then, that she now looked to another for direction? By the Goddess, would she destroy all his carefully laid plans, and all because of some passing fascination with an enemy? By mountain and sea, 'twould not be!

Riderch watched his daughter slide off her horse and lead the animal away before turning back to Marcus. "You weren't content, were you, until you corrupted Rhianna's affections?" he hissed. "Well, once I asked you as a friend to respect her vows of betrothal. But no more. Now, I order you. Come near Rhianna again and 'twill mean your death. Do you hear me, Roman? Do you finally understand?"

Marcus nodded, his expression calm, implacable. "I understand. You are wrong in this, though. We've done nothing to be ashamed of, only followed the call of our hearts. I may be of another people, a soldier in an army subjugating your land, but that makes me no less a man. A man who loves your daughter."

He mounted, then looked down at Riderch, shaking his head in wonder. "I tried to forget, to set myself apart from her, but I couldn't. I was wrong to have promised what wasn't mine to give. For that I am sorry. I never meant to deceive you. But it changes nothing. Rhianna is mine, as I am hers."

Marcus turned then and rode back down the hill to his awaiting troops. Riderch watched for a long while until the Romans disappeared back into the forest, struggling with his roiling sense of frustration and futility. Then, with a deep sigh, he turned and headed back to his house. 'Twas past time to tell Rhianna all.

Twelve

She awaited Riderch in their timbered house, nervously warming her hands over the hearth fire. At the sound of heavy footsteps, Rhianna whirled around. She met her father's gaze. "I see you've dispensed with Marcus. Is it now my turn? 'Twill do no good, no matter how hard you strike. I regret naught."

Slowly, Riderch shook his head. "Nay, lass. You are long past the switch or strap. 'Tis time for us to talk." He motioned toward the door. "Would you walk with me?"

Rhianna's eyes widened, but she obediently followed him from the house. They walked for a long while, out of the fort and into the forest. A rich, earthy smell clung to the crisp autumn air, the fallen leaves rustling underfoot as they walked. She kicked at a pile, and the leaves spewed up in a spray of vibrant reds, golds, and browns.

How like other days long ago, Rhianna mused sadly, when she and her father had had leisure to take a long stroll together. Even now Rhianna could recollect the scene. Riderch, tall, strong and omnipotent, and she but a small child, gazing up at him in loving adoration.

A bittersweet sorrow welled within. How long had it been since she'd cast aside her dependence on her father, begun to see him as a man, albeit wise and good, rather than an infallible god? Life had been so simple then, no problem or question too difficult for him to solve. But now? Now, the answers came not as readily, the solutions rarely clear. And the call of the heart was suddenly of more import than filial honor . . .

"Do you remember that day—you were but five—when I found you trapped in that old birch tree?"

Riderch's rich voice intruded on Rhianna's poignant reverie. She shot him a quick look, then nodded. "Aye, I remember it well."

"You cried for me to help you, your chubby little arms reaching down in terrified entreaty." He chuckled. "I gave you two choices, either climb down the way you came or jump into my arms. Do you recall what you said?"

"I told you to make the choice for me."

"Aye, and I told you to leap down and I'd catch you. You began to cry then, sobbing you were afraid, that 'twas too far to jump."

Rhianna smiled softly. "And you said trust you, that you'd never ask anything that would hurt me."

"Was I wrong, even that day so long ago?"

"Nay, Father." She halted and turned to face him. "Save in the matter of Cador, you've always had my best interests at heart, always wished for my happiness. I count myself fortunate to have you as sire—and always will."

"Then will you trust me once more?"

She knew what he was asking. Rhianna sighed and shook her head. " 'Tis too late, Father. My choice is made."

He frowned. "And what choice is that?"

"I will not wed Cador. We bear each other no love. 'Twould be a serious mistake to take him as husband."

"And 'twould be more serious if you did not." Riderch led Rhianna over to a fallen tree. He sat down upon it, motioning for her to do the same.

Rhianna complied, confusion darkening her eyes. "But why? Who'd suffer if I failed to wed Cador? With Marcus to support you, Cador won't dare challenge you. And there are maids aplenty who wish to take Cador as husband, many far more desirable than I. All he'd lose is what he perceives as a higher standing in our clan. That's all wedding me would have given him. Our marriage won't make him chieftain—you're bound to live many a year, and then my three brothers stand in line. So, tell me, with Marcus at your side, who's really to suffer?"

"Your people."

She blinked in bafflement. "My people? How?"

"If you don't wed Cador, our clan will surely split into two warring factions. My hold as chieftain is not as strong as of old. And Cador is determined to lead us into war with Rome." Riderch sighed, the sound laden with despair. "Our young men chafe under Rome's yoke, as do those of many of the other Britanni clans. Nay, it has never been the issue of Cador's potential challenge to me, though I admit to a selfish desire for a long life. 'Tis the threat of Cador leading the Trinovante against Rome. He'd have easy allies—the Iceni, for one."

"Then bring his selfish maneuverings to the attention of the Elders, the clan," Rhianna countered, her ire rising. "He cannot be allowed to threaten our people. But I won't forsake Marcus when there's still so much that can be done to control Cador."

"Do you think so, lass?" As if weighted down with a sorrow too great to bear, Riderch's head and shoulders sagged. "How little you know of the burdens of leadership. Few things are so simple, so easy to resolve as you would have them be. But I tell you true," he said, lifting his gaze to hers,

"I do the best I can. And I need your help desperately. I wouldn't ask otherwise."

Frustration swelled in Rhianna, frustration and a growing fear. "But surely there's enough support for your cause. Our clan isn't a pack of war-hungry wolves."

"There's enough of them, lass. And 'twould do no good for the clan to be divided over this, either. Not now, not with things so unstable. There are rumors the governor intends to—" Riderch paused, then shook his head. "Nay, there was naught left me but the wits experience had earned. And, right or wrong, I exploited them the best way I could."

Once more, he lowered his head. "Forgive me, lass, for using you as my bargaining piece." He inhaled a steadying breath before meeting her gaze. " 'Tis a heavy burden, a cruel responsibility, this weight of the chieftain's torc. Why do you think I've always striven to instill honor and love of one's clan in all my children? Do you imagine the ruler's torc will never be yours? Mayhap not. Yet, woman though you be, I felt compelled to prepare you as I did your brothers."

Riderch laughed, the sound bitter, ironic. "And indeed, did not a sacrifice fall to my daughter long before any was asked of my sons? Will you turn from it now because 'tisn't to your liking?"

Like waves crashing to their destruction on the shore, her father's words washed over Rhianna. She closed her eyes, feeling trapped, her heart torn. 'Twas so unfair—to give up the man she loved, then wed another and watch her life wither away in obedience to him. Where was the honor in that?

Even the thought of parting from Marcus sent a naked anguish lancing through Rhianna. Yet in light of what she'd just been told, did she not owe some measure of loyalty to her father, her clan?

"I will not force you, Rhianna," came the gentle voice beside her. "But these are issues that cannot be shared with the Tribune Paullinus. If he knew what our young men plotted . . ."

"I know, Father. I understand."

He took her chin in his hand, turning her gaze to his. His eyes gleamed with love . . . and unshed tears. "I ask only that you give my words consideration. Will you promise me at least that?"

She nodded, unable to hide the bleakness of her despair. "Aye. Be assured, Father. I'll consider your words well."

Riderch rose. "I thank you. Now come, 'tis time we were returning to the fort. A message has arrived from Queen Boudicca, bidding me join her in a gathering of Iceni and Trinovante chieftains. I am overlong in departing." He paused. "Ride with me to Venta Icenorum. 'Twill do you good to visit the Iceni capital, and 'tis only for a few days. Are you not good friends with the queen's daughters?"

"Aye." Rhianna nodded, her spirits lifting at the thought of seeing Temella and Goronil again. Her father was right. Mayhap a time at the Iceni court would clear her mind, allow her the opportunity to sort through this horrible dilemma. There had to be a way to have all that she wanted—a life with Marcus *and* continued peace for her people. There just had to.

She forced a wan smile. "Aye, Father. 'Tis a wonderful idea." She tugged at his arm. "Let us hurry. I've much to do to prepare for the journey."

"At last," Catus Decianus breathed triumphantly. He broke open the imperial seal and unrolled the scroll. "At last I've my answer to the issue of the Iceni queen."

Marcus set down his cup of wine. An uneasy premonition swept through him. Gods, not now, he thought. Not on top of everything else did the procurator need to receive permission to begin his greedy takeover of the Iceni kingdom.

"As I had hoped." Decianus chuckled. "The Emperor Nero has granted me leave to seize all Iceni lands, livestock, and items of royal wealth." He tossed the scroll onto his desk. "We've not a moment to lose. Enough time's been wasted in bringing that arrogant Queen Boudicca to heel. It'll take nearly two-day's ride to reach Venta Icenorum. We must depart at once."

Marcus shook his head. "I want no part in this. My business today doesn't include the theft of Britanni possessions. You've enough men to do the job."

Decianus wheeled around, his eyes narrowing in sudden anger. He was a portly man, florid-faced, balding, with dark, porcine eyes and a shrewd look about him. His apparel was of the finest quality, from the purple-trimmed white tunic to his finely crafted, bronze medallion-decorated sandals. He eyed Marcus for a long moment, then smiled.

"Do I hear you correctly, Tribune Paullinus? Are you calling an imperial decree an order for thievery? And have you also overlooked the governor's instructions that you cooperate with all Roman officials in his absence and serve as requested? Pray, don't forget I report directly to the emperor. Not only your career, but that of your illustrious uncle, could suffer if this order isn't carried out promptly." Decianus cocked a speculative brow. "Think long and hard, Tribune. Your words border on treason. And you know full well how Rome deals with disobedience in its Army."

Gods! Marcus thought. He returned the procurator's questioning gaze, his jaw tightening in anger. He was trapped at every turn in his attempts to help the Britanni. Though he fought hard to contain it, a sense of impending doom rose within him.

Rome had indeed set its own course of destruction in this land with its heavy-handed government and its choice of greedy, self-serving officials like Catus Decianus. He wanted no part in any of this but, as Decianus had said, military disobedience was anathema to the army. Better, indeed, to attend the disinheritance of the Iceni queen. Though he might be powerless to prevent it, his presence could at least control the extent of any atrocities.

Marcus shrugged his reluctant acquiescence. "As you wish, Excellency. I ask only that I be allowed to restrain the populace while you secure the emperor's will in the palace. One wrong move and we could have a rebellion on our hands."

Decianus nodded. "I bow to your greater military expertise. As long as the queen accepts the decree as befits a loyal subject of the Empire, no harm shall befall her or any of her people. I want war no more than you. My task is to collect what's rightfully due our emperor." He took up an indigo-colored cloak, flung it over his arm, and motioned for Marcus to accompany him from the room.

And is the whole of the Iceni kingdom the right of Nero? Marcus wondered grimly as he followed the procurator out of the room. The deceased Iceni king's will left only half of his holdings to the emperor. But now, it seemed the Divine Nero was determined to have it all. Queen Boudicca had no further avenue of redress. In truth, the Britanni had lost everything at the Conquest, however misled they might have been in thinking otherwise.

As they walked out onto the parade grounds, the procurator tersely barked orders. Soldiers scurried from barracks and stables, preparing for departure. Marcus shoved his helmet onto his head and watched as his own horse was brought forward.

Thank the gods this distasteful task will be over in five days' time, he thought as he rode out to inform his men of the impending journey to Venta Icenorum. I want nothing to interfere with my marriage to Rhianna. Thank the gods that Venta Icenorum is far from the Trinovante hill fort. It would have been more than he could endure if Rhianna and her family had become embroiled in this sad, sordid mess.

The sky was a leaden gray, looming heavy and foreboding over the Iceni palace. The air, unnaturally warm and moisture-laden, encompassed the courtyard garden like a pall. What *was* it about the foreshadowing of a storm? Rhianna wondered. She lifted her face to the stagnant heavens, searching vainly for a current of air, any hint of a cooling breeze that might herald the storm's arrival. There was none.

She turned back to the garden and her friends. The two princesses were engrossed in play with a small puppy. Rhianna's mouth curved in affectionate amusement. Though both sisters were within two years of Rhianna's age, she couldn't help but view them as much younger. Pampered, protected from the harshness of life outside the Iceni court, Temella and Goronil had little else to concern them but issues of such minor import as this small dog. Life, at least until the death of their father three months ago, had been sweet and gentle.

Temella glanced up at Rhianna. "Come, my friend. Help teach our new puppy tricks. You're always so good with animals and—"

A faint rumble teased their ears. Rhianna's eyes lifted to the sky. Had it been a roll of thunder?

The noise grew louder, closer. She climbed to her feet. 'Twas the sound of horses, a large mass of them, headed through Venta Icenorum toward the palace. Rhianna's glance caught the growing uncertainty in the other girls' eyes. She managed a reassuring smile. "Mayhap 'tis more chieftains arriving for the queen's council. They're tardy, I fear, and will surely incur your mother's wrath . . ."

Further words died as the troop of horses and riders pulled up at the front gate, their progress halted by a loud command.

"Who goes there?"

"Open in the name of the Divine Emperor Nero!" came the imperious reply.

The three girls' gazes met. Romans!

From the other side of the garden wall, there was movement, the hushed murmur of voices from inside the gate. The imperious order came again.

"Open in the name of the emperor!"

With a creaking of ancient hinges, the heavy gate swung open. "Who goes and what is your mission?" the Iceni guard asked again.

"The Provincial Procurator, Catus Decianus, demands a meeting with Queen Boudicca."

"She is in council. If you wish an audience, return on the morrow—"

"She will see him now, you fool!"

From the vantage of the nearby garden, Rhianna heard a dull thud and a cry. Horses thundered into the palace courtyard. Angry shouts rang out, then the sounds of battle.

Temella and Goronil ran to Rhianna. "What is happening? Are the Romans fighting our guards? Our men have no weapons save a few ceremonial spears and wooden staves. What shall we do?"

Rhianna gathered the two terrified girls in her embrace.

"From the sounds of it, I'd wager the procurator's men are forcing their way into the palace."

A sudden thought assailed her. Her father and the other chieftains, as well as Boudicca, were in the palace. Blessed Goddess, what if they chose to fight rather than submit? She must do something, but what?

She turned to the two princesses. "Stay here and hide in the bushes. 'Tis as safe a place as any. I'll see what's happening."

"Nay!" Goronil cried, grasping her arm. "Don't leave us here. Let us go with you."

" 'Tisn't safe for all of us to rush out into this." Firmly but gently, Rhianna pried Goronil's fingers free. "Let me go first. I've at least a dagger for protection. I'll return as soon as I can. I swear it."

Goronil stepped back, though her eyes betrayed her misgiving.

Temella smiled bravely. "Go, Rhianna. I trust your judgment."

Not nearly as confident as her outward demeanor suggested, Rhianna returned the girl's smile. Then, whirling about, she sprinted for the garden's door.

The scene outside the little haven immediately halted her. Men were everywhere. Though virtually defenseless, the Iceni guards strove valiantly to keep the Romans back from the palace doors. And, as valiantly as they'd lived, they died, Decianus' personal guard sparing no mercy as they slashed and hacked at their human barricades.

Rhianna's horror at the merciless bloodbath yielded quickly to anger. Would no one stop this senseless massacre? Her glance swept the enclosure. The luxuriously dressed form of a man who was apparently the procurator caught her eye.

He sat his horse, arrayed in a purple-trimmed tunic and indigo cloak, seemingly unconcerned at the violence around him. She heard him laugh. Was the slaughter little more than entertainment then? A seething rage swelled at his callous indifference. Moved by the need for revenge, long-suppressed and dearly treasured, Rhianna unsheathed her dagger.

Strong young legs carried her forward. If she were to kill him, mayhap the soldiers, then leaderless, would pull back. 'Twould most likely cost her life but the memory of her father, trapped, unarmed, in the palace, drove her on.

The Roman, seated as he was upon his horse, was too high off the ground for a fatal blow with but a dagger, Rhianna realized. Unless . . . unless she could manage to reach the soft area of his back just below his ribs. If she drove the dagger deeply enough there . . .

Fortune was with Rhianna. All attention seemed directed toward the ornately carved palace doors, where the soldiers now used a large log with determined intent against the wooden portal. The sickening thud and splintering of wood each time the battering ram made contact only heightened Rhianna's rage. Her resolve to slay the Roman hardened until her world narrowed to just the sight of him.

In the last few feet before she reached him, Rhianna leaped into the air. The dagger, glinting a deadly gray in the subdued light, slashed upward toward the unsuspecting man's back. Yet even as her weapon ripped through cloak and tunic, strong arms jerked her roughly away.

As the dagger sliced a long, shallow gash down his back, Decianus screamed in pain. He wheeled his horse about. One of his retired centurions fought to hold a beautiful, golden-haired girl while wrestling a small dagger from her grip. The procurator watched them struggle, saw her cloak fall open to expose, through the woolen dress, a sensuously rounded young body and long, slender legs.

He motioned to the soldier. "Bind the wench and don't lose her. Later," he snarled, his face livid with rage, "I'll see personally to her proper punishment."

At that moment, the battering ram smashed through the palace doors. With a cry of triumph, Roman soldiers streamed through the shattered opening. The awful sounds of battle reached Rhianna's ears, more horrible than before.

Frantically, she fought to free herself. Her elbow found an unprotected part of her captor's anatomy. He grunted in pain and, in a swift move, flung her to the ground. Before she could rise, a length of cord was tightly wrapped about her wrists. Then Rhianna was jerked back to her feet.

"Move, woman!" the soldier snarled, shoving her forward. "You have overstepped yourself in attacking the Provincial Procurator. Follow your new master and see what happens to rebellious Britanni dogs."

Rhianna shot a hateful glare at the soldier. Too old to be a legionnaire, the man was quite evidently one of the veterans who had settled in the area since his discharge from the Roman Army. They were perfect accomplices to their despicable pig of a procurator.

She forced her attention back to the scene in the main courtyard. Nausea rose within her. The fighting had ceased and bodies were strewn in a gory, heart-breakingly haphazard fashion. Soldiers ran to and fro, carrying out articles from the palace to be thrown into cloaks spread on the ground.

Rhianna fought back her rising sense of unreality. How could all of this be happening? Why hadn't her Gift warned her? This, she might have had some ability to prevent. This, she would have gladly shared with Cunagus and her father.

Escorted by two armed soldiers, Boudicca strode into the

courtyard. Tall, proud, with long red hair flowing to her hips, she came, her glance never wavering, her head held high. The soldiers forced her to a halt before Decianus.

"You discover at last the folly of resisting Rome," the procurator taunted, gesturing about him at the carnage. "I was prepared to be generous, to allow you continued use of your palace, even the retention of a few small land holdings, but in your arrogance you have lost even that. From this day forth all of your wealth, all of your possessions, as well as those of your tribal chieftains, shall be seized. Your actions are deemed as rebellion and will be treated as such. What have you to say for yourself?"

Boudicca gave a haughty laugh. "I care not for your sniveling words, little man. They make me no less a queen—and you no more than the fat worm that you are. In the name of your debauched emperor, you think to take what is legally mine. You think to strip us of our honor, our pride, but 'twill never be. If fighting for what is ours is rebellion, then so be it. There's naught you can do to make me recant or grovel before you."

Decianus' face purpled with rage. "Think again, woman," he sneered. "A taste of the lash will sweeten your disposition." He motioned to the weapon stone standing in the courtyard. "Tie her to it and flog her!"

"Nay!" Rhianna cried from her vantage nearby. "You cannot do this. 'Tis the act of a coward to dishonor a queen in such fashion."

The procurator graced her with a mocking, cold-eyed smile. "I do whatever I wish, wench. Now, hold your tongue or, when I'm done with Boudicca, I'll have you flogged as well."

She opened her mouth to protest further, then realized 'twas futile. She could do naught to halt what was to come.

Indeed, her own fate hung by as precarious a thread as did that of Queen Boudicca's.

They tied Boudicca's hands to the weapon stone, then ripped open the back of her gown. Rhianna's eyes clenched shut. She could bear no more. As the lash cut through the air to imbed itself into the soft, white flesh of the queen's back, Rhianna's grief could no longer be restrained. She screamed—a high, anguished, keening that rent the air, carrying far beyond the palace walls.

"My lord! A battle has broken out within the Iceni palace!"

The auxiliary sent to check on the progress of Catus Decianus and his personal guard reined his horse to a halt before Marcus. Marcus wheeled his stallion about, riveting his full attention on the soldier. From their post outside Venta Icenorum, where he'd set his men to guard the roads leading into the city, they were too far away to hear much of what went on in the Iceni palace.

Marcus' jaw tightened. Had he been played the fool, keeping guard to preclude any messengers being sent for help, yet far enough away to allow the procurator full opportunity to murder and pillage?

"A battle, you say?" he demanded tersely. "And how is that possible? The Iceni are all but unarmed."

"The procurator has set his men against the Iceni guards. That is all I know."

Curse Decianus, Marcus thought, his anger rising. The man had lied, had never had any intention of a peaceful takeover of Boudicca's holdings. His hands, gripping his horse's reins, grew white with the fierceness of his rage. He'd been used, manipulated into providing the military presence while the procurator committed legal thievery and murder. And he, as a loyal soldier of Rome, owed his first allegiance to his country's official representative. Yet to stand by and, through his own inaction, condone the murder of defenseless people!

"Hold the line until my return!" Urging his stallion forward, Marcus forged through his soldiers and down the road leading back to Venta Icenorum, his thoughts, his emotions in a chaotic turmoil.

His past two years in the Roman Army had been hard, eye-opening, but always before he'd participated in honorable battle against well-armed warriors or dealt with officials who were more concerned with fair dealings. Yet now the corruption, the utter contempt for the lives and feelings of the Britanni had brought him to the very brink of disillusion—disillusion with a system he'd heretofore respected and blindly obeyed.

His horse's hooves, clattering down the cobbled streets, echoed the tumult in his mind. The tall stone ramparts of the Iceni palace came into view, then a gathering of people milling outside the palace gates. Sounds of fighting, shouts, and screams, filled the air. Marcus urged his mount on, terribly, heart-stoppingly afraid he'd be too late. Too late to salvage anything—for the Iceni *or* Rome.

Then, suddenly, the sounds within the palace faded. The crowd standing outside quieted, their looks of anger transforming gradually to ones of anxiety.

Had the queen surrendered? Was the fighting at an end? Hope welled in Marcus. Perhaps there was yet a chance the situation could be controlled, politically minimized.

The crack of a whip, followed closely by a woman's agonized scream, reverberated through the air. Marcus' heart sank. Despair slashed through him as viciously as the whip cut through human flesh, shattering his last hopes for a humane solution to this day.

As he galloped through the gate and across the huge courtyard, his glance swept the chaotic scene. A red-haired woman, her back laid bare, was tied to a tall, carved column of stone. Already the lash had torn into her fair flesh several times, but she made not a sound. The scream had evidently not come from her, but from a golden-haired woman struggling with one of the soldiers standing near the procurator.

Marcus reined his horse to a sliding stop and flung himself down. There was no time to further contemplate the golden-haired woman, as familiar as she seemed. The whip was once more raised to strike.

Boudicca. Decianus was having Queen Boudicca flogged!

The whip man's arm moved forward. Marcus grabbed his wrist in a clasp of steel. "Lay the lash upon her again and I'll break your arm!" he snarled.

The man turned upon his unknown assailant—and met the smoldering eyes of a Roman officer. He paled, his gaze dropping to the ground. "Pardon. I ask pardon, Tribune Paullinus," the veteran stuttered in abject terror. " 'Twasn't my doing, but that of—"

"The Provincial Procurator," Catus Decianus smoothly supplied as he dismounted and strode over to Marcus. "Unhand my man. This woman," he said, indicating Boudicca with a disdainful sniff, "has insulted both the high office of procurator as well as our emperor. She has admitted to open rebellion against Rome. She deserves much more than a simple flogging, but I, in my great mercy—"

"Spare me tales of your great mercy, Decianus." Marcus glanced around at the bodies littering the courtyard. "I've seen more than I can stomach of your compassion this day. The queen will be set free. You've accomplished your task. Her palace has been thoroughly inventoried," he added, making note of the numerous piles of goods heaped throughout the yard. "I'd say your obligation to the emperor is complete. Gather your booty and prepare to depart."

The procurator's face contorted in rage. "You agreed to assist me in this, Paullinus, and now you *dare* impede an imperial decree? Treason is too fine a word for such a foolhardy act. Think again—"

"I've impeded nothing save the onset of outright revolt. My actions will speak for themselves when the governor returns. You insisted I lend my military authority to this . . . this ill-conceived debacle. Well, you've more than overstepped yourself this time. If you've any desire to reach Londinium alive, I suggest you prepare for immediate departure."

The movements of sullen-eyed, enraged royal servants filing into the courtyard caught Decianus' gaze. Gradually, the true peril of his situation permeated his skull. If a call for assistance had managed to reach nearby clans . . .

Imperiously, he gestured toward the royal treasures. "Gather them and let us make ready to vacate this town. As the tribune said, our task is done, the property seized, the Iceni taught their place. It is indeed time to depart."

The soldiers hastily complied with the procurator's order. Decianus mounted and rode toward the palace gate. Marcus turned to Boudicca. A muffled cry drifted to him.

"Marcus!"

He whirled about, the familiar voice wrenching him from his grim contemplation of the queen. There, a hand over her mouth to prevent further outcry, was Rhianna, slowly being dragged away.

"Centurion, halt!" Marcus shouted, quickly striding toward the man.

The soldier froze.

"Where do you think you're going with her?"

Though couched as a question, the barely veiled fury in Marcus' voice unnerved the man. "Th-the procurator ordered me to bring this woman along as part of the booty. H-he wants her for himself."

"And he'll die before he lays a hand on her." He gripped his sword. "Do you wish to join him?"

The old centurion vehemently shook his head. He released Rhianna and stepped back. "N-no, my lord. I bow to your higher authority. If you've an itch for her, so be it."

The soldier fled. Drawing his dagger, Marcus turned to Rhianna's bonds. "By the gods, Rhianna, what brought you so far afield on such an inauspicious day?" he demanded hoarsely as he sliced through the cords.

Her hands freed, Rhianna rounded on him. "Mayhap an opportunity to see how you really work, Roman? When I first saw you here, I thought you'd arrived to save us. And then . . . then I realized you were a part of this. How *could* you accompany that maggot here on so cruel a task?"

Her glance snared on Boudicca, still bound to the weapon stone. Rhianna grabbed the dagger from Marcus and ran to the queen's side.

Boudicca nearly fell as her hands were freed and, save for Marcus' timely arrival and strong arms to support her, Rhianna would have been hard-pressed to keep the taller woman upright. As she sheathed his dagger at her waist, Rhianna glared up at him. "Your services come far too late," she hissed. "Look, her servants hurry to us even now. Begone. I can help the queen until they arrive."

His mouth tightened in anger. Rhianna was merely overwrought, Marcus told himself, and who could blame her after the events she'd just witnessed? She wasn't really angry at him; all she needed was time to calm and put things in their proper perspective.

Gently, Marcus pushed her back from the queen. "Let me have her. She's too weak to walk and her women can't carry her." He carefully swung Boudicca up into his arms and strode toward the palace. Rhianna and the serving women had little choice but to follow silently in his wake.

Marcus didn't pause until he stepped inside the main door. "Where's the queen's chamber?" he demanded, glancing over his shoulder.

The terrified women merely pointed. A few minutes later, Boudicca was lowered to sit on the edge of her bed. Marcus, noting Rhianna was no longer with the group, turned to go, then hesitated. He looked back at Boudicca. "It shouldn't have happened like this, lady. To slaughter unarmed citizens, to loot . . . this isn't Rome's way."

She smiled grimly through her pain. "Young Tribune, today was a time for the loss of innocence. Yours to the true nature of Rome, and mine of my dead husband's hope of maintaining a peaceful coexistence. I am grateful for your kindness, but it changes naught. I no longer need your services; my people will care for me. Go, seek out Rhianna. Find her; comfort her. She has suffered a loss as great as ours."

At the sadness in the queen's eyes, a heavy foreboding flooded Marcus. He turned and ran down the smooth stone corridor, searching vainly for Rhianna. He found her in a colonnaded outdoor pavilion, bent over the still body of a man. Her arms clasped about him, she slowly, rhythmically rocked him back and forth as a mother would her babe. His heart pounding in his chest, Marcus stepped closer.

It was Riderch, his head half-severed from his body. Rhianna held him to her breast, his blood drenching her gown of pale-green wool. Softly she crooned to him, but otherwise her face was expressionless, her eyes blank and staring.

Marcus squatted beside her. "Rhianna?" He lightly touched her arm. "Let me help you."

She turned to him. Recognition flared. "H-help me. Haven't you helped enough for one day, Roman? Nay," she murmured, shaking her head, "henceforth no hands shall touch my father's body, save those who loved him. Get away from me. I can't abide your presence."

Marcus' hands fell to clench at his sides. "Don't turn from me, Rhianna. I love you. Your pain is my pain. Let me share this with you."

Eyes, bright with unshed tears, stared up at him. "L-love me? How can you utter such lies after what you've done here today? You made your decision for Rome and against me when you rode with Decianus. And you killed my father, just as surely as the man who wielded the sword." Fiercely, she shook her head. "Nay, this day's act has severed our vows. You've dishonored not only me and my people, but our love as well. Do you think I'd wed you now? You, my father's murderer?"

Anguish twisted Marcus' heart. Gods, what had his ambition, his unthinking obedience to Rome, wrought this day? In trying to straddle two worlds and have it all, he might have well lost what truly mattered, what he'd come just so late to love.

He grasped Rhianna by the shoulders. "Don't lay this at my feet, lady. I'd no intention of this happening. I'd hoped my presence instead would prevent it."

She averted her face.

Panic gripped him. Marcus' hold on Rhianna tightened. "Don't turn from me. Not now, not when you need me the—"

Loud wailing accompanied two girls being carried through the colonnade to the queen's quarters. Their torn gowns barely covered their young, budding bodies. Marcus uttered a low, savage curse. Decianus' men had been viciously thorough in seeking out all spoils of war.

"Goronil! Temella!" Rhianna cried. "Blessed Goddess, what have they done to you?"

Lightning flashed across the sluggish skies as the two princesses disappeared from view. A sharp crack of thunder quickly followed. Then, as if by some unseen signal, the rain began. Large drops fell upon the pavement, splattering wetly to stain the tiles in ever-darkening circles.

The droplets splashed upon Rhianna, mingling with her father's blood to run in pink-tinged rivulets down her arms, damply molding the scarlet-stained gown to her body. She noticed nothing, her gaze still locked upon the door through which Goronil and Temella had been carried.

Marcus gave her a gentle shake. "Come, Rhianna. Let me help you out of the storm."

Woodenly, Rhianna turned to him. "Nay, Marcus." Her tears fell at last to mix with the rain. "This day has severed what was ever between us. 'Twas never meant to be, the joining of Roman and Trinovante. My father knew this and begged me to part from you. His death but confirms his wisdom. To wed you now would be to count his life and love for me as naught."

She shrugged his hands from her shoulders. "Go. Leave me."

Disbelief, then denial, flooded Marcus. He shook his head. "No. You're hurting and confused. You don't know what you're saying. Now, more than ever, you need me, Rhianna."

"N-need you?" The question rose on a shrill edge of hys-

Now, for the first time . . .

You can find Janelle Taylor, Shannon Drake, Rosanne Bittner, Sylvie Sommerfield, Penelope Neri, Phoebe Conn, Bobbi Smith, and the rest of today's most popular, bestselling authors

. . . All in one brand-new club!

Introducing KENSINGTON CHOICE,
the new Zebra/Pinnacle service that delivers the best
new historical romances direct to your home,
at a significant discount off the publisher's prices.

As your introduction, we invite you to accept 4 FREE BOOKS worth up to $23.96

details inside...

We've got your authors!

If you seek out the latest historical romances by today's bestselling authors, our new reader's service, KENSINGTON CHOICE, is the club for you.

KENSINGTON CHOICE is the only club where you can find authors like Janelle Taylor, Shannon Drake, Rosanne Bittner, Sylvie Sommerfield, Penelope Neri and Phoebe Conn all in one place...

...and the only service that will deliver their romances direct to your home as soon as they are published—even before they reach the bookstores.

KENSINGTON CHOICE is also the only service that will give you a substantial guaranteed discount off the publisher's prices on every one of those romances.

That's right: Every month, the Editors at Zebra and Pinnacle select four of the newest novels by our bestselling authors and rush them straight to you, usually *before they reach the bookstores.* The publisher's prices for these romances range from $4.99 to $5.99—but they are always yours for the guaranteed low price of just *$4.20!*

That means you'll always save over 20%...often as much as 30%...off the publisher's prices on every shipment you get from KENSINGTON CHOICE!

All books are sent on a 10-day free examination basis, and there is no minimum number of books to buy. (A postage and handling charge of $1.50 is added to each shipment.)

As your introduction to the convenience and value of this new service, we invite you to accept

4 BOOKS FREE

The 4 books, worth up to $23.96, are our welcoming gift. You pay only $1 to help cover postage and handling.

To start your subscription to KENSINGTON CHOICE and receive your introductory package of 4 FREE romances, detach and mail the postpaid card at right *today.*

We have 4 FREE BOOKS for you as your introduction to KENSINGTON CHOICE

To get your FREE BOOKS, worth up to $23.96, mail the card below.

FREE BOOK CERTIFICATE

As my introduction to your new KENSINGTON CHOICE reader's service, please send me 4 FREE historical romances (worth up to $23.96), billing me just $1 to help cover postage and handling. As a KENSINGTON CHOICE subscriber, I will then receive 4 brand-new romances to preview each month for 10 days FREE. I can return any shipment within 10 days and owe nothing. The publisher's prices for the KENSINGTON CHOICE romances range from $4.99 to $5.99, but as a subscriber I will be entitled to get them for just $4.20 per book or $16.80 for all four titles. There is no minimum number of books to buy, and I can cancel my subscription at any time. A $1.50 postage and handling charge is added to each shipment.

Name ______

Address ______ Apt. ______

City ______ State ______ Zip ______

Telephone (   ) ______

Signature ______

(If under 18, parent or guardian must sign)

KC0195

Subscription subject to acceptance. Terms and prices subject to change.

We have
4
FREE
Historical
Romances
for you!

(worth up
to $23.96!)

Details inside!

AFFIX
STAMP
HERE

KENSINGTON CHOICE
Reader's Service
120 Brighton Road
P.O.Box 5214
Clifton, NJ 07015-5214

teria. "Need you? Do I need to be reminded of my father's murder? Do I need to remember what was done to Boudicca's daughters? Do I need to recall the butchery, the cruel humiliation of the Iceni this day? 'Twas Roman doings and you, Roman that you be, embody it all." She glared up at him through a haze of wrathful tears. "I hate your kind! Do you hear me? I hate all of you!

"To bear even one more moment in your presence—" with a swift motion she reached down to slip Marcus' dagger from her belt, "—is worse than death itself." Before he could halt her, she placed the dagger's point against the slender shaft of her throat. "Depart from me, Roman dog. Now, or I swear I will kill myself."

He looked deep into Rhianna's eyes and read her resolve. In her overwrought state, he knew she'd indeed do as she threatened.

Marcus rose to his feet. She didn't want his help, didn't want him. Perhaps in time Rhianna would realize how innocent both of them were in this bitter, spiraling clash of their cultures. Perhaps, then, she'd once more admit her love for him. But not now. His continued presence would only drive her over the precipice of grief. Wordlessly, Marcus turned and walked away.

Rhianna lifted her face to the heavens. At that moment, the sky opened to release a torrential downpour. *The Goddess, too, mourns the loss of her children,* she mused, her mind numb from the torment of losing two men she loved in but the space of a few hours.

Let the Mother's tears wash me clean—of the sorrow of my father's death and the unholy love of an enemy, Rhianna prayed, her anguish rising like some shimmering mist about her. *Soon, I'll have no time for regrets, for feelings that cloud the heart and weaken the sword arm. Soon, the weapons so long hidden from Roman knowledge will be unearthed again. And soon, all too soon, the time will come to think only of vengeance!*

Thirteen

In the waning light of yet another sunless day, a procession of black-garbed mourners wound its way across the vale toward the level spot commanding an unbroken view of the hill fort and surrounding lands. Behind them, borne on a wagon, was the body of Riderch, late chieftain of the clan Trinovante. Far ahead near the burial site, the form of Cunagus could be discerned, dressed in a goose-wing headdress and bull-hide cloak.

The somber column halted at last. The funeral wagon, laden with horse trappings, fine fabrics, ceremonial spears, and other weapons, was reverently pulled into a huge wooden box and sealed. Cerdic, Kenow, and Emrys, as Riderch's closest male relatives, stepped forward. Joined by their cousin Idris, they shoved the burial chamber down a small dirt ramp into the grave. Then, all turned expectantly to hear the Druid's words of comfort.

Cunagus, his ancient features ravaged with grief, lifted his gaze to the heavens. He stretched out his arms. Yet, as the minutes dragged on, he said nothing.

Watching him, Rhianna sensed his hesitation. Tears, long-suppressed since that day at the Iceni palace, burned at the back of her throat. Wise man, seer that he was, Cunagus, too, had lost much in the death of his only son. His hope for the future, for the peace and prosperity of the clan, now lay in that burial box. She but mourned a father. Cunagus, in his far-seeing wisdom, grieved for a whole people.

"Hear me, Trinovante!" the Druid finally said, his resonant voice carrying to the furthest reaches of the gathering. "We come to honor. We come to bury. We come to lay to rest the bones of our chieftain. And, though the parting is painful, for we loved him well . . ." He paused, his voice breaking. ". . . 'Tis a goodly thing this ceremony, this last proof of devotion we pay him. Without a fitting burial, his spirit cannot flee his prison of flesh to soar to the heavens, to live again in the body of another. This we believe. This we revere!"

An answering murmur spread through the crowd. Faces brightened with hope. Hearts stirred, lessening, for a brief time, the universal terrors of death. The Druid's arms lifted, the long sleeves, like giant bird wings, fluttering in the chill breeze.

One by one, from the chieftain's family to the humblest villager, the clan moved past the pile of excavated dirt. Each tossed a handful of the land Riderch had loved and died for onto his burial chamber. Finally, when all had tendered their respect, the late chieftain's sword brothers took over the task of covering the grave.

While the men worked, the light dimmed, until bodies blurred in the rising darkness. A signal was given and the torches lit. Fire sprang from one brand to another, ringing the mound in reddened tongues of flame.

Rhianna pulled the cloak of coarse black wool more tightly about her. A freshened wind gusted by, whipping the burning torches until sparks scattered like so many glowing motes of red. The scene around her acquired a sense of unreality—the blackness, save for the meager illumination at the gravesite; the darkly shrouded forms; the ever-growing mound of earth. Earth that covered her father's body.

Father!

The finality of his death struck her like a blast of frigid wind, tearing the breath away, numbing her heart and soul and body. How could she go on without him? How could any of them?

At last Riderch's barrow was complete, the high dirt mound smoothed, the stones lining its perimeter lain. The mourners wended their way back to the fort and the funeral feast—the ritual meal of roast boar sacrificed to appease the gods of the underworld and assure the free flight of their chieftain's soul. Though she'd no stomach for the meal, Rhianna forced her feet toward the fort and the feasting tables. As Riderch's daughter, to do less would be to shame his memory.

Despite the lilting beauty of Kamber's songs, the mood at the feast was somber and subdued. After making a show of tasting the boar, Rhianna slipped from the fire's light to be alone with her sorrow. The release from the compassionate looks and speculative stares, though, was short-lived.

A hand settled on her shoulder. "Come away, lass. I've a need to speak with you."

Rhianna wheeled about. Cador stared down at her. She sighed and shook her head. "Not now. I've no heart for any more talk."

" 'Tis important. Do you wish to discuss our marriage before everyone?"

Their marriage. Goddess, how could he consider such a thing at a time like this? She glanced around. A few were already beginning to study them with curiosity. Rhianna shook her head. "Nay, Cador. I've no wish to be this eve's entertainment. Lead on."

She followed, away from the brightly lit feasting place to the relative privacy of a cluster of round huts. Gathering her resolve, Rhianna halted and grasped Cador's arm. "I'll tell you now the discussion of our marriage is the last thing I wish this—"

He covered her mouth with his hand. "Hush, lass. 'Tis a difficult time, that I know, but we must move quickly. I ask your leave to arrange our wedding on the morrow."

Mouth agape, Rhianna stared up at him in speechless horror, struggling for words to convey her outrage. They finally came, in short, sputtering bursts. "O-our wedding? A-are you daft, man? My father's barely in the ground and y-you want to wed?"

" 'Twill bring you solace," he smiled smugly down at her, "to have a man's strong arms around you, to busy your mind with the pleasuring of a husband. 'Tis for the best, lass, no matter how unusual the haste."

"Haste?" she asked, barely able to control her impulse to slap the look of arrogant self-confidence off his face. "The only haste you feel is the need for winning the chieftainship! 'Tis your true reason for pushing forward our marriage, considering the decision for our new leader is the day after. Well, I'll not be a part of your ambition. I sever our betrothal vows!"

He stared down at her in disbelief. "Sever our betrothal? Woman, have you taken leave of your senses? I understand your distress at your father's death, but don't allow it to affect your judgment. 'Tis true I long for the chieftainship, but who else is better qualified? Am I not the bravest, the strongest warrior in the clan? Who better than I to lead the Trinovante now that war with Rome is imminent?"

"There are many men better suited to lead than the likes of you! You've never cared for anyone but yourself. Our chieftain must have more than his own interests at heart if he's to govern well." Rhianna vehemently shook her head. "Nay, I'll not wed you just to lend credence to your right to rule."

"And who will have you if not I?" he snarled, jerking her to him. "Sullied by a Roman, sighing after him even when he'd long ago lost interest in you . . ." His grip tightened. " 'Tis only to honor the memory of your father that I even now take pity on you."

She twisted free of his painful grasp. "Then pity me no more. I want naught from you. Do you think I care if none other offers for me? I've lost more love in the past few days than you'll ever know in a lifetime!"

Even as she spoke, the memory of a darkly handsome face, of warm, tender green-gold eyes, flashed before Rhianna. *Marcus* . . . The recollection was more than she could bear. She *had* to get away, now, before she burst into tears.

Run. . . . Run away, a small voice mocked her. It followed Rhianna as she turned and fled to her house, to the curtained haven of her boxbed where she threw herself onto its comforting softness and buried her face in her arms. *Run, fool that you be,* the voice derided in endless repetition until it reverberated through her skull. *Run . . . but carry the shattered dreams, the broken promises wherever you go—and never forget you gave your love to an enemy . . .*

Four days later, all inhabitants of the hill fort crowded the entrance to the main gate, eagerly awaiting the arrival of their new chieftain, back from Queen Boudicca's war council. Rhianna was one of them, standing on tiptoe, craning her neck to catch a glimpse of her brother Cerdic and his men. At first sight of their band of warriors, the Trinovante let out a jubilant cry. Like a troop of victorious soldiers, Cerdic led the parade through the fort until they reached the chieftain's timber-framed house.

He dismounted and held up a hand for silence. "I'll not mince words with you, for I know your question. 'Tis war against Rome. All Iceni and Trinovante chieftains have cast their lots for rebellion. Already, messengers have gone out to the Cantiaci, the Catuvellauni, the Dobunni, Atrebates, and Belgae, inviting them to join with us. In but two days time we march. Unearth the weapons long denied us by Roman law. Sharpen your swords; prime your bows. Prepare yourselves, for the time has come to drive the enemy from our land!"

The crowd dispersed with a wild cheer, each hurrying to his task. Cerdic's glance caught that of his sister. He shot Rhianna a triumphant smile. "Come, little sister, and we'll talk over a cup of beer. Though the past few days have been exhilarating, I fear I must soon find rest or drop where I stand. Gunnella is busy with our son, and I've a need for a woman's gentle voice."

Rhianna followed him into the house. After bringing him water and a cloth to cleanse himself, she sat down beside Cerdic with two cups of dark beer. She handed him one and watched as he thirstily downed its contents. With an affectionate smile, Rhianna handed him her cup.

Pride swelled within her. There had been a great uproar from Cador's band of hotheaded followers when Cerdic's name had first been raised as their next chieftain. The majority of the Trinovante, however, had seemed to view the tall, strapping, golden-haired son of Riderch as a fine warrior and able leader. Despite the heated debate and veiled threats from Cador's men that had spread through the gathering, stirring an unsettling talk of war, Cerdic's more direct lineage had finally prevailed. Her father's misgivings notwithstanding, Cador's influence over their people was, as yet, not quite as pervasive as he'd imagined.

"There's more news to tell than I dared reveal just now," Cerdic began finally, between more temperate sips. "But before I share it with the others, I thought it prudent first to speak with grandfather. 'Tis only kind to tell him, before the rest, of the massacre on Mona."

Rhianna paled. "Massacre? On Mona, the Druid teaching center? Who would do such a thing, and why?"

"The governor-general, Suetonius Paullinus, of course," her brother grimly replied. "He and his legion forded the Menai Straits and murdered every man, woman, and child they found, including our priests. They razed the sacred groves, destroyed the Druidic college, and built a garrison on holy ground."

"Ah, nay!" Rhianna buried her face in her hands. "Not this on top of father's death! 'Twill be too much for grandfather to bear."

"He is Trinovante, as are you, sweet sister. 'Tisn't the time to quail before our fate, but to accept it bravely. 'Tis the only way to drive the conquerors from our land."

The determination in Cerdic's voice gave Rhianna pause. She lifted her eyes to his in wonder. His expression was set in a firm resolve. For a fleeting instant, Rhianna imagined she saw her father. They'd chosen well, she thought, when they'd chosen Riderch's first born. If war there'd be, the Trinovante were once more in capable hands.

War . . . Her chance had finally come. *Honor, glory, service to her people.* At last she'd fulfill her dreams. At last she'd go to battle.

"I want a sword, Cerdic," Rhianna stated firmly. "I want to ride with the warriors against Rome. I, too, want revenge!"

For a moment Cerdic just stared at her. "There's no need to call our women into battle. Even now, we outnumber the Romans ten to one, and once the other tribes join us . . ." At the look in Rhianna's eyes, his voice faded. "I'm not being fair, am I, little sister?"

"Nay, Cerdic, you're not. I've trained just as fiercely as you with sword and spear. My blood boils just as hotly for vengeance. Don't deny me this, I beg of you. It may be the only chance I'll have to taste of glory before I'm forced to settle down to the dull, staid life of a married woman."

Cerdic laughed and took her chin in his hand. "I always told father you'd the heart of a warrior. And now I see you've also a warrior's lust for battle. 'Twill be a bloody fight, though, this first encounter against the Romans, for our cause is lost if we fail at the onset. 'Twas decided at the war council no prisoners will be taken, no Romans spared, save a few for sacrifice to our gods."

Rhianna met his gaze squarely. "I am ready. I ask only for the chance to prove myself."

"Then you have it, little sister." Her brother frowned. "And what of your Roman? What if you met him in battle?"

For a fleeting moment, Rhianna's eyes clouded in pain—and remembrance. Then she turned away. "What was between us is over, done with. My people, my land, are all that matter. I would kill him, Cerdic, cut him down just as surely as I would any Roman who stood in the way of our victory."

"Well, I pray such a fate will never be yours—or his. Until that incident at Boudicca's court, he seemed to me a fair and decent man. As fair and decent as a Roman could be at any rate." Cerdic set down his cup and rose. " 'Tis time I found my rest. The day of march is close at hand."

She lifted her gaze to his. "And where do we march, mighty brother? Where will we first lay sword to Roman flesh?"

His countenance darkened. "Where else? Camulodunum."

It had happened then, Marcus thought grimly. The cataclysm he'd been dreading was at last upon them. Barely five days since Boudicca's disinheritance, the wheels of war had already begun to turn.

With a gesture of despair, he flung the scroll aside on his desk. Its bearer had arrived but a few minutes before the patrol had returned, breathlessly warning of a massing of Britanni troops near Venta Icenorum. There was no doubt of their intentions. The only question remained as to where they'd strike first.

His uncle, with the Fourteenth Gemina, had just recently completed the conquest of Mona. According to the scroll the victory had been theirs, the Druids on the isle almost totally annihilated. The news would travel fast; the Iceni might know of it already. News that would only add fuel to the conflagration of their anger and hunger for revenge.

With a rising swell of presentiment, Marcus recognized Camulodunum's danger. The Ninth Hispana and the nearest legionary fortress at Lindum were over one hundred miles away. Militarily, the city would be ideal for a first battle. Camulodunum was virtually indefensible and would be easily overcome, raising the hopes of the people and drawing other tribes to their cause in the first flush of victory. In the bargain, there would be the satisfaction of razing the Temple of Claudius.

Yes, he'd wager Camulodunum, with its meager garrison, would be the first. But how long did he have, and what was the best approach to ensure the safety of the inhabitants? Londinium was the nearest large town, but it, too, was unfortified and could only bolster his small complement of men with a meager two hundred or so troops. Yet a mass exodus of civilians to Lindum would take them right through Iceni territory. An untenable position at best, with a certainty of quick slaughter.

There was no choice but to attempt the defense of Camulodunum. He'd send out messengers this very day. One to the governor apprising him of the situation; one to Petillius Cerealis, the commander of the Ninth Hispana, requesting immediate reinforcements; and one to Catus Decianus at Londinium, ordering him to send his troops to Camulodunum. Considering the procurator's known distaste for a fight, Marcus knew the man would be more than happy to let another take over the responsibility of putting down a rebellion, a rebellion Decianus had instigated in the first place.

Marcus rose from his desk. There was no time to spare. Letters had to be written, messengers dispatched, and the problem of Camulodunum's non-existent defenses addressed. For a fleeting instant he allowed himself to wonder how Quintus was faring, ensconced at last in his cavalry unit at Lindum. Their visit together—had it been but a few weeks past?—now seemed like a lifetime ago. He prayed he'd live to see his friend again. And Rhianna . . .

Grabbing his helmet from a nearby table, Marcus strode for the door. No time left for fruitless wondering, for nonproductive thoughts, he harshly reminded himself. There was work of immense proportions before him. In but a matter of days, he might well have a battle to the death on his hands.

* * *

The sky was unnaturally bright with Britanni campfires, the flickering light encircling the city as far as the eye could see. Wood smoke hovered on the still, night air, lingering like a pall over the land. The citizenry of Camulodunum had retired early that eve, silent and depressed after viewing Boudicca's army—a mass of wicker chariots, mounted troops, and well-armed infantry. Hopelessly outnumbered, all that was left to the beleaguered city was one last night of futile dreams and tender farewells.

Marcus and Cei made a final tour of the hastily constructed vallation of defensive earthwork, ringed by a wide and deeply dug ditch. Though almost ludicrous in light of the overwhelming numbers facing them, it was all that stood between the city and immediate destruction. As they walked, all was still, the night unnaturally quiet. Like the calm before a storm, Marcus thought sardonically.

"Have you heard of the signs and portents heralding this battle?" Cei asked, trying to make light of the somber mood that had settled over them. "The statue of victory on the provincial altar was said to fall face down as in retreat. Shouts in foreign tongues have been heard in the Senate House, and there've been howling noises in the theater. And I won't even begin to tell you what was seen reflected in the River Tamesis or the things said to have washed up from the sea."

He chuckled. "One only wonders how many of these tales were spread about by the Britanni for the benefit of our more superstitious citizens."

Marcus sighed. "Nonetheless, it won't require the gifts of a priest to foretell the future. The legionnaires that arrived from Londinium early today are some of the most poorly armed soldiers I've ever seen. Even with the repair of that cache of rusty weapons we found and the armament of all able-bodied men, we'll be fortunate to hold out against the first onslaught. Once the earthworks are breached, the temple is the only defensible place."

"You've done all you could, my friend, prepared for every eventuality." Cei grasped Marcus' arm, halting his forward progress. "No one, in the time you had, working with such meager resources, could have done more. None of this is your fault, yet you are forced to bear the brunt of it all."

Marcus shook his head. "Perhaps, but in a day, two at most, it'll not matter whose fault it was. The Iceni will have sealed their fate, the senseless destruction will have been set into motion. The saddest, the most heartrending part is the innocent loss of life that'll ensue—the women, the children, the non-fighting citizens. I'm a soldier. I've faced the possibility of death every day since I first donned this uniform. But you, Ailm . . ." He dragged in a shuddering breath. "Gods, not sweet, gentle Ailm!"

"We both stand to lose the women we love before this is over," Cei murmured. "What of Rhianna? Surely the Trinovante have joined forces with the Iceni. They're allies, are they not? What would you do if you met her in battle?"

"What choice would I have?" Marcus shoved a hand raggedly through his curls. "I could never raise sword to harm her. I love Rhianna and had hoped someday she'd realize she still loved me." He turned, pounding his fists on the top of the earthen battlements. "More than anything, I regret never having the opportunity of seeing her again, of holding her in my arms, of loving her one more time."

"You were wrong to leave her that day, no matter how she railed at you. More than she could have ever said, or even known herself, she needed you. Once again that cool, calm logic betrayed you." Cei sighed and joined his friend at the earthworks. "You cannot be in control of everything at all times, you know."

"Speak to me not of my failures, not now, not tonight of all nights!" Marcus rasped, wheeling to confront his friend. "She needed time, a space to heal, and I gave it to her."

"Nay, you deceive yourself if you think that. You ran from Rhianna and your own emotions," came the unperturbed reply. "I'll not soften the truth, not tonight, not when it may possibly be the last night of our lives. 'Tis the kindest thing I can offer, this final bit of knowledge about yourself. You're a good man, Marcus, the best of friends, but you hold back much of yourself from others. True, Ailm and I, and probably your friend Quintus, have never lacked for your love, but I'd yet to see you give of yourself to a woman until Rhianna. With her, I'd hoped . . ."

"And what more could I have done for her that day?" Marcus demanded harshly, his big body going taut with his frustration. "She told me she hated me so much she'd kill herself if I didn't leave. Would you have had me stay and force her to act on her threat?"

"No matter what Rhianna said, she needed you, deeply, desperately, and you weren't there for her. There are moments in a man's life when 'tis better to admit one's helplessness and confusion, face it squarely rather than run away. Somehow, though, 'tis easier for us to risk pain and the death of our bodies than to open ourselves to the dangers of love." Stirred by memory, Cei chuckled. "I, too, erred greatly with Ailm, almost lost her because of my own fears of commitment. There's no reason why we should both be fools, is there?"

A slight smile tipped the corners of Marcus' mouth. "No, Cei. I only hope I've the sense to benefit from your wisdom, if and ever the time comes again. You've been a dear and true friend. For all my reticence on matters of the heart, I hope you realize that."

"Aye, I know it well. 'Tisn't so hard to die when one dies loved, is it?"

"No, I suppose it isn't." Marcus paused. "Go, return to my quarters. You've a wife who awaits you there. A night like this should be spent in the arms of a lover."

Cei hesitated. "And you? Will you not come back, too?"

An owl hooted far in the distance, the sound sad, haunting. Marcus shook his head. "In time, my friend. In time."

The tall blond Celt nodded, then strode away. As he disappeared into the night's blackness, Marcus turned back to watch the hills and the eerie, flickering light of a thousand campfires.

Was Rhianna indeed out there somewhere? Did she wonder about the morrow or care what would become of him? Gods, Marcus thought in a sudden, bitter surge of frustration, if only they'd had a few more days before all of this had happened, they'd have been wed!

Wed . . . In truth, they'd been wed since that night at his quarters. Had she forgotten their vows so easily or did they mean so little in light of the impending devastation, the long awaited vengeance against Rome? Despair rose from the depths of Marcus' lonely soul. *Ah, Rhianna! To die with you hating me is more than I can bear!*

His eyes strained to pierce the darkness shrouding the hills, to find her in the shapes moving before the blazing fires. *If only I could see you once more, tell you how much I love you!* he called silently out to her. It would be enough to last a lifetime, though that lifetime spanned but another day. Yes, it would be enough, but it was a dream that would never see fruition. Not now. Not ever.

With a determined straightening of his shoulders, Marcus turned from the hill encampments—back to the only reality left him. He was *Praefectus Alae* of Camulodunum. The city was his responsibility. He needed rest to muster all the strength he could for the morrow.

Yes, it was past time to find his rest, to forget, for even a short time, the horrors that awaited. And time, he thought with a small flare of hope, perhaps even, to dream . . .

The morn dawned, gray and cold. After a hurried meal of bread and cheese, Marcus took his place atop the vallation. Even now the Britanni were massing for battle, their overwhelming numbers a disheartening sight. Striding along the rampart, Marcus did his best to encourage the men.

"We've defeated this people before. . . . Forget not your shields when the arrows fly. . . . Thrust and withdraw, thrust and withdraw in close combat. . . . Remember, the Celts are easily provoked and lose all battle strategy when the blood lust is upon them."

Whether the soldiers absorbed some of the confidence of their leader or perhaps were desperate for even the tiniest ray of hope, Marcus left a renewed vigor and determination wherever he went. The effects of his exhortations were soon put to the test.

The harsh blast of the carynx rent the peaceful morning air. Tens of thousands of voices rose in a fiercely exultant battle cry. The rumble of thunder echoed about the hills as the warriors charged the city.

With a crash of wooden shields against bronze, the two forces met at the narrow bridge spanning the ditch. Short swords clashed with the longer swords of the Britanni. In the close combat of the narrow space, the Romans were able to hold their own. As the hours passed, though, the attackers' superior numbers began to tell. There were few to replace even one of the auxiliaries and hundreds for every Britanni who fell.

From his vantage point on the rampart, Marcus saw the inexorable press backward on his troops. Time and again, he called for reinforcements, knowing all the while it would do little more than forestall the inevitable. Soon, he'd have no more men to call.

Marcus looked up at the sun, a hazy orb behind the overcast sky. It was nearly at its zenith. Midday, he thought dazedly, as he blocked yet another javelin thrust with his shield. It was a miracle they'd held this long. Soon, he'd be forced to call for an orderly retreat through the city streets to the temple. Cei was there, left in charge of barricading the building and the safety of the women and children already waiting inside.

If only he and his men could buy a little more time at the vallation, impede the progress of the Britanni through the city, and hold out long enough in the temple . . . The Ninth Hispana was on its way—a messenger from Cerealis had arrived a few hours before the city was surrounded. If they could just—

A loud tumult of voices, of despair mixed with jubilation, rang out. The defenses at the bridge had been breached. Marcus leaped down and ran to the phalanx of densely massed soldiers, shouting loudly to close ranks. Urged on by their leader, the auxiliaries tried mightily to beat back the surging pack of Britanni pouring through the hole, but to no avail. In but a matter of minutes, every man was engaged in individual combat. The opening in the line widened rapidly.

Marcus called for a retreat and the men desperately closed ranks. He leaped to the forefront to control the withdrawal. Sword blows came at him from every direction. Men fell at his side, to be replaced by yet another stalwart troop. Slowly, painfully, they inched their way back through the city.

His sword arm grew numb from the reverberating force of the thrusts he parried. The bronze oval shield began to weigh heavily. Sweat trickled into his eyes, blurring his vision. His muscles ached, burned. His breath came in quick, painful gulps.

Just a little farther, Marcus told himself over and over. Just a few more steps and they'd be there. And, finally, they were. The journey up the temple's broad, white steps was the longest one of Marcus' life. Men fell beside him, before him, staining the snow-white marble crimson.

At last he felt himself pulled inside and the huge bronze doors slammed shut before him. He turned and almost fell into Cei's arms.

"Thank the Good God, Marcus!" his friend exclaimed in joyous relief. "I feared none of you would make it back. You managed to save more men than I dared dream."

"I . . . I'd hoped to buy more time," Marcus gasped between ragged breaths. "I-I fear it may not be enough."

A clattering of swords against the outer doors arose, but the weapons made little impact upon the thick metal. Marcus and Cei exchanged glances. That barrier, at least, would give them a time of respite.

"Come, my friend," Cei said, drawing him back with him. "You look exhausted. Have a cup of wine and something to eat. Ailm will tend to your wounds. 'Tis time to rest and replenish your strength. The battle will resume soon enough."

Marcus glanced down at the numerous cuts and gashes marking the exposed parts of his body. Strange, but he'd not even noticed them as he'd fought. Well, no matter, he thought. Cei had spoken true. It was time to rest—until the Britanni found a way to break through the temple's defenses. He only prayed the Ninth Hispana reached them before they did.

The next night in the declining hours before dawn, Marcus awoke to the acrid smell of smoke. He climbed to his feet, Cei beside him. Stealthily, so as not to disturb the others, they made their way to the huge bronze doors.

Marcus touched it and quickly pulled back. It was hot. He turned to Cei. "They mean to draw us out."

"That or burn us to death," Cei commented wryly. "So kind of them to give us a choice, either fried or smoked."

"Considering the temple's marble walls, it's more likely the smoke will kill us long before the heat. But whatever the way, I prefer neither. My taste is to die fighting."

"No matter the choice, 'twill have to be made before the day's done, my friend. Even now I hear them outside, heaping more brushwood."

"The Ninth Hispana won't make it in time." Marcus searched out his friend's face in the flickering light of the wall torches. "Even at a forced march, they'd not arrive for another day and a half. We'll never last that long."

"Aye, that I know." Cei sighed. " 'Tis the end, then."

"What will you do with Ailm?"

"She'll stand by us until the last. She refused my dagger to open her veins. 'Twas a coward's way out, she said." Cei smiled. "My Ailm, always the fighter. By your leave, I'd like to stay with her until you give the call to attack. Then, I'll join you. Friends should fight and die together, don't you think?"

Marcus clasped Cei by the arm. "I'd consider it an honor. Now, go to your wife. I'll come for you when it's time."

The sun drove away the night before the smoke awakened

the temple's occupants. By mid-morn, the fumes had become so thick that everyone was choking. Marcus knew they'd soon succumb. He also knew that he, as well as his remaining men, preferred a cleaner death. Preparations were made for one last battle.

He and Cei then took their leave of Ailm, sending her to the back of the temple with the rest of the women and children. Massing the auxiliaries behind them, the two friends shoved open the bronze doors. For one final moment, they stared out upon the square fronting the temple—and into the eyes of a thousand Britanni warriors.

Then, with a fierce war cry, the *Praefectus Alae* of Camulodunum signaled his men forward.

Fourteen

Billowing clouds of smoke rose to foul the eastering sun, filling the blood-red sky with sooty flecks of ash. All night the city burned and not until dawn's first light was it finally safe to enter. As Rhianna walked through the devastation that was now Camulodunum, the acrid stench of smoldering shops and houses assailed her. Finally, it was too much and she raised a cloth to cover her nose and mouth.

She gazed about her, astonished at the totality of the destruction. The temple and the last of its defenders had been overrun but a day ago. After another day of rampant looting, the ransacked city had been put to the torch. For one entire day and night Camulodunum had burned, the first revenge upon Rome at last complete. Soon the tribes would march onward, to Londinium and the Procurator, Catus Decianus. All that hampered their departure was the return of the battle party sent out to ambush and, hopefully, annihilate the Ninth Legion.

Rhianna prayed her people's brave spirits and strong arms would prevail against the better-trained and well-disciplined Roman troops. Here, they'd triumphed only by dint of sheer numbers and, even so, the victory had been dearly won. She recalled the long hours she'd fought, hacking away at the Roman soldiers until the Trinovante force had finally broken through at one of the earthworks farther down from the main force battling to breach the bridge. They'd arrived at the temple in pursuit of the retreating Romans, only to have the huge bronze doors slammed in their face.

Cerdic, then, had sent her back to camp, claiming naught more could be done that night. And Rhianna, exhausted, covered with gore and grime, had gone willingly. Though her sword had at last tasted blood in defense of her land and people, surprisingly, she had found little pleasure in the actual act of killing.

Back at camp, Cunagus had asked her to assist him with the wounded. When finally relieved of those duties, Rhianna had fallen into an exhausted slumber, not awakening until midday. The Temple of Claudius had fallen by then, its inhabitants put to the sword and the city set afire.

Rhianna suppressed a small shudder. Once again her glance strayed to the smoldering ruins. Had Marcus made it to the temple or died earlier in defense at the earthworks? One way or another, he was dead. Aye, dead . . . as was their love.

A single tear trickled down her cheek. Was it but two weeks ago she'd lain in his arms, their hearts joined as surely as their bodies? How much had transpired since then, enough to irrevocably separate them forever! But she must not look back, must not question the course her life had taken. She had made a choice, as her father had always said she must.

Rhianna choked back a sob. Marcus was dead, killed by her people, their love, their time together little more than bittersweet memories. Indeed, memories were all that were left of a lost happiness, a burning city.

The recollection of a fiery vision overwhelmed her, of flickering, amber-red flames and the crimson-stained bodies of people scattered upon the temple's white steps. That awful vision of Camulos—why, oh, why had it been granted her? Had she been meant to warn against it and failed in her duty?

Yet what could she have done? Who would have listened? All these years she'd hidden the truth about her Sight, the strange, erratic ability known to none but Cunagus.

The vision of the white boar had visited her time and again as well. She'd had it just last night, waking drenched in sweat, her heart thundering in her chest. Once more the boar had attacked, the faceless man laughing in glee as she fell in bloody agony. The dream had foretold something, warned of a danger. To her, mayhap? But from whom?

She'd denied her Gift for too long now, avoided it when she should have instead been learning how to use it. If she had, mayhap she'd understand the vision of the white boar. Mayhap she could have prevented the destruction of Camulodunum. Mayhap Marcus, though never to be hers, would still live.

Rhianna's knees buckled. She sank into the cinders and charred wood of what was once a humble wattle-and-daub home. The cloth fell, unnoticed, from her mouth. She buried her face in her hands and cried.

" 'Twill do no good, you know. 'Tis better not to look back, to go bravely on, ever forward to meet one's destiny."

Her head jerked up and she glared furiously at the white-robed Druid. "My destiny, Grandfather?" Rhianna motioned about her. "Mayhap the prevention of all this *was* my destiny. I saw the destruction of Camulodunum long before it happened. Saw it in time to put a halt to it if I'd dared."

"But you didn't."

"Nay." She sighed. "I didn't. You know my hatred for this detestable power. I . . . I want no part of it, yet time and again it forces itself on me. I grow weary of fighting it." Entreaty tightened her voice. "Take it from me, I beg you. Surely, after how miserably I've failed in using the Gift this time, I'm no longer worthy."

"Worthy, child?" Cunagus smiled. "Worthiness comes with the Gift's proper use for the good of others, not in any inherent abilities or merit of your own. The choice of who receives the Gift isn't mine to make. The gods alone decide that. You must accept their decision, as you must accept their gift, if you are ever to utilize it properly. 'Tis for the benefit of your people that you were chosen."

His hand settled on her shoulder. Dark old eyes, filled with compassion, peered down at her. "You must accept it, child, or your heart's strife will never cease."

Time flitted by on the delicate wings of a shared pain, a common destiny, a heart-deep understanding, until a flame-eaten timber crashed to the ground. With a start, Rhianna disengaged herself from Cunagus' clasp and climbed to her feet. "Mayhap I must but, for now, 'tis past endurance. Let us speak of it no more."

Cunagus nodded. "I understand, child." He made a motion toward what was left of the city gate. "Come. No purpose is served in remaining here. Come back to camp. 'Tis time to tend the wounded. Let us leave the dead behind and look to the living."

Silently, Rhianna followed him out of Camulodunum. Her gaze lifted to the rising sun, free at last of the dark hindrance of the forested hills. It burst forth in a great flare of gold, blanketing the quiet countryside in burnished splendor.

A new day, she mused. Cunagus was right. Time to get on with life and learn to accept the inevitable. If only she could . . .

Rhianna scanned the other women busily working around her. After organizing the nursing of the wounded, she had set herself to planning the preparations for the evening meal.

Though normally a task Savren assumed as chieftain's wife, since Riderch's death she'd slowly relinquished her authority, slipping away, bit by bit, into a land of unreality. And Gunnella, overwhelmed by *her* role as the new chieftain's wife and mother of a small babe, had all but begged Rhianna to take over in her stead.

A heavy burden, on one hand to fight as a warrior and on the other then to turn to the nursing of the sick and wounded as well as see to the feeding of an entire war camp of Trinovante, but she'd help Cerdic in any way she could. With a small sigh, Rhianna returned to the bread she was kneading. Back and forth she worked the pliant mass, her tumultuous thoughts venting themselves in the hapless dough.

The scent of wood smoke rose from her hands. Her nose wrinkled in distaste. Goddess, would the burning of Camulodunum permeate even this night's meal?

After her early morning journey to the city, she'd labored throughout the day, not daring to allow herself a moment in which to think of Marcus. It didn't matter what had happened to him, Rhianna harshly reminded herself for the hundredth time. 'Twas war and he was the enemy.

Yet still the image of loving green-gold eyes, the memory of strong arms clasping her to a broad, powerful chest, rose to taunt her. She'd thought she'd put their love behind her that day at Venta Icenorum when she'd discovered Marcus' involvement with the provincial procurator. But she couldn't, not anymore. The battle, the horror of the slaughter, the destruction of Camulodunum—*Marcus'* Camulodunum—had ripped open anew her tightly guarded emotions.

Her throat tightened. Her fingers clenched in the bread dough. Was she never to forget him? He was gone, and life must go on. More than ever in this time of war, her people needed her.

Her people . . . A sharp swell of gladness rose in Rhianna. Thank the Goddess she would always have her people.

Leaning back, she brushed a stray wisp of hair aside with a flour-dusted forearm. Someone shouted her name. Rhianna glanced about. It was Emrys.

A slow, affectionate smile curved her mouth. Sweet, exuberant Emrys. Rhianna motioned for him to take a seat at her side. "So, little one," she said, turning her attention back to forming the bread dough into loaves, "what news have you, in your self-appointed role as camp crier, been spreading this day?"

Emrys wiped the smudge of flour off his sister's forehead before replying. "The battle party's advance messenger arrived but ten minutes ago."

When he paused in dramatic expectation, Rhianna impatiently urged him on. "Aye? Aye? Play no games with me, brother. How went the attack?"

"We routed the Ninth Legion!" A broad grin split his face. "The Romans were in such hurry to reach Camulodunum they sent out no advance scouting parties of their own. We caught them in an extended line of march and 'twas a simple matter to cut them into isolated groups. They never had a chance. Only the commander and his cavalry were able to break through and escape back to their fortress."

" 'Tis good news indeed. When will our warriors return?"

He shrugged. "Soon. That's why I sought you out. Cerdic said to hurry with the bread baking. There's to be a great feast this eve to celebrate the victory." Bright blue eyes shone with excitement. "Ah, what a time this has been! The battles, the feasting—do you think Gunnella will make some of her delicious honey cakes?—and, on the morrow, the long-promised sacrifice to our gods. I've not seen such entertainment in many a year!"

Rhianna frowned. "To sacrifice helpless people, enemies or no, isn't my idea of entertainment."

"But 'tis necessary, sister," Emrys protested. "Queen Boudicca promised human sacrifice to our gods if we were victorious. She is honor-bound now to do so. We can't afford to anger the Morrigan or Camulos, not to mention all the others, at a time like this."

Ever so carefully, Rhianna slid the loaves onto a wooden platter and covered them with a light cloth. "Aye, I know, but still I dread the next sunrise. You'll not find me present at the sacrifices, and 'twould be better if you weren't there, either."

She climbed to her feet and, with Emrys' assistance, carried the bread to a warm spot by the ovens to rise. Emrys lingered even when the task was done, etching swirling designs in the dirt with his toe. Rhianna cocked her head in bemusement. "And what else, little brother?" she finally prodded. "Is there yet more to tell?"

"A-aye," he began hesitantly, not quite meeting her gaze. " 'Tis . . . 'tis the prisoners."

"They are grandfather's responsibility. If one of them is ill or has some need—"

"I-I think I saw your tribune among them," her brother blurted.

The blood drained from Rhianna's face. "What? What did you say?"

"I think I saw the Tribune Paullinus among the prisoners."

She stared down at him, her heart thundering suddenly in her chest. "I saw no Roman soldiers brought in as prisoners."

"He must have arrived in the second party, when you were busy tending some of the wounded in the Iceni camp. I didn't see him, either, just heard talk that a few more had been added to the stockade. I only discovered him when I entered there today to deliver news of our victory to the guards." He flung back a shock of hair that had fallen into his eyes. "He was among the prisoners set aside for sacrifice. He suffers sorely from his wounds. Mayhap 'tis a mercy he dies on the morrow—"

Rhianna wheeled about, all thoughts of her brother and bread baking gone. She ran toward the prisoners' stockade, a high, circular fence constructed of sharpened tree trunks shoved into the ground, her mind churning with mixed emotions. Trepidation at confirming Emrys' words battled with a joyous relief that Marcus might still be alive. Ah, to be able to see him again, to touch his dear face, to tell him of her love . . .

She forced her steps to slow. Marcus might not share the same pleasure at their meeting. After the merciless, almost exultant slaughter of his fellow Romans and wanton destruction of his city, mayhap he now hated her. He'd have every right, if her response to him that day at the Iceni court wasn't reason enough. Yet she had to see him. Marcus would die on the morrow.

Rhianna quickened her pace. If she turned from him now, she'd live with the remorse the rest of her days. 'Twas a gift from the Goddess, this precious time left with Marcus. His reaction notwithstanding, she would go to him. She owed him—husband of her heart—at least that much.

The aroma of roasting meat and baking bread wafted to Marcus. He licked his dry, cracked lips, the pang of hunger once more twisting his gut. For the past two days he'd had little more than a bowl of runny gruel and a few cups of water. The tantalizing scents of the evening's meal were almost more than he could bear.

The last meal of his life, and he'd not even partake of it . . .

The thought elicited a brief, sardonic smile. Thank the gods he'd be dead on the morrow. The hunger, the burning thirst, combined with the strength-sapping, agonizing pain of his wounds were inexorably draining him of all will to live. And he'd only to gaze up at the smoke-tainted sky or glance at the other prisoners to wring the last bit of fight from him. He had failed, he who'd been charged with the responsibility for the citizenry of Camulodunum. He, who had never failed at anything in his life, was now bound and awaiting sacrifice like a lamb to the slaughter—vanquished, impotent, disgraced.

I've failed at everything that truly mattered, Marcus thought bitterly. My command, my brilliant career, my relationship with the woman I loved. Yes, even with the woman I loved . . .

With a growl of disgust, Marcus wrenched himself from his self-pity. Regrets were but fruitless pastimes for the weak and hopeless. He'd be neither, he vowed with renewed determination, until he last drew breath.

He turned to the man lying bound at his side, "The Ninth Legion might be our salvation after all, old friend."

Cei raised weary eyes. "How so? Think they'll come back as ghosts to frighten the Britanni away?"

"No," Marcus replied slowly. "I think, instead, there'll be a great feast this eve to celebrate the legion's defeat. And the guards have grown careless of late. If they drink a little too much of their potent beer . . ."

The Celt snorted in derision. "And do you imagine our bonds will magically fall away and that we'll walk from here unnoticed? Your wounds have made you sick in the head, my friend."

Marcus rolled his eyes. "I think nothing will come easily, but tonight's our last chance. If we can but loosen these ropes . . ."

At the entry of a white-robed Druid into the stockade, his voice faded. Though every Britanni tribe had its own holy men, each dressed alike, there was something familiar about this particular one. Marcus scrutinized the Druid closely. Yes, it *was* Rhianna's grandfather, but what was the old priest doing here?

The answer was forthcoming as the Druid opened a box and withdrew ointments and bandaging supplies. For a while, Marcus watched the man's efforts at tending the wounded, then turned away with a disgusted sound. "A waste of time, to my thinking," he growled. "Our injuries won't kill us before dawn, and to give false hope seems a greater cruelty than allowing us to endure the pain of our wounds."

" 'Tis his calling. He is vowed to aid the sick and wounded, no matter who they are."

Marcus looked at Cei. "And vowed to sacrifice us at sunrise, too," he added tautly. "I care not for the Celtic way of looking at things or for their priests who can heal and kill all in the same breath."

"Our religion is a difficult thing to explain, even if we were permitted to delve deeply into it with those outside our faith." Cei smiled. "Suffice it to say not all Druids agree with human sacrifice or engage in the ceremony."

"Well, in our case, it takes only one."

They fell silent for a time as again they watched the Druid work his way around the stockade. At last he reached the spot where Marcus and Cei lay.

Cunagus immediately recognized the tribune. His heart sank. Sweet Goddess, the Roman was still alive. If Rhianna should find out . . .

He expelled a deep breath and squatted beside Marcus. Their gazes locked and, for a long moment, neither spoke.

"Rhianna. I wish to speak with Rhianna," Marcus said, finally breaking the silence.

"Nay, it cannot be." Cunagus turned to the supplies in his box. "Let her go, Roman. Already she thinks you dead. Her wounds have begun to heal; don't tear them open again."

"And what of mine? I'm to die on the morrow. Is it too much to ask to see the woman I love one last time? There are things unspoken that must be said. I've no wish to cause her further pain, but I *need* to speak with her!"

Cunagus saw the entreaty burning in the Roman's eyes. 'Twould be cruel to deny such a request on this last night of his life, yet to do so was the lesser of evils. Rhianna must be protected at all costs. If it required the denial of the Roman's plea, so be it.

He shook his head. "Nay. I say again. It cannot be. I am truly sorry, but—"

"Waste not your sorrow on vermin such as he, old one!"

All eyes riveted on the blond warrior, flanked by two of his men, towering over them. Cador stared down at Marcus, a sneer curling his lip. One hand clasped the hilt of his sword, fingering it as if he itched to draw it.

"Cador, 'tis of no concern what passes between—"

"On the contrary, Holy One," Cador interjected, "everything about this Roman concerns me." He turned back to Marcus. "At last you'll pay for all your meddling in my life and plans. I'd kill you myself, this very moment, if not for the satisfaction 'twill give me watching your slow death on the morrow. What's your pleasure, Roman? Death by burning, drowning, or hanging on one of our sacred oaks?"

"Choose yourself, Trinovante," Marcus snapped. "It matters not to me, save that you remove your vile presence from my sight."

"Dog!" Cador took a threatening step forward. His sword slid from its sheath and slashed down to rest against Marcus' throat. Cei made a warning sound and struggled in his bonds, but Marcus did no more than calmly eye his assailant.

His visual challenge only served to enrage the Trinovante further. "You dare speak to your conqueror in such a manner?" Cador all but choked on his fury. "Sacrificial victim or no, I'll have your head for that!"

"Nay, Cador!" Cunagus rose and, with a sweep of his arm, knocked the younger man's sword aside. " 'Tis exactly what he wants—a clean death to one of slow torment. Go. Begone before you fall prey to his clever game and commit a sacrilege."

The Trinovante warrior hesitated. Then, with one final, murderous glare at Marcus, he resheathed his sword. "Aye, old man. There's truth in your words. Mayhap—"

A commotion at the stockade drew their attention. Rhianna stood there, arguing with a guard. Though her words didn't reach their ears, it was evident by her stance and gestures that she meant to enter the enclosure.

" 'Tis sorry I am, lady," the guard tried patiently to explain, "but no one's permitted—"

"No one?" Rhianna cut him off, her hands fisting on her hips. She made an impassioned gesture toward where Cunagus and Cador stood beside Marcus. "I see Cador, two of his men, and my grandfather within the stockade. Cunagus' presence I can well understand, for he tends the wounded, but the others'?"

She smiled beguilingly. " 'Tis of no import at any rate. I'm here to assist Cunagus with the wounded. Pray, let me pass."

The guard eyed her uncertainly, then finally relented and

waved her in. "Go. 'Twill be your last chance to tend the Romans before the morrow—one way or another."

Rhianna hurried inside, not wishing to allow the guard opportunity for second thought. Keenly aware of their stares, she resolutely strode to the men.

"Woman, why are you here?" Cador immediately stepped forward to keep her from Marcus.

She returned his glare with one of her own. " 'Tis no concern of yours, Cador."

"N-no concern?" Cador's freshened anger made him sputter. "Despite the fact you now gainsay our betrothal, you are still mine. 'Tis of great concern to me when your conduct borders on the shameful."

"Shameful?" Rhianna gave a withering laugh. "Get out of my way. I am *not* yours and I've no further time to waste on the likes of you."

When Cador's fisted hand rose, Cunagus quickly stepped between them. " 'Tis wiser if you left, lad." His penetrating gaze intercepted the dangerous glint in Cador's eyes.

"A-aye," Cador mumbled, a strange lethargy stealing into his expression. Without further protest, he turned and walked away.

Immediately, Cunagus wheeled to confront Rhianna. "And you, lass. 'Tisn't your place to be here, either. I didn't request your services."

"Nay, you didn't but, though I honor you as clan Druid as well as grandfather, 'tis my place to be where I choose." Her glance flitted momentarily to where Marcus lay. "And I choose to be with my husband."

"Husband?" The Druid's voice echoed his surprise. "And how can that be? I wed you not."

"We exchanged vows and, in our hearts, are wed as surely as from any pledges spoken by you."

Cunagus shook his head. "Nay, child. 'Twas never meant, this marriage of yours to the Roman. I cannot allow it."

A soft, sad smile touched Rhianna's lips. "I have caused Marcus enough pain in the past. Though I mean you no disrespect, I won't gainsay my vows to him, no matter what you or anyone wishes. Now, please, Grandfather. Permit me a few moments alone with him."

Cunagus hesitated, then sighed his acquiescence. He motioned her toward Marcus. "I know your determination well enough to realize I'll not sway you in this. 'Twill only serve to deepen your pain, child, but I give you leave. He'll still die on the morrow, marriage vows notwithstanding."

The old Druid walked away, leaving the box of bandages and ointments behind. Rhianna watched until he disappeared from the stockade, then turned to Marcus. Kneeling beside him, her gaze swept his bruised and bloodied form.

He wore no armor and was dressed in only his undertunic, half-torn from his body, and military sandals. The furred expanse of his chest was unscathed, but his arms and legs were marked with wounds. A long slash ran the length of his right arm from shoulder to elbow and a deep, gaping gash traversed the muscled expanse of his left thigh. Both were red and inflamed from two days of neglect. Cei, lying nearby, looked little better, but at least he bore no life-threatening wounds.

A small sound of compassion escaped her. "Ah, Roman, what have we done to you? Your wounds are sorely in need of cleansing or they will surely fester."

Marcus' gaze raked her with a hungry, joyous eagerness. "Let them fester. They'll not kill me before sunrise and I've much to say to you."

"And I, to you." She flushed. "I was unfair to you the last time we met. My confusion . . . and grief . . ."

"I understand now, as I did then." He shifted and winced in pain.

Rhianna noted the action. She rose.

"Wait. Where are you going?"

His sharp concern gave her pause. She smiled. "I cannot bear to look at you in such condition. Spare me but a moment to fetch water. We can as easily talk while I tend you as not."

As she walked away, Marcus turned to Cei. A joyous smile lit his pain-wracked features. "My dearest prayers are answered. I cannot believe my good fortune in finding Rhianna!"

"Aye, my friend. And, from the look she sent your way, I'd wager all is forgiven."

Marcus nodded. "I pray you're right." Cei rolled away, distracting Marcus from his fond scrutiny of Rhianna. "What are you doing?"

Cei smiled. "Merely placing a discreet distance between us. You've much to say to each other. My presence would only hamper the full expression of your feelings."

"Ever the solicitous friend, eh, Cei? Even in your own tormented uncertainty over Ailm?" Marcus sighed and shook his head. "Well, in one form or another, we'll have both soon lost the women we love."

"Aye, but at least Ailm will never suffer the anguish of seeing me die. 'Twon't go so easy for Rhianna."

A freshened pain slashed through Marcus. "I know. But speak no more of that," he said, noting Rhianna's approach. "We may yet escape and, if not, I've a wish to savor this time with her to its fullest."

Rhianna knelt beside him and placed a large bowl of water on the ground. Marcus glanced at it. "It's hard to drink from a bowl of water, and my thirst is more powerful than the pain of my wounds."

Smiling, she produced an earthenware cup. "I expected as much from you." She dipped a cupful of water from the bowl and offered it to him.

He shook his head. "Give it to Cei. I'll drink when he's done."

Rhianna opened her mouth to protest that his need was greater, then, seeing the resolute look in his eyes, silently carried the water to Cei. Supporting Cei's head while he drank, her glance anxiously scanned the stockade. No sign of Ailm. Dread filled her. "Ailm?" she whispered when Cei had finished drinking his fill.

His blue eyes brimmed with emotion. "I . . . I don't know. We left her in the temple with the other women and children. I tried to fight my way back to her when we were overrun, but . . ." Cei looked up. "Surely you must know what became of the women and children. Is Ailm being held prisoner or taken as a battle prize?"

She lowered her head, the tears welling in her eyes. Blessed Goddess, how could she tell him?

"Rhianna?"

His harsh plea wrenched her from her anguished thoughts. She lifted her face, her answer in the twin tracks of moisture trickling down her cheeks.

"D-dead?" The word escaped him in a low croak.

"Aye," she whispered achingly. " 'Twas said our warriors took no prisoners save those in this stockade, and I've seen no others in our camps. Ah, Cei, I'm so sorry. So very, very sorry. Ailm was the sister I never had. To think I'll never—" Her voice broke. The cup fell as she buried her face in her hands.

"Rhianna, Rhianna," Cei murmured. "Weep not for the dead while the living still need you. Marcus awaits and his time is not long. Go to him; comfort him while you may."

"A-aye." She wiped away her tears and picked up the empty cup. "But what comfort can I possibly offer him, knowing the horrors he'll face on the morrow. You're Celt. You know what they do at sacrifice."

"Think not of the morrow. That you love him and he, you, is enough for this moment. An eternity can pass in the hearts of two lovers. And that, I think, is time enough for any."

Gently, she touched his face in parting. " 'Tis true enough. Fare you well, sweet friend."

"Fare you well, Rhianna."

Rising, she made her way back to Marcus. Though out of earshot, he'd watched their actions and guessed what had transpired. Noting the pensive expression lingering on Rhianna's face, he said nothing as she offered him a drink, then proceeded to cleanse his wounds.

He gritted his teeth against the pain her ministrations, however gentle, elicited, forcing himself to bear the agony rather than intrude on her intent care. And Marcus was successful until she reached his thigh. Then, in spite of all his iron control, a sibilant hiss escaped when she began to bathe the gaping wound.

Startled from her anguished thoughts about Ailm, Rhianna looked up. Marcus' drawn face gleamed with sweat. His bound fists clenched tightly at his side. She put down her cloth. "Why didn't you say something? I didn't realize . . ."

"And what could you have done to spare me pain?" A weak smile touched his lips. "You were determined to cleanse my wounds, and every moment spent with you is dear to me. Besides, I didn't wish to intrude on your sorrow."

"Ah, Marcus," she sighed. "I know I'm acting selfishly, but to stand by and watch my friends die is a hard burden to bear. Ailm is already gone, and you and Cei are to face sacrifice on the morrow." Her voice wavered, but she forced herself to go on. "I can do naught for Ailm—'tis too late for her—but I'll not watch you and Cei die. Somehow, some way, I'll devise a scheme to free you. I swear it!"

"No, Rhianna! It's too dangerous for you. I'll not have you risking your life for my sake."

"And what manner of wife would I be, husband dear, if I deserted you now?" She resumed her cleansing of his leg, as much to complete the task as to silence his argument. "You'd do no less for me, so gainsay not my right to do the same." He didn't answer. Rhianna began to apply a soothing ointment.

Marcus expelled a shuddering breath and relaxed his tightly coiled body. "It's good to see you, to be near you again. So much has come between us in but the course of days." He paused until Rhianna glanced up from her task. "I've never stopped loving you, sweet lady, and never will, no matter what happens. Remember that, when I'm no longer there to hold you in my arms."

Soft color bloomed in her fair cheeks. " 'Tis a declaration I'll not forget, my love." Her gaze skittered off the cords binding his hands and feet. "Ah, if only I could feel your arms about me even now! But no matter. Soon enough we'll be together, and no man will separate us again."

Marcus moved closer. "Perhaps, but I've a need to talk of other things. Tell me what has happened with you since we last saw each other. What have you been doing? I've missed you so and envy others the time spent that should have been mine."

She laughed softly. "You talk like some besmitten suitor. I do naught special—" Rhianna sensed a presence behind her. She turned. A guard frowned over them.

"You tarry too long with this prisoner, lady," the man

stated. "Orders are that no one save the guards remain here overlong. Come away."

She looked at Marcus and bit her lip at the sudden anguish that ripped through her. 'Twasn't fair. They'd had so little time.

"I understand you but do your job, warrior." Rhianna lifted her gaze back to the guard. "But I must do mine, too. A few moments more and I'll have his wounds bandaged."

The man nodded. "Then I must wait while you do it. 'Tis as I said before. Orders."

Choking back the angry question of whose orders they were, Rhianna made a hasty wrapping of Marcus' wounds. The last bandage in place, she paused an instant longer, her hand brushing his cheek in silent farewell. It was all Rhianna could do to force herself to rise and turn away.

Only the thought she'd find some way to rescue him, that they'd soon be back together, kept her feet on a steady course out of the stockade. Yet once she'd walked through the gate and heard the wooden barrier latched shut behind her, panic crashed through the last barricade of her heart.

Rhianna's hands clenched into tight fists as she forced herself onward. How indeed shall I free Marcus and Cei? she cried inwardly. I need help, no matter what I do. But who? Who will help me?

Cerdic is clan chieftain now. He will not, cannot risk the welfare of our people for the sake of two prisoners, no matter how important they are to me. And Kenow and Emrys have no influence with the guards. Yet who else dare I ask?

Gradually, a thought insinuated itself into her desperately searching mind. Cunagus . . . Grandfather. He loves me. Surely, in spite of his misgivings, I can convince him to help.

Rhianna's steps quickened, her hopes bolstered by the realization that the old Druid, with his powers and special Sight, might indeed be the perfect accomplice. She broke into a run, her heart pounding with renewed hope. Grandfather, Rhianna thought, is indeed my last—and only—chance.

Huge bonfires lit the Iceni and Trinovante encampments, their blue-streaked flames leaping, laughing at the somber blackness of the night. Around the blazing fires the warriors danced in noisy, drunken revelry or lolled on skins spread on the ground, gnawing hungrily on haunches of roast stag and chunks of fresh-baked bread. The beer, foaming and rich, passed 'round and the shouts and exaggerated boasting increased with each keg broken open.

From the shelter of the forest skirting the edge of the stockade, Rhianna, Kenow, Emrys, and Cunagus watched. Though the guards maintained their post outside the enclosure, their supplies of food and drink were frequently replenished by solicitous friends and relatives. It had been a simple matter to slip a sleeping potion into one of their pitchers of beer. Now, they had only to wait for it to take effect.

The night drew on before the boisterous celebration slackened and the revelers sought out their pallets. Kenow and Emrys, armed with daggers and carrying cloaks to cover Marcus and Cei on the return journey, slipped toward the stockade when the last of the guards succumbed to the drug's soporific effects. Rhianna, along with Cunagus, stayed behind with the horses.

" 'Twill not be long now, Grandfather," Rhianna whispered, fighting back the surge of bitter despair the remembrance of her bargain with the old Druid had once more stirred. "I pray no one sees Kenow or Emrys bringing them out. If they can just make it to the safety of the trees . . ."

" 'Tis the perfect night for such an act, " the old man agreed. "Fortune, for a time more, has smiled on you and your lover." His hand settled on her arm.

She looked over at him. "Aye?"

"I am sorry that it had to come to this."

"Are you, Grandfather?" Try as she might, Rhianna couldn't keep the harshness from her voice. Cunagus had turned a deaf ear to her pleas when she'd first approached him, refusing to help her rescue Marcus. Desperate, Rhianna had offered him anything, if only he would lend his aid.

"Even if 'twas the renunciation of your vows to the Roman?" the Druid had then asked. "Even if 'twas necessary to wed another?"

Renounce Marcus? Wed another? Rhianna had listened in disbelief. How could Cunagus ask such a thing? How could he be so cruel? Yet one look at the steely eyes staring back at her, eyes that were suddenly those of a stranger, told Rhianna everything she needed to know.

"I would have willingly given all for the sake of my people—even my life," she had hoarsely replied. "Cannot they give me just this one thing in return? All I want is Marcus."

"It cannot be, child," her grandfather had said. "You were granted the Gift for a purpose. 'Twas meant to serve your people, not to be squandered in the bed of some Roman." He had paused then. " 'Tis best if the Roman never know the terms of our pact. 'Twill be a greater kindness if he imagines you've turned from him of your own accord than have him bear the endless frustration of a love never meant to be."

She had lowered her head then, hiding eyes suddenly too burdened with pain to bear the sight of the future—a future that now wailed, like the rising storm wind, of heartache and loneliness. Yet what good would it do? She had offered anything to save Marcus' life. And her grandfather had named his purchase price.

"You must trust me in this, child. 'Tis for the best."

His reply, so hauntingly reminiscent of the words her father had once spoken, recalled Rhianna to the present. There was naught left to do. The bargain had been made, the vow given. For the rescue of Marcus, his nursing back to health and eventual freedom, Rhianna had agreed to renounce him and wed Cador.

Four figures, one of them heavily supported by two of the others, came into view. Rhianna hastily choked back the tears. *Ah, Marcus,* she silently cried out to him. *My life, my love. How can you understand or even accept what I cannot, though it be couched in terms of my people's welfare? For me to turn from you now will surely break your heart. Break it as it already has mine.*

She turned and, heavy with a mindless despair, looked once more toward her grandfather. To love Marcus had never been her fate, no matter how hard she'd fought against that knowledge. Better to fight no longer. Better to let their love die at last.

Fifteen

"The bleeding won't stop, Grandfather. What shall we do?" Rhianna asked anxiously four hours later after a stealthy escape and ride deep into the forest to the old Druid's secret dwelling. Marcus' thigh wound had broken open during the arduous journey, and no amount of bandages or pressure would staunch the bleeding.

Cunagus glanced up from stoking the hearth fire. "It must be cauterized." He shoved an iron poker into the flames.

Rhianna shuddered. 'Twas necessary, this burning of flesh if they were to stop the bleeding, but to cause Marcus even more pain . . .

She turned back to him and renewed the bandage yet again, wrapping it tightly in an attempt to staunch the bleeding. Marcus stirred and opened his eyes.

"Rhianna," he mumbled weakly.

"Aye, my love?" Tenderly, her gaze scanned his pallid features, noting the fine sheen of moisture bathing his brow, the dark curls clinging damply to his forehead. Her heart swelled with compassion. Ah, hadn't he suffered enough?

"Wh-where is Cei? He came with us, d-did he not?"

She nodded. "Aye. He's but outside helping put away the horses. Shall I call him to you?"

"No." The negative movement of Marcus' head was barely

perceptible. "He is ever-loyal but, in-in his heart, he yearns to search for Ailm. Give him my leave to do so."

"He'll want to stay until he knows you're out of danger."

Marcus' mouth lifted. "I-I'm in the best of hands. There's no more he can do. Please, go to him. Send him on his way."

Out of the corner of her eye Rhianna saw Cunagus approaching, the fire-hot poker in his hand. She stroked Marcus' cheek. "In a moment, my love. First we must stop your bleeding. Do you know what must be done?"

He looked over at Cunagus. "Yes."

Rhianna's head inclined toward her grandfather and she pitched her voice low. "Could we not first give him some opium to ease his pain? 'Tis such a horrible thing, to burn him so."

"Nay, child. 'Twill take too long. The bleeding must be staunched now, before he loses yet more blood. Go aside, if you lack the stomach for this."

She shook her head fiercely. "Nay. I'll not desert him." She uncovered Marcus' wound, then moved back to take him in her arms and grasp his hands. Crossing them over his chest, Rhianna held them tightly in place. "He is ready. Let us be done with it."

Cunagus lowered the glowing poker to Marcus' leg. Hot metal seared flesh with a sizzling, sickening crackle. Marcus shuddered, his body tightening convulsively but, except for a low hiss of pain, he was silent. The smell of burning flesh filled the air. Rhianna's gorge rose in her throat. With an effort, she forced it back down.

At last the Druid pulled the poker away and leaned close to study the wound. The bleeding had stopped. He grunted his approval. Laying the poker aside, Cunagus rummaged through his medicine box on the rough hewn table.

Ever so slowly, Marcus relaxed in Rhianna's arms. He

groaned. She held him to her, rocking him in her arms, crooning words of comfort. Finally, she gently disengaged herself.

"Wh-where are you going?" he rasped.

"Nowhere, my love. I must tend to your wound, rebandage it. That's all."

She joined Cunagus across the room. He turned to her, a small cup in his hand. "What's that?" She eyed the liquid in the cup suspiciously.

"But a small dose of opium to ease his pain."

Rhianna took the cup. " 'Tis only enough for his pain, is it not? You wouldn't—"

"Nay, child. I do not wish his death. You made your vow. I know you will keep it."

Her gaze locked with his. " 'Twould be kinder, I think, to end both our pain now, spare him the anguish and put an end to mine."

"You cannot escape your destiny. 'Twould be a coward's way, and you are no coward." Cunagus motioned toward Marcus. "Now go. His pain is great; he needs the opium."

She hesitated an instant longer, then returned to Marcus. Kneeling beside him, Rhianna lifted his head and guided the cup to his lips. "Drink."

Marcus opened his eyes. "What is it?"

" 'Tis opium. 'Twill help you rest."

He drained the cup. Rhianna lowered him back to the pallet and finished the task of rebandaging his wound. She pulled the blanket up around him once more.

"You'll go to Cei?" The unexpected question startled her.

"Aye, love," she whispered. "Just as soon as you sleep." Rhianna dampened a cloth and wiped the sweat from his brow. "Now rest. 'Tis the best thing for you. Rest, and grow strong."

His lids, fringed with dense, dark lashes, slowly lowered and, a short time later, Marcus' breathing grew deep and even. Rhianna sighed. Rising, she walked outside to find Cei.

He was talking with Kenow. Seeing her approach, Cei excused himself and strode over. "Marcus?"

She smiled. "The bleeding has stopped. He sleeps." She paused. "He sent me to bid you go and search for Ailm."

"Aye, 'tis like Marcus to worry about me, even in the midst of his own suffering." Naked anguish flared in his eyes. "I-I am afraid, Rhianna. Afraid of what I'll find, yet just as afraid not to go, for then I'll wonder the rest of my days."

Rhianna reached out, lacing his fingers with hers. "I know. Come." She tugged on his hand. " 'Tis nearly dawn. Let me prepare you something to eat. 'Twill be several hours' ride back to Camulodunum and you've not yet broken fast."

Cei followed. An hour later, he was mounted and on his way. Rhianna watched him ride off, dreading what he might find or, worse, not be able to find in the destruction that was now Camulodunum. This war was spiraling rapidly out of control and boded ill for Roman and Celt alike. Aye, no control, no control at all, a tiny voice taunted her—so much like the course her own life had suddenly taken.

Days passed and, after the sacrifices were complete and Boudicca's army moved on to fresh battles, no further news reached them of the war. Hidden in the little glade deep in the forest, isolated from the outside world, Rhianna could almost imagine that the cataclysmic events of the Iceni court and Camulodunum had never happened.

Marcus grew stronger. He chafed at having to stay abed,

but Rhianna feared an early use of the wounded leg would only break it open again. At last Cei returned, exhausted and despairing. He'd found no sign of Ailm. Heartbroken at his haggard, hopeless look, Rhianna tried her best to cheer him.

"Mayhap she still lives. Mayhap she escaped and even now searches for you. 'Tis too soon to give up hope."

Cei shook his head glumly. "Nay, Ailm is dead. Your people took no slaves and I saw for myself what remained of Camulodunum. My wife is gone. I must live with that." He walked out of the hut.

Rhianna made a motion to go after him.

"No." Marcus levered himself up from his pallet. "Let him go. You do him no service by keeping alive hopes that should be buried." He paused. "Yours as well as his."

She sat down beside him on the pallet. "Is it that evident?"

"You loved Ailm. It's understandable." Marcus took her hand. "But you must let go of what's gone, my love. Cei needs us now. And I need you."

Must let go . . . need you . . . Marcus' words echoed in her mind, clawing at her heart with tiny talons of remorse. Goddess, how would she be able to turn from him when the time came—when she couldn't even find the heart to give up Ailm? Rhianna looked down at his beautifully hewn features. Tears filled her eyes.

Marcus, misinterpreting her sorrow, pulled her down to him. "Sweet lady, don't weep." He stroked the shiny mass of her hair that tumbled onto his chest. "This time of horror will soon pass and we'll go on with our life—a life full of love and happiness. My service in the army will end in less than a year. We can journey to Rome then, visit my family."

"Your f-family?" Rhianna sat up, gulping the words through her tears.

"My father, Claudius Suetonius Paullinus, and my sister,

Suetonia, live in a fine house near the Circus Maximus. My father's a lawyer and an important official in the government. Suetonia's engaged to a young nobleman, but until they wed, she still lives at home."

"And your mother."

A dark, angry expression settled over his countenance. "She's dead."

The flat tone warned Rhianna the subject was best dropped. She quickly moved onto other topics. "I . . . I wouldn't mind seeing Rome someday, but I'll never live anywhere but this island. 'Tis the only home I know; 'tis where my people are."

He pulled her back to him. "You're my wife now, Rhianna. Is it so wrong to desire the best life has to offer for you? To want the things only Rome can give? I've a very prominent government position awaiting me once I've completed this last of the *tres militae.* Come back with me to Rome for a time. Give it a chance."

"Nay!" Rhianna jerked away. "Never ask me such a thing again. I cannot, I *will not,* leave my people!" At the remembrance of her vow to Cunagus, tears sprang anew to her eyes. That vow notwithstanding, there seemed a chasm of hopes, of personal expectations widening between them at every turn.

Marcus took her hand, eyeing her with growing concern. "Come, Rhianna. Come back to me. These things aren't indisputable. I love you. In time, we'll work it all out."

Rhianna swiped her tears away and returned to him, creeping into arms that, for a time more, held the world and all she ever cared to know of it. But just for a time more . . .

And then what? Outside their insular world here in the forest, Roman and Celt battled, the outcome surely of shattering consequence to the losing side. Soon that, too, must be faced. So many changes, she thought, and the hardest of all was a vow given to a Druid . . .

Late one afternoon, scarcely two weeks after Marcus and Cei's rescue, a bedraggled group of people came stumbling through the forest toward Cunagus' hut. Rhianna, outside washing clothes in a small barrel, was the first to see them.

"Cerdic! Emrys! Mother!" She stood, wiped her wet hands on her gown, then ran to them. "Thank the Goddess you're safe! What news have you of the rebellion? How goes it with Queen Boudicca?"

Cerdic and Savren exchanged glances.

"The rebellion is no more," her older brother began brokenly. "After great victories at Londinium and Verulamium, we met the governor-general and his legions near the River Anker. He had gained the tactical position before our army arrived. Though we outnumbered them, after a long day's battle he routed us. Our people are scattered and those I've managed to find I've sent back to the hill fort to await us."

"Boudicca?" Rhianna whispered, horror filling her. "How does she fare?"

"The queen escaped, but even she cannot evade the Romans for long. We have lost, sister, and now 'twill go hard—very hard—for us."

"Nay!" Rhianna grabbed her brother's arm. "Surely the governor will be merciful, Cerdic, once he understands what drove us to such measures."

"Do you think so, daughter?" Savren cut in bitterly, her voice shrill and unsteady. "We already have had a taste of his 'mercy' at Anker. Our supply wagons, laden with women and children watching the battle, were in our rear. When our warriors were forced to retreat, the Romans drove them back into the wagons. The Red Crests spared no one in their heartless slaughter, butchering women, children, even the baggage animals in their relentless pursuit."

She gestured about her. "Do you see us, daughter? We are all who are left of your family. All . . . all . . ." Her strident voice faded into low, gut-wracking sobs and, if not for Cerdic's arms about her, she would have slipped to the ground.

Rhianna went waxen. Her grip on her brother's arm tightened. Anxiously, her gaze locked with his. "Kenow? Gunnella? D-Dagolit?"

Agony burned in Cerdic's eyes. Agony . . . and the flickering image of something huge and white, bearing down on her. With a sickening rush, the Gift descended.

A vision of the white boar, tusks gleaming, flooded Rhianna. A loud roaring filled her ears. Her heart pounded. Her breath came in ragged gulps, but there seemed no way to free herself from the hated, horrible vision.

Instead, she was forced to watch as the beast attacked not just her this time, but plowed into a mass of people, slicing through them without mercy, bringing them all down one by one as he charged, then turned and charged over and over again.

Sudden understanding swept through her. Death, destruction—all had followed on the heels of that day of the white boar and her first meeting with Marcus. Was that what the vision had meant to warn her of all along? The terrible danger Marcus presented not just to her, but to her people? And, if she didn't turn from him, resist his appeal, he would eventually destroy them all?

But none of this destruction was Marcus' fault, a tiny voice within Rhianna cried out in his defense. He had tried always to be a voice of reason, a man of fairness and honor in a world gone insane. Yet still the fact could no longer be denied that every time she attempted to turn to him and from her people, an even greater tragedy occurred. Did she dare renounce her true destiny again?

"N-nay. Goddess, nay!"

Her scream tore through the air, its piercing cry carrying to the hut where Marcus lay. He jerked upright, grabbing for his gnarled walking stick. An instant later, he was at the door. "Rhianna!"

At the sound of her name, she wheeled about. Tears glistened on her pallid face. She stared blankly in his direction. He struggled toward her, limping painfully even with the cane's support. "Rhianna, what is it?"

"Nay, not him!" Savren shrieked. "I cannot bear it. Not a Roman, not now. We are doomed! Blessed Goddess, we are dead!"

Marcus spared not a glance at the hysterical woman, his only concern Rhianna. As he moved forward he also noted, with little regard, Cunagus stride out from the trees with Cei. Onward he staggered until his free hand reached out to pull Rhianna to him.

She jerked away with a shudder. "Nay, 'tis over, Marcus. 'Twas never meant to be. . . . I see it now, now when 'tis too late . . . too late to help anyone." She lifted her gaze to his. "We must part. Go back to your own kind, as I must to mine."

"No!" Marcus gripped his walking stick to steady the dizzying sensations suddenly engulfing him. "You vowed to be mine. Whatever it is, we can see it through together. Just give us a chance. But you must choose, Rhianna. Choose to be my wife; stand by my side."

She shook her head. "I gave what wasn't mine to give," Rhianna whispered. "I-I am sorry. I must choose my people."

He stared back at her, stunned. Though he heard the words,

the acceptance wouldn't come. "You don't mean that." He ground out the words, his voice raw, ragged. "You're just overwrought." Marcus glanced around him. "What have they told you to make you turn against me? Gods, Rhianna, at least give me a chance to defend myself. Tell me what's wrong!"

Cunagus stepped up to Marcus and Rhianna. " 'Tis naught you have personally done, Roman. 'Tis the vagaries of Fate that you and my granddaughter were never meant to join. Once before I asked you to let her go before you tore open her heart anew. Now, you see before you the fruits of your selfishness. Now, I ask you, no more."

The Druid turned and, wrapping an arm about Rhianna's shoulders, began to lead her away.

"No!" Marcus moved to block the old man's path. "I won't let you take her from me!"

Cerdic strode over, his sword drawn. "Stand aside, Roman!"

Marcus wheeled around. "Heed me well, Trinovante. No one, *no one,* keeps me from Rhianna. We are vowed to each other. I'll not let her go!"

"And I, as clan chieftain, am vowed to protect her as my own." Cerdic motioned with his sword. "Roman that you be, I've no wish to kill you. In the past you've treated us with honor and kindness. But if you don't step away from my sister in peace, I swear I'll strike you dead."

Cei quickly hurried to Marcus' side. "Come away, my friend." He grabbed Marcus' arm. "You're no match for the Trinovante, unarmed and weak as you are. Let Rhianna go with them. Time enough to seek her later."

Marcus fiercely shook his head. He sensed he'd lose Rhianna forever if he let her leave now. "No. I'll not let her go. If you're friend to me, stand by me now. Help me!"

The Celt inhaled a sharp, frustrated breath. Then, in a lightning quick move, he struck Marcus in the jaw.

Multi-hued lights sparkled before Marcus' eyes. Pain reverberated through his skull. His head snapped back and he fell.

"R-Rhianna . . ." Helpless rage surged through him as reality hit full-force. He'd been betrayed, not only by Cei, but Rhianna. Curse her, curse the people who had taken her from him!

A hand—*his* hand, yet strangely disembodied—floated before him, reaching out toward Rhianna. Then everything went black.

Reprisals, under direct order of the governor, followed swiftly on the heels of the Battle of Anker. All rebels—even those who, by their lack of active support of the Roman cause, were considered indifferent—were endlessly harried and either executed or sold into slavery. Rumors abounded. As the legions made their inexorable sweep of the land south and eastward from the last battle site, fear and panic spread like wildfire.

The Eve of Samain, the feast marking the beginning of the Celtic New Year, ushered in the Roman month of Novembris. Its dark significance, laden with the forces of magic, faeries, and monsters, only served to stir the cauldron of rising terror. Cerdic, however, knowing the people's need for the comfort of old traditions to cling to in this time of uncertainty and strife, insisted the festival customs be honored.

The death of summer and birth of the winter season were heralded with all the pomp and solemnity of other years. Cattle were brought in from the fields to the safety and shelter of the hill fort's cow houses and cattle sheds. Excess beasts that grain stores weren't adequate to feed were slaughtered and salted down.

Led by the Druids, the Trinovante lit bonfires and marched from house to house soliciting contributions of coin and food. In turn, these offerings were set out to propitiate the spirits of the dead in the hopes of renewing earthly prosperity and tribal success and to ensure the germination of good fortune for the ensuing spring and summer.

Watching the beloved ceremonies of her growing years, Rhianna felt as if she stood on the crumbling precipice of her life. Any day now the Romans would reach the hill fort and the Trinovante lands it protected. What would Cerdic do then?

She glanced at him. Tall, strong, and handsome, her oldest brother, in spite of the brevity of his six and twenty years, bore the burden of chieftain well. To the casual observer, at least, the precarious state of the times seemed of little concern, as Cerdic threw back a tawny head and laughed at some comment of one of his sword brothers.

Yet Rhianna knew what lay beneath his calm, sure demeanor. In the aftermath of Gunnella's and Dagolit's deaths, Cerdic had turned to her in his grief. The bonds of brother and sister, already powerful, were forged yet stronger in the inferno of their mutual pain. In that sharing of hearts she'd learned of the true gravity of the current problems, the now-dire responsibilities of his position.

Noting Cador and his group of followers conspiratorially gathered at one end of the feasting tables, Rhianna realized Cerdic had much to concern him of late. She prayed he'd be given the chance to demonstrate the courage and sound judgment she knew he possessed. Yet barely weeks after they'd returned to the hill fort, Cador was once more maneuvering for power within the clan.

Playing on the younger men's desire for revenge, fanned to a fever pitch once more by the news of Boudicca's suicide by poison, Cador strove constantly to portray Cerdic's prudent restraint as bordering on cowardice. Fear of the unknown, combined with the impulsive, highly emotional Celtic nature, proved fertile ground for Cador's seeds of discontent. If only they'd a little more time before the Romans arrived, Rhianna thought in rising despair. If only the Romans were led by a man who could be reasoned with, one with compassion, like . . . Marcus.

Yet since that day she'd left him in the forest, still unconscious from Cei's blow, she'd no news of him. He knew where to find her, but never sought her out.

She sighed. 'Twas for the best. What could she say to explain her desertion, her refusal to remain his wife? Though, for the time being, she still chose not to approach Cador and beg him reconsider her as his betrothed, she knew the bonds between her and Marcus were irrevocably severed. His rescue that night in the war camp had sealed her vow. Soon, though she fought against it with all her heart, she'd have to relent and wed Cador.

But not now, not while he so openly opposed her brother. To wed Cador now would be to undermine everything Cerdic was so painstakingly trying to rebuild. Even Cunagus couldn't justify such an act. At least for a time, Rhianna thought as she turned from the feast and made her lonely way back to her house, she was free. Free to dream, to pretend she was no man's woman, save that of a dark-haired Roman named Marcus.

A harsh cry from the fort's lookout tower woke them the next morning. Cerdic, sword in hand, his heavy cloak flowing behind him, was out the door before Rhianna could barely leave her boxbed. She turned to Emrys, who was tugging a woolen tunic over his head.

"What's about, little brother?"

"The guards sighted a large troop of Romans headed this way. I fear our turn has come."

Rhianna grabbed her own cloak and clasped it shut over her right shoulder. "Then let us show them how we defend our home!"

She grabbed a sword and ran from the timbered house, heading across the fort to the main gate. Quickly climbing the stairs, Rhianna joined her brother.

Cerdic glanced down at her, his grim countenance relaxing for a moment into a smile. "It seems, little sister, we've some uninvited guests. Guests to whom I am loath to offer Trinovante hospitality." He gestured down at the hundreds of Red Crests amassed before the walls.

Rhianna's gaze followed the sweep of his hand. Lined in orderly rows, the legionnaires, well-armed with spears, swords, and shields, presented a formidable appearance. Goddess, she thought in growing horror, they mean to attack us!

Her brother leaned forward. "Who is your leader? Let him step forward so I may speak with him."

"I am he!"

A tall Roman rode up on a prancing black horse. Rhianna inhaled a ragged breath. Quintus!

"And what brings you to the Trinovante, Tribune?" Cerdic coolly demanded.

"Orders of the governor, Gaius Suetonius Paullinus." Quintus paused. "I've a wish to speak with you, Chieftain. Have I your permission to enter?"

Cerdic nodded. "Aye, but you and only you. Move your

troops down to the bottom of the hill. I promise no harm will befall you within my fort."

Quintus turned and gave a curt order. The legionnaires immediately marched down the hill. He stared up at Cerdic. "I but await your convenience."

A small hand settled on Cerdic's arm.

"Aye, sister?"

"Let me accompany you. I know the tribune. He is Marcus' friend. Mayhap I can be of assistance."

Her brother eyed her consideringly. "Come. 'Tis past time I stopped protecting you from life. You're a woman now, though it seems but yesterday I tugged at your braids and hid your dolls. I'd be proud to accept your assistance."

She shot him a loving smile. Together, they walked down the stairs and over to the main gate. Cerdic gave the command. The gate swung open to allow Quintus to ride through.

He swung down from his horse and, with red cloak swirling, strode over to Cerdic. His glance swept Rhianna and he bowed. "Lady. You're even lovelier than I remembered, if that is possible."

Rhianna nodded curtly in acknowledgment, her mouth grim.

Quintus turned back to Cerdic. "Is there someplace we can speak in private?"

Cerdic motioned toward a small guard hut. "Follow me, Tribune."

Once inside, Quintus removed his helmet and tucked it under his arm. "I'll not mince words, Chieftain. As part of the governor's resumption of provincial control, he demands all tribal chieftains implicated in the revolt surrender and peacefully submit to imprisonment. I am ordered herewith to take you into custody."

"And if I refuse?"

"Your fort will be burned to the ground and all your people enslaved."

"Nay!" Rhianna cried. "You cannot take our chieftain. Who will guide us, protect us?"

Quintus impaled her with a silver stare. "The governor's thoughts exactly. I am sorry, lady, but those are my orders."

Rhianna turned to her brother. Rising panic widened her eyes. "Tell him to leave, Cerdic. Tell him we're not afraid to fight and die rather than surrender our honor."

Cerdic shook his head. "Nay, little sister. You know as well as I 'tis a chieftain's responsibility to lay down his life for the clan. 'Tis a small price indeed, if 'twill buy the lives of our people."

"Nay. Ah, nay, Cerdic," Rhianna sobbed, the tears at last breaching the barrier of her resolve. " 'Tisn't fair! First Father is lost to us, then so many of our people in the Rebellion. Must we now lose you as well? What is left to us if you leave? How will we go on?"

Powerful arms gathered her to a broad, hard chest. "Hush, little sister," her brother crooned. "You must be strong, not for you, nor me, but for our clan. You and Emrys are the last of our father's blood, and Emrys is still too young. The people will look to you when I am gone. For their sake, you must be brave and sure. 'Tis all that's left them in times such as these. Promise you'll weep no more, that you'll do this for me."

She gazed up into eyes of deep, aquamarine blue. "Aye, that I'll do, though it near to breaks my heart." Rhianna disengaged herself from her brother's clasp and wiped away her tears. She turned to face Quintus. "And you. You call yourself Marcus' friend, yet you come here to carry out such orders. You are a coward, as is the man who gave you such a mission."

Quintus' jaw tightened. "Then call Marcus coward. As the new commander of the legionary fort at Caesaromagnus, he gave the order that sent me here."

"Marcus?" A suffocating sensation swelled in her chest. Goddess, not Marcus. Not Marcus.

And why not Marcus, she asked herself bitterly. In the end, was he not a Roman? From deep within, Rhianna summoned forth the strength to go on. She swallowed hard, lifted her chin, and boldly met his gaze.

"Then so be it. I call that tribune coward as well. All of you would rather blindly obey an order, no matter how much pain it causes, than follow your heart and brave the awful wrath of Rome." She turned back to Cerdic. "Fare you well, dear brother. I'll keep our people safe until your return."

Cerdic bent to kiss her forehead. "Until my return." His lips lingered a moment more, then he straightened. His eyes met those of Quintus. "Let us leave now, before my people have time to react. I'll tell them I go but to have a meeting with the Tribune Paullinus and that Rhianna stands in my stead until my return. They know him and will think 'tis but a simple matter."

Quintus bowed. "As you wish."

The two men turned and walked out of the hut, Rhianna following. No one questioned them as they strode toward the gate. No one protested when Cerdic called for his horse. He made the announcement of his departure, of Rhianna's assumption of temporary chieftainship in his absence, and then mounted. For one last, bittersweet moment Cerdic, Chieftain of the Clan Trinovante, gazed down at his sister, his eloquent eyes saying what lips dared not utter.

As they stood there, the sun broke through the clouds. Gold-fire, in a blinding flash of light, glinted off the chieftain's torc about Cerdic's neck. Then the huge oaken gates swung open. In a flurry of dust and flying hooves, brother and sister parted.

Sixteen

Rhianna stared down from the ramparts, her brows knit in concern. So, she thought, this was what had been so important to call her from a meeting with the clan elders. Below her at the main gate, Quintus and his troops stood once more. What did they want now?

Anxiety rose within her. Barely a week had passed since her brother's departure. Hadn't Cerdic's sacrifice been enough?

"Cerdic was a fool to imagine his noble gesture would placate the Romans," Cador muttered from beside her. "Even so, 'twas better he went with them that day. He was weak and misguided. What's needed now, more than ever, is a strong, decisive leader."

She turned to him. "Like you, mayhap, Cador?"

"Aye, sweet lass." He smiled smugly. "We can tarry yet awhile longer for your brother's return, but a chieftain's council must soon be called. You know that as well as I. And, though you and Emrys are the last of Riderch's line, who would dare choose a lad or lass over me?"

"There's still Idris."

Cador laughed. "That weak, strutting peacock? We're at war, lass, whether we bear sword and shield or no. The Trinovante need a warrior, tried and true in battle, with the strength of character to mold the wills of other warriors to his way. I'd wager in times such as these 'twill take more than proper lineage to do that. Do you think Idris is the stuff of chieftains?"

"Nay." Rhianna turned her gaze back to the legionnaires massed before the gate. "But neither are you. We can only hope Cerdic will yet return and the terrible choice of our next chieftain will never be forced upon us. In the meanwhile, I, at his request, stand in his stead to protect his rights and position as chieftain. And I have more pressing matters than you to deal with."

She made a dismissing motion with her hand. "By your leave, Cador. There are Romans awaiting me."

He glared down at her, his inner battle with his rage contorting the handsome planes of his face. "You'll soon regret those haughty words. The time fast approaches when you shall, as will the entire clan, bow to my control. On that day you'll rue your shameful treatment of me, and rue it well."

As he stalked away, foreboding swelled within Rhianna. She forced herself back to the more immediate problem at hand. Leaning over the wall, she stared down at Quintus. "So, Roman. Have you brought us news of our chieftain or is your visit one of more sinister intent?"

Quintus squinted up at her in the glare of an overcast, rain-swollen sky. "I wish a meeting with your new leader, whoever that may be. My message is not for shouting from horseback."

"Then enter as before," Rhianna cried. She hurried down the stairs, meeting him inside the entrance.

He dismounted and strode over to her, wrenching off his helmet as he did. "And your leader?" he demanded, halting before her. "My time is short and the task distasteful. Most unfortunately, it cannot be spent in conversation with you no matter how much I'd prefer such a pleasant interlude."

Rhianna regarded him impassively. "Until my brother's release, *I* am the leader. Follow me to the guard hut."

A bemused smile on his face, Quintus shrugged and fell into step beside her.

She confronted him as soon as they entered the hut. "What is it now, Roman? If you've not come to tell me of Cerdic, there's naught for us to speak about."

"Lady, you forget yourself." Quintus frowned down at her. "Rome is once more in command here. You court great danger in your arrogant reception of its representatives. Even Marcus, for all his kindness to your people, never stepped beyond what was politically and militarily permissible. He was no fool. I suggest that you not be, either."

A flush warmed Rhianna's cheeks. Quintus was right, no matter how she hated to admit it. "My brother then, my lord. What can you tell me of him?"

The tall Roman sighed and shook his head. "He was sent away. That's all I know. I am sorry."

"And who would know more?"

"You know the answer as well as I."

She wheeled about to hide the tears. Marcus. Marcus had sent Cerdic away. Did he hate her so fiercely that he'd seek to hurt her through Cerdic? What manner of man had Marcus become since they'd last parted?

Rhianna turned back to Quintus. It mattered not what Marcus thought or did anymore. She had put him behind her. Her people were all that mattered now. "If you came not to tell me of my brother," Rhianna said, lifting her gaze to lock with his quicksilver stare, "you've yet to reveal the true purpose of your visit. What is it, Tribune Marcellus?"

Quintus exhaled a deep breath. "Your food stores. I am ordered to confiscate all grain and livestock."

The color drained from Rhianna's face. "You . . . you'd

take our food? Now, with winter fast approaching and no means to procure more? If you wish for our death, why not kill us now? The end result's the same."

"It's not my wish, lady," Quintus growled. An uncomfortable expression stole across his face. "I only follow orders."

"Whose orders?" she cried, her hands fisting at her sides. She took a step toward him. "Marcus'?"

He vehemently shook his head. "No, not Marcus'. He'd never request such a thing and you know it. The governor ordered it. The punishment is to be carried out against all tribes that rose in rebellion, not just yours. Marcus, whether it is wise or no, will permit you to hold back one month's supply of food."

"And how will that help, save to prolong our misery? There's four months of winter still before us. What will we do then, when all the food is gone?"

"A month will buy you time to search out game, roots, other foodstuffs." Quintus shook his head. "Ask me not what to do. I've no stomach for this any more than Marcus."

"Yet you obey him without question. Does he obey the governor as blindly?" She made a sudden decision. "Mayhap 'tis time to find out."

Quintus' eyes narrowed. "What do you plan, lady?"

"Plan?" Rhianna gave a strident laugh. "Why, travel to Caesaromagnus and talk to Marcus, of course. What other choice is there? 'Tis our only hope, it seems, in a world suddenly bereft of hope."

"I don't recommend that." Quintus' glance skittered away.

"Oh, and why not? What have I to lose?"

"He will not see you." Gray eyes turned back to capture hers. "You have hurt him deeply; he is angry. I cannot swear to what he might do if he saw you again."

"And I ask again, Quintus. What have I to lose that I didn't forfeit the day I last left him? I've lost Marcus, that I well know. Naught else matters to me now, save securing the welfare of my people." Her eyes shut briefly in anguish before opening once more to meet his. "I cannot stand idly by and watch them die if some way of helping them remains."

He grasped her by the shoulders. "I understand, lady, but still I fear for you. Your loss festers within Marcus, gnawing at his very soul. He's not the same man you knew. I don't know how he'd treat you if you forced your way into his presence. I don't want to be responsible—"

" 'Tis *my* doing, *my* responsibility." She gazed up at him. "Will you take me to him?"

A sudden realization flared in his eyes. "You love him still, don't you?"

Rhianna glanced down, not quite able to face him. "Aye," she whispered finally, "but it changes naught. Let us speak no more of it." She looked up. "Take me to him. Please, Quintus."

The Roman released her and stepped back, a puzzled look in his eyes, a wondering smile on his lips. "You're both the greatest of fools, but I'll not come between you and whatever fate has in store for the two of you. Let us depart. The day draws on and the journey's long. Let us go to Marcus."

Through the fog and chilling drizzle, the timbered parapets of Caesaromagnus came into view. A brisk wind blew, adding to the general misery of the waning day.

Rhianna shivered, the bone-numbing damp seeping through her heavy cloak. She'd never been in a legionary fortress, and this one was larger and far more imposing than the small garrison at Camulodunum. Though she yearned for the promise of warmth and shelter its dark expanse was sure to offer, Rhianna wondered if any welcome truly awaited her.

The thought of meeting Marcus filled her with conflicting emotions. She had missed him so. Though she no longer had the right to foster such feelings, time hadn't dulled the love or aching need for him. And it never would, Rhianna realized with a sudden, piercing clarity. Their hearts were eternally bound even if their bodies would never be again.

Yet for all her eagerness to see him, for all the urgency to resolve the impending confiscation of the Trinovantes' food, Rhianna also wondered—and worried—if going to Marcus now wasn't once more putting her people in jeopardy. Her vision that day in the forest, when she'd finally turned from Marcus, had seemed so potent, so vivid, so undeniably clear. 'Twas Marcus who was and always would be the danger—not just to her peace of heart, but to the continuing welfare of her people.

Yet there seemed few other options, and confronting the man who must carry out the governor's orders—a man who she knew was capable of reason and compassion—seemed a far more prudent act then going to the governor himself. He, Rhianna thought with a swell of bitterness as they neared the main gate, when it came to the Britanni, was incapable of either reason *or* compassion.

A sentry halted the troop. Quintus rode forward to identify himself. The soldier saluted and waved them through. Down the long street running the length of the fort they rode, Rhianna's head swiveling in fascination.

'Twas true, what they said about the Roman Army's famed orderliness, even to the layout of their forts. The main street was intersected at right angles by two other avenues and, between the sections formed by the streets, various leather tents were laid out in precise military fashion. Ahead, in the middle of the fort, sat a large, imposing tent surrounded by several smaller tents.

Quintus caught the direction of Rhianna's gaze. "That's the *Praetorium.* The commander's tent is always placed there."

They halted before it. Quintus dispersed his troops. That task complete, he swung down and moved to Rhianna's side. His clear gray gaze sought out hers. "Though I hate to ask you to wait out in this wind and damp, it would be better if I talked to Marcus first."

Rhianna smiled wanly. "I understand. I'll await you here."

He helped her down from her horse. Then, raising the flap lowered against the chill day, Quintus disappeared inside the tent.

Marcus was seated at his campaign desk, deeply immersed in the study of a large map. At the biting blast of air accompanying Quintus' arrival, he glanced up. Despite the day's end, he was still dressed in full gear, from his corselet and woolen tunic down to his heavy military sandals.

When he saw his friend, his mouth twisted in a grim smile. "Back so soon? I'd envisioned a little more difficulty appropriating the Trinovante food stores."

Quintus girded himself for the storm to come. "There was a change of plans. Instead of the Trinovante food, I brought a Trinovante."

Green-gold eyes narrowed. "Oh, did you?"

Curse him! Quintus thought. He's not going to make this easy for any of us. "Rhianna's here."

Fury flared in Marcus's eyes, darkening them to glinting shards of jade. His jaw tightened, his scar flaming crimson. *"You brought her here?* After all that's happened between us, you *dared* bring her here?"

He rose from his desk and strode to the serving table. With

tense, jerky movements, Marcus poured himself a goblet of wine and downed its contents. "Have a care, my friend," he growled from over his shoulder. "You overstep yourself this day. First, you disobey a direct order to confiscate the Trinovante stores. Then you presume to bring back a woman I've no desire ever to see again."

"You know why I brought her."

Marcus wheeled around. His jaw muscles jumped in enraged spasms. "I warn you, Quintus. Stay out of this. The wench has played my heart false one time too many. Take her away; take her anywhere, but I *will not* see her!"

"And will you turn away an official Trinovantian representative? Rhianna also comes here on behalf of her people. You owe her an audience for that, if for nothing else."

"Do I now?" A bitter smile curved Marcus' lips. "Then send her in. Mark my words, though. You'll both rue this day. No one manipulates me, Quintus. No one!"

Quintus turned and departed the tent, an uneasy sense of foreboding settling over him. Gods, what did Marcus have in store for Rhianna? Perhaps it would be better to urge her to leave without seeing him. Somehow, though, he doubted she'd turn from her duty any more than Marcus would. Yet that look just now on his friend's face . . .

As he stepped outside, Rhianna ran over to him. The drizzle had intensified to a steady downpour. She was soaked to the skin. Though he knew she must be nearly numb from the cold and damp, her look of eagerness belied her apparent discomfort.

"Marcus. Will he see me?"

Quintus nodded. "Yes, he'll see you, but I'd advise against it. He's in a foul mood, Rhianna, and the news of your arrival did little to sweeten it. You may well harm your people's cause by going in there, not to mention what he might do to you."

Her chin lifted. "My people will starve if I don't talk with Marcus, and they matter more than silly concerns for my personal safety. Besides . . ." She sighed, her defiance melting in the face of her sudden surge of pain. ". . . what can he do to me that I've not already done to myself? Can his hatred be any greater than my own regret and self-loathing?"

Quintus shrugged. "Perhaps not but, until now, you've never confronted his pain. He's hurting, Rhianna, like a wounded animal. And wounded animals can be very dangerous."

" 'Tis long past time for fear," Rhianna said with fierce resolve. " 'Tis too late for regrets, though still I fight against them. And what I've done cannot be called back, though I'd give my life for it to be any other way." Gathering her cloak about her, Rhianna looked pointedly at the tent flap. Quintus eyed her for a moment more, then raised the covering and, with a gallant sweep of his hand, waved her in. She ducked her head and strode into the warm, brightly lit interior.

Marcus, his eyes narrowed to predatory slits, watched her approach from his casual slouch in a chair near a serving table. In one hand he clasped a goblet.

Rhianna drew up before him. He sat there, the man she loved, and, for an instant, she couldn't control the hunger that swelled within her.

He reclined in his chair, his long, heavily muscled legs stretched out before him. Powerful and iron-thewed, she could barely repress the urge to run her hands up them, once more to feel the play of sinew and muscle beneath her fingers. Goddess, but until this moment, seeing him again in all his virile masculinity, she hadn't realized how deeply she'd missed him!

Under the intensity of his unrelenting scrutiny, the color rose to her face. She forced her gaze upward, past the tunic and corselet covering his awesome form until, at last, her glance met his. The eyes staring back were flat, hard.

He urged her forward with a careless motion of his hand. "Come, come, lady. Quintus told me you've important business and the eve draws on. You keep me from other, more pressing matters. Let's finish this as expeditiously as possible."

Anguish stabbed through Rhianna. He hated her. Though she'd told herself over and over she could endure it—nay, deserved it—at this moment its reality was almost more than she could bear. Yet bear it she must, for the fate of others now lay in her hands. There was no time left for personal needs, not now, not in times such as these.

"My brother, Cerdic," she forced herself to respond. "I seek knowledge of his fate."

Marcus' gaze lowered to his cup. Long minutes passed as he swirled the ruby-colored liquid, the impulse to spare her further pain warring with his need to extract a measure of that same torment he'd suffered. His hunger for revenge finally vanquished any softer emotions.

He looked up. "The governor ordered all rebel chieftains executed."

Rhianna blanched. "N-nay. 'Tisn't true. Ah, I beg you, Marcus. Tell me 'tisn't true!"

His jaw clenched. *Gods!* he thought. *How can I do this to her, no matter how much she's hurt me? Yet I must or I'll never be free of her.*

"It's true enough," he muttered. "What did you think would happen if you and your people dared rise against the might of Rome? We can't afford the other tribes thinking they can revolt and not face dire consequences. The governor must make an example of your people."

"But the war is over. We've surrendered!"

Marcus set aside his goblet and straightened in his chair, leaning forward to rest his elbows on his thighs. "Do you know how close we came to total annihilation? Do you realize Boudicca nearly managed to wipe the presence of Rome from Britannia? My uncle has no choice but to punish the rebels severely. It's the only way to prevent future thoughts of rebellion."

"And . . . and you agree?" The words were choked out in a raw voice.

Dark brows slanted into a frown. "My uncle doesn't confer with me before making provincial decisions. Not that it would matter what I thought anyway. I'm a Roman soldier. My job is to obey."

"Aye." She lashed out at him in her blind anguish. The hand holding her cloak closed twisted the cloth into a tight knot. "Obedience is a brave word for Roman cowards to hide behind. You should have a fine and prosperous military career."

With a low growl, Marcus sprang from his chair. "I've heard enough. I'll not stand by and bear your insults, woman. Go; leave while you still can!"

"N-nay." Rhianna wrenched herself back from her futile attack. To anger him now when she needed his cooperation was foolish and of no service to her people. And no kindness to Cerdic, either.

"I beg pardon for my impertinence, lord." Tears of humiliation welled in her eyes and she furiously blinked them away. "There is yet more I would ask you. My brother's b-body. Could I have it, take it back to bury in the manner of my people? 'Tis all that's left me and 'twould set his soul to rest."

"No!" Marcus rasped. "He . . . he wasn't executed here. I know not where his body lies."

Rhianna forced herself to go on. "Then tell me where he was sent. I will journey there and seek out his remains."

"No! Do you hear me? I said no. And that's the end of it!"

The end of it? Rhianna thought, dazed. But he didn't understand. Not to bury Cerdic in sacred ground, not to free him from his earthly form and grant his soul liberty to find its ultimate rebirth, not to feast his memory and appease the gods . . .

The strength drained from her; the room began to whirl crazily. Marcus didn't understand—or just didn't care. That last realization was more than her tormented mind could bear. The blackness rose around her. For once, Rhianna was tempted not to fight it.

Oblivion. Blessed oblivion. 'Twas no solution but, for a brief time, 'twas all the respite she had. Her lashes fluttered down onto her cheeks but, in that last instant, Rhianna's pride rose to shame her. How could she flee from reality, no matter how painful, when Trinovante lives hung in the balance? To do less would dishonor all she held dear.

"Rhianna!"

From a place far away, she called herself back. Strong arms caught her as she struggled to dispel the encompassing mists, gathering her to a strangely unyielding body. Rhianna moaned and pushed away. She touched a hard, leather-covered chest. Marcus. The realization of who held her jerked her back to full consciousness.

Her eyes snapped open. Marcus' face, set in grim determination, was disturbingly close as he strode across the room with her. She glanced in the direction he headed. He carried her to his bed.

Warmth flushed her. Goddess, she was the envoy of the Trinovante and here she was being carried to bed like some . . . some weak, swooning girl! Shame sent the blood pounding through her body. Renewed strength coursed through Rhianna. She began to struggle.

"Let me go! Please, let me go!"

Marcus halted, his tumultuous emotions frozen into icy disbelief by the frantic plea. He looked down at Rhianna. Was that loathing he saw in her eyes? Did even his touch now disgust her?

He lowered Rhianna to her feet and released her. "Are you certain you're well enough to stand?"

She swayed unsteadily, then straightened. "A-aye." She stepped back from him.

At the action, something in Marcus hardened. Nothing had changed between them. Nothing ever would. "Then, since there's nothing I can do about your brother, it's best you leave." He turned on his heel and walked away.

"Wait! A moment more of your time, my lord. Then I promise to go."

With a weary sigh, Marcus turned. "What is it?"

Rhianna inhaled a deep breath and squared her shoulders. "Our food and livestock. Surely you cannot mean to take it from us?"

"I'm only obeying orders."

"Orders? Goddess, Marcus, must you always hide behind the safety of orders?" she railed at him. "What of innocent people, the women, the children who'll suffer because of those orders? What has happened to you? Don't you care about anything anymore?"

"Yes, I care, and deeply so," he gritted. "But you have happened to me; this war has happened; and, suddenly, it seems I've no control over anything. My career is all I have left. I've no intention of sacrificing it for a people who have betrayed me every step of the way."

His words knifed through Rhianna. He thinks *I've* betrayed him and, in a sense, I have. Because of that, my people will suffer. Ah, is there naught that will turn his wrath aside?

Desperation welled inside her, blotting out all pride, all reason. With a small cry, Rhianna flung herself at Marcus' feet. "Nay, ah, nay, my lord! Punish not the Trinovante for the pain I've inflicted. Turn your wrath from them; direct it where it truly belongs—on me. Leave them their food and I'll do anything, even offer up my life, if 'twill appease your anger!"

"Will you now?" came the bitter rejoinder. "How noble of you to sacrifice yourself to the Roman monster you now envision me to be."

"I-I only wish to help my people."

Her words tore through Marcus, twisting his heart in an excruciating vise. He threw all reason, all control aside. Leaning down, Marcus jerked Rhianna to her feet. "Your sweet entreaty, couched as it is in such glowing regard for me, does have its merit," he snarled. "You said you'd do anything. I assume that includes the offering of your lovely body?"

Rhianna looked up, transfixed, her eyes wide and staring.

Marcus gave her a small shake. "Well, does it, wench?"

A tear trickled down her cheek. "A-aye."

He steeled himself against the sudden impulse to pull her to him and comfort her, to whisper that he was sorry and never meant to hurt her. She deserves this, Marcus told himself. Indeed, she has brought it to a head in coming here and must suffer the consequences.

"And whom shall I choose to give you to? Perhaps Quintus? He's always favored you. Surely he'd be a kind and gentle lover." Marcus gave her another small shake. "But you'd like that, wouldn't you? To pay my price with little or no suffering?

"No, I think Quintus would be too kind a fate for one such as you. You deserve a far greater torment than he'd ever bestow. Perhaps *I* would be more appropriate, disgusting brute that you now find me to be."

He released her and strode back to fling himself into his chair. "Yes, only I could exact the full purchase price. Have we a pact then? The Trinovante food stores for one more night with me?"

Though the tears coursing down her cheeks belied her, Rhianna lifted her chin in quiet dignity. Never, no matter the cost, would she let him defeat her. "I'll do whatever is necessary to save my people. If it requires a night with you, then so be it."

Marcus grabbed his wine goblet from the serving table and took a deep swallow of its contents. "Good. I've a mind to begin immediately. Remove your garments."

She gasped. "N-now?"

Not a flicker of emotion touched his face. "Yes, now. Have you lost heart for our pact so quickly?"

Rhianna shook her head, the tears evaporating in her shock and rising anger. "Nay. 'Tis just that I've never played the Roman whore before."

His low rumble of laughter startled Rhianna. "Be assured, lady, that whore or no, you've sold yourself dearly. Now, disrobe, for I mean to take my money's worth."

Her hand moved to the clasp on her cloak. "As you wish, *my lord.*" With more bravado than she felt, Rhianna unfastened her cloak and let it drop to the ground. Her gaze never leaving his, she untied her girdle. As it fell away, she freed the fibulae holding the shoulders of her long-sleeved, woolen gown closed.

The fabric slid from her chest. Rhianna made a quick grab at it, stopping the gown where it rode the swell of her breasts. Her modesty protected, she lifted defiant eyes to Marcus.

He sat, his body tense, his bold gaze boring into her in silent expectation. Finally, he made an impatient motion with his hand. "Finish with your games, wench!"

Rhianna let the gown fall. A dark flush crept up to suffuse Marcus' striking features. Though his gaze was lazy as it roved over her body, the erratic rise and fall of his broad chest, combined with his taut vigilance, gave lie to his casual pose.

A dizzying current of excitement raced through her. *He wants me! In spite of everything that's come between us, he still desires me! Just as I desire him . . .*

Her flawless perfection took Marcus' breath away. She was everything he'd ever dreamed of in a woman. Beneath his corselet, Marcus felt his heart pound so hard he thought it would burst. Yes . . . everything he'd ever dreamed of or ever wanted.

Curse her, Marcus thought. Curse the spell she has cast over me. Even now, when I seek only to shame her, to hurt her as she has hurt me, I hunger for her still.

Desire, hot and savage, swept through him. His glance raked her naked form, taking in the creamy swell of her breasts, the gentle indentation of her waist and provocative flare of her hips, the golden triangle of curls at the apex of her long, shapely legs. His sex filled, engorging until it was throbbing hard. Gods, how he wanted—

A cold blast of air wrenched Marcus from his heated reverie. His gaze moved to the source of the disturbance, the raised tent flap. In the doorway stood Quintus.

"By the gods!" Quintus let the flap fall as he stepped farther into the tent. "What is going on here?"

Rhianna glanced over her shoulder and gasped. Her hands moved instinctively to cover herself.

Marcus stood. "Get out of here, Quintus." He poured himself another goblet of wine. "This is no longer your concern."

"You're wrong, my friend," Quintus rasped. "I brought Rhianna here. Until she bids me otherwise, she remains my concern." His glance strayed to the ivory-hued form of the woman standing between him and Marcus.

"And I say again," Marcus growled in warning, noting the direction of Quintus' gaze, "get out of here. You've interfered enough for one day. What is between Rhianna and me is not your concern."

Quintus ignored him. "Rhianna?" He moved closer. "Has he hurt you? Do you wish to leave?"

"Quintus!"

The harsh rasp of a sword being drawn jerked both his and Rhianna's attention back to Marcus.

"You stretch the limits of our friendship," Marcus snarled, his voice harsh. "Go, now, before I'm forced to forget what we've meant to each other."

"Friendship or no," Quintus ground out, his hand going to his own sword, "I'll not leave until I'm assured of Rhianna's safety."

Marcus waved his sword in her direction. "Then answer him, lady. Are you in any danger from me? Have I forced you to do anything against your will?"

Again, Rhianna glanced back at Quintus. "I-I am here of my own accord. Please go. I do not wish to be the cause of enmity between you." She lowered her eyes and turned away. "Marcus won't hurt me."

"Is that true, Marcus?" Quintus prodded. "Do you swear not to hurt her?"

"You dare ask such a thing of me?" Marcus' demand was taut with anger. "You dare question my personal integrity?"

Quintus eyed him calmly, though his hand tightened about his sword hilt. "I ask only for assurance that the lady will be treated with the respect she deserves. Is that such a hard pledge to give?"

Marcus glared at Quintus, the seconds passing with tension-fraught slowness. Finally he sighed and threw his sword onto the campaign desk. "No, it isn't." He shook his head. "I won't hurt her. It seems I haven't the stomach, no matter what she does to me."

"Then I bid you farewell." Quintus turned to Rhianna. "Lady." He rendered her a small bow.

Rhianna answered with a nod and wan little smile.

The tent was briefly inundated with another gust of frigid air. The flames in the braziers fluttered erratically, then Quintus was gone. Marcus strode back to the serving table and poured himself yet another goblet of wine. He raised the cup to his lips, then paused as his gaze met Rhianna's.

Feelings too deep for words arced between them, building until the emotions seemed too great to bear. With a low oath, Marcus threw the goblet across the room. Grabbing his heavy military cloak, he strode to Rhianna and flung it over her shoulders. Then, without another word, he left the tent.

In the waning hours of the night, a sound woke Rhianna. Clutching Marcus' cloak about her, she shoved to one elbow. The tent flap lifted and Marcus stepped in. The rhythm of her heart quickened. Had he come back at last to claim his due?

She'd dared not leave even after he'd left her earlier, not certain if his departure had signaled a fulfillment of their pact or not. Yet though she now waited with baited breath, he never glanced her way. Instead, in the dying light of the braziers, Marcus disrobed.

Rhianna lay back on the bed but, with hooded eyes, continued to watch him. His corselet and sandals were the first to be removed, soon followed by his belt and tunic. Then his loincloth joined the rest of his clothing.

Her gaze slid down his body, past the powerful, furred expanse of his chest to his narrow hips and taut buttocks, to hungrily traverse his hair-roughened, steel-tempered thighs. She bit into her lower lip, battling desire that swelled deep within her. How she wanted, needed to go to him and beg him not to hate her.

She opened her mouth to call to Marcus, but the words wouldn't come. Fool, she berated herself. What good would it do in the end, save worsen the pain between us? Better to remain silent, to endure the waning hours of this endless night, and leave him behind on the morrow. Better to remember my vow and the wise words of Cunagus . . . *a greater kindness that he not know.*

Marcus wrapped himself in a blanket and made a bed on a rug lying in one corner of the tent. Soon, the heavy, even breathing of sleep filled the room. With a small sigh, Rhianna turned from him and pulled the coverlet over her. 'Twas a greater kindness indeed, she mused, yet had she the strength to leave without attempting to assuage some of the pain of her rejection?

And hurt him she had. The evidence had been there, even in the midst of Marcus' cruel treatment of her. That look of anguish, of bewilderment burning in his eyes, lingered in

Rhianna's mind, tormenting her even now. If only she could ease a little of that pain . . .

She slipped from the bed before the sane voice of reason could call her back. The cloak wrapped about her, Rhianna crept to him.

Marcus jerked around, half-rising before his eyes made out her slender form. "Rhianna!"

Kneeling beside him, she tenderly stroked his face.

He inhaled a ragged breath and gripped her hand. "Why? Why, Rhianna?" he groaned. "Why did you leave me?"

" 'Tisn't mine to tell. Let it be enough that I did so most unwillingly."

"But it's *not* enough," he cried, grabbing her to pull her up to lie beside him. "It can never be enough. I love you. Torment that it has become, I will always love you. Tell me why. I demand it!"

She tried to pull away but he held her to him, his fingers gripping her like iron talons. Even in the amber glow of the fading embers, Rhianna could see his eyes, intent, beseeching, searing to her very soul. The warmth of his body, his heady scent surrounded her in seductive bonds, weakening her strength to resist him.

Goddess, why had it come to this, that she must constantly struggle against her need for Marcus? Rhianna sighed her defeat. "And I will always love you. But I say again, the reasons for our parting are not mine to tell. 'Tis a fact that must be accepted, as I have come to accept all the other losses in my life."

"You accept things too readily, I think." Marcus sat up. "Where is the fiery, unquenchable girl I first met? All I see now is a dispirited, acquiescent woman."

"This *woman,*" she bristled, "has had to learn there are things of more import than her own childish, self-centered wishes. I'm a chieftain's daughter and, until late, the sister of one as well. Now, my brother is no more. Until a new leader is chosen, I am left with the responsibility for my clan. How can I now bemoan my fate—when Cerdic sacrificed his very life—even if it requires the renunciation of our love?"

"It seems you can't," Marcus muttered bitterly. "For what little it matters, though, your brother isn't dead. I sent him away before the other chieftains were taken to my uncle."

Rhianna gripped Marcus' arm. "Cerdic's alive? Ah, thank the Goddess! Where is he? When can I see him?"

"You can't. Though I rescued him from certain execution, I'd no choice but to send him into something akin to a living death. Even now, he's gone from Britannia, on his way to a slaver's market."

"Slavery?" She choked out the words in horrified disbelief. "You sold my brother into slavery?"

"Yes," was the calm reply. "To spare his life, it was the only recourse. Coward that I am, I dared not let my uncle discover his whereabouts or more than just your brother's head would have rolled."

She stared at him, the realization of what he'd risked in saving Cerdic warring with her horror at her brother's fate. Sweet, brave Cerdic. Would she ever see him again?

Rhianna sighed. She laid her hand alongside his cheek. "You're no coward, my love. You did all you could for him, and I thank you from the bottom of my heart. He has his life. Mayhap someday he'll return to us."

Marcus kissed her palm. "As I pray that someday you'll return to me. No matter how you deny it, you are mine. Our hearts are wedded, the vows spoken, and nothing—neither man nor an uncaring fate—can come between."

She opened her mouth to refute his words, to slay the hope

smoldering beneath them, but couldn't find the heart. Let time perform the onerous task, Rhianna thought, for I haven't the strength.

His hands moved to the cloak covering her, spreading it to bare her nakedness. "Let me love you, sweet lady. I will not force you to stay with me. Yet for this night, let us join once more as husband and wife."

With a soft cry, Rhianna came to him, melding into the whipcord muscle and sinew of his body. Her vow to Cunagus remained but, for this glorious moment in eternity, it mattered not. On the morrow they'd part, each to their own separate destinies, but for one last time they'd savor the joy of their love.

Mouths met and melded, tongues united in a fiery dance of passion. Bodies hungry for the feel of the other moved with a frenzied urgency, legs entwining, hands caressing. The touch of Marcus' hair-roughened body drove Rhianna mad. She slid her trembling fingers across his chest, down his hard, flat belly, circling, kneading, drawing ever closer to the center of his manhood.

Her teasing fingers hesitated a heartbeat from his heated, straining arousal. Finally, with a groan, Marcus took her hand and guided it to him. "Touch me; hold me, my love. Don't torment me when I ache for you so."

Eagerly, Rhianna grasped the thickened shaft, stroking its throbbing length in an ever-increasing ardor. He shuddered at her touch, his breath escaping through tightly clenched teeth. The evidence of his wild arousal, his sweat-dampened body straining toward hers, struck an answering chord. A primitive, feminine urge to feel his strength and hardness within her filled Rhianna. Goddess, how she needed him, wanted him to satisfy once more that sweet, exquisite ache!

As if he sensed the urgency now driving her, Marcus

pushed Rhianna onto her back and moved over her. The iron planes of his chest crushed the soft mounds of her breasts, the rigid tumescence of his masculinity moving to nestle in the bed of curls between her thighs. He placed a hand on either side of her hips, and she opened to him in loving surrender.

Slowly, unerringly, he fit Rhianna to his need, her cry of ecstasy shattering the last of his control. Together they joined, the rhythmic, thrusting movements of their impassioned bodies carrying them upward on dizzying currents of pleasure.

The bonds fettering her spirit fell away. Like the goshawk of her now-dead girlhood, Rhianna flew. On wings of glittering, golden joy, she soared high above the firmament, skimming the heights of enchantment and love. Drinking in the heady intoxication, the delicious hysteria, Rhianna fought against the ultimate release until, at long last, she shot downward into a whirling maelstrom of fire, passion—and the sweetest freedom she'd ever known.

Seventeen

Gathered about a huge circle, the people of the Clan Trinovante sat and listened to the pounding drums. From the furthest reaches they had come—warriors, teachers, farmers, and craftsmen—to choose a new chieftain. White-robed Druids paced the circle's perimeter, sacred oak boughs held high in their hands, murmuring prayers for the propitious selection of clan leader.

From her position near the head of the circle, Rhianna scanned the myriad expectant faces. The solemnity of the occasion filled her with awe. A sacred trust, this decision affecting the lives and welfare of hundreds of families. A grave choice, touching even their children and children's children—if only the right choice were made . . .

A freshened breeze whipped the folds of her heavy cloak about her. Rhianna stole a glance at the brilliant blue sky. Wispy clouds raced across the heavens, herded along by the strong winds. In the distance, heavy gray thunderheads hovered over the sea, forewarning of the storm to come. A storm . . . terrible and destructive . . . like the consequences to the tribe if Cador were chosen chieftain.

"Look at him," Cordaella murmured, as she squatted beside Rhianna.

Rhianna glanced up. Cordaella's adoring gaze was riveted

on Cador, seated with his sword brothers on the other side of the circle.

"Is he not the finest, the most handsome of all our warriors?" the red-haired woman sighed. She turned to Rhianna. "His name will be offered for consideration this day. Will you, as chieftain's daughter and sister, tender your approval of his election? 'Twould greatly improve his chances."

Rhianna studied Cordaella for a moment. "And what weight would the opinion of a woman carry among so many warriors? Surely Cador didn't ask you to gain my vote?"

"If he did, what of it?" Cordaella's lips tightened. "Now that your betrothal is ended, he has all but promised to wed me when he's chieftain. As his intended wife, do I not owe him some loyalty? 'Tisn't something you ever gave him, but I feel differently." She smiled knowingly. *"Much* differently."

Rhianna stared at her friend in disbelief. Goddess, what could she say that Cordaella wouldn't construe as evidence of jealousy? Yet Rhianna knew Cador would never marry the red-haired woman, no matter what happened. Cordaella's position in the clan wasn't high enough; her father was only the fort cobbler. Cador's lust for power was too great to marry so low. He used her solely to garner support for his chieftain's bid. But would her friend ever realize that?

She swallowed hard. "What you do on Cador's behalf is your own affair, Cordaella. As for me, I will not support his cause. I truly believe he cares only for himself and won't help the clan."

"Then whom *do* you choose to support?" Cordaella demanded indignantly. "Your little brother, Emrys?"

"There are other choices besides Cador," Rhianna muttered, "and all almost sure to be a better chieftain than he."

Cordaella glared at her. "Well, I'll not sit here and listen to a brave, wonderful man spoken ill of." The rising tone of her voice was beginning to draw attention. "Cador has supporters enough and I go to join them."

She climbed to her feet and strode around the outside of the circle to join Cador's group. Rhianna stared after her. What had happened to their childhood friendship? The division had occurred so gradually until it now seemed they'd naught in common. So much had changed in her life. The growing estrangement between her and Cordaella, the loss of her father and two brothers, the revolt—and Marcus.

It had been hard to leave him that morn, now but two weeks past. So very hard, after waking in his arms, knowing she must go and 'twas the last time they'd ever lie together. He'd said little as he'd helped her to depart, then insisted on riding with her for a short while after she left the fortress. Rhianna closed her eyes, the bittersweet pain of their leave-taking flooding her once more.

"I won't ask you to stay," Marcus had said, "though to let you go is the hardest thing I've ever done. But I will. Our love can never be one of coercion or guilt on either side. But nothing, neither time nor distance can diminish our love, nor change the destiny we must ultimately share . . ."

An anguished lump rose in Rhianna's throat. He'd been so serene, so accepting, so certain she'd soon return to him. The agony of parting was pain enough; she hadn't the heart to tell him 'twould indeed be forever. Better to let time do what she'd no courage for.

A hand on her arm drew her from her poignant thoughts.

" 'Tis nearly time for the choosing to begin, daughter," Savren rasped, her voice barely carrying over the rhythmic pounding of the drums. "The clan respects you and what you did to spare our food supplies. You must speak for your brother when the time comes. 'Tis his only hope."

Dazed, Rhianna stared up at her mother. "Emrys? You

wish me to offer Emrys as chieftain? But he is too young, too inexperienced. The warriors would laugh us to shame."

"He is the last male of your father's blood. Young or no, he *must* be chieftain. 'Tis our only hope."

Savren plucked at her clothes as she spoke, arranging and rearranging the folds in an endless, fussing motion. Rhianna's eyes narrowed, as if observing her mother for the first time. Savren's once shining, smooth braids, coiled about her head in a woman's crown, now hung loose and unkempt, long past stranger to a comb or washing. Dark circles smudged her emotionless eyes, eyes that stared out of a gaunt, haggard face.

She mourns father still. Compassion flared in Rhianna. To leave Marcus, to give him up, had been the most heartrending torment of her life. How much worse for her mother, who'd loved and lived with a man for over seven and twenty years?

Moving close, she wrapped an arm about Savren's shoulders. In her father's memory, in honor of the pain of their mutual loss, Rhianna's long-standing antagonism with her mother faded. In light of all that had transpired, 'twas now of such little consequence.

A flash of deep insight pervaded her and, in its own mystical way, filled Rhianna with a strange sense of peace. In the eternal rotation of life, daughter had now become mother and mother, child.

The drumbeats suddenly ceased. Cunagus, as clan Druid, stepped into the circle's center. All eyes turned to him; all tongues stilled. His arms lifted, the full, white sleeves falling back to reveal gnarled, ancient limbs.

"Hear, oh Trinovante, the call to chieftainship," he intoned. "Hear and ponder the lineage of eligible candidates. In the first generation, Brennus, who was chieftain, wed Idha. Their children were Gai, Riganna and Cunagus. In the second generation, Brennus' son Gai, by his wife Maga, bore Taran, who became chieftain and died in the Conquest without issue, these seven and ten years past. Cunagus, who as Druid forswore his own claim to chieftainship, had three children by his wife Ana—Riderch, Dagma, who later died in childbirth, and Una. At Taran's death, Riderch was elected chieftain. In the third generation, Riderch and Savren had four living children—Cerdic, Kenow, Rhianna and Emrys. Of these four, only Rhianna and Emrys remain. Una bore one son, Idris, whose living children are one daughter, Mandua."

Cunagus' piercing gaze swept the gathering. "This is the lineage of our chieftains. Let the choice be made with prudence and courage."

As the old Druid took his place with the other Elders beside the chieftain's stone, a tall, smooth monolith where the newly chosen leader would pledge his vows, Maddan, one of Idris' sword brothers, rose to his feet. By tradition, it was considered bad form to propose oneself and the honor of doing so usually fell to kin or one's sword brothers. Here it comes, thought Rhianna, as the ruddy-faced man walked to the center of the circle. The contest begins.

Maddan glanced about him, then self-importantly cleared his throat. "A fine lineage, a noble lineage, that of Riderch and his son Cerdic. They served our people well and died as bravely as they lived. 'Tis time, though, to consider the other branch of that fine tree, Riderch's sister Una and her son, Idris. I offer Idris for consideration as our new chieftain."

A murmur of approval spread through the crowd to mingle with the scowls and angry mutterings of the group surrounding Cador. Cunomorus, Cador's sword brother, stepped forward imperiously. He raised his arms for silence.

" 'Tis true enough that Idris is of the blood of chieftains, but in times such as these other things must also be considered. For one, 'tis law a minimum of two candidates be put forth. And, for another, the ability to lead combined with true warrior talents are now, more than ever, greatly needed if we're to prevail against Rome. Cador, though not of the blood, is high born and meets all other considerations. I offer Cador as second candidate."

A loud shout of approval rang out from the group gathered around Cador. He grinned, making the appropriate gestures of humility but, as his gaze caught Rhianna's, she noted his feral gleam of triumph. Fear swept through her. For her people's sake, if for naught else, she must find some way to prevent Cador from winning the chieftainship. But how?

Kamber, his oakwood harp tucked beneath his arm, calmly strode to the middle of the circle to stand beside Maddan and Cunomorus. Surprised murmurings leapt through the gathering like the spreading tongues of wildfire. Everyone had known of the first two offerings, but who would the bard propose?

Rhianna's brow wrinkled in puzzlement. Kamber was an Elder, a highly respected member of the clan, in standing only less than chieftain and Druid. Whatever his words, they were sure to be seriously considered. A wild hope flared in her breast. Mayhap Cador hadn't won after all.

As he patiently awaited his turn to speak, fiery red lights glinted off Kamber's hair. A gust of wind sent the gut strings of his harp vibrating, filling the air with a soft, sweet sound. At last the crowd quieted. Ever the actor, the bard's glance scanned the circle in a slow, assessing movement—until his gaze met Rhianna's. For a long moment their eyes locked, and he smiled. Then he turned back to Cunagus and the other Elders.

"Though Cador is indeed a mighty warrior," he began, "there is no need to propose one who is not of the lineage.

Yet another of chieftain's blood remains. I stand here now to speak that name."

"And who might that be?" Cunomorus demanded. "Surely you speak not of Emrys. He is but a lad of two and ten. No matter his blood, he is not ready to lead."

"Nay." Kamber tossed Cunomorus a tolerant smile over his shoulder. "I speak not of the lad, but of his sister, Rhianna."

"A maid?" Maddan joined Cunomorus in incredulous laughter. "In times such as these, you propose a maid lead us rather than a warrior?"

The blood drained from Rhianna's face. Her heart thudded heavily in her breast. Her hands clenched tightly at her sides as she waited, dreading Kamber's reply. What was he about, to offer her as chieftain? Had he, too, become addled in the recent tragedies? Never, in her wildest dreams, her strangest visions, had she seen herself as chieftain. A warrior, yes, but never, ever, leader.

Kamber nodded, his smile unwavering. "Aye, I propose the maid, Rhianna. She is of age, is she not? She is a warrior and fought bravely and well in the battle of Camulodunum. And who would question her devotion to the clan? She has matured much in the past months. Did not her own brother Cerdic lay his chieftainship in her hands when he left us? And has she not carried the burden well?"

He glanced about him. "Does that not speak, more eloquently than words, of the high esteem our last chieftain held her in?"

Cador strode forward. "Aye, but that was a temporary measure to hold his place for his return. And Cerdic hasn't returned, so her guardianship is at an end. We'll have no woman as our leader!"

"The Trinovante will have whomever they choose!" Cunagus' voice rang through the gathering. "The law does not speak of male or female, but of lineage. Have not other tribes had women as leaders? Did we not follow Boudicca into battle as eagerly as any man?" The Druid shook his head. "Nay, Cador. Kamber is right. Rhianna's prerogative is greater than yours. You must step aside."

"S-step aside?" Cador rasped. "For a *woman?*"

"Aye, Cador," Kamber said. "For a woman who has proven her claim in more than just blood. Already Rhianna has accomplished as much as any warrior when she saved our food stores from the Romans. While other tribes around us face starvation, their homes piles of cinder about them, thanks to Rhianna, we are warm and well fed."

"And what did she offer to gain such concessions?" Cador snarled, his face contorted in a livid mask of rage. "Ask her what she gave to the Romans to save our food?"

"It matters not what she offered." Kamber's voice carried to the furthest reaches of the crowd. "What matters is that she was willing to do anything to save the clan. 'Tis the hallmark of a true chieftain, is it not, be it man *or* woman?"

Maddan looked around in rising consternation as Cunomorus sullenly withdrew with Cador and his sword brothers. "Forget not Idris' claim!" he shouted. "Idris is of the blood and a warrior as well."

A hoot of laughter drifted to him. "Aye, a warrior he is, at least in name, yet I'd wager Rhianna could best him in a chieftain's battle."

Flushing red, Maddan shot Idris an imploring look. Idris, white-faced, answered with an impatient motion for him to continue. Though Maddan tried valiantly to plead his cause, as the minutes passed it became increasingly evident fewer and fewer were listening.

Mutterings arose in various parts of the circle, men with

their heads together, women chattering behind their hands. Rhianna watched them, the realization they were seriously considering her filling her with a rising anxiety. She turned to her mother, seeking a way out of the trap about to be sprung.

Savren's head was bent to the endless task of straightening the folds of her cloak, humming a mindless tune as she worked. Rhianna suppressed an urge to shake her from the safe little world she'd escaped into. 'Twasn't fair! Her mother, in her sorrow, was permitted to run away, to hide from the harsh realities of life, while she . . . Goddess, she was being thrust into the forefront!

"Let Rhianna lead us!"

The cry came from Rosic, one of Cerdic's sword brothers. "Cerdic always said she'd the heart of a warrior!" He drew his sword and waved it above his head. "Let Rhianna lead us. I, for one, will follow no other!"

"And neither will I!" Maglor leaped to his feet, lifting a beefy arm to the sky.

From around the circle, man after man rose to lend their support to Rhianna's cause. Soon, their combined shouts reached deafening heights. Iron swords lent their flashing brilliance to the maelstrom whirling about her until light and sound melded into one.

"Rhianna! Rhianna! RHIANNA!"

"Rhianna?"

She blinked, clearing her vision of the blur of faces standing before her. Cunagus stood there, a mixture of pity and pride etched into the weathered planes of his face.

"A-aye, Grandfather?"

His hand entered her line of sight. Rhianna accepted it unthinkingly and rose to her feet. Dark eyes bored into hers. She felt a drawing sensation. Then it was gone.

Her grandfather sighed. " 'Tis your destiny, child. Go forth to meet it." Then in a louder voice so all could hear, Cunagus continued. "The people choose you. Will you be their Lady and wed your life to them and the land?"

The ritual words of chieftainship reverberated in Rhianna's mind. Only a few months past she'd heard the same phrases repeated to Cerdic, requesting that he be their Lord and promise himself to lifelong service to the clan. And now?

. . . a heavy burden, a cruel responsibility . . .

Her father had spoken of the chieftainship in such terms that day, now so long ago, when they'd walked through the autumn forest. A sob caught in her throat. Had he sensed even then, only two days before he died, that the ruler's torc would eventually fall to her?

. . . and will you turn from it now, because 'tis not to your liking?

Riderch's words danced in the air, rising to encompass her in a haunting recollection of the past and shimmering specter of the future. Rhianna struggled to breathe, to cry out against the unfair demands, the terrifying trust inherent in such a position. Yet no words would come.

She was of the lineage. In her veins flowed the proud blood of her forefathers. Blood that must be spilled, if need be, in defense of her clan. Her clan . . . her people . . . her beloved Trinovante.

Peace flooded her. Rhianna lifted serene blue eyes to her grandfather. "Aye," she said, her voice becoming stronger, more sure, with each word she spoke. "I'll be their Lady and plight my troth to the dear Mother Earth and her children, the Trinovante."

"And do you do so unreservedly, with full realization that ever to betray that sacred trust will result in your death?"

She nodded. "I do so unreservedly and with full realization."

"Then come." Cunagus took her hand and led her to the stone monolith. " 'Tis time to pledge your vows."

Rhianna followed him to the chieftain's stone, the words of a long ago Lughnasa day echoing in her head. *Neither human love nor life itself will ever separate me from an unswerving devotion . . .*

Human love. Marcus.

The chasm between their destinies widened until she could no longer distinguish his face. The features that now rose before her were familiar and dear. Her people. Ah, how she loved them!

The chieftain's stone loomed before her. Rhianna banished further regrets. The past was over; there was no looking back. Honor now lay in the future, no matter how lonely the path might be. Rhianna raised her hands to touch the stone—and closed her mind to everything but her destiny.

With a soft sigh, Rhianna paused in the reception of her people to readjust the heavy gold torc hanging about her neck. Heavy, so heavy . . . like the burden of chieftainship so lately lain upon her shoulders. Kamber, in his high position as bard and one of the last to complete the ritual ceremony, approached to render his obeisance. Rhianna eyed him wryly as he knelt before her.

"Rise, honored bard." She leaned down to draw him to his feet. "I accept your act of homage." Her voice lowered as their heads met. "I pray your faith wasn't misplaced. 'Tis an awesome task you've set me."

Kamber smiled, the act lighting the planes of his nondescript face until Rhianna thought him almost handsome.

"You are the best of us, Lady, though you have yet to plumb the depths of your courage and devotion to our people. I have watched you grow all these years and seen you blossom into the rich, vibrant woman you now are. You are equal to this."

At his expression of confidence in her, Rhianna's mouth curved into an unconscious smile. "I will need advisors, men more experienced than I. Will you be one to me?"

"Aye, Lady. That I will."

From the corner of her eye, Rhianna saw Cunagus approaching. 'Twas time to dismiss Kamber. She took his hand and gave it a parting squeeze. "Then, for now, I bid you farewell. Go, enjoy the feast. The morrow is soon enough to call together my new council."

Kamber bowed low and walked away. But a moment later, his place was filled by the old Druid. As he lowered himself to one knee, Rhianna bit back the impulse to halt him.

He bows not to me, she reminded herself, but to the high office of chieftain. I must remember that always and let it humble me to the reality of my position. Though placed at their head to lead them, I am yet servant to the lowest. If I fail in my obligation I am not above punishment, even to the loss of my life.

The ritual words were spoken yet one time more, the allegiance offered and accepted. A joyful shout rang out from the onlookers. The ceremony of chieftainship was consummated at last. Kegs of dark beer were broken open and the revelry begun.

Cunagus remained at Rhianna's side during the increasingly boisterous merrymaking. A warmth and heightened affection flooded her. They were her children now and she, their mother. As the Goddess was to the land, she was now to her people. And, though forever denied the man she loved, ceaseless service to the Trinovante could still fill her life. Some secret corner of her heart would always be empty and aching but, for the first time since she'd left Marcus, Rhianna thought she could bear it.

"The acceptance begins, does it not, Lady?"

Rhianna turned to her grandfather, her eyes mirroring her surprise. "Aye, so it does, Druid," she murmured, returning his respect for her new position with the appropriate distancing response. Yet, as she spoke she felt a small twinge of pain. Never could she call him grandfather again or find comfort in his arms. No comfort, not from him or anyone . . .

Had that been the true purpose of her visions then? Not only to warn her against Marcus, but to prepare, to strengthen her for the enormity of the lonely, heartrending task now facing her? Was she then free of them at last, in fulfilling what now seemed to be her ultimate destiny—the chieftainship of her people? Rhianna prayed so. She needed no further burdens laid upon her shoulders.

'Twas enough she must now govern the Trinovante, must appear strong and sure. Her thoughts skirted the edges of the frightening responsibility, then fled. It did no good to dwell upon it. The knowledge alone was enough to bear.

"You have carried yourself admirably this day, Lady," Cunagus said, interrupting her train of thought. "Yet there remains one thing more to ensure tribal unanimity. Cador, though he offered his obeisance, must still be brought to heel. 'Tis time to wed him."

She stiffened. Goddess, so soon, before she'd even had time to ease the fresh wounds of her parting from Marcus? The thought was too much to bear. Yet she knew her grandfather spoke true. Now, more than ever, a marriage to Cador would strengthen her standing in the tribe, soothe his seething discontent, and bind the most dangerous faction to her side.

Rhianna met Cunagus' gaze. "Your words are wise, Druid. I'll speak to him this very eve." She paused, her resolve hardening. "You'll have the fulfillment of your vow, but I require a time to prepare for my wedding. In a month, and no sooner, will the ceremony take place."

Cunagus nodded. "A month's time is soon enough." He glanced about him. "By your leave, Lady. I've a wish to enjoy the feasting, and you've matters of your own to attend."

She made a motion of dismissal, her mind already elsewhere, steeling herself to the unpleasant task ahead. *Matters of my own.* Rhianna sighed. 'Twould do no good to prolong the inevitable. She rose and set out to find Cador.

Rhianna held the little glass flagon in her hand, her nimble fingers turning it over and over as she contemplated its liquid contents. In size and shape it resembled the flagon of poison Cador had wanted her to use on Marcus that last Lughnasa eve.

Had it been just five months since she'd first met Marcus? It seemed a lifetime. In a sense, it had been. She was now chieftain—had been for a month now—and was no longer the girl of that summer's day. Then, she'd been so sure. Everything had seemed so simple. Even her antipathy toward Marcus.

With a deep sigh, Rhianna shoved the flagon into her girdle. 'Twould serve no purpose to ponder it any longer. No purpose, save to worsen her growing dread over the wedding night to come. Cunagus had said the flagon's potion would ensure Cador's deep slumber, and that was enough. Though of necessity they must share the marriage bed this eve,

Rhianna was determined their union would be consummated only in Cador's mind. Husband he might be in but an hour's time, but husband in name only to the end of their days.

Rhianna's hand slipped to her belly, resting in gentle wonderment over the life growing within. The time of her monthly flow had come and gone without the return of her woman's blood to the earth. She was with child—Marcus' child—a child conceived that night at Caesaromagnus.

She smiled a secret smile. Though Cunagus had seen to her separation from Marcus, he could never divide them totally. She would always possess a part of her love in their babe. And that babe, though he might never know his real father, would be raised with all the love born of his parents' union.

The bone earrings carved in the shape of hawks lay in the small wooden box on her lap. Rhianna hesitated. Did she dare wear them today of all days, knowing they were yet another reminder of Marcus? And yet, dare she not, desperately needing the strength, the secret solace they would give her? She picked them up and donned them. 'Twas all she'd soon have left of Marcus—her earrings and his babe.

A sharp tug on her hair jerked Rhianna back from her bittersweet musings. She winced and half-turned to glance up at Ura. "Have a care, will you?" she pleaded. "Isn't my wedding day painful enough without your trying to pull the hair from my head?"

Ura smiled. "Hush, Rhianna. I'll not have you shaming your family and friends by going to Cador improperly prepared. A moment more and I'll have this last ribbon braided into your hair."

"And who, pray tell, save you will notice? Cador will have me, prepared or no, and my mother is all but oblivious in her grief. And Cordaella . . . Cordaella refuses even to speak to me, much less attend the wedding."

The brown-haired woman expelled an exasperated breath. "Cordaella is so love-struck she can't think straight. The maid has gone daft. She cannot see Cador for what he truly is or she'd be mourning *your* unfortunate fate rather than her own for losing him."

Rhianna's head lowered. "She accused me of using my influence as chieftain to take Cador from her, of forcing him to wed me against his will." She gave an unsteady laugh. "Can you believe that, Ura? As if I'd ever wanted him!"

"Give her time." Ura tied the last braid in place. "In time, Cordaella will see Cador for the man he is. Be patient with her; try to understand. She has lost the man she loves, however unworthy he is."

Try to understand. A wry smile twisted Rhianna's mouth. 'Twas easier than her friend could ever imagine to understand Cordaella's pain. And yet in a time when she and Cordaella most needed the solace of each other, they were torn apart by the very thing that should have brought them together—the loss of the men they loved. Goddess, why must the fulfillment of her destiny also be the cause of pain to so many others? Why?

"Rhianna! Rhianna!" Emrys excited voice clamored from the other side of the bridal bower. "Come! Come quickly before Cador brings the wrath of Rome down on us!"

The two women exchanged startled glances. Rhianna rose and hurried to the bower's entrance. Shoving aside the checkered wool hanging, she stared out at her brother. "What are you about, to carry such news? How can Cador bring disaster on us, on this day of all days?"

Blue eyes gazed up at her, a shock of blond hair tumbling onto a forehead flushed and freckled. "A tribune, *your* tribune, waits outside the gates, demanding to speak with you. He has brought a large troop of soldiers with him and refuses to leave until he sees you. Cador is arguing with him even now. I fear there'll soon be blood letting if you don't put an end to it."

Ura ran over and handed Rhianna her heavy winter cloak. She flung it about herself to cover the robin's-egg-blue wedding gown, then grasped Emrys' arm. "Let us begone," she muttered in irritation. "I've no wish to allow such actions on my wedding day."

Yet even as they strode across the hard, frozen ground, its meager grass crunching crisply underfoot, Rhianna's heart began a crazed pounding beneath her breast. Marcus was here and once again she must confront him. Would it never end then, this eternal torment, the endless heartbreak?

Time, the final healer of all wounds, would never be permitted its chance. Instead, she must plunge the dagger of her rejection yet deeper into Marcus' heart, twisting it hard with the knowledge of her impending marriage to Cador. The realization rimed her soul with ice, chilling the blood until she felt one with the day's winter cold. Then so be it, Rhianna resolved. Let us kill, once and for all, the love between us.

"Begone, Roman!" Cador's voice, from high atop the parapet, rang across the fort. " 'Tis your last warning. We'll offer no hospitality to dogs such as you."

Clutching her cloak tightly to her, Rhianna ran the last few feet to the parapet steps. Sweet Goddess, let him not start another war in his arrogance! As she climbed toward Cador, Marcus' voice, calm and sure, carried to her ears.

"I come to speak to the Trinovante chieftain, not an underling. I suggest you carry that message—"

"*I* am the chieftain, Tribune Paullinus," Rhianna cried, drawing to Cador's side. "Say what you will to me."

Cador grabbed Rhianna's arm. "You'd undermine my authority, humiliate me before the Roman, on this of all days?" he whispered harshly. "Have a care, woman. You risk much."

"Enough, Cador!" Rhianna twisted free of his grasp, her voice low but tinged with anger. "As chieftain I risk naught. Naught, do you hear me? This matter is my concern, not yours. What we ultimately share as man and wife has no bearing on my authority as chieftain." She forced her voice to soften, already aware there were other ways to handle Cador. "I've no wish to humiliate you, but to weaken my chieftain's status in the eyes of others will only weaken yours, too. Surely you can see that?"

He studied her, the anger still roiling beneath the surface of his pale blue eyes, his long, blond mustache twitching with the effort to stay his heated reply. At last, as if realizing to remain would be to unleash things he'd no desire for, Cador strode away.

Rhianna turned back to Marcus, still quietly waiting astride his white stallion. "Well, Tribune? What would you say to me?"

"What I've to say is for your ears only."

She expelled a shuddering breath. There was no way to avoid it then. He was set on a confrontation. With a curt wave of her hand, she indicated the gate. "Enter, Tribune. I'll await you."

The main gate swung open and Marcus rode through. He dismounted and strode to meet Rhianna as she climbed down the steps from the parapet. Their eyes met warily, the coiled tension creating an almost palpable aura between them.

"Come, follow me to the guard hut," Rhianna finally forced herself to say.

He wrenched off his helmet and, shoving it beneath his

arm, gave a stiff bow and motion of his hand. "After you, lady."

She rounded on him as soon as they walked inside. "Why did you come, Marcus? Why can't you let it be?"

"I come to discover if the rumors were true." His glance fell to the heavy, ceremonial torc about her neck. "One at least was accurate. I congratulate you on the attainment of the chieftainship. A singular honor, is it not, for a woman to lead a Britanni tribe?"

Rhianna ignored the sarcasm in his voice. "And the other rumors? What were they?"

He gave a sharp bark of laughter. "The other rumor I found most ludicrous, though my sources insisted that it, too, was accurate. They said you were to wed."

"They also spoke true."

Marcus' eyes narrowed to glittering slits. "And who is that most fortunate of men?"

Despair rose in Rhianna's throat. "Cador."

"When?"

"This very day."

For a fleeting instant Marcus' features twisted in pain. Then a mask of cold indifference settled over them. "Indeed? And have you suddenly discovered you love him, too?"

High color swept Rhianna's face. Her lips tightened. 'Twould do no good to debate the reasons with him, nor would it ease the agony of the act. "I owe you no explanation. 'Tis enough to say some choices aren't mine to make."

His eyes widened in mock disbelief. "Are you telling me as chieftain you've no say in whom you wed? Or was it rather, in your newly exalted position, you no longer had a taste for a Roman lover?"

"It matters not what my reasons are." She lashed out at him, her anguish hovering on the edge of control. "I cannot wed you, Marcus. I've tried to tell you that, over and over, even that night at Caesaromagnus. Why can't you let it be?"

"Because I love you, and you love me."

With a swift motion, he took her into his arms, his mouth descending savagely to crush her lips. Like the searing heat that joins metals, his kiss burned through Rhianna, setting her blood afire to course in molten rivulets through her body. She moaned, her arms encircling his neck. For one ecstatic moment, she gave herself up to the singing, joyous abandon of her love.

Yet when his mouth moved to trail kisses across her cheek and down her neck, Rhianna stiffened. Reality, in all its piercing intensity, rushed back. She pressed against him, pushing herself away. "Nay!" she gasped. "Nay, Marcus! 'Twill do no good. 'Twill change naught no matter what you do to my body. I'll not wed you, now or ever."

Marcus went rigid, the shock of her rejection finally filtering through his love-besotted mind. He stepped back, his hands clenching at his sides. The scar marking his face flamed scarlet. "I should never have allowed you to return to your people that morn at Caesaromagnus. I could have kept you with me as part of our bargain." He ran a shaking hand through his black curls. "But no, I had to be calm, logical about it all. Give her time, I told myself. She loves you and will come back of her own accord."

He laughed, the sound harsh and jarring. "You've used me from the start—haven't you?—for your own amusement and pleasure. There was never anything in your heart for me. It was all but a clever way to exact some small bit of retribution, to avenge your hatred of Rome by flaying the heart of one of its citizens."

"Nay, Marcus." Tears flooded Rhianna's eyes. "I swear, 'twas never my intent. 'Tisn't my doing—"

His hand, upon her lips, silenced her. "Spare me your lies. In the end you're like every other woman. Like—like *her!*"

His anguished fury grew until Rhianna wondered if he might not lose control and strike out at her. She almost wished he would, if 'twould ease his pain.

"You care only for yourself," he said, his voice catching, "not for the ones who love you, need you. At the first opportunity you betray everything, with no concern for the pain left in its wake." Marcus shoved his helmet back onto his head. "Go, wed that pale excuse for a man. You deserve each other. As for me, I'm not some sniveling cur that returns repeatedly to be kicked. Have no fear, Rhianna. I'll not disturb your well-ordered existence again."

In stunned disbelief, she watched him turn and stalk from the hut, heard his harsh command to reopen the gate and then the thunder of hooves as he rode away. Time passed, enshrouding Rhianna in its heavy, numbing protection, until the world about her assumed an unreality that hardly seemed to touch her. A curious sense of relief filled Rhianna—a finality, a completeness. 'Twas over then; the final purchase price had been paid, the visions heeded at last.

Surely there was no further pain to be elicited, no sacrifice remaining greater than the one she'd just given. 'Twould be easy to bear anything after this . . . even her marriage to Cador.

Marriage . . .

Time to see that through, too, Rhianna thought. See it through to its bitter, loathsome end. See it through and fulfill, at last, the vow that had bought Marcus' life—and turned him from her forever.

Eighteen

Rhianna eyed Cador's sleeping form. Sprawled out flat on his back beside her, a fur pelt only half-covering his nakedness, he lay mired in the throes of a drug-induced slumber. Her husband, she thought, barely suppressing the surge of bitterness that admission stimulated. If only he knew how little of his husbandly rights he'd taken last night.

Considering how heavily Cador had imbibed of the potent Trinovante beer, it had been a simple matter to instill the sleeping potion into his cup. And, if he'd no memory of their nonexistent lovemaking, 'twould be an easy task to blame his drunkenness for the slip of mind. Nay, the issue of last night's activities would be no problem at all; 'twas the task of convincing Cador there would be no further sharing of the marital bed that worried Rhianna.

Despite her vow to Cunagus, she would *not* be a wife to Cador in any way save name. She would *not* submit her life or body to him—not now or ever. She was now chieftain, leader of her people. She refused to be manipulated further.

Yet how to couch her intentions to Cador in the least offensive way? He was a proud, vainglorious man—a man, nonetheless, who was a force to be reckoned with. And a wise leader attempted to use all to further the best interests of her people.

As Rhianna watched him, various approaches to the dilemma whirling through her mind, Cador awoke. Heavily muscled arms stretched above his head and he yawned hugely. Pale blue eyes opened to focus blearily on her.

"Good morrow, wife," he rasped, his voice still hoarse with sleep. He stared at her for a long moment, then made a move to pull her to him.

Rhianna scooted out of his reach and sat up, kneeling on the pallet. "Nay, Cador."

A perplexed frown etched his brow. "What troubles you, lass?" His gaze roved over the thin shift covering her. His eyes narrowed in lust. "I but desire to mate again. Though I've no memory of last night, surely you found me to your liking. I've yet to disappoint a maid."

She grimaced, not at all impressed by his cocksure assessment of his lovemaking. "Oh, aye. 'Twas better than I'd ever dared hope. After last night we are indeed man and wife."

Cador moved, reaching out for her once more. "Then come, lass, and let me taste anew of your breathtaking body."

In a quick movement, Rhianna swung off the pallet and covered herself with a cloak. She shook her head firmly. "Nay, Cador. There are first a few things that must be settled about our marriage."

He sat up, wariness now glinting in his eyes. "And what might those be?"

"Though after last night we are fully wed in the eyes of the clan," she carefully began, "we can nevermore be lovers. 'Tis enough we've both gained something—you, your greater standing and power and I, well, suffice it to say that I, too, have gained. But that's all there will ever be between us. Do you understand?"

"Aye, I understand." His features hardened in anger. "And you forget I'm your husband now and won't be dictated to."

He made an imperious motion. "Now, enough of the shy maiden. Come here, wench."

'Twas too much to hope Cador would be swayed by logic or a sense of fairness. She should have known only power could influence him. A small, pitying smile formed on Rhianna's lips. She shook her head. "Nay. You forget who you speak to, husband. First and foremost, I am chieftain. Never forget that. And never tell me what to do again."

"By the Goddess!" Cador leaped from the bed and, wrapping a pelt about him, strode to Rhianna. "Do you think I wed but to turn into a simpering, feeble-minded fool?" He shoved his face down to meet hers until he was but a stale, beer-tainted breath away. "You stand here and dictate your terms, and what is it to me? What have *I* gained from this unnatural alliance?"

"What have *you* gained, Cador?" Rhianna pulled back and cocked her head in mocking consideration. "Quite a lot, if you but pause to think on it. You're my champion. You bear the title of chief sword brother to the chieftain and gain responsibility for the young men's battle training." She smiled sweetly up at him. "And no one need know we don't share the marriage bed. I care not if you take a mistress; I ask only for your discretion. And that, husband, is what you've gained. Does it satisfy you?"

He glowered back at her but his words, when he spoke, were taut and controlled. "Aye, for the moment at least. It matters not to me if I lie with you. You were always but a means to an end, no matter what your parents ultimately hoped to gain. I can have any woman I want and any," he sneered, "is far preferable than one sullied by a Roman dog."

"Cador," Rhianna said, her voice tightening with warning, "you press where you've—"

"Everyone knows you lay with the Roman to save our

food," he savagely cut her off. "Though many admire your brave 'sacrifice,' I know how eagerly you went to him. Do you think I don't have my pride? Do you think I don't see the men laughing at me behind their hands? Well, I'll not beg for affection from a Roman's whore. Your terms are *quite* satisfactory."

He threw aside his pelt and dressed, then stalked out of the marriage bower. Cador strode across the fort, wending his way through the huts and people already up and about to the house of Cordaella's family. *Dare put me aside, will you?* he thought in a mounting fury. *You'll rue this day, Rhianna. Cordaella will take me back and gladly so. I've but to tell her I wed you solely out of clan loyalty after you begged me to rule at your side. I've but to assure Cordaella that I love her still, then seal my vow between her legs.*

Beware, my fair and haughty bride, Cador taunted silently. *What chance have you when I've a dear friend like Cordaella to use against you? But first, I've a long overdue score to settle with a certain Roman. And then . . . then I'll turn at last to your chieftainship!*

Clutching his woolen military cloak to him, Marcus strode through the blustering spring winds across a large, tiled courtyard to the governor's palace. The month of Martius was like a fickle girl, he mused, wild and unpredictable one moment, gentle and seductive the next. The winds gusted about him, suddenly tearing his cloak from his grip to swirl it wildly in the air, carrying to him the sounds of hammering, of men shouting orders. The harsh, discordant noises drew Marcus from his uncharacteristically poetic thoughts.

He glanced around. Like the phoenix of ancient Egypt, Londinium was rising from the ashes of its destruction. Barely six months since the Revolt had ended, homes of brick and stucco were springing up all over the town. New warehouses to store Britanni imports and exports were being thrown up along the River Tamesis, and gutted marble government buildings were once more inhabited.

How quickly normalcy had returned, Marcus marveled, even after such utter devastation as the rebel Britanni had wrought. Life went on, he reminded himself bitterly, no matter how difficult. These two months past since he'd last seen Rhianna had been hard, but he'd buried himself in his work, driving his mind and body to the point of total exhaustion until even the nights had little opportunity to torment him.

The pain, whenever he thought of her, had eased a little with time, the agony dulling to just a throbbing, lonely ache. Time . . . that was all that was needed. Time . . . and the end of his term in Britannia.

But that was hardly an issue worth dwelling on today. His uncle's missive had reached him at Caesaromagnus late yesterday. Now, after a hard day's ride, he was about to learn the reason for the summons. It was all very strange, that terse message requesting his presence, Marcus thought as he mounted the palace's stone steps, but—

From out of the open bronze doors strode a Britanni warrior surrounded by others of his kind. For a moment, in the bright glare of the white marble, Marcus wasn't certain who it was. Then recognition came. His eyes narrowed. His fist clenched in the red wool of his cloak.

Cador!

Releasing his cloak to furl about him in the stiff wind, Marcus made a quick move to his sword hilt and strode over to stand in Cador's direct line of sight. The Celt noted his approach and halted. His mouth spread into a thin-lipped sneer and he impatiently waved on his men who had stopped behind him.

The two men eyed each other, Marcus' angry scowl only enlarging Cador's mocking grin. " 'Tis quite amazing," the Trinovante finally said, "how prompt the Roman system of justice is. I've only now left the Provincial Governor after a four day visit to Londinium, and already you've arrived to be disciplined."

"What are you talking about?"

Cador's eyes widened in feigned disbelief. "Come, come, Tribune. Surely you didn't think your disobedience would be long ignored? The rumors of Roman officers refusing to confiscate food stores, of aiding and abetting—or, shall we say, 'bedding'—certain rebels, couldn't fail eventually to reach the governor's ears. As a loyal Roman subject, 'twas my duty to bring such traitorous activities to his attention, was it not?"

Marcus' grip on his sword tightened. "And your hatred of me is so great you'd endanger your own people to gain your revenge? Or have you even thought that far?"

"Fear not, Roman." Cador chuckled. "I've given thought to that and far beyond. 'Twon't hurt me if our food's taken. 'Twill hurt Rhianna and her standing as chieftain. 'Twas one of the main reasons she was chosen leader, you know. To lose our food supplies now, when her position in the clan is still so new and unstable, would serve me well. 'Twould be a simple matter to dethrone her and step into the chieftainship myself.

"Aye," he sneered, stepping close to confront Marcus, " 'twould serve me very well indeed. I'll have my revenge on you for interfering between Rhianna and me, and I'll have the chieftainship besides. Then my proud little wife will come crawling back on her hands and knees, begging for me to spare her life, for just one more chance to serve me as a woman should."

With a rasping, metallic sound, Marcus unsheathed his sword. "You'll die before you see that day!"

At the unleashed fury emanating from his opponent, Cador gave an unsteady laugh. "And would you kill an unarmed man?" He spread his arms wide. "Do you see any weapons to match your sword? 'Tis forbidden once again, you know."

He made a quick motion to stay his sword brothers who, with daggers drawn, had begun to creep up behind Marcus. To kill him now would be too kind a fate, Cador thought. Better to send him to face a destiny far more horrible from his own kind. He smiled. " 'Twon't do any good slaying me at any rate. Your uncle would know why you killed me."

"You're more deadly than a snake, your tongue more vicious than any weapon made by man," Marcus growled. "Thanks to you, I've little honor left. Killing you can't do much more harm, and if it'll spare Rhianna—"

"Enough, Marcus! Enough I say!"

At the sound of his uncle's voice, Marcus wrenched his heated gaze from Cador.

Accompanied by his guard, the provincial governor stood at the top of the marble stairs. His expression and stance mirrored the smoldering anger in his voice. "The Britanni isn't the issue here. Your conduct as a Roman soldier is. I wish to speak with you about it. *Now!*"

After a long moment, Marcus resheathed his sword. Not awaiting a reply, his uncle turned and strode back into the building. Marcus knew he was expected to follow. He spared

Cador a final, smoldering glance. "It's not over, Trinovante. If it's the last thing I do—"

Cador threw back his head and laughed. "It may well be, if the look on the governor's face is any indication. We shall see, won't we, who has the final revenge?"

He turned and walked away then, down the smooth expanse of stone steps and across the courtyard, his men following in his wake. Marcus watched until they exited through the gate. Squaring his shoulders, he then climbed the steps toward the open doors and a now-uncertain fate.

The older Paullinus was seated behind his parchment-strewn desk. Striding to him, Marcus halted and rendered the proper military salute. The governor stared silently up at him through steepled fingers. The tension grew to palpable proportions, but Marcus maintained his military stance. No permission had been given to do otherwise.

"I recall a similar conversation several months ago," his uncle finally began. "It had something to do with words and actions that came perilously close to disobedience. You were young, headstrong, and I overlooked them then. But now . . ." He paused, lowering his hands to rest them upon his desk. "Now, I find I can no longer ignore them.

"That Britanni." He motioned toward the open doorway leading back to the outside. "He was but the last piece in the case growing against you. For the past weeks, no, months, I've heard nothing but disturbing rumors about you. Rumors that the Britanni tribes in the vicinity of Caesaromagnus aren't being punished as severely as the rest of the rebels, that none of their food stores have been confiscated as ordered. And now that Britanni comes to me and confirms everything." The governor paused. "What have you to say in your defense?"

Marcus continued to stare straight ahead, his body rigidly

at attention, his gaze unwavering. Fleetingly, he considered claiming Cador lied, that it was the word of a Roman tribune against a Britanni rebel. But to lie to his uncle was dishonorable, and he'd shamed himself and his family name enough as it was. He was tired, tired of fighting against the rising tumult in his heart and mind. Tired of endlessly justifying Roman policy in this land, a policy that possessed neither compassion nor wisdom where a vanquished people were concerned.

"I saw no point in relegating the Britanni to certain starvation," Marcus finally said.

"*You* saw no point?" The words were uttered with calm incredulity. "And since when does one of my soldiers feel free to make such decisions, to supersede my orders? Have you lost your wits, Nephew, that you risk dishonor, even death, for a pack of rebellious Britanni?"

The governor rose and, hands clasped behind his back, left the sanctum of his desk and strode around to circle his nephew. Marcus neither moved nor replied, knowing to attempt explanation or protest would do little more than bring the full brunt of his uncle's anger down on him. As the seconds passed and the older Paullinus continued to circle him, the room grew unaccountably warm. A fat black fly buzzed in the window, frantically flinging itself against the glazed panes in a futile attempt to escape.

Gods, Marcus thought. His uncle was waiting for him to say the right words, words necessary to divert the full force of his wrath from him. But what *were* those words, and could he, in all honesty, say them even if he knew?

"Your actions demand punishment." The governor halted before Marcus. "There is one chance left, however, to redeem yourself."

For the first time, Marcus allowed himself to meet his

uncle's gaze. For the first time a flicker of compassion gleamed in his uncle's eyes. "And what might that be?" Marcus forced himself to ask.

"I demanded the Britanni reveal the name of his clan, a clan I'm certain was one of those you so magnanimously spared. He suggested I ask you." The governor cocked his head in query, a slight smile glimmering on his lips. "He said, as a loyal son of Rome, you'd be more than eager to provide the information. Will you prove him wrong?"

Marcus swallowed a savage curse. Cador had set the trap all too well. His military career, all his plans, not to mention his very life, now hung in the balance. So simple a thing, to name the Trinovante, and yet to do so would endanger Rhianna and her people.

Rhianna.

A sudden, frustrated rage flooded him. Why should he care what happened to her, she who had so callously discarded his love? She, who had betrayed him? Why, indeed, should he destroy himself because of her? He had bought them time, far more time than other clans. It was enough he'd risked his military career in his blithe disobedience of orders.

Orders.

What had Rhianna once said about his following orders? Marcus could almost hear her voice, see that dear, sweet face as she spoke. *What of the innocent people, the women, the children who will suffer because of those orders? Don't you care?*

Her face, tear-streaked and pleading, flashed once more through his mind. In spite of his resolve to the contrary, a fierce longing, a poignant tenderness, welled inside him. Gods, how could he harm her, even if indirectly by betraying the name of her clan? And how could he be the cause of innocent people's suffering?

He couldn't, Marcus realized, no matter how much she'd hurt him. No matter, even if in the doing, his own life were lost. His conscience, his honor, would allow no less.

Marcus slowly shook his head. "No, Uncle. I'll not condemn a whole clan to death because of your bloodthirsty need for endless retribution. For six months now you've persecuted them. I beg of you, let it end. The Britanni have been punished enough."

"And who are you to tell me what to do? You, who are little less than a traitor?" The governor's face purpled with rage. "You misguide yourself in thinking our kinship will protect you from your well-deserved punishment. First and foremost you're a Roman soldier. And, as one of those soldiers, you shall suffer the fullest extent of my wrath."

He glared at Marcus, his fists clenching and unclenching at his sides as if he didn't know quite what to do with his anger. Marcus watched him impassively, though a faint tremor of apprehension rippled through him. His uncle, as provincial governor and military legate, had full authority to condemn him to death, and many had died for crimes of lesser magnitude than he had committed.

"You are hereby relieved of your command and placed under arrest," the older Paullinus finally said, once more in control of his faculties. "In a week's time you'll be taken to the town square, formally stripped of all military privileges and discharged *missio ignominiosa.* Then you'll be publicly flogged and sent back to Rome in disgrace. Only because you're my brother's son," he continued, less harshly, "have I spared your life, though to punish you so will dishonor you until you will wish you were dead. Have you anything to say?"

"Caesaromagnus. The fort will need a new commander."

Admiration flared in the governor's eyes, then was gone. "Ever the soldier, eh, Marcus? And who would you suggest?"

"The Tribune Quintus Marcellus stands next in line."

"And is he not a close friend of yours?" The governor shook his head. "No, I think not. I'll not reward a man who most probably aided and abetted in your treason."

For the first time, emotion flared in Marcus' voice. "He's a loyal Roman. He was only obeying my orders."

His uncle smiled. "Nonetheless, the Tribune Marcellus won't assume your command. I think, rather, I'll assign him to temporary duty assisting the new provincial procurator, Caius Julius Classicianus. Considering the financial state of affairs Decianus Catus left things in when he fled Britannia, Classicianus will need all the help he can muster." He shouted an order and two guards strode in. "Now, no more of this. I tire of your disobedient presence. These guards will escort you to quarters where you will remain at house arrest until the day of your punishment."

Marcus rendered his uncle a closed fisted salute and, without further comment, wheeled to meet the guards. Together they exited the palace and made their way across the windswept courtyard, their heavy cloaks swirling about them. Never once did Marcus look back or allow himself to question the wisdom of the choice he had made—a choice for Rhianna and her people over his honor and career.

His life, as he'd once envisioned it, was over, his dreams forfeit, the woman he loved wed to another. There was nothing left in Britannia for him. It was too late to mourn what might have been. It was far too late and had been since that day he'd rescued Rhianna from the boar.

No matter how hard he tried to call it back, his life would never be the same.

* * *

It was late morning and Rhianna was busily engaged in washing her mother's hair. Though, as chieftain, she'd several servants to attend to her family's daily needs, Rhianna always insisted on spending some time each day with her mother. She told herself her actions were merely those of parental respect, but in her heart Rhianna secretly cherished the hope she would someday break through the bonds chaining Savren to her madness. In an odd way, she felt closer to her mother now than she had in a long time and dearly wished for the chance to speak to her again, woman-to-woman.

"Emrys," Rhianna called out to her brother who sat nearby, engrossed in sharpening a set of knives. "If you will, fetch me more hot water. 'Tis time to rinse Mother's hair, and you know how she hates it if the water's too cool."

Emrys dipped an earthenware pitcher into the cauldron of water steaming over the fire and carried it to her. "Pour it there," his sister said, motioning with a soapy hand toward a nearby bucket.

The hiss of hot water then a flurry of steam briefly pervaded the room. Rhianna resumed the scrubbing of her mother's hair. Finally, lowering Savren's head over an empty bucket, she began the rinsing. Once that task was completed, she wrapped her mother's head in a clean cloth and sat back to dry her arms.

" 'Tis a fine wife and daughter you've become," Savren observed dreamily. "I always told your father you'd the sense to overcome your infatuation with the Roman and see Cador's true worth. He was an evil one, that tribune, and the Goddess has at last seen to a fitting retribution."

"What are you about, to speak like that?" Rhianna asked

as she dried her mother's hair. "The Tribune Paullinus has done no wrong. On the contrary, he has helped us as no other Roman has."

Savren cackled in glee. " 'Tisn't our people, but his own who punish him. He will get what he deserves at last, and yet we'll be innocent of blame."

'Twas no use, Rhianna realized. To glean any coherent information out of her mother was next to impossible. Marcus was in no danger. Most likely 'twas just the deranged ravings of her sick mind. Rhianna picked up a comb to free the tangles from her mother's hair.

" 'Tis true, what Mother says, Rhianna."

She jerked around to find Emrys standing there. "What do you mean?"

"Cador's bragging all over the fort how he went to the governor-general and told him about your tribune. Cador says your tribune was arrested and will soon be severely punished . . ."

Emrys' voice faded as Rhianna shoved the comb into his hands. "Here, finish Mother's hair. I go to speak with Cador."

Grabbing a cloak, Rhianna flung it over her shoulders and hurried out of the house. After questioning the men, she soon discovered Cador down at the horse stables. He was grooming his favorite mount.

"Why, Cador?" she demanded without preliminaries. "Why did you betray Marcus to the governor-general?"

Cador shrugged and lay down the grooming rag. "He's Roman and our enemy, though you've conveniently forgotten that at times. He deserves his punishment and more, but his public humiliation will do for a start."

The color drained from Rhianna's face. "What are you talking about?"

"Why, his dishonorable discharge from the Roman Army

and public flogging, of course. The governor-general was rather incensed when he discovered one of his tribunes has been flagrantly disobeying his orders to gather our grain." A grim smile spread across his face. "If I hadn't a hunting party to lead, I'd be tempted to attend the spectacle. 'Tis a long time coming, but that Roman cur has finally gotten what he deserved."

She bit back the impulse to rail at him for his stupidity and shortsightedness, knowing it wouldn't change Cador's outlook one way or another. At this moment, Marcus and the danger he was in were all that mattered. Rhianna schooled her features into an inscrutable mask. "When is the flogging to occur?"

"On the morrow."

Rhianna struggled to control her rising fury. "Where? Where is Marcus now, Cador?"

A blond brow arched in amusement. "And why would you ask, wife? Surely you've no plans to hurry to his side?"

"Where is Marcus to be punished?" she demanded through clenched teeth. "As chieftain, I order you to tell me."

Anger flared in Cador's eyes. "You dare much, woman, ordering me . . ."

"Cador! Don't bandy words with me. You've made a grave error this time. If the clan were to discover what you've risked in your selfish search for revenge . . ."

Cador eyed her narrowly. "And would you tell them?"

"Aye, and gladly."

"Londinium," he muttered after a few seconds more. "The Roman's in Londinium."

Londinium! Rhianna thought as she ran from the stable. Over a day's hard ride and Marcus was to be punished on the morrow. She hurried to the smithy's hut.

"Maglor!"

The burly blacksmith looked up from his forge. Sweat glistened on the grimy planes of his rough-hewn face, but he smiled when he recognized Rhianna. "Aye, Lady?"

"Find Rosic and prepare your horses and supplies for a day's journey. We ride to Londinium in an hour's time!"

Barely breaking stride, Rhianna headed back toward her house. There were food parcels to wrap, warm riding clothes to don, not to mention the preparation of her own horse for the trip ahead. Too much to do and too little time left, if she were to arrive in Londinium before Marcus' punishment. Rhianna didn't know what she could truly do to save him, but if she could reach the governor-general, mayhap she could speak to him, explain the fault lay with her, not Marcus. Mayhap then his punishment, as well, would fall on her.

Fault . . . 'twas all her fault, and once more Marcus would bear the consequences. Rhianna quickened her stride. Blessed Goddess, he had suffered enough for her sake! Let her, just this once, bear it instead.

The palace guard eyed Rhianna disdainfully. "The governor isn't here." His gaze slid down her body. "Not that he'd see the likes of you even if he were."

She bit back a sharp retort. Granted, she, Rosic, and Maglor weren't in the most presentable of conditions to meet with the governor-general but, after riding nearly nonstop since yesterday, their dusty, bedraggled appearance was unavoidable. To anger the soldier further, though, would serve little purpose. Rhianna schooled her face into a bright, cajoling expression. "And where, brave centurion, might I find the governor?"

The man, little more than a common soldier, swelled

visibly at her mistaking him for a centurion. "Why, fair lady, the governor is where most of the townspeople are, gone to watch the public punishment of one of his tribunes at the town square." The guard paused to sigh morosely. "Would that I, too, could be there, rather than forced to remain at my post. It isn't everyday one can watch the spectacle of a high and mighty tribune brought low. A rare treat, to be sure."

"My thanks," Rhianna muttered, turning from him in disgust. She strode down the steps to where Maglor and Rosic waited with the horses. "We are too late to see the governor. Already they gather at the town square to watch Marcus' punishment. Do either of you know the way?"

"I do, Lady." Maglor stepped forward. "I've had several opportunities to visit Londinium in the past."

Rhianna swung up onto Demetia's back. "Then lead on. I've ridden too long and hard not to reach Marcus in time."

They made their way toward the center of town, the size of the crowd increasing the further they went. As they rode through the milling throng, an almost festive air permeated the surging mass of humanity. Vendors hawked meat pies, haunches of roast fowl, and mugs of dark beer. Others elbowed their way through the people, artful displays of trinkets and brightly colored ribbons arranged in the wide wooden boxes slung from leather bands around their necks.

As if they were at the fair, Rhianna thought.

The realization sickened her.

At last, far ahead, Rhianna could make out a tall column of stone, one she recognized as commonly used for corporal punishments such as flogging. The stone was surrounded by a large, open space, the curious onlookers kept back by a phalanx of armed soldiers. The area in the center was empty, save for two men. One was dressed in the garb of a centurion;

the other wore more ornate cloak and armor. The governor, Rhianna thought with a wild swell of hope. Mayhap she wasn't too late after all.

She reined in Demetia and turned to Maglor and Rosic. "Await me. The crowd's too thick to ride any farther. I'll go on from here on foot."

Maglor opened his mouth to protest, when Rosic's hand came down on his arm. The smithy turned to the blond giant beside him. Rosic said nothing, only shook his head, a warning light gleaming in his eyes. Maglor sighed and nodded his acquiescence. " 'Twill be as you ask, Lady."

Rhianna dismounted. She handed Demetia's reins to Rosic and began to push her way through the densely packed crowd. 'Twould be difficult to gain the governor's attention now, but 'twas her last hope of saving Marcus. In the jostling of the people, all jockeying for a prime viewing spot, the hood of her cloak fell back from her head. Sunlight glinted off her pale gold mane. Heads turned. Suddenly, Rhianna heard her name shouted.

She looked about, searching for the origin of the voice. A hand settled on her back and she wheeled around. "Quintus!"

Silver eyes stared down at her. "Thank the gods I found you! I was afraid you'd come."

"I-I had to. Marcus . . . Blessed Goddess, what has he done to deserve this?"

Quintus' mouth tightened. "The governor discovered Marcus' 'omission' in not confiscating the food stores of the Trinovante and some of the other clans. Your man Cador brought it all to a head."

Rhianna sighed. "Aye, I know." She attempted to free herself from Quintus' clasp and failed. Puzzled, Rhianna lifted her gaze back to his. "Please, let me go. I must speak to the governor, tell him 'twas my doing, not Marcus'."

"Are you daft, woman?" Quintus pulled her to him, his voice lowering. "It'll do no good, save to draw you into the punishment as well. Marcus made his choice, and it was to refuse to reveal the names of the clans he'd helped. *That's* why he's being punished."

"Then I will go to the governor, tell him . . ." Her voice faded.

"Tell him what, Rhianna?" Quintus prodded ruthlessly. "That the Trinovante were one of the clans? What do you think that would do to your food stores?" He sighed and shook his head. "Whatever you do, it's too late for Marcus. The governor is committed now, no matter what you might tell him. And I'll not have you adding to Marcus' torment by sacrificing yourself as well."

Rhianna struggled in his grasp, pummeling futilely at his corseleted chest. "I care not how hopeless 'tis. I must try; can't you see that? 'Tis my fault, all my fault. All he's ever suffered has been because of me. If I allow this to happen, I'll have finally destroyed him." She choked back a strangled sob. "And that is more than I can bear."

"Lower your voice!" Quintus rasped, giving her a quick shake. "People will hear, and I may not be able to save you if the governor learns of your presence. There's nothing you can do, Rhianna. *Nothing!* Don't you think I'd have done something if there were? If you go to the governor now, you'll only worsen Marcus' pain—and do irreparable harm to your people. Don't you see that?"

All the fight suddenly drained from her. Rhianna ceased her struggles and wearily rested her head on his chest. Once again, she thought miserably, it came down to a choice between Marcus and her people. "I just don't want him to s-suffer anymore," Rhianna whispered, her voice breaking.

"Neither do I, but—"

A murmur of anticipation ran through the crowd. Rhianna whirled about, her heart hammering wildly. Flanked by four guards, Marcus, hands bound before him, strode through the people toward the stone column and the governor. Shouts rang out, ugly and derisive. Rhianna paled. They were demanding Marcus' death!

She turned to Quintus, her eyes wide, beseeching. He smiled down at her and wrapped a strong, well-muscled arm about her shoulders. "Fear not, Rhianna. The governor has already decided Marcus' fate. He'll not be swayed by the demands of a few bloodthirsty citizens."

A weak smile of relief touched her lips. She turned back to the scene at the flogging stone. Marcus was led to stand before the governor. Dressed in but tunic and sandals, he stood in the late morning sun, the chill breeze ruffling his dark curls, his handsome countenance stoic, unreadable. A bittersweet swell of emotion flooded Rhianna. Goddess, how she loved him!

The centurion unrolled a scroll and the crowd quieted. "Citizens of Londinium!" the soldier read. "Before you stands a Roman soldier of the high and noble rank of tribune, one who has shamed himself and his country by his failure to obey a lawful order. His acts, in a time of civil unrest, border on treason, for he sought to give succor to the enemy. He has disgraced himself, his command, and his family name.

"For these and other crimes too numerous to recount, the Tribune Marcus Suetonius Paullinus is hereby stripped of his commission and discharged *missio ignominiosa,* to be sent back to Rome on the next galley. But before he departs, he is sentenced to one humiliation more—a flogging of forty lashes."

Rhianna gripped Quintus' arm. "Nay," she cried. "Not forty lashes! 'Twill kill him!"

Quintus exhaled a frustrated breath. "In the governor's eyes, Marcus has disgraced not only himself, but the governor as well. The family name of Paullinus must, it seems, be scourged clean—on the back of Marcus." He turned to Rhianna and cupped her chin in the callused expanse of his hand. "Marcus is strong; he can bear it. There's no need for you to watch. Leave now, before it begins."

She twisted free of him, the action punctuating the firmness of her resolve. "Nay, Quintus. 'Tis my crime as much as his. If I cannot spare him this, nor bear the flogging myself, I can at least be with him in spirit. Mayhap, in some way, 'twill give him an extra measure of strength."

He eyed her closely, then nodded. "As you wish, lady, but before it's over, you may well rue your words. Forty lashes will lay his back open. Not a piece of flesh will remain."

Rhianna shuddered in horror, but didn't falter. The sound of cloth tearing recaptured her attention. She turned to face the flogging stone. Marcus, his upper torso bared, was tied, hands above his head, to the tall column. As she watched, the centurion stepped into place several yards behind him and unfurled his lash.

Her eyes moved to Marcus, drawn to his undraped expanse of skin. Smooth, bronze flesh stretched tautly across a powerfully corded back, flesh that would never look nor feel the same after today. For an instant slowed in time Rhianna remembered the warm, satiny texture of it, the play of muscle and sinew beneath her fingers when they'd last lain together.

Her hands clenched at her sides, her nails scoring her palms to stay the poignant hunger the memory elicited. Then the lash arced forward, cracked, and tore across Marcus' back.

One . . .

The lash snapped again, and once more the leather slashed across his back.

Two . . .

Sweat beaded on Marcus' body. The lash sliced into him again and again. He jerked backward with each stroke, his neck straining with the effort.

S-seven . . . Eight . . . N-nine . . .

The sweat rolled down his skin, trickling into the long, gaping gashes across his back. At the next slice through his skin, his hands opened in grotesque spasms. He fell against the column.

As if fighting to hold back the agonized cries, Marcus shook his head to and fro. Crack! Crack! Crack! The lash snaked again and again. His legs began to tremble.

How many had it been now? Rhianna wondered through the blood-red mists of her horror. Fifteen, twenty? Goddess, she didn't think she could bear much more!

Yet on and on the lash fell. Each stroke tore open Rhianna's heart until it, too, seemed a gaping, aching wound. At last Marcus' form went limp. The bite of the leather now jerked his body with the force of its own momentum. Still, the centurion continued, adding more and more red streaks to crisscross Marcus' back until it was nothing more than a bloody pulp.

Thirty-nine . . . Forty!

Rhianna could barely stand. Her breath came in sharp, panting gasps, the tears coursing down her face. Marcus hung fully suspended from his wrists, his head bent between his arms, the blood streaming down his back staining his tunic crimson.

Goddess, surely this soul-searing torment must equal his bodily pain, Rhianna thought, yet why was she still conscious? How she longed to escape to that sweet oblivion that was now his! Yet her agony must perforce continue, even after Marcus had mercifully found surcease.

Gradually, the noise of the crowd pierced her despairing haze. She became aware of an iron clasp about her. 'Twas the only thing that kept her on her feet, Rhianna realized numbly. Quintus. 'Twas Quintus.

Rhianna whimpered softly and turned in his arms, gazing up at a face that mirrored the same pain she felt.

"Rhianna," he groaned. "I should have never let you watch this."

She shoved away from him and, after a moment of unsteadiness, righted herself. "You couldn't have stopped me and you know it."

Rhianna turned back to the flogging stone. Already they were cutting Marcus down and Cei, ever faithful, stepped forward to accept his unconscious friend. She suppressed an urge to go to Marcus. A sob rose, forming a hard lump in her throat. 'Twasn't her place anymore—she'd forfeited that right the day of her wedding to Cador. But Marcus still had two good friends to aid him.

"Go to him, Quintus." Rhianna motioned for him to leave. "Cei will need your assistance."

"And what of you, lady? Who will help you?"

"No one, Quintus." She lifted burning, tormented eyes to him. "My course was decided long ago and must be traveled alone. But Marcus . . ." Rhianna choked back a sob. "Go, Quintus. I can manage."

He hesitated. "Is there anything you wish me to tell Marcus, when he wakens?"

Tell him I love him and always will, she thought, then

immediately recognized the cruelty of such a message. Rhianna shook her head, fresh tears stinging her eyes. "Nay, naught save I pray he finds a happier life in Rome. He deserves much better than he ever received here."

"I'll tell him, Rhianna." Quintus touched her lightly on the face, his fingers tenderly tracing the delicate line of her jaw. "If you've ever need of me, I'll be found here in Londinium at the office of the new provincial procurator, Julius Classicianus."

"I'll remember, Quintus. My thanks."

She turned from him then and walked through the rapidly thinning crowd to where Rosic and Maglor awaited. Demetia was wordlessly mounted and the trio set out again, away from Londinium, toward home.

Home . . . Rhianna thought in a hazy, dreamlike state as they rode along. Home was all she had left, the only certainty remaining in a world that had all but tumbled down about her. Time to go home, to rebuild a life, to start anew.

Surely the vision had finally run its course, surely Marcus was no longer a threat to the Trinovante. He would be gone in but another day or two, sailing far from Britannia, never to return. Though Rhianna still couldn't help but believe he was an innocent pawn to the will of the gods, he'd at last been destroyed, his proud military career and fine aspirations beaten to as bloody a pulp as his body. And she . . . she was as ground down as he.

But she had done what had to be done, followed the call of her visions at last. Marcus had been brutally excised from her life. He could never be a threat to her people again.

Cunagus would be proud.

Yet one question remained. Would living with the horrible consequences of following the bidding of her Gift be any easier than avoiding them had been? She didn't think so.

A strange, fluttering sensation moved within her. The babe. Rhianna's hand slid to her belly, a belly now beginning to round with life. Time to rebuild the shattered remnants of her life, to heal her ravaged heart, to start anew. For the sake of the babe—Marcus' babe—if for naught else.

Nineteen

Rhianna's gaze swept the semicircle of men sitting before her. Cunagus, Kamber, Maglor and Rosic. The clan Elders, her trusted advisors. She settled more solidly in her chair, and steeled herself to the difficult decisions ahead.

"Rosic." Rhianna turned her attention to the burly Celt in charge of the food stores they'd managed to hide prior to the Romans' return over a month ago. "What remains of our grain and other supplies?"

He sighed. "A few weeks more, and then we must save the rest for seed. Soon, there'll be no flour for our bread. 'Twill be a long summer with only the winter barley to feed us before we can once more harvest the wheat."

"Aye," Maglor agreed, "but we can gather roots from the forest and hunt the abundant game roaming there. And summer is nearly upon us. Soon, we'll have fresh greens from our gardens. 'Twill be hard, but by next Lughnasa we'll feast as before. Try as he might, the governor-general hasn't destroyed us."

"But what of our brothers, the Iceni?" Kamber interjected, his voice impassioned. "They have been decimated. They starve, and illness runs rampant among them. Now that we are safe, are we to forget them and all the other clans the governor still unmercifully persecutes?"

"Aye, 'tis a sad state we have fallen into if we ignore the

plight of our brothers." Cunagus rose to stalk the room. "Yet what recourse have we? Who can we turn to?"

"We can send a portion of what food we have left to the Iceni, for one," Rhianna said. "Kamber is right. We cannot forget their need, which is far greater than ours." She glanced at her four councilors. "But Cunagus, as well, is right. We must do even more."

"I've heard tales of the growing enmity between the governor and the new provincial procurator," Kamber offered. "It seems that Classicianus also views the governor's continued policy of retribution as ruinous, if only from a financial standpoint. After all," he paused to smile grimly, "where will the monies for taxes come this year if the people are barely able to feed themselves, much less survive?"

"So, what do you propose, Kamber?" Rhianna eyed him consideringly. "That we pay the procurator a visit?"

The bard shrugged. " 'Twould be worth a try, if we're careful not to let the governor-general get wind of it. Classicianus is a Gaul, a fellow Celt. Fiscal policies are but one of many ways to approach him, I think."

She nodded. "Aye, 'twould be dangerous indeed but worth a try." A plan began to form in her mind. "The Tribune Marcellus has the procurator's ear. I could mayhap gain an audience with his help." Rhianna rose from her chair. "I'll journey to Londinium the day after the morrow. But first, we celebrate our feast of Beltane. Then and only then will we see to the matter of the Roman governor. He has caused us all far too much pain and sorrow. If there's any way we can effect his recall . . ."

Rhianna paused, impaling each man with a fierce look. "No one, do you hear me? No one outside this room must know of our decision. There are those among us who would gladly betray me if they learned of what we plan."

The four men nodded their understanding, Rhianna knowing one name above all flashed through their minds. Cador. Cador, in his ceaseless pursuit of the chieftainship, couldn't be trusted with such dangerous information. Though she had yet to reveal his involvement in the loss of their food stores to any but the clan Elders, choosing to use the knowledge as an inducement to gain Cador's obedience, he'd continued to prove his lack of trustworthiness time and again in countless small ways.

How deep the consequences of her vow to Cunagus ran, she thought bitterly. Even to continued clan unrest and disunity. Rhianna wondered if the Druid had realized Cador's disruptive ambition would lead this far. Not only her life and happiness had been sacrificed in this unnatural union, but clan integrity as well. If Cador wasn't to betray them again, they must appear to travel to Londinium on other premises.

Rhianna's glance moved about the room. She smiled. Her Elders. All good and loyal men. Though she as chieftain gained the credit for the successes, 'twas these men who, in their wisdom, supplied the solid judgments on which she based her decisions. They were the real reason she remained chieftain in times such as these.

A knock sounded at the door. Rhianna's gaze swung to the portal of the council chambers. "Enter!"

One of the guards posted to prevent unwanted eavesdropping hesitantly peeked in. "Pardon, Lady, but there's a woman outside who insists on seeing you. I-I told her you were in council, but she's very ill and on the edge of hysteria. If you could but spare her a moment . . ."

Rhianna smiled. "Did she give you a name?"

The guard nodded. "Aye, Lady. She calls herself Ailm. If you—"

She was halfway out of her chair and across the room

before the man could finish. Ailm, Rhianna thought, excitement pounding through her. Was it possible? Was she indeed alive?

As she exited the building, a small, ragged form standing at the main gate caught her eye. Rhianna's pace quickened. The woman saw her.

"Rhianna!"

Joy flooded Rhianna. The voice. She recognized that dear voice even if the woman before her was a mere shadow of the friend she knew. She gathered the frail form to her. "Ailm! Thank the Goddess, you're alive!"

"A-aye," the russet-haired woman cried, her thin body wracked with sobs. "It has been so long, so hard a journey back. Sometimes I wondered if I'd ever s-see you again."

"Fear not," Rhianna crooned, stroking the other woman's dull, matted hair, "you're safe now. Come, let me take you to my house. You can stay with me and my family."

As Rhianna began to gently lead her forward, Ailm drew back. Dark eyes burned in a gaunt face.

"Cei. Is he alive?"

"Aye." Rhianna smiled. "Cei survived Camulodunum, as did Marcus."

Relief swept across Ailm's features. "Thank the Goddess! I have my husband still. Where is he?"

Rhianna inhaled a deep breath before replying. So much had happened since Camulodunum. "In Rome by now." At Ailm's look of horror, Rhianna wrapped an arm about her shoulders and resumed their walk toward her house. "We'll find him, Ailm. I promise. Now, come. You need a bath, clean clothes, and a good, hot meal in your belly. There's time enough to talk about Cei and how we'll get you to him later."

Ailm nodded. “Aye, time enough. We’ve much to share.” Quietly then, she followed along to the house.

After some explanation to Savren and Emrys, Ailm and Rhianna were left to themselves. Rhianna assisted Ailm with her bath, then helped her don a clean gown and comb out her long tresses as they sat before the hearth fire. Ailm sipped a mug of steaming soup and, for a while, both women were contentedly silent.

Finally, the dark-haired woman sighed. “ ’Tis a long time since I’ve been so clean and warm. There were days and nights when I wondered if I had the strength to go on. Only the thought that Cei might still be alive, that I was coming back to him, kept me going.”

“What happened? How did you escape Camulodunum?”

“When the Britanni overran the last of our men and poured into the temple, I was struck unconscious and left for dead. Later, I awoke in the gathering dusk to dead bodies strewn around me. I . . . I searched for Cei and Marcus among the men I found lying in front of the temple, but they weren’t there. After that, I didn’t know what to do.” Ailm set her cup aside and buried her face in her hands. “I remember stumbling through the city and hiding from the looting parties, hearing the cries of the dying, smelling the stench of burning buildings. ’T-twas a nightmare, Rhianna!

“And the worst part of all was not knowing what had happened to my husband or what I should do or where to turn next.” She lifted a memory-ravaged face. “Then, in all my confusion and despair, I was captured by a Britanni. I thought ’twas all over, but he was an older man and not set on murder. He took me back with him to his clan in the North to care for his dying wife, not even remaining to fight further battles.”

“Aye,” Rhianna interjected bitterly. “ ’Twas the case with many of the clans. Once they’d tasted Roman blood and filled their wagons with booty, they saw no further need to swell the ranks of our army. 'Twas our undoing in the end, I think, this inability of our people to maintain a common unity against Rome. But enough of that. How did you finally escape?"

"The man treated me well enough while his wife lived. But after her death, just a month ago, he turned to drowning his sorrows in wine and beer. He became mean, abusive, and I began to fear he meant to ravage me. One night while he slept off yet another drunken stupor, I escaped. The journey back to Camulodunum was long. I found little to eat save what I could steal." Ailm's hands tightened around her mug. She lifted it and drank deeply. "Viewing the carnage around me," she then continued, "I dared not trust anyone, neither Britanni nor Roman. After a time only hope drove me onward, the hope somehow, if Cei were still alive, he'd be waiting for me at Camulodunum. When I couldn't find him . . . well, I had nowhere to go save to you."

"And thank the Goddess you did!" Rhianna laid down the comb and moved to sit before her friend. "After all these months I'd given up hope of ever seeing you again. 'Tis one of the happier surprises of my life."

Ailm glanced down at the rounded belly protruding beneath Rhianna's gown. "It seems you and Marcus have been busy with happy surprises since I last saw you. When is the babe due?"

At Ailm's artless words, a sharp pain lanced through Rhianna. To lie to Ailm was hard, but to do less would risk Marcus eventually finding out. And that, after everything else she'd done to him, was too cruel an act even to imagine. To lose his child, as well as the woman he loved . . .

"The babe is due in Lughnasa time," she replied gently,

"but Marcus isn't my husband. I am Trinovante chieftain now and wed to Cador, one of our warriors."

"Rhianna! Nay! How can that be? You made your vows to Marcus. You loved him."

Rhianna sighed. Aye, indeed, how *could* that be? " 'Tis a long story, my friend, and time enough to tell later."

As if to signal the end of the conversation, Rhianna picked up Ailm's empty mug and rose. She walked to the iron pot suspended over the fire and filled the mug anew with the rich, nourishing soup. Kamber, his harp tucked under his arm, entered as she strode back to Ailm and handed her the mug.

" 'Tis time, Lady, for the eve of Beltane to begin."

Rhianna smiled. "Aye, so it is." She gazed down at Ailm. "As chieftain, I must lead the festival rituals. 'Tis best if you rest. On the morrow, when you're feeling stronger, you can join in the feast, such as 'twill be."

Ailm took a few deep swallows of her soup, then set the mug aside. "I am indeed weary. Where would you like me to sleep?"

Though Rhianna, as chieftain, had taken possession of the large bed her mother and father had once shared, Cador had slept elsewhere ever since their wedding night. "There's plenty of room in my boxbed. You can sleep with me."

Her friend spared her a brief look of puzzlement, then followed Rhianna without protest. Rhianna tucked her in bed, then returned to Kamber. "Let us go, bard. The people await."

The eve was mild, and Rhianna left behind her cloak. The clan was already gathered, some bearing branches budding the fresh yellow-green of spring and others, armloads of yellow flowers. Around the fort Rhianna led them as they decorated the doors and windows of the dwelling houses and cattle sheds. As harbingers of spring, these first signs of renewed life were strewn to symbolize rebirth and power in all growing things. Yet the greenery and blooms served a dual purpose as potent protectors from witchcraft and the influence of the evil eye.

Flowers and fire, Rhianna mused as she later led them out of the fort to the surrounding countryside to set ablaze the bonfires on the hills. Both were integral to the feast of Beltane. While the twigs and flowers protected home and hearth, the fires actively drove out the witches, the smoke blowing over fields to purify both land and cattle.

Save there were no cattle to purify this Beltane. The governor-general had seen to that. The skin drums would be beaten, the horns blown all through the night, but in the morn there'd be no cattle to drive out onto the rich new grass. Not this year, but if she were successful in putting an end to the ceaseless vengeance . . .

She *must* succeed in her mission to Londinium, Rhianna thought. The governor would never stop until he'd driven them all to destruction. That much she knew. She'd seen it all too clearly that day of Marcus' flogging. She'd watched the governor's face as the lash fell again and again onto Marcus' back and had seen the pleasure, the cruel satisfaction etched deeply into his features and burning in his eyes. 'Twasn't Marcus, his nephew, he saw being beaten into a senseless mass of bloody flesh, but the Iceni, the Trinovante, and all the other tribes of the Revolt. Marcus was but an unfortunate symbol of the governor's undying rage. Nothing short of his recall would end the atrocities.

For a long while Rhianna stood there, her heart troubled, watching the gorse fires blaze, the hedges alight, the hillsides criss-crossed with walls of flame. Had these been the feelings of Cerdic that eve of Samain? He, too, had then carried alone the burden of an uncertain future.

Samain . . .

But a few months ago, and yet it seemed so much longer. Cerdic had been chieftain then. Now, 'twas she. Rhianna turned to the fort, leaving behind the happy festivities.

Let them have their night of hope, of rejoicing that the hard times were over at last. If her mission on the morrow finally set the wheels of their salvation into motion, mayhap they were.

"You're mad, to think you can go up against the governor!" Quintus turned from the window of his tiny office to confront Rhianna. "His power on this island is absolute. Do you wish to bring down his wrath on you and your people even worse than before? I understand your worry. I even agree with your concern, but you're only one person."

Rhianna rose from her chair. "Aye, I *am* only one person, but if I find powerful allies, then I'm no longer one—and not quite so powerless. Take me to the provincial procurator, Quintus. Let me speak to him. I've heard he's no friend to the governor. Mayhap he can help."

Gray eyes examined her intently. Then Quintus sighed. "As you wish. It's evident you'll not be swayed from this. Stay here while I see if the procurator will receive you."

He left the room. For what seemed a long while, Rhianna awaited his return. Doubts whirled through her mind. What if the procurator wouldn't see her or, if he did, what if he refused to consider her request? What would she do then? Blessed Goddess, he *had* to help them!

By the time Quintus returned, Rhianna's state of mind had disintegrated to a near panic. At the sound of footsteps, she ran to the door. "What did he say?" she demanded immediately when she saw it was Quintus. "Will he see me?"

Quintus smothered a grin. "Yes, the procurator will see you. Come with me."

She followed him down the marble-floored corridors and into a large room ornately decorated with murals, fruitwood tables and chairs, and low-slung couches. A tall, sandy-haired man dressed in a white toga was pouring himself a cup of wine. He turned to greet them, his glance appreciatively skimming Rhianna.

"You should have told me such a lovely lady was waiting, Quintus," Julius Classicianus said, moving to stand before her. "And, as if your striking beauty weren't enough, Quintus tells me you're also a tribal chieftain." He made a motion toward a setting of chairs. "Come, sit with me. You've some matter you wish to discuss, have you not?"

"Aye, my lord." Rhianna accompanied him to the chairs and took the one he indicated. " 'Tis the problem with the governor-general. He means to destroy us. 'Tis said you bear him no love. Will you not help us?"

"Rhianna!"

At Quintus' horrified exclamation, Classicianus threw back his head and laughed. "Are you always so direct, Lady? Most would feel me out a bit first, see which way the wind blows. But you, you throw yourself right into the fray."

Unflinching, Rhianna returned his amused gaze. " 'Tis said that you, too, are Celt, Lord Procurator. If that is true you, of all people, understand my disdain for honeyed words and politics. Even as we speak my people are suffering and dying as a result of the governor's heartless persecutions. I've no time to mince words and tiptoe about the subject."

"And neither do I." Classicianus lowered himself into a chair opposite Rhianna. " 'Tis true. I greatly oppose the governor's policy of retribution. My duty is to promote the economic growth of this province, something that's virtually impossible considering the current state of things. But only the emperor can recall the governor or reprimand him."

"Then ask the emperor to do so."

Classicianus exchanged a meaningful look with Quintus. " 'Tis a matter the tribune and I have given much thought to of late," he said softly. "I've been contemplating sending Nero a letter detailing him to expect no end to the hostilities if a replacement isn't found for Paullinus but, unless I can effectively convince the emperor, all I may do is jeopardize my own position."

He paused to lock gazes with Rhianna, his concern gleaming in his eyes. "I need someone who can speak eloquently for the Britanni. You know your people better than I. Know you of someone like that, Lady?"

To leave the island, to travel to faraway Rome? The consideration filled Rhianna with a sense of foreboding, yet she knew now where her destiny next called her. Indeed, how could she turn from the task, she who had strode in here and demanded that something be done? If 'twas necessary to go as far as to confront the Emperor Nero to save her people, then so be it.

She fixed him with a bold stare. "Aye, my lord. I'll take your letter to Rome."

"You?" His brows lifted in surprise. "And why should I let you go?"

"I am a tribal chieftain. I have lived through the Revolt, lost family and friends. And, because I am also a woman, there's a chance my presence, my pleas to Nero will be taken all the more seriously." She smiled bitterly. " 'Twas a woman who led the Revolt and vanquished Rome on this island.

Who better now than another woman to seek to end the terrible repercussions and animosity stirred by that revolt?"

Classicianus' gaze never left hers. "Your argument has merit."

"No, Rhianna!" Quintus stepped between them and turned to confront Classicianus. "She cannot bear such a journey, not now, not so near her time of childbirth. It'll be impossible for her to make it back here before the babe is born, not to mention what the hardships of the travel will do to her. Let me take the letter in her stead. I've powerful friends in Rome. I'll find a way to procure an audience with Nero."

Deep in thought, Classicianus stroked his chin. "Aye, 'twould be a prudent thing to send you, too, Quintus. But Rhianna is right. The emotional appeal could only be supplied by her. Without her, I fear our cause might still be lost." He turned back to Rhianna. " 'Tis your choice. I intend no pressure on you, but I fear the letter won't be as effective without your presence.

The longer Rhianna thought about it, the stronger her conviction grew. "I'll go, my lord."

"Good. I'll fund the journey. Take what men you'll need from your own tribe. In two weeks time, leave for the port of Rutupiae. Quintus will meet you there with my letter. Use the utmost discretion in preparing for the journey, for if the governor discovers it prematurely . . ."

Rhianna nodded. "I'll take the greatest care. I swear it." She rose. "If there is naught else, my lord, I'll be on my way. There's much to be done to prepare for such a journey."

He stood and rendered her a slight bow. "You've my leave. You're a brave woman, Rhianna of the Trinovantes. I wish you well in your travels and much success with the emperor. He can be difficult, but if anyone can convince him, I believe you can."

"Too much hangs in the balance," Rhianna said, a resolute gleam in her eyes. "I won't fail." She turned and strode out the door.

Quintus and Classicianus stared after her.

"This may well be the death of her. Surely you know that, my lord?" Quintus finally broke the silence. A worried frown creased his brow.

"Aye, and 'tis apparent to her, as well. A rare woman, is she not?" the procurator replied. "Is she mayhap the one the Tribune Paullinus sacrificed his career for?"

"Yes, Lord."

Classicianus smiled. "A woman like that is worth such a gamble. He was a fool to part from her."

Quintus sighed and shook his head, his eyes darkening with painful memories. "Marcus was no fool. A cruel destiny tore them apart. And now it seems that same destiny might soon force them back together again. I only wonder if it will finally destroy them when it does."

The salty wind stung Rhianna's face, the surging gusts of air whipped her long, flaxen hair about her. Beneath her feet, the wooden deck of the Roman merchantman rolled up and down as the ship fought its way across the turbulent channel waters. Rhianna's fingers gouged into the deck railing as she leaned over to peer into the ocean's wild, dark depths, heedless of the vessel's erratic movements, heedless of the spray rising to dampen her from the waves breaking below on the curved bow.

On the sea the day was clear, the sky a sharp, achingly intense shade of blue. Wind-swept clouds, in pristine contrast, stood out in such relief one could almost reach up and touch them. The stiff breeze beat the square sails unmerci-

fully, snapping the cloth tautly to and fro. The shouts of th
burly sailors mingled with the haunting cry of gulls as the
soared overhead, then hungrily dove into the white-cappe
waters. Behind them, the coast of Britannia slowly slippe
away, the morning mists rising from the land engulfing it i
a thick blanket of white.

Her last sight of home, Rhianna thought sadly as sh
watched the ship race out to sea. Home, the dear, belove
land she'd thought she'd never leave. Yet what choice ha
she, when to remain would be to watch its destruction? Th
only hope for her people lay ahead now, in the hands of
foreign emperor in a city called Rome.

"It's hard, is it not, to say goodbye to one's country?"

Rhianna turned to find Quintus at her side. She nodded
"Aye, 'tis hard but necessary." She gazed back to the shad
owy, blue-green depths of the sea. "When shall we reac
Rome?"

"If all goes well, in about six weeks. Once we dock a
Gessoriacum, we'll try to join a caravan to Lugdunum. It'
the capital of Gaul and all major roads diverge from there
We're sure to catch a caravan that'll take us through th
mountains to Italia in Lugdunum."

"Six weeks." Rhianna sighed. "How very long and fa
away. 'Twill be over three months before I'm back hom
again."

"A long journey, to be sure." Quintus leaned against th
rail, facing her. "And doubly so considering your condition
Perhaps it would be wise to go below and rest. It'll be severa
hours more before we reach the coast of Gaul."

She smiled at his solicitous concern. "Not yet, Quintus
I've a wish to watch until I can no longer see the island
Then I'll seek my rest."

He paused to tuck an errant lock of hair behind her ear. "See that you do."

Quintus strode away, but not before a strangely tender light flared in his eyes. How odd, Rhianna thought, the gradual change in their relationship. Once she despised him and now . . . now she warmed to his kindness, his solid strength. Marcus had indeed chosen well when he'd taken Quintus as friend. Mayhap he was slowly becoming hers, too.

She turned back to the sea. Friendship . . . how blessed she was with good and true friends. There was Ailm, who of course had to accompany her on this journey. 'Twas the perfect solution to reuniting her and Cei. Kamber, as representative of the Elders, was an obvious choice to come as well. And how could she refuse dear, loving Ura's pleas?

It had been more difficult deciding which of her warriors to bring along, but she'd finally settled on Maglor and his two sons. Rosic, with his imposing size and presence, she'd reluctantly left behind, needing him to rule as interim chieftain. He was one of the few men, outside the rest of the Elders, not overawed by Cador. Rosic would guide the clan well in her absence.

Three months . . . time enough for Cador to cause more problems. It had been a difficult decision not to bring him along, to keep an eye on him if for naught else. But the thought of being free of him for even a short while was too great a temptation. She'd made her authority clear when she'd chosen Rosic over Cador to rule in her absence. Now, she'd just have to trust that Rosic could handle him. At least she'd been able to buy Cador's silence, Rhianna consoled herself, when she'd threatened to reveal his role in the loss of their food stores if he dared betray their plans to the governor. A small consolation at best, but all she—

"Rhianna."

Recognizing the voice, Rhianna smiled. Cordaella drew to her side. The red-haired woman's request to come on the journey was the most surprising aspect of this whole trip. Just when she'd ceased to hope Cordaella would ever forgive her, her friend had sought her out to beg for the honor of accompanying her to Rome.

Rhianna couldn't help but wonder if Cador hadn't sent Cordaella to spy on her, but decided to accept Cordaella's offer nonetheless. Though the hope might be a foolish one, mayhap, with time away from Cador, Cordaella would finally see him for what he truly was. And mayhap, just mayhap, she and Cordaella could once more be friends.

She released her grip on the railing and turned to the red-haired woman. After a brief hug of greeting, they entwined arms and ambled down the deck to the ship's stern. There, in a poignant, companionable silence, the two women watched until the mist-shrouded cliffs of their beloved land disappeared over the horizon. Then, they went below.

The journey to Italia was tedious and tiresome, but relatively uneventful. Once on the Via Aurelia out of Genua, however, the road became more dangerous. Robbers frequently harassed the caravans. The weather only exacerbated the increasingly miserable conditions, raining often and hard. The nights not spent in roadside inns were wet and cold.

Though the women rode in a four-wheeled *raeda* drawn by two oxen, each day seemed to drain yet a little more of Rhianna's strength. The incessant dampness, the jolting ride of the large wooden wagon, the long hours on the road, took their toll on all of them, but Rhianna was the only one unable to spring back after a night's rest. She fought against the insidious weakness, hiding her growing infirmity with an iron-willed determination.

'Twould do no good to reveal it, she told herself on yet one more dreary, drizzling day five weeks into their journey. They couldn't spare even a day's extra rest. The caravan would move on without them, and they needed its relative size for protection against the bandits haunting the roadways. Besides, too much time had already passed since they'd left home, time in which the governor continued to harass and punish her people. In but a week more, a few hundred miles, they'd be in Rome. She could hold on until then. She had to.

That night, however, a chill began to wrack her body and Rhianna flushed hot with fever. Try as she might, she couldn't hide the true state of her health any longer.

"Are you daft, Rhianna?" Ailm demanded as she wrapped yet another blanket around her huddled, shivering form. "How long have you been ill like this? Why didn't you tell anyone?"

"I-I saw no reason," Rhianna replied through chattering teeth. "We must stay with the caravan. I can rest as well in the wagon as in some inn. 'Tis but a small thing; 'twill pass."

Ailm poured her a mug of hot broth and shoved it into her hand. "Here, drink this. 'Twill warm you." She rose.

Rhianna looked up at her. "W-where are you going?"

"To find Quintus. 'Tis past time he know of your condition."

"Ailm, nay! He'll only make matters worse." Rhianna set down her mug and made an attempt to stop her, but the awkward weight of her swollen belly precluded any rapid movement.

Ignoring her pleas, Ailm had already hurried off. She found Quintus near the water barrel tied to one of the wagons. He was bare-chested, his tunic top rolled down about his waist as he washed his upper body. Droplets of water glinted in his damp hair, and his face was once more cleanly shaven.

Ailm hesitated, then forced herself onward. "Quintus, a moment of your time."

He stopped washing, the soapy rag in his hand. "What is it, lady?"

" 'Tis Rhianna. She's ill, has been so for some time now, if I guess correctly."

"Gods!" Throwing the rag aside, Quintus stooped to sluice water from a wash bucket over his arms and chest. "Why hasn't she said something before now?"

"She didn't want us to halt the journey because of her. You know Rhianna, know how stubborn she can be."

Grabbing a clean cloth, Quintus hurriedly dried himself as he strode back toward the campfire and Rhianna, Ailm following in his wake. "Yes, I know," he muttered, "but I'll not have her endangering her life and the child's for a few days' delay."

Rhianna sat before the fire, pretending fascination with her mug of broth. Quintus squatted before her. "Rhianna. Look at me."

Blue eyes, their usual glinting brightness dulled with fever, reluctantly lifted. He grasped her chin with one large hand while he touched the back of the other to her forehead. For the first time Quintus noted the dark circles under her eyes, the translucent sheen to her skin, the hectic flush to her cheeks, and her unnatural warmth. Gods, she'd been suffering, slowly weakening all the while, and hadn't said anything!

He scowled blackly. "You're ill and feverish. Are you fool enough to risk the child's life as well as your own?"

"I risk neither." Rhianna smiled. "We'll both live to see my childbirth purification. I have seen it in a vision."

Quintus laughed in disbelief. "Well, I care not for your Celtic superstitions. All I know is that I'm responsible for your safe arrival in Rome. We'll rest here a few days until you're better."

Rhianna shook her head, her lips tightening in defiance. "Nay. I leave with this caravan on the morrow, with or without you."

"And if I choose to stop you?"

Her eyes filled with tears. "Don't, Quintus. I couldn't bear it if you were hurt, but I'd be forced to order my warriors to protect me."

She lowered her head, her hair tumbling down to hide her face. "Please, I beg you; don't try to stop me. You cannot shield me from my destiny. No one can."

"Rhianna, Rhianna." He gathered her to him, pressing her head to his hair-roughened chest. "I've no heart for this, no desire to hurt you. But to stand by and watch you kill yourself by little steps . . ."

How like Marcus he was in so many ways, she thought, finding comfort, for a brief moment, in the solid warmth of his body. Yet she dared not let herself weaken or he, too, would keep her from her mission. With a resigned sigh, Rhianna pulled away.

Better to divert both their attention to a more neutral topic. She shoved the hair from her face and gave him a small, arch smile. "So many pretty girls in the caravan, and you waste your time on a married woman bloated with child? Why hasn't such a handsome man as you taken a wife by now?"

A slight flush crept up his neck to tinge his rough-hewn features. "For a long while I wasn't looking and when I finally did, the one I found was already in love with my best friend."

There was no mistaking the meaning in his words or the emotions glinting in his silver eyes. Rhianna averted her gaze. "I-I am sorry. I didn't know."

Quintus took her chin back in his hand and lifted her eyes to his. "What good would it have done? You loved Marcus as much as he loved you. I never had a chance."

"I-I didn't like you at first," she volunteered, eager to change the subject. "You seemed arrogant, shallow, everything I supposed a Roman soldier to be—and everything I hated." A slow, shy smile curved her lips. "I was wrong about you."

He shrugged. "And how were you to know otherwise? I'm not in the habit of letting people get too close. Most aren't worth the potential pain."

"Have *I* hurt you, Quintus? I pray not."

"No more than I can bear, and one's masculine ego heals in time." He took her hand, turning it over to stroke her palm. "I'd like very much, though, if you'd be my friend. It's something I'd value greatly."

She squeezed his hand. "I'd be honored." The babe within her moved suddenly. Rhianna gave a small gasp. The reminder of the life growing inside filled her with a renewed joy.

As if noting the change in her, Quintus' gaze sharpened. "The child's active, isn't it? It'll be a strong boy."

Rhianna laughed. "You men are all alike. You think only of sons, and yet where would you be without the daughters to bear those sons?"

His keen eyes knifed into hers, piercing to her very soul. "Marcus would have been happy with the child, no matter what it was. But he'll never know, will he, Rhianna?"

The smile died on her lips. Goddess! "Cador's my husband."

"But not the child's father, is he?"

" 'Tisn't your concern, Quintus."

He rose to tower over her. "Perhaps not, but how do you plan to hide the fact once the child's born."

She blinked in confusion. "I-I don't understand."

"Don't you, Rhianna?" Quintus' voice took on a pitying tone. "Both you and Cador are fair, blue-eyed, and yellow-haired. What if the child's born darker, with green eyes and black hair? It's possible, isn't it, Rhianna? What will you do then?"

Before she could reply, Quintus walked away. She watched his tall, powerful form until it disappeared from view, her hand all the while unconsciously caressing her belly. Indeed, she thought, what would she do if the babe looked like Marcus? They'd soon be in Rome. What if the babe were born early, while they were still there? And what if Marcus found out? What would she do then? To turn from him, to deny their vows was hard enough. But to take his child away . . .

'Twouldn't happen. It couldn't happen. Rhianna quashed the sudden surge of panic. All would go well in Rome, the letter soon delivered to Nero, and then they'd be on their way home again. Why, there wasn't even a need to see Marcus. Quintus could deliver Ailm to Cei. Aye, no need at all to meet him again, she reassured herself, to submit either of them to further pain.

No need at all.

Twenty

They left the caravan on the northernmost outskirts of Rome and took a road south to the summer villa of Quintus' family. A sprawling estate of stucco buildings and red-tiled roofs, it stood in the midst of well-tended gardens and bountiful orchards. Though surprised at their son's unexpected arrival, not to mention his Britanni guests, Quintus' parents nonetheless welcomed them warmly.

Rhianna, Ailm, Ura, and Cordaella were given a large, lovely room complete with four wooden beds on slim frames ending in sturdy legs carved into animal heads. While Cordaella and Ura, who'd never been inside a Roman house, walked about the room examining the smallest detail, Ailm set about putting the exhausted Rhianna to bed. Rhianna slept until early evening, when Quintus, accompanied by a servant bearing the supper meal, arrived.

"Wake up, sleepy one," he said, chuckling, prodding her awake with an insistent finger. "You need more than rest if you're to bear a healthy child."

With Ailm's assistance, Rhianna raised to a sitting position in bed. She gazed, bleary-eyed, at the small table that was moved beside her. On a tray sat a simple but attractively prepared meal of succulent slices of roast pigeon, freshly baked bread, a generous wedge of goat's cheese, and a bowl of berries. Next to the red-glazed Samian-ware plates and the silverware was a flagon of wine and two goblets. Quintus poured out a cup for himself and Rhianna.

Turning to the three other women, he motioned toward the quietly waiting servant. "Julia will take you down to the *triclinium* where the others await. I'll join you soon, after I've had a few minutes to speak with Rhianna."

The women left with Julia. Once they were alone, Quintus turned to Rhianna. He filled a plate and placed it before her. Then, retrieving his wine goblet, he pulled a chair up to the bed and sat down. "On the morrow, I'll take Ailm to Cei."

And Marcus is with Cei, Rhianna thought, finishing his unspoken words. She smiled sadly. "Aye, I thought as much. 'Twill be hard to say farewell, but I know she'll be happy."

Quintus waited for her to say more. "And what of you?" he demanded finally. "Have you no words for Marcus, no wish to see him?"

"What I want is of no import. 'Twould only hurt to see him again." She laid her hand on his. "Let it be, Quintus."

"We need his help, his father's contacts in the Senate, if we're to gain an audience with the emperor." He withdrew his hand. "I must speak to him, Rhianna."

She bowed her head, suddenly weighted down with the seemingly incessant demands she must make of Marcus. Would she never be able to let him be or end her torment of him? Were they bound by invisible bonds pulling one to the other, no matter what the distance?

All she'd ever wanted was to spare him pain and, most particularly, the agony of her presence. Yet what could be done, when the needs of her people constantly forced them together?

"Do what you must, Quintus," Rhianna whispered, lifting her gaze to his, "not because of me, but for my people."

He rose, his gray eyes as dark as slate. "And why not for

you? Aren't you entitled to a little happiness, Rhianna? I don't understand what drives you to such lengths of self-sacrifice. You Celts speak so highly of honor, but I find nothing honorable in the way you're ruining not only your life but that of Marcus as well. If this is honor, you can have my share."

"There are many forms of honor," she replied quietly. "Do not denigrate what you cannot understand."

A muscle leaped in Quintus' jaw. "Cannot understand? So that's how it is, is it? I'm but an ignorant Roman, too stupid to grasp the higher principles?" At the anguished look in Rhianna's eyes he paused, fighting to master himself. His voice, when he finally spoke, was husky but controlled. "You're tired, as am I. This isn't the time for a discussion about personal integrity."

Quintus glanced at her plate. "Eat, then rest. The morrow is soon enough to seek further understanding, to learn more of honor."

She watched him stride from the room. Honor, understanding. What were they to her—she, who had sacrificed everything of personal value for the sake of her people? Was it true, what Quintus had said about her ruining Marcus' life? Was that the punishment for turning from her Gift, for fighting so long against her true destiny—to watch Marcus' destruction by slow, painful degrees?

With an explosion of pent-up anger and pain, Rhianna swept the tray of food off the little table. The contents spattered the bed and nearby walls, the plates and silverware crashing to the floor. Burying her head in her hands, Rhianna cried until she could weep no more and then fell into an exhausted, fitful slumber.

* * *

The next morning Rhianna saw Ailm off. Her eyes still puffy from her long hours of crying and intermittent sleep, she teetered on the verge of collapse.

Ailm's worried gaze swept her face. "Fear not, I'll have Cei bring me to visit as often as I can." Tenderly, she stroked Rhianna's cheek. "Today isn't our final parting, dear friend. We've a time yet before that happens."

"Aye, I know, but still I cannot bear to see you go." Rhianna gathered Ailm to her, her words muffled in her friend's hair. "I'm not as strong anymore, Ailm. Sometimes I . . . I feel so alone, so afraid."

"These past months have been hard on you, but 'twill soon be over. Hold on; have faith. For your sake, for the babe's . . . for Marcus'." Ailm disentangled herself from Rhianna's clasp and stepped back. She ran to the chariot where Quintus awaited. Not daring a backward glance, she gazed up at him tearfully. "Go. Now, before it breaks my heart."

Reins snapped across the horses' backs and, in a flurry of dust, the chariot rolled away. Out toward the Appenninus foothills they sped, drawing ever farther from Rome and toward the palatial summer villa of the Paullinus family.

A peephole opened when Quintus knocked on the thick, wooden door of Marcus' home. Alert dark eyes set in an ancient face stared blankly back at them. Gradually, recognition dawned.

"Master Quintus!" the servant exclaimed. "What an unexpected surprise. Master Marcus will be overjoyed!" The guide bolt slid back and the heavy, carved door swung open. "Come in, come in," the old man motioned.

With a wry grin, Quintus led Ailm into a long, cool hallway. As Ailm stared in interest at the bright, intricate scenes of the tessellated floor, Quintus turned to the servant. "Marcus and his man, Cei? Are they about, Lucius?"

Lucius nodded. "Yes, Master Quintus." He gestured to a nearby room. "If you will, there is wine and fresh fruit to enjoy while I bring them to you."

As the little man excitedly hurried off, Quintus and Ailm walked into the room. Lavishly furnished with several couches upholstered in shades of emerald green and peacock blue that accented the colors of the mosaic floor, the chamber was airy and relaxing. On a table of ebony wood set against one wall were a long-necked bronze flagon, four cups, and a bowl of fruit.

Quintus strode to the flagon. "A cup of wine, perhaps, Ailm?"

"Aye, please. 'Twas a long, dusty ride and my throat's parched." She accepted the proffered cup. "And I must admit to a need, as well, to calm my nerves."

"It's an exciting moment, isn't it?" Quintus smiled down at her, sipping from his own goblet. "And perhaps one of the happiest, too."

At the sound of rapid footsteps, Quintus took Ailm's cup from her then wheeled about, effectively blocking Ailm from view. Marcus strode into the room, closely followed by Cei.

Marcus halted, an incredulous grin spreading across his face. "I can't believe it! What brings you all the way from Britannia? Surely you, too, haven't so soon managed to anger my uncle?"

"Not yet," Quintus said with a laugh, "but quite possibly after this trip. My visit here today, however, is one of pleasure as well as business." He stepped away from Ailm, gesturing to her with his goblet. "First, though, let us deal with pleasure."

Ailm's eyes locked with Cei's and, for a moment, both stared at each other in speechless wonder. Then, with a soft cry, Ailm sprang forward into the welcoming arms of her husband. They stood wrapped in a passionate embrace until Marcus cleared his throat. Cei glanced up, his gaze ecstatic, bedazzled.

"Why don't you finish your reunion in the privacy of your quarters while Quintus and I talk here?" Marcus suggested, smiling. "Time enough later to share Ailm's company with the rest of us, wouldn't you say?"

His only reply a grateful nod, Cei gently guided his wife from the room. Marcus turned to Quintus. "Where did you find her, Quintus? I'm eternally in your debt for what you've done for Cei." As he spoke, Marcus strode to clasp his friend's arm."

"I had nothing to do with it. Ailm found Rhianna. It was she who nursed Ailm back to health."

At the mention of Rhianna's name, Marcus winced. Would he never be free of her, even now, halfway across the world? He schooled his voice to a calm, even tone and kept his face an inscrutable mask. "Then I'm also grateful to Rhianna." He walked to the table and poured himself a cup of wine. "You said something about business."

"I've a favor to ask, but first, tell me of you. What has happened since your untimely departure from Britannia?"

"Untimely departure?" Marcus gave a bitter laugh and ran his hand through his dark curls. "You've become quite the diplomat, eh, Quintus? I've taught you well." He downed the contents of his cup and, setting it back on the table, strode to the nearest chair and flung himself into it. "Strange how Fate can deal you a painful blow with one hand and, with the other, pick you up and set you on your feet almost better than before. I returned to Rome thinking I'd brought shame not only upon myself but my family. I even contemplated suicide, for the honor of home and hearth and all that. But

I couldn't bring myself to it, for I honestly felt I'd done no wrong."

He smiled grimly. "Besides, I wasn't about to let others dictate my death for me. My father, though very perturbed at the conflict between his brother and me, accepted me back into his home despite the censure of many. And, not long after, I received a summons to a private audience with Nero. I went, fully expecting further reproof and perhaps even an imperial request for my 'honorable demise.' Instead, I was warmly welcomed and informed that, though he couldn't, because of current political difficulties, reinstate my military commission, Nero didn't view my actions as treason."

Quintus arched a dark brow. "Indeed?"

"Indeed," Marcus replied. "It seems the reports filtering out of Britannia of late have increasingly concerned the emperor. He asked me to bear with him for a time while he gathered a more conclusive case against my uncle. Then my honor would be restored and I'd be reinstated with a comparably prestigious position. Needless to say, I left greatly heartened, with Nero's assurances that he still had need of me."

His friend gave a snort of surprise. "For your sake, I'm glad the emperor views you favorably, but his regard is notoriously fickle. I pray the opportunity for reinstatement occurs before he has the opportunity to forget you." Quintus paused, a sudden thought flashing through his mind. "Perhaps that opportunity has indeed arrived. You said Nero needs further proof of the governor's lack of ability to rule Britannia. Well, I may have just the proof he seeks."

"And what might that be?"

"The new provincial procurator, Julius Classicianus, sent me here with a letter for Nero. In it he details the havoc the governor's cruel policies are wreaking on the southern provinces. He begs the emperor to recall the governor."

Marcus' brows knit in puzzlement. "And what is my part in this?"

"I need an audience with Nero. You're in a position to obtain it for me."

Marcus studied him intently. "Do you realize what you're asking of me, Quintus? That I aid you in the political destruction of my uncle?"

"And what is that to you, after the treatment you received in Britannia? I should think you'd be eager to seek revenge against him."

"If only it were so simple." Marcus rose and returned to the wine table. He poured himself another cup and took a long swallow before turning back to Quintus. "I have a political career to rebuild. I have my family to think of. To turn against my uncle would hurt my father deeply, not to mention stir the gossip and speculation anew." He shook his head. "I'm sorry, Quintus. My life is here now, where it was always meant to be. There's nothing left for me back in Britannia—nothing."

"Marcus—"

"I said no, Quintus. There are other channels. You can procure an audience through the usual means."

"It needs to be secret. I can't use the 'usual means.' "

Marcus' mouth twisted wryly. "Oh, and why not?"

Quintus sighed in exasperation. He'd have to tell him about Rhianna, and he'd hoped to have had more time to feel Marcus out before breaking the news. But now, what other recourse was there? He took a fortifying swallow of wine. "Too many lives would be endangered if the emperor decided against taking action and the governor found out. Lives of people like Rhianna and her clan."

Marcus scowled blackly. "And what does Rhianna have to do with this?" When no answer was forthcoming, he slammed down his cup of wine on the table. "Well, Quintus? *What does Rhianna have to do with this?*"

"She came with me to add her plea to the procurator's. She intends to speak with Nero."

Green-gold eyes narrowed to angry slits. "And where is she now?"

"At my parents' home," Quintus replied calmly, undaunted by the growing rage on his friend's face.

As the seconds sped by, Marcus stared at him, the muscle jumping in his jaw the only hint of his inner turmoil. So, he thought, even now she torments me, following halfway across the world to complete my destruction. But not this time. She'd not succeed this time. He'd not let her.

Slowly, Marcus shook his head. "I see you, too, have fallen under her spell and now she seeks to use you. But I'll not help her in this, and I advise you to disengage yourself as well. As you said, lives are in danger, and one of them could well be yours." He gave a bitter laugh. "Beware, Quintus. Rhianna's love is a deadly thing. She'll suck you dry, then toss you aside when you're no longer of use. Leave her now, before it's too late!"

"You speak as if she intentionally chose to hurt you," Quintus growled. "That couldn't be farther from the truth. You say I've fallen under her spell and, in a sense, I have. I respect her deeply, but as far as cherishing any hope of winning her love . . ." It was his turn to laugh. "Any man who sought such a prize would be doomed to failure. Rhianna's never stopped loving you."

Marcus smiled grimly. "And you're a greater fool than I if you believe that. Cease your futile matchmaking, Quintus. It's over, dead between us, and I'll hear no more."

"Does that mean you won't help us?" Anger smoldered just below the surface of his words.

"Exactly."

"Then *you're* the fool, Marcus, and I'll not squander any more of your precious time. I bid you good day." He set down his goblet and stalked from the room.

Marcus made no move to stop him. Instead, he poured himself yet another cup of wine. Staring into its shimmering depths, he swirled it contemplatively. Rhianna in Rome . . . Gods, how he yearned to go to her, if only to refresh the memories still haunting him. Yet to do so would only admit to a weakness he dared not face—the fact he loved her and always would. If he saw her again . . .

He slammed the cup of wine down on the table. The burgundy sloshed over his hand, but he noticed nothing save the searing anguish tearing through him. Curse Quintus and, above all, curse Rhianna! Irritated, he rubbed the back of his neck and shoulders, then stopped as his fingers slid over the bands of raised tissue.

His scars. Even now, over five months since his flogging, they still burned and ached at times. Yet another reminder of the utter devastation of his life and heart thanks to Rhianna, he reminded himself bitterly. Well, this was one time he'd not weaken and be beaten down by his tumultuous feelings for the beauteous, golden-haired Britanni.

And he'd not help her—now or ever again!

Thanks to Cei's assistance and the grudging loan of Marcus' chariot, in the course of the next two weeks, Ailm managed to visit Rhianna several times. She faced a friend hovering on the brink of despair.

"Quintus doesn't know what else to do, whom else to turn

to," Rhianna groaned as she paced the room, massaging her aching back as she did. In but the past few days, the discomfort had seemed to increase tenfold. Goddess, would she be forced to bear her babe in Rome?

Ailm eyed her calmly. "Then the solution is simple. You must go to Marcus."

"Marcus?" The word was but an echo of the horror in Rhianna's sky-blue eyes. She vehemently shook her head. "Nay, Ailm. Never. Never will I go to him again. He turned away his best friend when he came to plead my cause. Do you think I'd fare any better? Nay, 'twould be more shame than I could bear. Let us speak no more of it."

"You won't go to him; he won't come to you." Ailm threw up her hands in exasperation. "What a pair of proud, love-struck fools! Why do you two insist on endlessly hurting each other?"

" 'Twas never my intent to hurt him, though it seems I've succeeded most admirably in the task. And that, dear friend, is exactly my point. Haven't I managed to ruin him, to nearly cause his death? To ask his help now would risk him yet again.

"Nay, Ailm," Rhianna whispered, lowering her head to hide her tear-filled eyes. "I can go no farther in this, not even for the sake of my people. I'll not put Marcus in such jeopardy again!"

The russet-haired woman clasped her friend by the shoulders. "Ah, Rhianna, 'twas never your fault, any of that. 'Twas the hand of an unkind fate. In his heart, Marcus knows that. 'Tis his pain at losing you that keeps you two apart. Go to him, tell him of the babe, his babe—"

"Stop!" Rhianna wrenched herself free of Ailm's hold. "You know naught of who my babe's father is! And I forbid you to speak of it to Marcus!"

" 'Tis a cruel thing, to hide the truth from Marcus," Ailm said, her gaze never wavering. "And no matter how you deny it, we both know what that truth is."

"And isn't it a crueler thing to tell him of a child he can never call his own?" Tears trickled down Rhianna's cheeks and, with an impatient gesture, she brushed them aside. "Ah, it seems I cry far too long and oft of late." A small, self-conscious smile wended its way across her face. "Think you 'tis but the effects of my childbearing?"

Ailm returned her smile. "Aye. 'Tis said it affects most women that way." She sighed. "I fear 'tis a thing I'll never know. We've tried mightily, Cei and I, to conceive a child and still I remain barren. 'Tis my greatest sorrow, this inability to grant my husband's fondest wish."

Rhianna patted her friend's hand. "There's yet time. You and Cei are still young, strong and—"

Cei stepped into the room. His glance swept the two women and, noting Rhianna's reddened eyes, he discreetly averted his gaze. " 'Tis time to leave, Ailm."

Ailm turned to Rhianna. "I must go, dear friend, but I'll return in a few days. For a time more I'll respect your wish not to tell Marcus, but we must speak of this again. All I ask is that you think upon what I have said."

She gently kissed the golden head and followed her husband from the room. The ride back to the Paullinus' villa, though long, was one of little conversation. Frustration at Rhianna's situation simmered within Ailm. By the time they reached the villa, her anger had reached the boiling point. Marcus, unfortunately, was the first person she saw when she walked into the house.

"Let it be, wife," Cei warned, as if sensing the cause of her anger and the intent of her determined movement toward Marcus.

She shook her head, not even gracing him with a backward glance. "Nay. I tire of the foolish pride keeping them apart." She resolutely walked over to confront Marcus. "Lord Marcus. A moment of your time."

Marcus' chiseled mouth tilted into an amused smile. "Lord?" He glanced at Cei questioningly.

Cei expelled a frustrated breath and shrugged.

Ailm ignored the two men's visual interchange. "I've just returned from a visit with Rhianna."

"So I gather," came the dry rejoinder.

"She has been here two weeks now, and still you refuse to see her."

Marcus' jaw tightened. "That's of no concern to you."

"No concern? You are both my friends! I care for you deeply. How can you expect me to stand by and watch this senseless self-torture, when both of you yearn to be together?"

"You mistake yourself, Ailm." Marcus strode to the wine flagon and poured himself a cup. "I long ago ceased to want or care about Rhianna."

"And I say you lie!"

Marcus' tall form went rigid.

"Wife," Cei growled, hurrying to grasp her by the arm and drag her from Marcus, "this time you've gone too far!"

Ailm, struggling in his clasp, however, was not to be silenced. "You know 'tis true," she cried as she was all but carried from the room. "She loves you, Marcus, and needs you as much as you need her. Go to her; help her. Now, before 'tis too—"

Her voice was abruptly cut off as Cei disappeared down the hall with her. Marcus emptied the contents of his cup in one gulp, then poured himself another. Raising it to his lips, he paused to eye it consideringly.

I've taken to the grape more and more oft of late, he thought. *If I'm not careful, I'll soon be one of those besotted, crimson-nosed drunkards who frequent the Roman alleyways. And all because of a woman.*

Impatient and self-disgusted, Marcus set down his cup and strode from the room. *A woman! First his mother and now Rhianna! Gods,* he silently cursed, *why were men so stupid, so governed by their loins they allowed themselves to be driven, like braying jackasses, by pretty faces and softly rounded bodies?*

He stalked to the stables and ordered his horse saddled. Then, mounting, Marcus signaled the animal forward. The stallion sprang out in a billowing cloud of dust, carrying Marcus toward the distant hills—and a fruitless search for peace.

In the early hours before sunrise, a loud, insistent pounding woke Marcus from a wine-besotted stupor. He opened his eyes to darkness. The pounding continued. The door . . . the main entry door. Gods, would no one answer it?

He swung his legs over the side of his bed and sat up. A rhythmic throbbing in time to the pounding at the door reverberated within his skull. He groaned and cradled his head in his hands. Too much wine . . . you fool.

The ride into the Appenninus Mountains hadn't eased his torment of heart and, when he'd returned hours later at dusk, he'd headed straight for the wine. Just a few cups to quench his thirst had led to several empty flagons before Cei had finally carried him to bed. And now to be woken in the middle of the night by some inconsiderate lout! Marcus rose to his feet and staggered from his room.

He met Ailm in the hallway, just as Cei was opening the

front door. Noting his bleary-eyed condition, her glance skittered guiltily away.

"What brings you here at such an hour?" Cei demanded of the man who stepped through the open doorway. His exasperation died as he recognized the nocturnal visitor from his visits to Rhianna. "Maglor!"

The Trinovante glanced about until his gaze found Ailm. "Ah, lady," he exclaimed in relief. "Thank the Goddess I've found you. The Lady Rhianna's time has come. She asks for you."

"Permit me a moment to dress and I'll—"

"What do you mean, 'Rhianna's time has come'?" Marcus interrupted Ailm huskily. His gaze narrowed. "Is she with child?"

Ailm nodded. "Aye, Marcus."

He ran a hand raggedly through his tousled curls. "Why wasn't I told?"

"She didn't want you to know."

"And why not?" The tone of his voice sharpened. "Why was it such a secret? What was there to hide?" His voice faded and he scanned the faces of the three people standing before him intently. Marcus' glance finally settled on Ailm. "Whose child does she carry, Ailm?"

"She claims 'tis Cador's." Ailm wouldn't look at him.

"Claims? Whose child do *you* think it is?"

She lifted her eyes. "You know the answer as well as I."

"Gods!" Marcus turned to Maglor. "There's wine in that room." He indicated the chamber on Maglor's left. "Take a moment to sate your thirst while we prepare to accompany you back."

Maglor nodded and walked away. A small hand settled on Marcus' arm. He turned to its owner.

"You'll go to her then?" Ailm whispered.

"She asked for you, not me, Ailm. I go only to see for myself the fruits of the birth and to discover who the father truly is. That, and no more."

The eyes staring down at Ailm were hard and unrelenting. She knew better than to press the matter. With a sigh, she hurried away, consoling herself with the hope that once Marcus was near Rhianna, his fierce resolve might finally soften.

A small hope at best, but all she had.

Dawn's lavender fingers spread their feather-light touch across the sky before they arrived at the Marcellus' villa. The chariot was barely halted when Ailm jumped down and ran inside. Marcus and Cei followed at a more sedate pace and met Quintus at the door.

Gray eyes met green ones. "It's good that you're here," Quintus said. "The birthing goes hard. She'll need you."

"She didn't ask for me, only Ailm," Marcus muttered, flushing hotly. "I came only to discover the truth that all of you have tried to keep from me."

Quintus' brow wrinkled in puzzlement. "And what truth is that?"

"The real father of Rhianna's child."

His friend sighed. "She didn't wish for you to know."

Marcus gave a harsh laugh. "Yes, that's more than evident. And it makes one wonder—does it not—about the reason behind her action." He glanced at the open doorway that Quintus' powerful form still blocked. "Will you permit me entry or does your protection of Rhianna extend to the barring of old friends from your home?"

Quintus stepped aside. "No, I'll not keep you from her. I ask only that you be gentle. It's enough she suffers the pangs of childbirth without your adding to them."

"I've no intention of even seeing Rhianna," Marcus stated flatly. He made a motion with his hand. "Now, play the host, Quintus. Show me where she is."

With Marcus and Cei in his wake, Quintus led them down the long corridor to the sleeping quarters. A low moan identified the location of Rhianna's room. Quintus turned to look at Marcus just in time to see the color drain from his face. He opened his mouth to speak, then thought better of it.

Instead, he gestured to a polished wooden bench placed against the wall outside her room. "You may wait here or rest in one of the guest quarters until the child comes. What is your wish?"

"Here," Marcus rasped. "I'll wait here." He sat on the bench and cradled his head in his hands.

Quintus shot Cei a quizzical look.

The Celt smiled crookedly. "Too much wine last night."

"I'll send for something to ease his misery." Quintus strode down the hallway.

"Well, my friend," Cei chuckled as he settled himself beside Marcus. "Now we engage in the traditional pastime of all males at birthings—a long wait."

Marcus looked up, his glance anguished. "Is the child mine? Tell me the truth."

The blond-haired man slowly shook his head. "I do not know, Marcus. 'Tis my strong suspicion, but if Rhianna's told Ailm, I cannot pry it from her." He gripped Marcus by the arm. "Time will tell, though, will it not? All we have to do is wait."

A louder moan emanated from Rhianna's room and Marcus grimaced. "Yes, and it may just be the hardest thing I'll ever have to do."

Hours passed and the child wouldn't come. Rhianna writhed on her bed when the contractions held her in their agonizing throes and dozed in limp exhaustion when they left her for all too brief, merciful moments. Ailm, Ura, and Cordaella did their best to hide their growing concern, but even Rhianna finally noticed the drawn, tight expressions.

Weakly, she reached for Ailm's hand. "Come closer," she whispered. "A word . . . with you."

Ailm squatted beside her bed. "Aye, Rhianna?" As she spoke, she moistened a cloth to sponge her friend's forehead.

"It goes badly . . . the childbirth, I mean." She intently searched Ailm's face. " 'Tis true, is it not?"

" 'Tis naught to trouble yourself about," her friend hurried to reassure her. "Many first births go as long."

Rhianna's grip tightened as yet another wave of contractions swept through her. For long seconds she fought the pain, struggled against the cry that rose to her lips, until it finally escaped in a strangled gasp.

"A-Ailm!"

Ailm grasped her hand. At last the contraction peaked and began to ebb. Rhianna expelled a long, shuddering breath and went limp.

"Tell me . . . the truth!" she cried. "Is it not . . . possible . . . I could die?"

Her friend hesitated until Rhianna could bear the wait no longer. "Tell me," she groaned. "Would you wish my motherless babe be given to Cador?"

"Nay, never!" Ailm whispered, choking back a sob. She stroked Rhianna's cheek tenderly. "Aye, 'tis possible you could die if the babe doesn't come soon."

"Marcus."

The word was spoken so softly Ailm had to lean closer. "What did you say?"

"M-Marcus. Send for him. I . . . I must speak with him."

A fierce joy welled in Ailm's breast. At last, at last they'd finally face each other. She took up a cloth and wiped the moisture from Rhianna's brow. "I'll fetch him. Marcus is but outside your door and has been since I arrived."

Pain-glazed eyes stared up at her. "H-here? Outside . . . all this time?"

"Aye." Ailm nodded, smiling. Ever so gently, she disengaged her hand. "But a moment and I'll have him at your side."

The door opened, drawing the gaze of Marcus and Cei.

"She asks for you, Marcus." Ailm extended her hand.

His bronzed features paled. Marcus rose. "How is she?"

"It goes hard for her."

He hesitated. Gods, but he wanted to see her, to be with her through it all. Yet what about his resolve to separate himself from Rhianna, to drive her from his heart and life?

"Marcus, please. She may not survive this birthing."

His iron will splintered. Wordlessly, he strode past Ailm and into the room. Rhianna lay in the bed, so pale, so quiet Marcus imagined for a moment she was unconscious. He pulled up a chair and sat down beside her. A slender arm lay atop the thin sheet covering her. He stroked it lightly.

"Rhianna?"

Long, thick lashes fluttered open. "M-Marcus?"

He smiled warily. "Yes, it is I."

"Thank . . . thank you for coming."

His hand slipped down to take hers. "Ailm said you asked for me. What is it you wanted?"

"The birthing goes poorly. I—"

She tensed with the building force of another contraction. Her eyes widened, then clenched shut, as Rhianna fought to ride the wave of pain. "Ah, Sweet G-Goddess!"

Marcus grasped her hand and clasped it to his forearm.

"Hold onto me, Rhianna. Squeeze as hard as you can. It'll pass, as surely as have all the others."

"Stay with me!" she cried. "Don't leave!"

"For as long as you want me," he assured her, his voice low and soothing.

The pain finally subsided and Rhianna relaxed once more. She opened her eyes and smiled. "The . . . babe. If I die, prom-promise to t-take it from me."

Marcus opened his mouth to protest.

"You must save the babe, Marcus," Rhianna interrupted him tearfully. " 'Tis yours."

"Ours," he corrected her, smiling, the truth at last filling him with a curious, heart-deep joy. "The child is the fruit of *our* love."

"A-aye." Her long fingers caressed the dark, curling hairs on his arm. "And all that is left of it, I fear." She forced her gaze back to his face and went on resolutely. " 'Tis all I have left to give you. If I die, I want my babe raised by his true father. Promise me you'll take him into your home, love him, and speak kindly of his mother."

"And if you live, what then? Do you think I can easily part from him, knowing what I know now? Will you then take him from me?"

Twin tracks of moisture coursed down Rhianna's cheeks. " 'Tisn't m-my desire."

"Yet, what choice have you, eh, Rhianna?"

She looked up into eyes glinting as hard as ice yet, beneath their frigid surfaces, she caught a glimpse of a searing anguish, a barely controlled need. She sighed. "I cannot remain in Rome, Marcus. My people . . ."

"Then promise me the child, whether you live or die."

The harshness of his demand sliced through her, just as deeply as the contraction that once more rose within. On and on it climbed in an ever-worsening crescendo of pain. It knotted her body into spasms until Rhianna arched from the bed. Her eyes snapped open at the unexpected agony of it.

"Goddess! Ah, M-Marcus!"

In an instant he was beside her on the bed, pulling her to him. "Don't fight it, my love," Marcus crooned in her ear, cradling her head to his chest. "Ride it; go with it. I'm here. I'm here."

The need for rest after the contraction waned lasted longer this time, but Rhianna finally opened her eyes. "You take unfair advantage of my weakness." She smiled wearily.

The merest hint of a similar smile touched Marcus' lips. "Then perhaps I've evened the odds at last. Pray, answer my question, for I'll not let you escape it."

Her gaze swept lovingly over his face, drinking in as one long thirsty the strong, handsome features, the compelling green-gold eyes, the firm, sensual mouth. The man she loved and would love until she died.

How could she deny him this one request, though to fulfill it would be to tear her heart from her body? Was this the final payment of her vow to the Druid—the sacrifice of even the smallest portion of Marcus she might ever have, in the form of her babe? She was so tired, so weary of the endless battles. Let him have it then; let it be finished. 'Twas the loving thing to do.

Rhianna gave a small nod, though the effort cost her dearly. " 'Twill be as you ask, whether I live or die."

Once more the pain engulfed her, more agonizing than before. Rhianna's body grew taut and she jerked back, hard, against Marcus' chest. "Hold me, ah, hold me!" she gritted through clenched teeth.

Marcus' grip around her tightened, but even the protective strength of his arms wasn't enough to ward off the excruciating inevitability of childbirth. As she struggled against the rising torment, her breathing quickened until it was little more than quick, shallow pants. 'Twas too much for Rhianna's labor-wracked mind and a scream—half-despairing, half-joyous—finally escaped her.

"Ah, Marcus, my love! It comes! Our babe . . . comes!"

Twenty-one

The huge golden doors swung open and Marcus, carrying Rhianna in his arms, strode through. On his right walked Quintus, garbed in full military dress, on his left, the bard Kamber. Across Nero's palace they went, through rooms gleaming with marble, bronze, and gold, past countless statues and paintings, ever onward—toward the emperor's private audience chamber.

Marcus glanced down at the once-more slender form of the woman he carried. She wore a simple, sleeveless gown of deep blue, sandals, and her chieftain's torc, but the contrast of the rich colors with her fair hair and pale skin was striking. He shook his head, a bemused smile twisting his mouth. "I still struggle to understand why, but three days after such a difficult childbirth, you insist on accompanying us to this audience. Even now you can barely walk or stand for more than a few minutes without weakening. Your place would've been better served at home, recuperating and caring for our son."

Rhianna gazed up at him with a sweetly indulgent look. "Deny me not what is mine, Marcus. I'm no less a chieftain, my responsibilities no less demanding, because I'm now a mother. For the moment, 'tis my proper place to be here. Later, 'twill be at little Riderch's side.

"And, despite your misgivings, I'm quite capable of standing on my own two feet. Permitting you to carry me this far was but a ploy to conserve my strength." She shot him an arch smile. "Not to mention steal some covert pleasure spending a time being near you."

Marcus grinned and shifted Rhianna's weight to carry her yet closer, allowing himself, for a brief, stolen moment, his own pleasure at feeling her soft woman's body next to his. "You're as willfully stubborn as ever, woman," Marcus growled, trying to hide the emotion that sprang, unbidden, to his voice. "I see you'll soon be back to your old vigor and busying yourself sticking that pretty little nose into everyone's affairs."

"That she will," Quintus said with a chuckle beside him. "And then we'll have our hands full, rescuing her from whip-wielding horse drivers and the like."

At the reminder of the cause for their first meeting, Rhianna tossed the silver-eyed Roman a light-hearted grin. Before she could reply, though, the small group halted at one last door guarded by two ornately garbed soldiers.

"Ah, the mighty Praetorian Guard," Quintus muttered dryly, eyeing Nero's hand-picked personal bodyguards. He stepped forward to meet them. "The emperor expects us." He handed over a small rolled document. "We've an official audience."

The senior of the two soldiers accepted the scroll and, unrolling it, proceeded to read. His head lifted to scan the faces of the four people assembled before him. Then, he nodded and snapped to attention. "It is as you say, Tribune." The guard motioned to his compatriot. "Open the doors and allow them to enter. The emperor awaits."

Once more huge, ornately gilded doors swung open. Rhianna turned to Marcus. "Put me down, please."

He shot her a quizzical look. "I don't mind carrying you. You're as light as a feather."

"Mayhap, but *I* mind being carried into the presence of your emperor. I'm not so weak I cannot walk a short distance. You can lend me support if I've need for it."

"As you wish." Marcus sighed and put her down. Together, they entered the room, Marcus and Rhianna in the lead followed closely by Quintus and Kamber.

Across the huge expanse of mosaic-tiled floor sat the form of a yellow-haired man on a gilded throne. Though he was dressed in the prerogative of royalty, a deep, rich purple tunic and toga, the regal color did little to hide the degeneration of the man. Rhianna knew him to be but four and twenty, but already Nero possessed a swollen paunch, weak and slender limbs, and a fat face with reddened, blotchy skin. She swallowed hard, choking back her surge of revulsion. Was this then, the emperor of the mighty Roman Empire?

"Remember what we talked about. You must bow when we reach his throne," Marcus muttered, as if reading her mind.

"And I say again," Rhianna whispered back, "he is your ruler, not mine, no matter how strong his armies."

"Then consider it a courtesy between two leaders!" His words escaped in a warning hiss. "This is no time to risk your cause over a few ceremonial bows. And don't forget to let him lead the course of the conversation. Quintus told me how you stampeded over Classicianus. Proper protocol is of essence here."

Before she could toss back yet another reply, they drew up before the throne. Shooting Marcus an exasperated glance, Rhianna turned to Nero and gave a full, elaborate bow.

"Rise, Lady," Nero commanded in a strangely musical,

lilting voice. "Marcus tells me you're a Britanni chieftain. I've a need to see what such a rare woman looks like."

Rhianna straightened and forced her mouth into what she hoped was a protocol smile. "No different from any of your own Roman ladies, I'm sure, Your Majesty."

Dull gray eyes thoroughly scrutinized her. "On the contrary. You are one of the loveliest women I've ever had the pleasure of meeting." His glance settled on Rhianna's hair. "And our Roman ladies would swoon over those golden tresses. It's quite the fashion now, you know." Nero turned to scan the men standing with her. "Besides this beautiful spokeswoman, was there not some letter from the provincial procurator?"

"Yes, your Imperial Majesty." Quintus stepped forward. He offered a military salute and then extended the wax-sealed scroll. "From the Provincial Procurator of Britannia, Caius Julius Alpinus Classicianus."

Nero accepted the letter and, unrolling it, began to read. Gradually, a frown marred his brow. He glanced up at Rhianna. "And you, Lady. What have you to add to this?"

Rhianna took a deep breath and shot a quick look at Marcus. Her heart began to pound beneath her breast. "Ah, where shall I begin, my lord?" she said, taking care not to "stampede" over the Emperor of Rome. " 'Tis all so horrible to recount. The Revolt has been over for ten months now, yet still the retribution continues. We have lost our fathers, brothers, sons, and husbands. Our grain and livestock have been taken from us, our homes destroyed. Countless thousands have died from disease and starvation, and the rest sold into slavery. Yet, even so, I come here today not to beg or grovel or to lie and say that our cause, though ill-fated, wasn't just. Righteousness is no longer of any import. Putting an end to the brutal punishment, the causes of the Revolt, is."

A blond brow lifted in amused inquiry. "And what do you consider the causes?"

As Rhianna opened her mouth to reply, Marcus' hand moved over hers to give a cautionary squeeze. Tact, diplomacy, she reminded herself yet again. Use it now or you'll ruin everything.

"The causes, my lord? Why, greed, corruption, lack of insight into the hearts of the people—the same problems plaguing all governments. Rome is no different from any other ruler. It has good leaders and bad." She looked at Marcus briefly and returned his squeeze. "My friend here was one of its good leaders. He tried to work with my father, who was then chieftain of our clan, to right the wrongs that drove such a wedge of anger and resentment between our two peoples. If he'd had more time, if there had been more of his kind, the Revolt might never have been. *He* is the stuff of Rome. 'Tis men like him who have made this land what 'tis today—strong, wealthy, and rulers of over half the world."

"Well said, Lady." A small smile creased Nero's lips. "It becomes increasingly apparent what attributes saw you chieftain of your tribe." He glanced down at the scroll. "Perhaps the time has come to put a rein on my provincial governor."

Gray eyes lifted to hers. "In a few months I'll send a trusted freedman to investigate the problems in Britannia with full authority to settle all disputes. I can trust what Polyclitus brings back to me will be an accurate accounting of both sides."

Rhianna released Marcus' hand and took a step forward. "A few months?" she repeated anxiously. " 'Tis too long, my lord. Even as we talk the governor continues to punish my people, sell them into slavery, execute them. How many more will have died in but a few months' time?"

"What Rhianna is asking, Royal Majesty," Marcus hastened to interject, noting the sudden narrowing of Nero's eyes, "is that you grant her an imperial decree placing a halt to my uncle's ongoing policies *until* your man Polyclitus has a chance to travel to Britannia. As Classicianus so aptly states in his letter, the longer the people are punished, the longer it will take to rebuild the provincial treasury."

Nero thoughtfully stroked his jaw. "Your words, though less impassioned than the lady's, are no less convincing, Paullinus. You'll have your decree." He paused to eye Marcus, consideringly. "I once spoke of officially reinstating you to another position. That time has come. You will return to Britannia with this lady and deliver my orders to your uncle." Nero smiled. "A most fitting revenge, is it not, to be the instrument of your uncle's censure?"

Marcus stiffened. "If it is your wish, Royal Majesty."

"This lady made mention of your strong talents in working with her people," the emperor continued. "I think those talents should be once more put to use. You're to remain in Britannia indefinitely, Marcus Suetonius Paullinus, with an appointment to work directly with the provincial procurator. Your commission will be to oversee the rapid regeneration of provincial health and welfare."

Marcus hesitated. All his plans, his careful reconstruction of his political career in the past months, stood in jeopardy once more. He didn't want to start anew, didn't wish to return to Britannia. Yet even as the rebellious thoughts flashed through his mind, a sudden realization filled him.

If the truth be known, his Senate ambitions no longer held the appeal they once had. Rome, as glorious, as mighty as it was, no longer seemed the epitome of all that was right and good. Though the admission was long in coming, his destiny had always lain along a path other than Rome's—a path with and for Rhianna and her people. His destiny *and* his ultimate happiness.

With a small, wondering smile, Marcus bowed. "It will be as you ask, Royal Majesty."

Nero rose. "This audience is at an end. When my imperial decree is dictated, a messenger will carry it to your home." Without a backward glance, he left the room.

There was a long silence, then all exhaled a sigh of relief. "My congratulations, lady." Marcus turned to Rhianna. "You handled yourself well and impressed the emperor. It seems that any man who comes under your influence cannot help but fall prey to your charms."

Yet the only one I've ever wanted to charm was you, she thought, gazing up at him. At the realization of what she'd accomplished, combined with her rapidly waning strength, a dizzying weakness washed over her. Rhianna went pale, then swayed.

Marcus quickly gathered her up in his arms. "I told you this would all be too much for you," he growled. "No more outings for the next few weeks."

"But we must leave for home," she murmured from the comforting haven of his broad chest. "There's no time to waste."

"You're not up to the journey and I'll not have you endangering your or our son's health in such thoughtless eagerness. A few weeks won't matter that much and, besides, we can't leave without the emperor's decree. You've given up quite enough for your people. I'll not have you sacrificing your life as well."

Rhianna snuggled yet closer. Marcus was right. She dearly needed the time to regain her strength. Mayhap 'twas wrong to feel so happy over the decision, but she no longer cared.

She smiled up at him, for once all feminine meekness and sweet acquiescence. "Aye, Marcus."

Rhianna cuddled the sleeping babe to her breast, smiling at the downy soft head and fat cheeks nestled so contentedly against her. A small drop of milk glistened on his pursed lips and she wiped it gently away. Her babe . . . sweet, tiny Riderch.

Chee-chee-chee-chee-chee! A flash of metallic green zipped past the edge of Rhianna's vision. She jerked her head up just in time to see a vibrantly red-throated hummingbird fly by. So delicate, yet endlessly energetic, she mused as she watched the diminutive bird disappear over the garden wall, its heart so brave and strong its wee body could barely encompass it.

Let your own heart be so, my son, Rhianna thought, glancing down at her slumbering child. Full of hope, never daunted, always striving for the best in life. 'Tis the only legacy I can offer and all I could ever wish for you. Your father will provide the rest in the long years ahead when I am no longer with you. But I'll not think of that now. 'Tis too perfect a day, this Lughnasa morn, and we are together.

Her thoughts flitted back to another Lughnasa but a year ago and yet, in another sense, ages past. She'd been so young, so carefree then, with no concerns save her lack of enthusiasm at wedding Cador. Yet even as she'd gaily skipped through the leafy forests and raced across the verdant meadows of Trinovante land, her life had reached a crossroads.

A white boar, sacred to the gods, and a handsome, dark-haired Roman . . . Why hadn't she seen it then? The boar's advent was but a signal of her entrance into a new era in her life, a life—her visions had heretofore seemed to warn—of death and destruction. Yet 'twas a signal, instead, that the next person or thing she'd encounter would profoundly affect her existence.

She shook her head, bemused. 'Twas all so clear now, looking back, yet what would or could she have done differently if she'd truly been able to interpret her vision correctly? As hard as they'd both fought against it, life and the vagaries of man had repeatedly come between her and Marcus. Yet however painful and frustrating their relationship had frequently been, she'd never regret the brief moments of happiness, the ecstasy they'd shared. 'Twould never be enough, but 'twas all she had. And she'd cherish the memories to the end of her days.

The past two weeks while she'd slowly regained her strength had been infinitely special, too. Though an unspoken barrier remained between them, Marcus had been kind and solicitous; and the times he'd spent with their son, holding him or watching her attend to his simple infant needs, had possessed an intimacy that made Rhianna's throat ache in the remembrance. The way of a family . . . if things had been different.

With a small sigh, she recalled her thoughts to a less bittersweet path. On the morrow they'd depart Rome, embarking, at last, on the journey home. All was in readiness, all had been seen to, even to the accomplishment of the childbirth purification ceremony. The chosen pool for the bathing had not been one sacred to the Celts, but it had still possessed, for her at least, a special significance.

Marcus had led them to it, explaining that, as a boy, he'd found the pool hidden in a nearby forest and had always considered it his secret haven. The setting was lovely, the waters of the tiny, ultramarine pool gently undulating in the warm, late summer's breeze, the thick stand of encircling trees walling it off from the rest of the world. A multitude of brightly hued flowers grew in dense profusion down to the water's edge, and bird-song filled the air. Mystical, magical—like the pool of her long-ago vision.

She had stood in the wind-lapped waters, her breasts blue-veined and milk-swollen, as Cordaella, Ura, and Ailm had taken turns pouring the ceremonial liquid over her. Strange, Rhianna had mused, that she'd not seen Ailm in her vision. Her friend had played such a vital part—

A scrabbling sound from the outer garden wall snagged Rhianna's attention. She turned her head just as a large, masculine hand grasped the top of the stone enclosure. Clasping Riderch to her, she rose and unsheathed her dagger. Blessed Goddess, who could possibly—

Shaggy blond hair framing a bronzed face appeared above the wall. The features were familiar, but the unexpectedness of the man's appearance caused Rhianna to stare in speechless amazement. His head turned then, his gaze intercepting hers.

"Rhianna!"

An intense, heart-stopping joy flooded her. "Cerdic!"

But an instant later and he was at her side. Though dressed in a ragged, thigh-length tunic of brown homespun with shabby sandals on his feet, her brother looked well if a bit thinner. At the sight of the child in her arms, Cerdic hesitated. His eyes met hers in silent query.

"His name is Riderch. He's Marcus' son."

"Riderch." Cerdic rolled the name on his tongue, a bittersweet smile touching his lips. "Father is reborn at last, then, in the body of your babe. My thanks to you, sister." His aquamarine eyes raised to the torc encircling her neck.

"So, they have chosen you chieftain in my absence. 'Tis well."

Rhianna touched the heavy, bronze neck-ring. " 'Tis a calling I'll gladly return to you, brother." A sudden thought assailed her. "Indeed, you can come with us, for we leave for Britannia on the morrow. Ah, Cerdic, how fortunate the fate that brought us together this day! 'Tis truly a happy Lughnasa."

" 'Tis indeed Lughnasa day?" Cerdic laughed. "In these many months, I'd lost count of the days and seasons." His expression clouded. "But I'll not be returning with you. I've still unfinished business here in Rome, a long dreamt debt to settle. 'Twill be too dangerous to return home directly once I've done what I must do. Rome's arm is long. I'll not risk the safety of our clan until the Red Crests have had a time to forget and turn to other matters."

"But why?" Rhianna cried, then quickly lowered her voice when Riderch moved restlessly against her in his sleep. "Why must you do all this? We need you. You're our chieftain."

"Nay, little sister." Cerdic stroked her cheek tenderly. "You're chieftain now and will remain so until my return. Tell no one of our visit or that I'm alive. To do otherwise might undermine your power in the tribe." He smiled wryly. "After all, 'tisn't possible to have two chieftains at the same time. Think of the conflict, the confusion. Nay, until my return, your authority must be complete. Besides, there's always the possibility I'll not survive long enough to make it back home."

Concern furrowed her brow. "I don't understand. Why wouldn't you make it back?"

"Because I'm an escaped slave, a hunted man. And, when I'm finished exacting my revenge on a certain Roman, I'm sure to be branded outlaw. Not the most promising circumstances under which to attempt a journey home, is it? But enough of that. My time is short. I must be going lest I risk recapture."

Before he could turn away, Rhianna halted him with a clasp on his arm. "A moment more, brother. How did you come to find me here or even know of my presence in a city as large as Rome?"

"Your audience with the emperor. News of even the private meetings eventually filters through the palace hierarchy. A friend of mine heard the tale from a serving maid of Nero's mistress. I couldn't be certain the female chieftain they spoke of 'twas you, but the more information I gleaned, the more hopeful I became." Cerdic gave her a quick hug. "I'm proud of you, little sister. You've borne the burdens well, carried high the lofty traditions of our family and people. The Trinovante are in good hands."

He paused to kiss her on the cheek and run a callused thumb along Riderch's tiny arm. "And this babe is the hope for all our futures."

"Cerdic—"

"Fare you well, Lady." Disengaging himself, Cerdic backed away before Rhianna could offer further protest. In a few quick strides he reached the garden wall, leaped up, and, grasping the top, swung his long legs over it. For one last, emotion-laden moment, Cerdic glanced back at Rhianna. Then, in a lithe movement, he disappeared.

She gazed at the empty wall for a time, the hot summer sun beating down on her, the buzzing and chirping of the garden but a backdrop for her tumultuous feelings. Riderch finally stirred in her arms, his small, rosebud mouth opening in a huge yawn, and then fell back asleep. Rhianna gazed down at him in loving wonder.

Then, with a sigh, she walked back into the house.

* * *

The trip home seemed interminable, twice as long as the journey to Rome. The roadways were so crowded with late summer travelers Rhianna wondered if the entire Roman Empire were on their way to somewhere else. Besides the common rank and file, they encountered philosophers begging their way from town to town, astrologers, doctors, wealthy Greeks traveling in style, and missionaries of many religions.

Thanks to the imperial decree they carried, Marcus was able to procure a diploma which entitled them to the use of the well-organized *cursus publicus* with its posting stations and relays of horses and carriages at regular intervals along the way. The four women and tiny Riderch traveled in one of the horse-drawn carriages, while the six men accompanied them on horseback. Nonetheless, Marcus watched Rhianna carefully and insisted on calling a halt to each day's travel much sooner than she would have ever done.

His prudent judgments as to her reserve of strength proved justified time and again. Once they were lodged for the night, Rhianna found herself fast asleep soon after consuming the evening meal. Fortunately, the inns of the Imperial Travel Service were but another welcome change from the usual hostelries—clean and safe from robbers and other cutthroats.

Thanks to the efficiently run *cursus,* their little group reached the Gaullish port of Gessoriacum a full ten days early. Three days later they were able to procure passage on a merchantman bound across the channel to Rutupiae. Rhianna remained on deck for the entire trip, leaving Riderch in the other women's care save for the necessary nursing visits. Barely able to contain her rising excitement as they drew near the island, she watched as the hours sped by, marveling at the wild beauty of the ocean.

Sea gulls swooped low, skimming the waters in search of food among the glinting, silver-tipped waves. Gray clouds scudded across the horizon, herded by the sharply impatient wind until they churned to dark, smoky gray on the cliffs of the nearing landfall. That first glimpse of the beloved coastline wrenched the first words from her.

"Home!" Rhianna joyfully cried. "Blessed Goddess, we're home!"

"Yes, lady, you're home at last."

Rhianna turned to the handsome, dark-haired man who had quietly moved to her side. " 'Tis your home now, too, Marcus. You've a new commission to serve here, the undying gratitude and friendship of my people, and a son whose blood will span both our cultures. As Trinovante chieftain, I give you my vow to aid in your task, for my people can bear no more war."

"And what of the war between us, Rhianna? Has it, too, come to an end?"

She gazed up into eyes smoldering with a green-gold fire. "On my honor, I never meant for that to happen, never meant to hurt you."

He took her hand. "Then let us be friends. I don't wish our son to grow up in the midst of two battling parents. Besides," he added, smiling, "I need your good will if I'm to visit him whenever I wish."

"V-visit him?" A fierce hope leaped in Rhianna's breast. "But I thought . . ."

"Did you think me so heartless I'd truly take your child?" Marcus chided her gently. "I was hurting when I asked that of you, even hoped, in some addle-minded way that to possess Riderch would be to possess you. I know it was a foolish, futile dream, but it's so hard, so very hard to stop loving you."

She opened her mouth to speak; tenderly, he silenced her with a finger pressed to her lips. "I fought against it for a long while, the anger and bitterness slowly eating me alive. In the end, it still changed nothing. Holding Riderch in my arms that morn of his birth made me realize that, set me back at last on the path of acceptance. Though I may never possess you as wife, I find a strange peace in the knowledge our destinies are as closely entwined as any who are wed."

Rhianna took his hand and, lifting it to her lips, kissed it. "You possess it all, my love, and always shall—my heart, my soul, my body. Though I be wife to another, 'tis only words that join us. *You* are the only man I have ever lain with, and I swear to you on my father's bones that you'll be my only lover. Our vows, spoken on that night so long ago, are as real, as important to me now. In my heart, I've never ceased to honor them."

Marcus pulled away. Gripping the ship's railing, he turned to stare out at the turbulently surging sea. His mouth tightened, his jaw clenched, as the inner turmoil twisted within. So, she loved me always, through it all, and I doubted her, almost hated her in return. Guilt and a searing regret flooded him. A need to cleanse himself of the gnawing, soul-numbing bitterness once and for all rose within him. *It's time,* he thought, *and long past, to speak of Mother.*

"For a time, I hated you," he began, his rich-timbred voice laden with pain. "I imagined you like another woman who long ago hurt and betrayed me. My mother, beloved and adored, was that woman. When I was but a boy of ten she left us—my father, sister, and me. I was distraught for a long while, confused, guilty, afraid my childish failings had driven her away. To protect myself, to heal the wounds her leaving had inflicted, I forced a barrier about my heart, a wall I've allowed few, and no woman until you, to breach."

He swung about, his eyes smoldering pits of anguished, haunted memories. "Yet from that first summer's day when I saved you from the boar and held you to me, I knew I was lost. Your flashing blue eyes, that wild mane of golden hair, and deliciously rounded and most feminine of bodies—all set afire by a fiercely proud but most passionate of spirits—was more than even my pain-hardened heart could withstand. Though caution warned me not to weaken, never to open myself to a woman again, I became besotted with desire for you. For a time, I dared hope we could be happy together, that the cares and conflicts of the world wouldn't intrude on our love. And then, for no apparent reason, you turned from me."

"Ah, Marcus," Rhianna cried, clutching his arm, " 'twasn't a willing thing! I swear."

"I know that now, sweet lady." He smiled down at her, his expression sad, loving. "I've learned much in the time since we parted. There were things to discover within myself, a need to reexamine my values and what I truly wanted out of life." The brisk sea wind ruffled his dark curls and whipped his cloak about him. "I was full of ambition when I arrived in Britannia. And then I met you. Suddenly my priorities changed; my ambitions became as of little import."

A wry smile skimmed his firm, chiseled lips. "Quintus told me you felt responsible for the ruination of my military career. In a sense, you were. You made me begin to question what I'd heretofore accepted without thought. But you didn't make me do any of what I did. What I did, I did of my own volition, because my heart could no longer bear any other course.

"To some I'm now considered a failure. Why, I can't even take the woman I love to wife. Yet, in spite of it all, I'm curiously at peace." Wonderment gleamed in Marcus' eyes. "Though I've lost much, I still possess all that truly matters.

I've a son, the certainty of your love, and a new sense of purpose in my mission to help your people. I had wanted to build the bridges of respect and cooperation between our two peoples before and hoped to succeed with your father's help. He was a wise and brave man, Rhianna."

"Is that why you made no protest when I asked to name our son after him?"

Marcus nodded. "Yes, for that reason and in the hope of assuaging some of the pain my presence that day of his death caused you."

" 'Twasn't your fault, Marcus." Rhianna moved toward him, halting only when she was so close she could feel the warmth of his body emanating from him. "We were both caught in a maelstrom of events and consequences beyond our control." She sighed, suddenly overcome with the cruel turn of fate that had taken Marcus from her. "If only things could have been different. If only the Revolt had never come to pass . . ."

Strong, heavily muscled arms gathered her to a broad chest. "Yes, 'if only,' sweet lady. But it did, and now we must find our peace where we may."

"Aye, peace." Rhianna's head found its haven over Marcus' heart. Yet, in spite of his comforting nearness, an uneasy premonition settled over her. " 'Tis long past time, my love," she whispered in weary frustration, knowing the unwanted feeling for what it was. ". . . if only the rest of the world lets us."

Twenty-two

"Ah, what a fair, lusty son you have, daughter." Savren laughed contentedly as she swung Riderch above her head in the warm, late autumn sun.

Rhianna glanced at her mother and smiled, her needle poised in mid-air over the new shirt she was sewing for her rapidly growing babe. Though the duties of chieftain since her return from Rome two months ago had demanded much of her time, she tried to find a few moments each day to spend with her son, attending to his childish needs, performing some of the motherly tasks she so dearly loved.

"Aye," she murmured softly, her blue eyes glowing with pride, "he well resembles his father in every way."

The shadow of an old enmity passed across Savren's face, then, with an effort, was banished. She lowered Riderch to cradle him once again in her arms. "You've never stopped loving the Roman, have you?"

"Nay." Unwaveringly, Rhianna returned her mother's gaze. "And I never will. No matter what happens, no matter the obstacles others place between us, Marcus will always remain my one true love."

The older woman studied her for a long moment, her glance lucid, free at last of the sorrowing madness of the past months. "I was wrong about him. I know that now, see things more clearly after the horrors of the past year. 'Tis just as evident he feels as strongly for you. Yet it must be hard, loving him and knowing you can never be together, that you must instead call another man husband." As if realizing the answer was apparent, Savren continued. "You still blame me, do you not, for a large part of these unfortunate circumstances?"

"Aye, Mother."

Savren smiled at her daughter's bluntness. "You thought me overly harsh with you."

Rhianna nodded. "Aye."

"Well, mayhap I was. Somehow, from your earliest years, I saw you were different, even before I knew of your Gift." At her daughter's look of surprise, Savren's mouth quirked. "Aye, I knew. Cunagus couldn't hide the truth from me for long. It frightened me; though, when he hinted of your destiny. I asked him what to do, how I could help." She paused to inhale a shuddering breath. "Do you know what he told me?"

"Nay, Mother."

Riderch stirred in her arms and Savren hugged him closer. "He told me to make you strong, to teach you obedience, responsibility. He said I must hold you to earth no matter how you yearned to fly away to things more gloriously beckoning, if yet less substantial. Mayhap 'twas why you always loved your father more. He stirred your heart, fed your dreams of honor and glory, allowed your hopes to soar unfettered toward the heavens while I . . . I constantly called you back to the sometimes unpleasant realities of life. Yet was I so wrong, in light of all that has transpired?"

"Nay, Mother." Rhianna's gaze softened. "I needed the best that both of you could offer. 'Tis a little late, my insight into your true motives, but I'm grateful nonetheless." Her smooth brow furrowed in puzzlement. "Father never knew of my Gift then? Only you and Cunagus?"

Savren nodded. "Aye, only your grandfather and myself. 'Twould have distressed Riderch if he'd known, realizing the heavy burden Fate had lain upon your shoulders in the granting of such a power. He'd tried so hard to prepare you for what he'd envisioned your life to be. To have discovered there were some things beyond even his loving efforts . . ." For a moment, her eyes clouded with bittersweet memories. "Mayhap I was wrong to spare him the full truth, but he'd so many responsibilities, so many cares, and I loved him . . ."

"I understand." Rhianna laid her hand on her mother's shoulder in a gesture that was both meant to comfort and to bind them closer in a woman's bonds of loving self-sacrifice. "He, in his own way, also tried to spare you pain and worry. When he finally admitted 'twas his idea, my betrothal to Cador, I at first refused to believe him, thinking only you could demand such a cruel thing of me. But 'twas never your wish, was it?"

"He did the best he could for the clan, even if, in the doing, it broke his heart in sacrificing you. Never forget that."

A sad smile touched Rhianna's lips. "I won't. I know he loved me."

Riderch stirred yet again, his small arms moving to stretch in tremulous jerks. As Savren shifted him in her arms, a wry chuckle escaped her. "Your son has need of a changing."

Rhianna hurriedly put down her sewing and reached out toward her mother. "Then let me have my soggy babe."

"Nay, I'll take the lad." Savren rose to her feet. "The day is warm; the sun feels good, and you've had little enough time to rest of late. Stay there and take your ease. I'll return soon enough."

Gratitude welled in Rhianna. "My thanks, Mother, for your consideration."

Savren glanced back as she paused in the house's doorway. "You've been good to me these many months, trusting your babe to me when others thought me mad. 'Twas my healing. 'Tis time enough to repay your consideration."

Her mother turned then, disappearing into the house. Rhianna stared after her, a deep sense of peace pervading her. Savren had indeed come to a healing, her mind once more whole and strong. Little Riderch had seen to that, for who could remain indifferent to him or fail to cast aside their pain with so sweet a babe in their arms? So much had begun to heal since their return from Rome.

The imperial decree had been delivered to the provincial governor, ordering him to halt further persecutions. Less than a month later, the emperor's freedman Polyclitus had arrived, and his thorough investigation had only served to further control the governor's harshness. Polyclitus was gone now, but not before meeting with Julius Classicianus and Marcus to assure them his report to Nero would faithfully portray the true state of affairs in Britannia, and cast the governor in a most unfavorable light.

Marcus had settled in Londinium with Cei and Ailm and thrown himself wholeheartedly into the task of restoring economic stability to the area. He seemed at peace, content with his new role and mission in life. For that, Rhianna was glad.

The horror was at last behind them, Rhianna thought, the Revolt finally laid to its long-awaited rest. Time now to rebuild, to—

"Ah, 'tis a scene of true domesticity you are, my friend."

At the sound of Ura's laughing voice, Rhianna's head jerked up. "Don't begrudge me my simple pleasures, few as they are of late." She patted the spot beside her. "Come. Sit and talk with me."

"I'm on my way to the well," Ura said, lowering her water jug to the ground, "but I'll gladly spend a few minutes with you." She settled herself next to Rhianna. "You're looking healthy and rested of late. Motherhood sits well with you."

"The world itself sits well with me of late, my friend. Our storehouses are full of grain, our new cattle fat, and the clan's busy with happy plans for the Samain feast. I've much to be content about."

"Aye, 'twill be a joyous celebration this year. I can hardly wait the next four days." Ura smiled. "You've been a good chieftain to us, Rhianna, as fine as any man. 'Tis proud I'll be to follow you in the festival procession."

"My thanks for your compliment." Rhianna bent her head over her sewing to hide her flush of pleasure. "I—"

The commotion of horses passing interrupted her train of thought. Rosic and several men were leaving, their destination Londinium. Rhianna knew of their purpose, having delegated Rosic to deliver the first of the required tribal taxes to the provincial procurator's office. What surprised her was the sight of red-haired Cordaella determinedly joining the group. The two women watched in silence until Rosic and his entourage departed.

Rhianna turned to her companion. "So, Cordaella's accompanying them to Londinium."

Ura gave a snort of disgust. "Aye, she claims a need for some shopping in the town. Did she not ask your leave?"

"Nay." Rhianna sighed. "Knowing her renewed 'friendship' with Cador, I assume she thought it enough to ask him.

Strange, though, how quickly our own friendship died once we returned home. I'd hoped—"

"She's naught but a love-besotted fool!" Ura interjected fiercely. " 'Tis an unholy passion she has for Cador. 'Tis a wonder they haven't yet bedded each other—" She stopped, suddenly realizing what she'd just said. "I . . . I beg pardon. I didn't mean that."

" 'Tis of no import, Ura." Rhianna leaned over and patted her friend's hand. "I care not where Cador beds or with whom, as long as he doesn't share mine. After all," she added with a wry laugh, "I can hardly point a finger, when my son isn't his."

" 'Tisn't the same thing at all!" Ura defended her stoutly. "Riderch was conceived before you wed Cador. There was no adultery in that. The clan holds you faultless, and your babe gains his legitimacy through you. He's as entitled to as full an inheritance as any children you might bear with Cador."

"Aye, the problem lies not with me or my babe," Rhianna agreed sadly, "but with Cador's heartless manipulation of Cordaella. He pays her little respect—'tis evident to all who care to see—and I've heard him mocking her devotion when she's not about. I want so badly to talk with her, to make her see what manner of man Cador truly is, but she'll have naught to do with me."

"Don't trouble yourself over Cordaella, my friend." Ura climbed to her feet and brushed off her gown, then bent to pick up her water jug. She settled it in the curve of her hip. "Only time will cure that one of her blindness. In the meanwhile, I say they deserve each other." She grinned down at Rhianna. "Now, back to your sewing, little mother. I must be off to the well."

Rhianna shot Ura an affectionate smile. "Aye, 'tis past time we were both back to work. Fare you well, my friend." As Ura disappeared behind a cluster of thatched huts, Rhianna resumed her careful stitching of Riderch's tiny shirt. The work was going well on the gay, blue-and-yellow-checkered garment. 'Twould be ready by the Samain feast.

Gradually, Rhianna's thoughts drifted back to their conversation—and Cordaella. Passing strange, she mused, how much both had changed over time. Once Cordaella had been the logical, level-headed one and she, headstrong and emotional. And now? Now, she was staid, even cautious, burdened with cares and responsibilities while Cordaella threw all caution, all logic, to the winds and gave her heart to a man who possessed no heart of his own.

A small, premonitory shudder coursed through her. A dangerous course at best, this "unholy passion" that Ura had called it. Fraught with the surety of heartbreak at the very least and something more tragic—even sinister—at its worst.

She heard her name called and glanced up to see Savren returning with Riderch. Laying aside the unpleasant thoughts with her sewing, Rhianna went to meet her mother and babe. Another visitation of the Gift or no, she hadn't further time just now to dwell on it.

Flickering tongues of firelight danced about the circle, throwing the faces of all into shadow, then red-gold illumination. The feasting meal of Samain had ended and, save for the occasional cup of rich beer, most at last were sated. One by one they had come, gathering to listen to the songs of the bard Kamber.

For a time Kamber did little but strum his oakwood harp, permitting the lilting melodies to soothe the boisterous revelers into a more receptive, reflective mood. Soft, beguiling strains floated over the people, drifting out into the cool night air until they died a gentle death in the distant, ebony stillness. At last the bard paused, his long, slender fingers lifting from the vibrating strings to rest alongside his harp.

Slowly, his glance scanned the faces gathered before him until it reached the chieftain's chair. There, cloaked in a mantle of rich crimson, her gold torc glinting in the firelight, sat Rhianna. Kamber smiled. "A song, Lady? One in thanks for all you've done for your children, the Trinovante?"

Rhianna nodded, the faintest hint of a smile touching her lips. "Aye, Bard. Play me a song."

Kamber's hand glided across the taut gut-strings. A lovely, haunting melody emanated from his harp, and he began to sing.

The lions of the hill are gone,
And I am left alone—alone—
Dig the grave both wide and deep,
For I am sick, and fain would sleep!

The falcons of the wood are flown,
And I am left alone—alone—
Dig the grave both deep and wide,
and let us slumber side by side.

The dragons of the rock are sleeping.
Sleep that wakes not for our weeping—
Dig the grave, and make it ready,
Lay me on my true-love's body.

Even as a girl, Rhianna had loved the song of Deidre, mourning the untimely death of her lover and his two brothers. And now, after all that had happened in the course of the past year, the poignant lament held yet more meaning. She, too, had lost much—father, brothers, lover. Dreams had died or become tempered in the harsh fires of reality. Had she truly once been that girl of a Lughnasa now long ago, racing down the hillside to the berry brambles, her life as fresh and bright as that sunny day?

Dreams had come easy then, of honor, glory, service to her people. Dreams that failed to foreshadow the sacrifice, the effort, the heart-wracking choices. She glanced around at the people seated about her—her people, but now in a form and depth she could have never imagined. Aye, Rhianna thought, she'd indeed fulfilled those girlish, idealistic dreams, but her honor was now to be found in peace, not battle.

O, to hear my true-love singing,
Sweet as sounds of trumpets ringing;
Like the sway of ocean swelling
Rolled his deep voice round our dwelling.

O, to hear the echoes pealing
Round our green and fairy shealing,
When the three, with soaring chorus,
Passed the silent skylark o'er us.

Echo now, sleep, morn and even—
Lark alone enchant the heaven!

"Lark alone enchant the heaven . . ." Why did the mention of birds always remind her of Marcus? Rhianna wondered. Because of the bone earrings, so cunningly carved in the form of birds, that he'd given her that night of Quintus' banquet? She'd cherished them, even as she'd fought against her feelings for him, fleeing from the attraction tearing at her heart and soul. And, even when they'd parted that day of her wedding to Cador and she'd finally gone to her marriage ceremony, the wearing of those earrings had provided her a curious sense of peace, symbolizing the man she would truly and forever love though she must take another as husband.

Her hand slipped within her cloak to pull forth a small parchment scroll tucked beneath her girdle. Once more she unrolled it and read the words written there. "Meet me at the pool at midday, the day after the feast of Samain. Marcus."

Strange, Rhianna mused, that Marcus would ask for a secret meeting, knowing the continuing difficulties she was having with Cador and the terrible risk of such an assignation. 'Twasn't as if he hadn't seen her since their return from Rome. In the past two months he'd visited the hill fort five times on one pretext or another. But all those meetings had been public and, though he'd had time to spend with Riderch, little opportunity had been found for them to speak in private. Had that frustrated him as much as her, until he finally felt compelled to send this request?

Stranger still had been the messenger who delivered his missive. Scarcely had Rosic and his group returned today from Londinium than Cordaella had hurried over and breathlessly pulled her aside. Shoving the sealed scroll of parchment into Rhianna's hand, the red-haired woman had excitedly explained how Marcus had found her when she'd accompanied Rosic to the procurator's palace, insisting that she carry his message back to the "Trinovante chieftain." Though initially reluctant, Cordaella had eventually agreed thinking 'twas some official bit of business.

Rhianna had left her with that same impression, loath to

share the true message with anyone. Yet even as she ached to see Marcus, to hold him just once more, Rhianna knew 'twas dangerous to meet with him secretly. She questioned why Cordaella would now act as messenger between her and Marcus, fully aware as the red-haired woman was of Cador's hatred for the Roman. Was it, mayhap, a trap devised by Cador, with Cordaella as accomplice, to harm her and Marcus?

She'd had no time to send a reply to Marcus, whether he truly had wished to see her or had, like her, been tricked into the meeting by Cador and Cordaella. If 'twere indeed the latter, however, Rhianna had no intention of letting Marcus ride, unwittingly, into a trap.

Nay, she decided, she'd go to him on the morrow, risk or no. But only for a quick meeting to warn him away and, to have a witness to their encounter, she'd bring along Ura. 'Twas mayhap still a dangerous plan, but for Marcus she'd hazard that and more.

As Kamber signaled the closing verses, the harp music rose in volume and poignancy. Chords vibrated resonantly, their piercing notes carrying to Rhianna's ears, gently yet insistently drawing her back. The familiar, well-loved words flowed over her, inundating her with a bittersweet pang, strengthening, yet the more, her resolve for the morrow.

Dig the grave both wide and deep,
Sick I am and fain would sleep!
Dig the grave and make it ready,
Lay me on my true-love's body.

Churning gray clouds sailed across a dismal, wind-swept sky. Skeletal tree limbs vibrated in the chill, sporadic breezes, their branches clattering together like so many rattling bones.

The air was damp, numbing. Though nearly midday, the cloud-shrouded sun had barely burned away the morning mists.

An altogether unpleasant morn, Rhianna thought with a tiny shiver. She tied Demetia to a nearby tree and, while she waited for Ura to do the same with her horse, Rhianna tugged her warm woolen cloak more tightly to her. She listened for sound of approaching hoofbeats or any suspicious movements in the trees and heard none. Indeed, the winter-barren forest was so silent it seemed pervaded with an ominous sense of anticipation. But for what? she wondered.

Rhianna shook off her odd feelings. 'Twas naught more than the lingering aftereffects of last night's dream. Once more the eerie white boar had appeared, thundering toward her with his lethally sharp tusks. And, as always, the mysterious man had been there, laughing triumphantly.

She'd woken in a gasping sweat, her heart pounding madly, wondering why, after over nine months now, the same, awful dreams had resumed. More intense than ever, they seemed to warn of an impending encounter. Rhianna shuddered. But why now? And what part would she play in it this time?

Cunagus would help her to understand it. At long last, she, too, wished to know, to understand and use that knowledge. Too long had she fled the Gift. Too long had she denied that part of herself because it didn't suit her dreams. But *'twas* a part of her. To turn from it any longer would be to deny herself—and her people—and she was forsworn now to bear all for their sake.

A sense of peace pervaded Rhianna. The distaste for a power that had never been of her choosing, and the terrible responsibilities inherent in such an ability, suddenly muted into a serene acceptance.

Just as her life had changed, her experiences leading her through a cauldron of pain and sacrifice to a richer, deeper appreciation of life, of joy, and of love, Rhianna now knew she'd fought where 'twas futile and foolish. Her gift was special, unique, and oh, so precious. Aye, so precious, Rhianna thought, so much a part of her that 'twas nearly a living death to go on fighting it. And a fate far worse than any meted out by man.

" 'Tis a strange, unsettling day," Ura murmured, drawing up at last to stand beside Rhianna. "I'll be happy when your Roman has come and gone and we're once more snug in our homes." She shivered. "And I like it not that no one has seen Cordaella since last eve."

"Aye," Rhianna agreed uneasily. " 'Tis passing strange, even for Cordaella. Mayhap she'll be out and about from wherever she was by the time we return to the hill fort."

"Out and about from yet another illicit coupling with Cador, do you think?" Ura couldn't hide the disgust in her voice. "While you, on the other hand, to avoid all hint of impropriety, must go so far as to bring me along for an innocent meeting with your Roman. 'Tisn't fair, Rhianna, and I grow weary of watching Cordaella's hypocrisy while you must—"

A distant sound reached Rhianna's ears. She held up a hand to silence Ura and listened intently. The pounding grew louder. Moving quickly, Rhianna pulled Ura behind a tree with her until she could ascertain who it was.

A white stallion came into view, ridden by a powerful, dark-haired man. Marcus! Rhianna's heart leapt in her breast. She glanced at Ura. "Await me here. I wish but a few moments alone with Marcus."

Ura smiled. "Go, my friend. You have my leave, but don't tarry long. Remember why you brought me."

Rhianna nodded, then turned and hurried to join Marcus.

Having caught sight of her, Marcus smiled and slid from his horse, striding to meet Rhianna. They halted a few feet apart. A long-suppressed joy and unquenchable hunger burned brightly in Rhianna's eyes.

In an infinitely tender gesture, Marcus reached out to tuck a wind-whipped lock of Rhianna's hair behind her ear. "I've sorely missed you, lady." His voice was husky with emotion.

"And I, you, Roman." Rhianna stepped closer. "But 'tis unwise to meet like this. You must go."

His glance snared on Ura standing several yards away near a tree. A deep chuckle rumbled in his chest. "So, you now need a chaperone to see me, do you?"

" 'Tis the wisest course." She placed a hand on his chest and pushed. "Now, away with you."

Marcus clasped her about the wrist and, before Rhianna could pull back, lowered his head to kiss her palm. "Wait a moment," he said then, smiling up at her. "I've some happy news since I last saw you."

"And what might that be?" Rhianna asked, suddenly as loath to leave him as he seemed to be to leave her.

"Ailm is with child."

Happiness flooded her. "With child? Ah, thank the Goddess! 'Twas her greatest sorrow, her failure to give Cei a child. I'm so happy for them."

"As am I, sweet lady. As am I."

"And what of Quintus?" Rhianna prodded, eager for just a bit of news about her friends, knowing, even as she did she was foolishly prolonging the inevitable parting. "I've not seen or heard from him since that first visit you two made to the fort. How fares he?"

"Our friend Quintus chafes rapidly beneath the yoke of paperwork and politics. He has tendered his request for a transfer back to the legions, preferably one that sees heavy action." Marcus shook his head ruefully. "I fear he'll not be long in Londinium."

A soft smile touched Rhianna's lips. "Dear, brave Quintus. I pray he someday finds a woman worthy of him."

"And preferably one not already taken."

At the wry tone in Marcus' voice, Rhianna gave a small gasp. "You knew—"

"That Quintus desired you? Loved you?" Marcus finished the sentence for her. "Yes, Rhianna, I knew. But I also knew I could trust him. Now you, and *your* feelings, I wasn't always so certain of. There were times when I was almost jealous of Quintus."

Smiling, Rhianna disengaged her hand from Marcus' clasp. "But that was long ago. Now, there's no need for doubt on anyone's part." She paused. "But come, 'tis past time we put an end to this meeting. Though I dearly cherish this time together, 'twasn't wise to request we secretly meet."

Marcus stepped back. A puzzled frown etched his brow. "What do you mean, ' 'twasn't wise to request we meet'? I didn't ask for it. You did."

"Nay, Marcus. I sent you no request."

"I don't understand this. Cordaella delivered a letter from you but two days ago—"

"As she did to me, from you, on her return yesterday from Londinium." Growing horror rose in Rhianna.

"What is it, lady?"

"A trap. I was afraid of this. Goddess, Marcus, 'tis a trap!" She gave him a shove. "Go, now! Before 'tis too late!"

" 'Tis already too late, wife."

Marcus and Rhianna wheeled about. There, slipping from their hiding places in the trees on the other side of the small glade, were Cador and his men. Following, reluctant, unhappy expressions on their faces, were Cunagus and the res of the Elders.

Rhianna stepped forward to confront the triumphantl grinning Cador. "What is the meaning of this, that you sp on me, Cador? This time you've gone too far!"

"Nay, wife. *You* have gone too far when you sought t cuckold me. 'Twasn't enough you bore another's child an expected me to accept it, but to continue to meet secretl time and again with your lover . . ." He sighed and shook his head. "Even a man as tolerant as I can only bear s many clandestine meetings where my wife repeatedly betrays me."

"Clandestine meetings!" Rhianna cried in outrage. "Thi is the first and only time I've met Marcus outside the fort You know as well as I this was but an innocent meeting arranged by you to ensnare us and ruin me." She gesture to Ura, still awaiting her by the trees. "Ask Ura. Naugh happened here between Marcus and me!"

Cador turned to the Elders. "And what do the words o Rhianna's friend and accomplice matter? You have seen fo yourself the loving words and touches they shared. Did i appear to you as an innocent meeting?"

Cunagus stepped forward, his weathered features shadowed in unease. "Appearances can indeed be deceiving. Unfortunately, we've little else to go on." He studied Rhianna "Why, Lady? Time and again have I warned you from th Roman, counseled you he would be your destruction. Wh did you repeatedly close your ears to me?"

Rhianna stared at her grandfather in disbelief. "Y-you' choose to give Cador's words more weight than mine, knowing him as you do, aware of his obsession with my chieftainship?" She glanced back at the other Elders. Kamber Maglor, and Rosic gazed at her in miserable dejection. God ess! she thought. They either believe Cador's accusations r don't know what to think. What can I do? What can I say) convince them otherwise?

And convince them she must. A chieftain caught in adul- ery, wed in the full marriage as she was to Cador, risked ss of the chieftainship, if not death itself.

Rhianna drew herself to her full height. She forced her aze, a gaze shining with a proud defiance, to swing from unagus to each of the Elders. "I am your chieftain and have d you well. Have I ever lied or led you astray? I lie not ow, when I swear that Marcus and I haven't been lovers ince before Cador and I were wed. Aye, my son is his. I'll ot gainsay that, but he was conceived the last time we were gether. 'Tis all I can say in my defense, save that you know ador and of necessity must consider his true motives in his."

The Elders exchanged looks. As if sensing the doubts be- inning to form, Cador's hand moved to his sword. " 'Tis y word against hers. She has failed in her obligation to us nd must pay the price. I challenge her to defend her hieftainship."

Cunagus' head snapped up, his dark eyes wide. "You'd emand Rhianna fight you—she, a woman, and you, a sea- oned warrior? 'Twould be murder, man! Do you desire the hieftainship so badly you'd willingly kill her?"

Marcus uttered a low curse and pulled Rhianna back to is side. "I've held my tongue long enough in this. Cador on't lay one hand on Rhianna while I live! If it's a fight he ants, let him cross blades with me!" He withdrew his short word.

Cador's men moved closer, unsheathing their own weap- ns. Rhianna glanced about, her panic rising. Goddess, they ad unearthed the swords hidden from Roman knowledge, weapons once more forbidden by law. And one look at the determined faces assured her they meant to use them, th Marcus' life was forfeit if Cador but gave the word.

She turned to Cunagus. "You are judge and law-giver. Ca Cador demand a battle with the chieftain over this?"

"Aye, Lady."

Her gaze met his and Rhianna read the hopelessness, th despair in the old Druid's eyes. Then so be it, she though "Seize him," she ordered, motioning toward Marcus. An instant later, four burly men leaped forward to capture Marc from behind. In a wild melee of flailing arms and strainin bodies, the sword was wrestled from his grasp.

"Rhianna!" Struggling to the last, Marcus was final forced to his knees. "Don't! Don't fight him. Don't sacrific yourself," he cried. His gaze locked with hers and somethin arced between them. Something deep, dark and anguishe "Let Cador have the chieftainship if he wants it that badl Please, Rhianna. Please!"

She stared down at him, her eyes filling with tears. "Na Marcus. As chieftain, I am sworn to defend my position the death, and I'd rather die then give the Trinovante over Cador." Her hand moved toward Marcus' sword, now hel by one of Cador's men. "Give it to me. I deserve at least weapon to defend myself."

The man glanced at Cador. At his leader's nod, he hande Rhianna the sword. She threw aside her cloak and turned face the tall blond man who was her husband. A grim smi touched her lips. "Well, Cador, your long-dreamt-of-mome has arrived, has it not? Have a care, though. Your destin may not be all it seems."

With a feral growl, Cador advanced on her. His lon Celtic sword rose above his head and, in a flash of silve slashed downward. Rhianna dodged the blow, then moved thrust toward him. With a mocking laugh, he easily escaped, then whirled to strike at her again. Once more she leapt aside, parrying his thrust with a swift angling of her blade.

Her breath coming in soft little pants, Rhianna settled into another fighting stance, her sword poised, two-handed, before her. Like a wild cat stalking its prey, Cador circled her lithely, his movements confident, negligent in his superior strength and skill. His arrogance struck at a deep chord of pride. Too long had she practiced with her father and brothers, too well had she fought at Camulodunum, to allow such a poor showing of her skill.

In a lightning swift move she lunged forward, then, in the last instant, changed her angle of attack. Cador was caught off guard. Rhianna's blade bit into the flesh of his thigh. With a harsh intake of breath, Cador jumped back.

"Curse you, woman!" he snarled, glancing down at his wounded leg. Though the cut was deep, it wasn't mortal. The pain only goaded him onward.

" 'Twon't be long now, will it, Rhianna?" Cador's smile widened wolfishly as he began a systematic series of sword thrusts to drive her across the glade and away from the others. " 'Twon't be long before you, too, share the same fate as Cordaella."

At Rhianna's look of surprise, Cador laughed. "She came to me last night, and when I told her that I planned to kill you today she turned coward on me, threatening to go to you and warn you of my plan. Foolish woman. I had no choice but to silence her—permanently."

"Y-you killed Cordaella? Curse you, Cador! Ah, curse you!" In a move more desperate then tactical, Rhianna's sword once again slipped past his guard and sliced, this time, across his face.

With an enraged cry, he quickened his thrusts until they

fell with dizzying speed. There was little Rhianna could do but ward off the blows. Once more, she was slowly driven backward toward the forest's edge.

Her sword arm grew numb. Her reflexes slowed. Fear snaked its slimy tendrils about her heart. If Cador didn't relent in his onslaught soon—

An exposed tree limb caught Rhianna. She fell, her sword arm striking the ground with such force the weapon sailed from her hand. She turned, grasping for it wildly, but 'twas too late. Even then Cador was lifting his sword for the killing blow.

"Rhianna!"

From across the glade, Marcus' impassioned cry rang out. She looked toward him and, for a fleeting instant, time slowed. She saw him twist free of two of his captors. Dragging the other two with him, he staggered toward her. Yet, though every ounce of muscle and sinew was thrown into the effort to reach her, Rhianna knew Marcus would never make it in time.

She smiled at him, all the love in her heart in her eyes. *Fare you well, my love.*

Rhianna turned back to Cador, her gaze fierce, challenging him even in her defeat. He hesitated but the briefest instant. And, in that flicker of time between life and death, a new sound intruded. The cracking and splintering of underbrush, followed by a harsh, discordant snorting, filled the air.

Cador wheeled around. There, but ten yards away, stood a white boar, prickly haired, sharp tusks gleaming. Then the creature charged.

A dizzying realization flooded Rhianna. Her dream, her vision—come to life at last! A sense of acceptance filled her. Even in her dying she'd protect the Trinovante by taking Cador with her. 'Twas enough . . .

As the boar thundered ever closer, an unsteady yet defiant laugh rose to Cador's lips. The laughter caught on the wind, gaining in force and intensity until it assumed a deranged reality of its own.

He's mad, Rhianna thought, to confront a wild boar with only a sword. Yet still Cador held his ground and, at the last minute, the white boar swerved, pounding past him and back into the forest.

Though the creature's retreat was startling, Rhianna spared not a moment more. She rolled over, shoved to her knees, and grasped wildly for her sword lying nearby in the grass. With a shout of fury, Cador tore himself from his stupefied staring after the boar. He turned on her with all the speed and might in his command.

Rhianna's fingers closed about her sword's hilt. With a fierce battle cry of her own, she swung and slashed upward. Miraculously, the tip caught Cador in the groin, slicing through a major vessel. He halted. He looked down to where the bright-red blood spurted around the end of Rhianna's sword. Shock, then disbelief, twisted Cador's features. His sword fell from his hand.

"Nay," he gasped. " 'Twasn't meant to be this way. 'Tisn't fair. 'Tisn't fai—"

With a strangled scream, Cador toppled over. Rhianna knelt there for a long moment. Then she moved, wrapping her arms about her.

It was then she noted the blood, warm, sticky and wet, covering her. Blood . . . just as in her dream. But not her blood. Not this time.

"Rhianna!"

With a cry that was both anguish and joy, Marcus reached

her. He pulled her to him, heedless of the blood on her hands and face and clothes.

"Gods, Rhianna," he choked out the single word and buried his face in her hair.

Twenty-three

"The will of the gods." Marcus rolled the phrase on his tongue as if he still couldn't quite fathom it. "That wily old Druid stopped everyone in their tracks with that pronouncement, didn't he?"

Rhianna glanced up from her preoccupation with Riderch. Her pace slowed as she shifted the babe in her arms. "And did you doubt for a moment his words weren't truth? Think on it, Marcus. Did the white boar not first bring us together that Lughnasa day and now, but a few hours ago, return to save both our lives? A more evident blessing by the gods I've yet to see."

As they walked through the hill fort, Marcus' arm encircled her waist. "Well, gods' wills or no, I'm content it finally silenced the faction against your chieftainship. Without Cador's malicious interference . . ."

She nodded. "Aye. Though I'm loath to wish death on any man, his dying will end most of the discontent, not to mention my personal difficulties with him."

His grip tightened but he remained silent. Together, they walked from the fort and down the hill. Instead of the forest path, Marcus and Rhianna chose the open meadows and farmlands surrounding the hill fort. As they moved, the sun, long hidden behind the surging, wind-harried clouds, broke through at last.

Golden beams bathed the land, their light turning the frost-browned grasses a delicate shade of flaxen. Rhianna's heart swelled with pride. How beautiful the land. The land of her people. A land that would soon blossom, once more, with the earth's generous bounty.

Aye, her land. A land neither human love nor life itself had ever separated her from. Yet, though the sacrifices had been great, in the end she had still gained so much. Marcus, little Riderch, the well-being of her people. And even Cerdic, though far from home across the sea, who might well return some day. Aye, she *had* gained so much.

'Twas enough. 'Twas more than most could ever hope for.

A stiff breeze whipped at the long cloaks both Marcus and Rhianna wore. She paused to tuck her cloak more snugly about her son. At the concerned effort, Riderch, sound asleep with a full belly, nestled yet deeper into the comforting warmth of his mother's body.

Marcus smiled down at his chubby-cheeked son. A fierce protectiveness, for the child as well as his mother, flooded him. To think he'd almost lost them . . .

A sudden determination rose in his breast. Marcus halted, his action forcing Rhianna also to stop.

She turned, a bemused, questioning smile on her face. "Aye, my love?"

His eyes locked with hers. "Too many times have I nearly lost you. Today was the last. I can bear no more. For whatever reason you chose to wed Cador instead of me, surely the reason is no more. Let us wed. It's past time I made you my wife in every way."

Rhianna's smile slowly saddened. "There's naught I desire more than proclaiming our vows before my people and our clan Druid. Yet life for me isn't as simple or as easy as that. I am chieftain. I cannot wed a man not sanctioned by my people." Her gaze lowered. "And I fear they will never accept a Roman as husband to their Lady."

"But why?" The old frustration welled in Marcus. The years of enmity, the brutalities so recently ended, rose like a mocking specter between them. Rhianna was right. Some of the Trinovante still looked upon him as enemy and might always, no matter what he did. Their spirits were too proud, too unquenchable ever truly to admit defeat. And, as long as they warred, even if only in their hearts, they'd never accept him.

He ran a ragged hand through his dark curls. "Then what is there for us?"

For a long while Rhianna was silent, her gaze never wavering from the gently rolling hills of Trinovante land. Finally, she turned to him. "There is but one hope for us. Cunagus is Wise Man and Judge. Whatever he decrees, the people will obey. We must go to him and plead our love."

"But he has always been against me!" Further argument died on Marcus' lips. The look in Rhianna's eyes spoke more eloquently than words. Cunagus *was* their only hope. "Then let us seek out your Druid," he rasped, his voice thick with emotion, "for I must know our fate before this day is done." Wordlessly, they turned and headed back to the fort.

Cunagus was in his thatched hut. Rhianna lifted Riderch from the warm haven of her cloak and handed him to his father. "Let me speak with the Druid alone."

Marcus exhaled a deep, shuddering breath. "As you wish."

She walked inside. Her grandfather was busily mixing potions in various earthenware jars. At her entrance he looked up briefly, then resumed his task. "I expected you."

Rhianna eyed him calmly. "Then you know why I'm here?"

He rose to his feet. "Aye. But before we end, at last, this battle of ours over the Roman, I must know one thing. Your Gift. Have you come to its acceptance?"

So, he guessed even that. Rhianna nodded. "Aye, Druid. 'Tis mine, even if not of my asking, and it now *feels* mine, *feels* right." As the words fell from her lips, a sudden, heart-deep happiness swelled within her. Freedom. 'Twas at last hers, though in a way and form she'd never have imagined. 'Twas complete then. The acceptance. The fulfillment of her destiny.

She smiled. "Will you teach me more of it?"

Cunagus nodded. "Long have I awaited this day. Aye, I'll teach you, for the learning will be as much to your good as to our people's." His dark old eyes studied her, a loving pride warming their depths. "The growing has been hard, has it not? Harder than for most, yet it has tempered you well. In time, you will serve the Trinovante as one of their finest chieftains."

At the unexpected praise, coupled with what Rhianna guessed was a pronouncement of his Gift, her eyes lowered. "My thanks for your confidence." Then, remembering herself, she swung her gaze back to his. "But what of my vow? Am I still bound—"

He raised a hand to silence her. " 'Tis past time to answer all things, to put to rest the final torment of your heart. Come."

When they left the hut, Marcus exchanged a quizzical glance with Rhianna. She shook her head, equally puzzled, then fell into step behind her grandfather. Staff in hand, Cunagus was already striding across the fort toward the main gate. Marcus shifted Riderch to a more secure position on his chest and hurried after them.

At the gate, Cunagus paused to deliver a terse order before stalking out of the fort and down the hill. "Sound the trumpets; call the people. I await them in the oak grove."

Rhianna waited until Marcus joined her. Taking his hand,

she followed after the Druid's rapidly retreating form. Though her mouth was dry, her palms clammy, she fought to hide the inward trepidation stirred by Cunagus' strange pronouncement.

A solemn meeting in the sacred grove. Her grandfather was indeed intent on settling this matter of their love once and for all. Goddess, she moaned silently, if only he'd allowed me a moment to plead our cause!

They waited until the entire clan had gathered. Then, the white-robed Druid lifted his hands. A hush settled over the assemblage.

"Much has transpired today," he finally began. "Much you have yet to fathom. A wound, long festering upon the Trinovante heart, has begun to heal at last. But, like all cures, the treatment has been long drawn, the cautery far too painful. Cruelties have been perpetuated in the name of honor, hearts nearly broken in the quest for peace. Mistakes have been made. I, like the rest of you, have suffered, lost—learned."

He turned to Marcus and Rhianna, gesturing toward them. "Aye, all have suffered, Roman and Trinovante alike, but these two have stood in the midst of it all and remained true, one to the other. Many have tried to tear them apart, to destroy the love that burned between them—myself included. All have failed.

"From the start I knew their destinies were entwined, but to what extent I was never certain. Yet still I ignored the signs, thinking I knew what was best for them. I see now 'twas wrong, my efforts an affront to the gods. The knowledge I suspected but feared to face was confirmed today, when the white boar returned once more. The purchase price has at last been paid. Woe to any man who comes between these two again!"

His gnarled fingers came to rest on Marcus' shoulder. Their glances met, melded, and mutual respect flared between them. "The Roman has proven his worthiness time and again. He is brave and strong. His love for our Lady has been tempered in fires hotter than most could even imagine, much less bear. I say he is worthy to wed her and rule at her side. Does any man gainsay my right to decide this?"

Cunagus paused to scan the crowd. No one moved nor spoke. A breeze rustled the dry grasses and, high above, a goshawk screamed.

"From the ashes of our terrible subjugation, 'tis time to accept the inevitable," he continued, his proud old voice ringing to the farthest reaches of the crowd. "The Trinovante must learn to adapt, to meld what is good of our conquerors with the ancient traditions, while always continuing to reject the bad.

"And what better way to begin," he demanded, reaching to join the hands of Rhianna and Marcus, "then with the union of Rome and our island—in the hearts and bodies of our Lady and the man she loves?"

As the Druid stepped away, a jubilant cry burst from the crowd. "Rhianna! Rhianna! Rhianna!"

The voices swirled around them, encompassing Marcus and Rhianna in a wild tumult of sound, yet their joyous, loving eyes saw only each other. They moved together, two hearts melding as one.

"Kek, kek, kek," came the cry overhead. Marcus and Rhianna lifted their gazes. Soaring high on the air currents, a swift, powerful goshawk claimed dominion of the skies—enchanting the heavens with the unfettered freedom of flight.

Author's Note

The two songs used in *ENCHANT THE HEAVENS* were taken from the *Lyra Celtica: An Anthology of Representative Celtic Poetry,* edited by E.A. Sharp and J. Mattay and published in 1932. The song, *March of the Faerie Host,* is an ancient Irish and Scottish verse and reminiscent of the type of songs sung by the Celtic bards of the ancient British Isles. Its origins are most likely from the time of Rhianna and Marcus, or even earlier. *Deidre's Lament for the Sons of Usnach,* however, is based on an Irish myth and originated much later than the time frame of *ENCHANT THE HEAVENS,* probably at least several centuries later. I used it anyway, feeling it was perfect not only for its reiteration of the book's title, but for the mood it set of star-crossed lovers whose love spanned not only the trials of life, but that of death as well. I hope you'll forgive that one purposeful but well-intentioned failing in the historical accuracy of this book. Sometimes, though, a bit of literary license can go a long way . . .

Kathleen Morgan

Dear Reader,

I hope you enjoyed *ENCHANT THE HEAVENS.* This was the very first historical romance I ever wrote and it took nine years from its inception to its publication. Still, I just knew I would sell it someday. *ENCHANT THE HEAVENS* is, and will always be, one of the books closest to my heart.

My next endeavor from Zebra/Pinnacle Books will be a futuristic romance. *FIRESTORM,* the second book in my Volan trilogy (begun with *FIRESTAR,* which is still available), will be released in September 1995. If you've never tried a futuristic romance, you're in for a pleasant surprise. And if you have, get ready for the tale of Raina (the friend of the heroine from *CRYSTAL FIRE* and leader of the Sodalitas, a militant society of outcast women) and Teague Tremayne, a warrior monk sworn to a most unwilling perpetual chastity. It's their turn to take on the problems caused by the alien race of Volan mind-slavers and, in the process, join forces in the fight to save their home planet from an evil dictator.

I'm also considering (amongst all the other story ideas churning in my mind) two sequels to *ENCHANT THE HEAVENS,* one featuring Quintus and the other Cerdic. I find them appealing as hero material and think they both deserve their own chance at a happy life, as well as their own special heroine. What do *you* think? Write me at P.O. Box 62365, Colorado Springs, Colorado 80962, and let me know. Enclose a self-addressed, stamped, business-sized envelope, and I'll also send you an excerpted flyer of my upcoming book. In the meanwhile, happy reading!

Kathleen Morgan

TURN THE PAGE
FOR A SNEAK PREVIEW OF

LISA JACKSON'S

INTIMACIES

A FEBRUARY 1995 RELEASE
FROM ZEBRA BOOKS

Prologue

The woman was lying. And she was good at it. Damn good.

Deputy T. John Wilson had put in too many years with the Sheriff's Department not to smell a liar. He'd seen the best the county had to offer—two-bit con men, thugs, snitches, and killers—and he recognized a rat when he was facing one.

This beautiful woman—this beautiful *rich* woman—was hiding something. Something important. Lying through her gorgeous white teeth.

The smell of stale smoke hung heavy in the interrogation room. Pale green walls had turned a grimy shade of gray since the last paint job before all the budget cuts, but T. John felt comfortable here. At home in the beat-up old chair. He reached into his breast pocket for a pack of cigarettes, remembered he'd quit smoking two months before, and reluctantly settled for a piece of Dentyne that he unwrapped slowly, wadded, and shoved onto his tongue. The gum wasn't the same as a good drag on a Camel straight, but it would have to do. For now. Until he gave up his continual battle with his addiction to nicotine and took up the habit again.

"Let's go over it one more time," he suggested as he leaned backward in his chair and crossed a booted leg over his knee. His partner, Steve Gonzales, was propped up against the door frame by one shoulder, his arms folded over his skinny chest, his dark eyes glued to the woman who was at the center of this mess—murder, arson, and probably much, much more. Casually, T. John picked up the file and began leafing through it until he came to her statement, the one she'd made without an attorney present just a few hours before. "Your name is—"

Her amber eyes blazed in outrage but he didn't feel one iota of guilt for putting her through it all again. After all she'd do it to him, if the situation were reversed, and she wouldn't give an inch—just set her teeth in and hang on. Reporters never let up. Always on the case of the law or the D.A.; it felt good to get a little of his own back.

"My name is Cassidy McKenzie. But you already know who I am."

"Cassidy *Buchanan* McKenzie."

She didn't bother responding. He shook his head, dropped the file, and sighed. Tapping the tips of his fingers together, he glanced at the soundproof tiles in the ceiling as if wishing God Himself were lurking in the joists and would intervene. "You know, I was hoping you were going to be straight with me."

"I am! Going over it again isn't going to change anything. You know what happened—"

"I don't know shit, lady, so cut the crap!" His boots hit the floor with a thud. "Look, I don't know whom you think you're talking to, but I've seen better liars than you and busted them, like that." He snapped his fingers so loudly the sound seemed to ricochet around the cinder-block walls. "Whether you realize it or not, you're in deep trouble here; deeper than you want to be. Now, let's get down to it, okay? No more bullshit. I hate bullshit. Don't you, Gonzales?"

"Hate it," Gonzales replied, barely moving his lips.

Wilson grabbed up the file again. He felt as if he were

losing control. He didn't like it when he lost charge of any situation. Especially one in which he thought his career was on the line. If he solved this case, hell, he'd be able to run for Sheriff himself and oust Floyd Dodds, who needed to retire anyway. Floyd was becoming a real pain in the ass. But if T. John didn't solve the case . . . oh, hell, *that* wasn't even a possibility. T. John believed in thinking positively. Even more, he believed in himself.

He glanced at the clock mounted over the door. The seconds just kept ticking by. Through the dirty window, the last rays of sunlight settled into the room, causing shadows to creep along the walls despite the harsh light from the overhead fluorescent bulbs. They'd been at this for three hours, and everyone was growing tired. Especially the woman. She was pale, her skin stretched tight over high cheekbones and sunken gold eyes. Her hair was a fiery red-brown that was pulled off her face by a leather thong. Tiny lines of worry pinched the corners of what might have been a pouty, sexy mouth.

He tried again. "Your name is Cassidy Buchanan McKenzie; you're a reporter with the *Times,* and you know a helluva lot more than you're telling me about the fire at your daddy's sawmill."

She had the decency to blanch. Her mouth opened and closed again as she sat stiffly, her denim jacket wrapped around her slim body, her makeup long faded.

"Now that we've got that straight, you might want to tell me what you know about it. One man's near-dead at Northwest General in CCU, the other in a private room unable to talk. The doctors don't think the guy in Critical Care is gonna make it."

Her lips quivered for a second. "I heard," she whispered. She blinked, but didn't break down. He hadn't supposed she would. She was a Buchanan for Christ's sake. They were known to be tougher than rawhide.

"This isn't the first fire to occur on your daddy's property, is it?" He climbed to his feet and began to pace, his gum popping in noisy tandem to the heels of his boots clicking against the yellowed linoleum floor. "And if I remember right, after the last one, you up and left town. Said you'd never come back. Guess you changed your mind—oh, hell, everyone has that right, don't they?" He flashed a good ol' boy smile. His best.

She didn't even flinch.

"But, now listen to this. It's what bothers me. You give up a job most men and women would kill for, come back home married to one of the McKenzie boys, and guess what? Lo and behold we have another hot-damn fire the likes of which we haven't seen in—what—nearly seventeen years! One guy killed from the explosion and two guys in the hospital." He threw up his hands. "Go figure."

Gonzales shoved himself away from the door, grabbed a styrofoam cup from a package on the table, and poured a thin stream of coffee from the glass pot warming on a hot plate. He brought the pot over and without asking poured a little more into the woman's cup.

Wilson turned his chair backward and straddled it. Leaning forward, he glowered at her. She held his gaze. "We're still trying to figure out exactly what happened and who was there. Fortunately your husband was carrying a wallet, otherwise we couldn't have recognized him. He's a mess. His face is swollen and cut, his hair singed, his jaw broken, and one leg's in a cast. But they managed to save the injured eye and if he works at it, he may even walk again." He watched as the woman shuddered. So she did care about her husband . . . if only just a little. "The other guy we don't know.

No ID. His face is busted up pretty bad, too. Swollen and black and blue. He lost a few teeth and his hands are burned. Hair nearly singed clean off. We're havin' a helluva time figuring out who he is and thought you might be able to help us." Leaning back in his chair again, he picked up his now-cold cup of coffee.

"What—what about fingerprints?"

"That's the hell of it. John Doe's hands are burned; no prints. At least not yet. With all those broken teeth and messed up jaw, dental impressions are gonna take some time . . ." Wilson narrowed his eyes on the woman and he scratched thoughtfully against the stubble of two days' growth of beard. "If I didn't know better, I'd think the bastard burned his hands on purpose; you know, to throw us off."

She grimaced. "You think he started the fire?"

"It's possible." Wilson picked up his chipped mug, took a long swallow, scowled and motioned for Gonzales to pour him a fresh cup.

"I told you I don't know who he is."

"He was meetin' your husband at the mill."

She hesitated. "So you said, but I . . . I don't keep up with my husband's business. I have no idea whom he met or why."

T. John's eyebrows quirked. "You got one of them new-fangled kind of marriages—you know, he does his own thing, you do yours?" Gonzales was at the hot plate again, tearing open a packet of non-dairy creamer—that god-awful white powder that in no way resembled anything remotely associated with a cow.

"We were thinking about separating," she admitted with a trace of remorse.

"Is that so?" Wilson swallowed a smile. He'd finally hit pay dirt. Now he had a motive—or the start of one. And that's all he needed. "The Fire Chief thinks the fire was caused by arson."

"I know."

"The incendiary device, well, hell, it could be the spittin' image of the one used seventeen years ago when the old gristmill was torched. You remember that, don't you?" She winced, her lips losing a little color. "Yeah, I guess you couldn't very well forget."

She looked away and her hands trembled around the thin styrofoam. Of course she remembered the fire. Everyone in Prosperity did. The Buchanan family—all of them—had suffered a horrible, tragic loss, one from which most of them had never recovered. The old man—Cassidy's father—had never been the same; lost control of his life, his company, and his willful daughter.

"Maybe you'd like to come to the hospital, see the damage for yourself. But I'm warning you, it's not a pretty sight."

She leveled steady whiskey-colored eyes at him and he was reminded again that she was a reporter as well as a Buchanan. "I've been demanding to see my husband ever since he was injured. The doctors told me I couldn't see him until the Sheriff agreed—that there was some question about his being a suspect."

"Well, hell, let's go!" he said, but as she started to climb to her feet, he changed his mind. "Just a couple more things to clear up first." Her spine stiffened and she settled slowly back in the worn plastic chair. She was a cool one, he'd give her that. But she was still lying. Hiding something. As Gonzales refilled his old mug, T. John reached into his pocket and pulled out a plastic bag. Within the clear plastic was a charred chain with a burned St. Christopher's medal attached to it. The image of the saint was barely recognizable, twisted and blackened from the heat and flames.

Cassidy's mouth rounded, but she didn't gasp. Instead she stared at the bag as Gonzales dropped it onto the battered old table in front of her. Her hands gripped her cup more tightly and she drew in a quick little breath. "Where'd you get this?"

"Funny thing. The John Doe was holding it in his fist, wouldn't let it go, even as much pain as he was in. We had to pry it from his fingers and when we did, guess what he said?" Wilson asked.

She glanced from one deputy to the other. "What?"

"We think he yelled your name, but it's just a guess because his voice wasn't working right. He was screaming his lungs out, but not making a sound."

Cassidy swallowed though she hadn't taken a sip of coffee. Her eyes seemed to glisten ever so slightly. He was definitely making headway. Maybe with the right amount of pressure, she'd crack. "I guess maybe he thought he needed to see you . . . or maybe he did see you there, at the mill that night."

Gonzales's dark gaze fixed on the woman.

She licked her lips nervously and avoided his gaze. "I already told you I wasn't anywhere near the place."

"That's right, you were alone in the house. No alibi." Wilson turned to his partner and picked up the plastic bag. "Has this been printed?"

Gonzales nodded slightly.

"Funny," Wilson said, staring at the woman as he pulled out the darkened silver chain. "Wonder why a guy who was being half-burned to death, would hang onto this damned thing—you know, like it was real important?"

She didn't answer as Wilson let the plastic bag fall softly back to the table and allowed the St. Christopher's medal to swing, like a watch in a hypnotist's hands, in front of her nose. "Wonder what it means?" he said and he saw the tiny spark of fury in those round eyes again. But she didn't say a word as he dropped the blackened links onto the table and they slithered together.

She stared at the charred metal for a minute, frowning, her throat working. "Are we finished? Can I go now?"

Wilson was pissed. This woman knew something and she was holding back, and here he was sitting on the biggest murder and arson case in his nine years with the department—his ticket to ousting Floyd Dodds. "You're not changing your story?"

"No."

"Even though you don't have an alibi?"

"I was home."

"Alone?"

"Yes?"

"Packing? You *were* planning to leave your husband."

"I was working on the computer at home. There are time logs, you can see for yourself—"

"That *someone* was there. Or that someone took enough computer courses and knows how to get into the guts of the machine—the memory—and change the entry times. Let me tell you, you're pushing your luck." He snapped up the chain and dropped it into the plastic bag. "You know, whatever you've done, it will go easier on you if you 'fess up. And if you're protecting someone . . . hell, there's no reason for you to take the rap for something you didn't do."

Her eyes shifted away.

"You're not . . . protecting your husband, are you? Nah, that's silly. You were gonna split anyway."

"Am I being charged?" she demanded. Two spots of color caressed her high cheekbones and beneath the oversized jacket she straightened her thin body, a body that must've dropped five pounds in the twenty-four hours since the fire.

"Well, not yet, but it's still early."

She didn't smile. "As I said, I'd like to see my husband."

Wilson sent his partner a look. "You know, I think Mrs. McKenzie—you don't mind if I call you that since you're still legally married—I think that's a damned good idea. Maybe you should see the other guy, too; there's a chance you can tell me who he is, though in the shape he's in I doubt if his own mother would recognize him."

Gonzales shifted against the door. "Dodds won't like it—not without him there."

"Let me handle the Sheriff."

"It's your funeral, man."

"I'll give old Floyd a call. Make it official, okay?" Wilson stretched out of his chair. " 'Sides, he don't like much that I do."

Gonzales still wasn't convinced. "The doctors gave strict orders that the patients weren't to be disturbed."

"Hell, I know that!" Wilson reached for his hat. "But how can they be disturbed? One guy's so far gone he's nearly in a coma and the other . . . well, he's probably not long for the world. This here's the wife of one of the men, for God's sake. She needs to see her man. And maybe she can help us out. Come on, Mrs. McKenzie, you wouldn't mind, would you?"

Cassidy tried to control her ragged emotions though a thousand questions ran in long endless paths through her mind. She hadn't slept in nearly two days and when she had managed to doze, horrifying nightmares of the inferno at the sawmill blended into another terrifying fire, that hellish hot beast that had destroyed so much of her life and her family seventeen years ago. A shudder ripped through her body and her knees nearly gave way as she remembered . . . oh, God, how she remembered. The black sky, the red blaze, the white-hot sparks that shot into the heavens as if Satan himself were mocking and spitting at God. And the devastation and deaths . . . *please help me.*

She noticed the deputy staring at her, waiting, and she remembered he'd asked her a question—something about going to the hospital. "Can we go to the hospital now?" she asked, steeling herself. *Oh. God, please, don't let him be in agony!* Tears threatened her eyes, riding like drops of dew on her lashes, but she wouldn't give Deputy T. John Wilson the satisfaction of seeing her break down.

She should have asked to have her attorney present, but that was impossible as her attorney was her husband and he was clinging tenaciously to his life. Though she hadn't been able to visit him, the doctors had told her of his injuries, the broken ribs and jaw, punctured lung, cracked femur, and burned cornea of his right eye. He was lucky to be alive. Lucky.

Pushing herself to her feet, she slid a final glance at the tarnished silver chain still coiled, like a dead snake, in the clear plastic bag. Her heart seemed to rip a little bit and she reminded herself it was only a piece of jewelry—not expensive jewelry at that—and it meant nothing to her. Nothing.

The hospital noises were muted. Rattling carts and gurneys, the sound of doctors being paged, quiet footsteps all seemed to melt away as Wilson held the door open for her and she stepped into the hospital room where her husband lay unmoving beneath a sterile white sheet. Bandages covered half his face, including his right eye as well as the top and back of his head. The flesh that was exposed was bruised and lacerated. Stitches tracked beside his swollen nose and yellow antiseptic sliced across the scratches of his skin. Dark beard-stubble was beginning to shade that part of his jaw that was visible, and all the while an IV dripped fluid into his veins.

Cassidy's stomach lurched and she gritted her teeth. So this was what it had come to. *Why was he at the mill that night? Whom was he meeting—the man who lay dying somewhere in the labyrinthine rooms of this hospital? And why, oh, God, why, had someone tried to kill him?*

"I'm here," she said quietly, walking into the room and wishing she could turn back time, somehow save him from this agony. Though they'd stopped loving each other a long while ago, perhaps never really been in love, she still cared for him. "Can you hear me?" she asked, but didn't touch the clean sheets covering his body, didn't want even the slightest movement to add to his discomfort.

His good eye was open, staring sightlessly toward the ceiling. Its white had turned a nasty shade of red and the blue—that clear sky-blue—seemed to have dissolved into the surrounding tissue.

"I'm here for you," she said, conscious of the deputy standing near the door. "Can you hear?"

Suddenly the eye moved, focusing on her with such clarity and hatred that she nearly jumped back. Her husband stared at her a long, chilling minute, then looked away as if in disgust, his gaze trained on the ceiling once more.

"Please—" she said.

He didn't move.

The deputy stepped forward. "McKenzie?"

Nothing.

She said softly, "I want you to know that I care." Her throat clogged painfully on the words as she remembered their last argument, the cruel words they'd hurled at each other. The eye blinked, but she knew it was useless. He couldn't hear her. Wouldn't. He didn't want her love now any more than he ever had and she was just as incapable of giving it. "I'll be here for you." She remembered her marriage vows and felt a deep rendering in her heart, an ache that seemed to grow as she stared at the broken man who had once been so strong.

She'd known from the start their marriage was doomed, and yet she'd let herself believe that they would find a way to love each other.

But she'd been wrong. So wrong.

She waited and eventually the eye closed, though she didn't know if he were sleeping, unconscious, or pretending that she wasn't in the hospital, that she didn't exist, as he had so many times in the past.

Cassidy walked out of the room on wooden legs. Memories washed over her, memories of love gained and lost, of hopes and dreams that had died long before the fire.

The deputy was in step with her. "You want to tell me about the chain and the St. Christopher's medal?"

Her heart jolted. "I . . . I can't."

"Why not?"

She wrapped her arms around herself and despite the soaring temperature felt a chill as cold as November. "It didn't belong to my husband."

"You're sure?"

She hedged because she wasn't certain. "To my knowledge, he never owned anything like that. It . . . it probably belonged to the other guy—the one who was holding it."

"And who do you think he is?" Wilson asked.

"I wish I knew," she said fervently, not allowing her mind to wander to another time and place, another love, and a shining silver chain with a St. Christopher's medal dangling from its links. "I wish to God that I knew."

They walked the length of one corridor and took the elevator down a floor to CCU. Wilson couldn't convince the nurse on duty or the doctor in charge to let them see the man who had been with her husband, so they passed through the exterior doors to the outside of the hospital and there, in the simmering afternoon heat, Wilson handed her a photo of a charred man, his face blistered, his hair burned off. She closed her eyes and fought the urge to retch. "I already told you. I—I don't know him. Even if I did, I don't think, I mean I can't imagine—"

"It's all right." For once Wilson's voice was kind, as if he did have some human emotions after all. "I said, it was a long shot." He took the crook of her elbow and helped her walk across the parking lot to the cruiser to which he'd been assigned. Glancing back over his shoulder to the white-washed hospital and the wing in which CCU was housed, he shook his head. "Poor bastard. I wonder who the hell he is."

**TODAY'S HOTTEST READS
ARE TOMORROW'S SUPERSTARS**

VICTORY'S WOMAN (4484, $4.50)
by Gretchen Genet
Andrew—the carefree soldier who sought glory on the battlefield, and returned a shattered man . . . Niall—the legandary frontiersman and a former Shawnee captive, tormented by his past . . . Roger—the troubled youth, who would rise up to claim a shocking legacy . . . and Clarice—the passionate beauty bound by one man, and hopelessly in love with another. Set against the backdrop of the American revolution, three men fight for their heritage—and one woman is destined to change all their lives forever!

FORBIDDEN (4488, $4.99)
by Jo Beverley
While fleeing from her brothers, who are attempting to sell her into a loveless marriage, Serena Riverton accepts a carriage ride from a stranger—who is the handsomest man she has ever seen. Lord Middlethorpe, himself, is actually contemplating marriage to a dull daughter of the aristocracy, when he encounters the breathtaking Serena. She arouses him as no woman ever has. And after a night of thrilling intimacy—a forbidden liaison—Serena must choose between a lady's place and a woman's passion!

WINDS OF DESTINY (4489, $4.99)
by Victoria Thompson
Becky Tate is a half-breed outcast—branded by her Comanche heritage. Then she meets a rugged stranger who awakens her heart to the magic and mystery of passion. Hiding a desperate past, Texas Ranger Clint Masterson has ridden into cattle country to bring peace to a divided land. But a greater battle rages inside him when he dares to desire the beautiful Becky!

WILDEST HEART (4456, $4.99)
by Virginia Brown
Maggie Malone had come to cattle country to forge her future as a healer. Now she was faced by Devon Conrad, an outlaw wounded body and soul by his shadowy past . . . whose eyes blazed with fury even as his burning caress sent her spiraling with desire. They came together in a Texas town about to explode in sin and scandal. Danger was their destiny—and there was nothing they wouldn't dare for love!

Available wherever paperbacks are sold, or order direct from the Publisher. Send cover price plus 50¢ per copy for mailing and handling to Penguin USA, P.O. Box 999, c/o Dept. 17109, Bergenfield, NJ 07621. Residents of New York and Tennessee must include sales tax. DO NOT SEND CASH.

Reach for the Stars...

and always Reach for Romance by these Zebra Superstars:

Coming in February 1995

Lisa Jackson

Intimacies

Coming in March 1995

Jo Beverley

Tempting Fortune

Coming in April 1995

Joan Hohl

Compromises

Coming in May 1995

Christine Dorsey

My Heavenly Heart

Coming in June 1995

Jo Goodman

Always in My Dreams

AND
RECEIVE

$1.00 REBATE

WITH PURCHASE OF

ENCHANT THE HEAVENS

To receive your rebate, enclose:

★Proof of purchase symbol cut from below

★Original cash register receipt with book price circled

★Print information below and mail to:

ZEBRA REACH FOR
THE STARS REBATE
POST OFFICE BOX 1052
GRAND RAPIDS, MN 55745-1052

Name____________________________

Address__________________________

City_____________________________

State____________Zip_____________

Store name________________________

State____________Zip_____________

This coupon must accompany your request. No duplicates accepted. Void where prohibited, taxed or restricted. Offer available to U.S. & Canadian residents only. Allow 6 weeks for mailing of your refund payable in U.S. funds. OFFER EXPIRES 3/31/95.